Cinderella

MYRNA MACKENZIE
TRISH WYLIE
DIANNE DRAKE

Printed and bound in Spain
by Blackprint CPI, Barcelona

Published in Great Britain 2014
by Mills & Boon, an imprint of Harlequin (UK) Limited,
Eton House, 18-24 Paradise Road, Richmond, Surrey, TW9 1SR

THE BACHELOR'S CINDERELLA © 2014 Harlequin Books S.A.

The Frenchman's Plain-Jane Project, His L.A. Cinderella and *The Wife He's Been Waiting For* were first published in Great Britain by Harlequin (UK) Limited.

The Frenchman's Plain-Jane Project © 2009 Myrna Topol
His L.A. Cinderella © 2009 Trish Wylie
The Wife He's Been Waiting for © 2008 Dianne Despain

ISBN: 978-0-263-91202-9
eBook ISBN: 978-1-472-04497-6

05-0914

Harlequin (U[...]
and recyclab[...]
The logging [...]
regulations o[...]

Printed and b[...]
by Blackprin[...]

THE FRENCHMAN'S
PLAIN-JANE PROJECT

BY
MYRNA MACKENZIE

Myrna Mackenzie never meant to be a writer. Writing was something that mysteriously famous people did, and she didn't qualify. Still, fate came calling in the form of a writing assignment in sixth grade, so Myrna got out her trusty blue pen, her lined notebook paper, and penned a murder mystery. It was titled something suitably gory and…um…embarrassing (Mackenzie doesn't remember the title, but thinks *The Terrible Mystery of the Bloody Glove* would have been about her style back then). The story was a mess, and the box containing that story eventually went missing somewhere between moves (hurray!). But the experience of writing a story turned out to be amazing and wonderful and fun and…you get the picture. She was hooked.

Years later Mackenzie discovered her true love: writing romances. An award-winning author of over thirty novels, Myrna was born in Campbell, a small town in the Missouri boot-heel. She grew up just outside Chicago, and she and her husband now divide their time between two lakes in Chicago and Wisconsin—both very different and both very beautiful. In addition to writing she loves coffee, hiking, cruising the internet for interesting websites and *attempting* gardening, cooking and knitting. Readers (and other potential gardeners, cooks, knitters, writers, etc.) can visit Myrna online at www.myrnamackenzie.com, or write to her at PO Box 225, La Grange, IL 60525, USA.

CHAPTER ONE

"I HATE to discourage you, but you're not going to be able to convince Meg to come work for you. And I'm afraid… I'm sorry, but I'm not at liberty to tell you why."

That small bit of information was all Etienne Gavard had been able to glean from one of Meg Leighton's former coworkers. It echoed in his head as he drove his sleek black Porsche into a rundown Chicago neighborhood, located the apartment building he was looking for and pulled into a parking spot two doors down. Not an especially promising situation, but Meg Leighton was the expert he needed to help him complete the near impossible task he'd taken on.

"So, this is what it's come to." He muttered the words as he stared at the dingy building where Ms. Leighton apparently lived. He had crossed the Atlantic and had been driven to following questionable women he'd never met to even more questionable neighborhoods. *Do you even know why you're here or what you're doing?* he wondered.

Of course, he did. His calendar said that it was June first. Six weeks from the anniversary of the worst day of his life, the day that would haunt him forever but which especially haunted him in June and July. And for the past two summers he'd handled things badly. He'd closed himself off from the world and tried to drink himself into oblivion to forget the death of his wife and the unborn child she had agreed to bear only because she'd thought he needed and wanted a Gavard heir. Not this year. This year he wouldn't allow himself to sully their memories that way. If he could just get through this one year without losing it…if he could just do one good thing to replace the bad memories…then maybe…

Well, never mind the maybes. The truth was that he'd built an empire saving dying companies and he was good at what he did, maybe even better since the tragedy and what had followed had led him to decide that this job would be his only life and love, his only world from now on. And this year, to keep himself sane, he would attempt the impossible. He'd located a company so far gone that it seemed beyond saving, one where no one cared that it was going under other than the people who worked there. Attempting to breathe life into it would take up all his time. He wouldn't have time to think about the past.

One task accomplished.

Now, he needed the right person to assist him. Usually this was the easy part. There was always someone who knew the details, had some idea what was going on and who knew at least a little about what had made the company a success in the first place.

This time with this in-a-total-tailspin company? Not so simple. Everyone was running around crying that the sky was falling, and the best person to help him, he'd been told by someone with an interest in his success, was no longer with the company. Furthermore, there was a mystery attached to her departure, one that her former coworkers had refused to discuss. But he'd been able to glean this much. The woman, Meg Leighton, was here in this building right in front of him.

Etienne stared at the crumbling brown brick and the unkempt lawn. One would think a person living in such a place would be easy to influence, but no. He'd been told that she would be extremely reluctant and he would have to find another avenue.

"Oh, but I'm a very determined man, Meg Leighton," he muttered to himself as he exited the car. "And I need you, mademoiselle. Very much. I intend to have you." Now that he'd made the commitment to save the company, there was no going back. He hadn't just bought a company. He had taken on the responsibility for people's lives and he absolutely was not going to fail them. That would be unthinkable, the past repeating itself, and it would be totally unbearable to damage another person again.

Besides, most people had tipping points. They could be persuaded once one discovered their weaknesses.

Etienne wondered what Meg Leighton's weaknesses were. Time to find out. He stepped forward and pushed open the door to the building.

"Lightning, there's a man coming to see us," Meg told her cat as she hung up the phone. "I hear that he's French. He's also tall, blue-eyed and very handsome."

Lightning looked incredibly bored. The cat yawned.

"I agree," Meg said to herself. "Who cares about that? Handsome Frenchmen come to our door every day."

The cat simply stared.

"All right, so maybe we *don't* have Frenchmen ringing our doorbell, or handsome men tapping on the windowpane or…well, let's face it, sweetie, we just don't get too many men around here at all. Even our mailman is a mail-woman," Meg conceded. "But that's not the point."

The point was that Meg's friend, Edie, from the home office of Fieldman's Furnishings, had just called. It appeared that the new owner of the company was going to try to persuade Meg to do something she didn't want to do; come back to the company. But that just wasn't going to happen. Fieldman's had once been the closest thing to a real home that Meg had ever had. Mary Fieldman had hired her when she had only been sixteen and an at risk teenager. She had literally saved Meg from herself, but after Mary's death, the business had also been the site of Meg's biggest and most public and painful humiliation. The once warm feeling Fieldman's had given her had been completely replaced by scalding regret, pain and anger directed at herself. She had allowed herself to forget the ugly lessons she'd learned growing up an outsider at home and in school and all that had followed as a result of her outsider status. The end result of that forgetfulness had been the shame-inducing fiasco at Fieldman's.

Nevertheless, Edie had told her that she should prepare to be wooed by a man who wanted her to return to the scene of the crime.

Meg closed her eyes and counted to ten. "I'll just

have to be strong and firm and make him understand that no means no," she whispered out loud. *I could never go back there after what happened*, she thought. The memory of the total humiliation when Alan Fieldman had publicly dumped her, fired her and thrown her out on the street, or that she had not taken it quietly or with any degree of dignity could still make her blush with shame if she allowed herself to think about it. She seldom did. She certainly wasn't going to do so now.

Not for all the blue-eyed men in France, she thought. Downstairs, she heard the outer door to the apartment building open. Immediately, Meg's heart started to race. She had done her best to move on past her life at Fieldman's, to let go of her stunned pain at having lost the business that had been her anchor, and she had come so close to succeeding. The fact that Etienne Gavard's impending visit was bringing back her ugly past…the fear that she might be asked questions about that day at Fieldman's and about her relationship with her boss…the waiting…she had always been so horrible at waiting…

"Darn it," she said, moving to the door and throwing it open just as the man made it to the top of the stairs.

So much for being standoffish. She hadn't even waited for him to knock.

Meg swallowed hard as she came face-to-face with Etienne Gavard. He was, as Edie had noted, very tall. Meg, no Lilliputian herself, was a good half a head shorter than he. With that dark hair, those silvery-blue eyes and that slightly amused smile…

"Mr. Gavard?" she asked, as casually as possible, hoping her voice sounded calm and disinterested.

"Yes, Mademoiselle Leighton. I'm Etienne Gavard. I see you were expecting me a little?" he said, raising one dark eyebrow that Meg was sure made any number of women feel dizzy and disoriented.

A little? She'd practically ripped the door off its hinges. If Meg had been a blushing kind of woman she would have blushed. As it was, her blush was only on the inside. "Edie called me. That is…Edie's a total sweetheart, but she's totally loyal to me. You probably shouldn't tell her anything you don't want her friends to know."

"Ah, loyalty," he said. "I see. I like loyalty." When he said the last word he looked at Meg as if he could see right into her heart where all her most fervent and darn irrepressible emotions lay no matter how hard she tried to repress them. This man was staring at her as if he knew things about her that no one else knew, the places she kept under wraps and hid carefully. Always.

A trickle of panic ran through Meg. No way was she letting some man rip off her carefully applied emotional bandages and make her consider going back to Fieldman's just because he could do that sexy eyebrow thing.

Meg, unable to raise her eyebrow, simply stared. "I'm not like Edie," she said. "Edie is a very special and nice person."

Etienne Gavard's smile grew. The man had dimples. Gorgeous, sexy dimples. Meg almost hated him just for standing here in her hallway spreading all that virility around. She was, as her father used to say, as plain as toast. Slightly plump. With a fading scar on her cheek that had caused her grief in her youth. And worst of all, an outspoken manner and attitude that had gotten her in trouble and kept her there all her life.

"I'm happy that on only ten seconds' acquaintance that you're willing to share that bit of information with me, but…are you trying to tell me that you would be disloyal to Edie?"

Meg blinked. "I would never harm Edie."

He nodded. "Excellent! Because Edie is one of my employees now. I have to have her best interests at heart, so the fact that you would care about her welfare is a very good thing to know. I like loyalty in my employees and…I'm hiring. I'd like to discuss hiring *you*." The man tilted his head. He studied Meg closely.

Meg felt suddenly naked. She most definitely didn't want to feel naked in front of a man like this. "I'm afraid that's not possible. Mr. Gavard, let me be frank. You obviously went to all the trouble of coming from France to buy a company, so you must be an incredibly busy and important man. I'm flattered that you would want to hire me, but I just… I don't want to waste your time."

"You're not." His voice was very deep with that enticing accent. Meg glanced up at him. That was a mistake, since she noticed the breadth of his shoulders and immediately felt a forbidden thrill slip through her body. Men who were that good-looking made her nervous. They were on her "don't touch, don't even notice" list. Especially since that incident with Alan Fieldman. Besides, she didn't want or need to notice anything more about this man. He'd be gone in minutes.

"Mademoiselle Leighton, I understand that this…my methods today are…abrupt and unconventional, but the situation at Fieldman's is complex. I'm not sure how much Edie or any of the others understands about this, but... Is there somewhere we can go to talk?" he asked. "I don't want to alarm you by suggesting your apartment, but surely..."

"I'm never alarmed," Meg said, lying. "And it's not as if you're a stranger. You own Fieldman's. You're Edie's boss. Still, I'm sorry, but there's no point in the two of us continuing this conversation. I don't have any idea why you would want me to come back to Fieldman's, other than the story Edie told me about you needing an expert on the company, but if that's the case, then I'm afraid you're mistaken. I'm not who you need."

"Who is?" he asked, studying her intently. Meg almost felt as if she couldn't tear her gaze away. As if she had no brains or self-control at all, her heart began to pound in a terribly disconcerting way. She ignored it. She'd always had brains, and she was working on the self-control. It was, in fact, the prime goal of her life, to escape her past and become a strong, successful woman. Eliminating her too impetuous, reactive ways was a necessary part of that plan. Self-control was key.

She hesitated.

Etienne raised that dark, expressive eyebrow again, and Meg's breathing hitched in her throat. She wondered just how many strong women he had won over with that seemingly insignificant move. "I'm truly sorry for this intrusion, Mademoiselle Leighton, but the company seems to be in total disarray," he said. "The books are in arrears, production has all but shut down, confusion reigns. Even the most mundane things are out of order. There's not even any soap in the washroom, and no one seems to know where it's kept."

"Third aisle of the stockroom on the fourth shelf from the bottom. Or at least that's where it *was* kept," she said.

He smiled. "See. You know things."

"No," she said, trying not to smile at his blatant attempt to stroke her ego. "I know how things *were* when I was there, but I've been gone for a year. Besides, Mr. Gavard, I hardly think that knowing where the soap is kept is going to help you very much."

"When I wash my hands it will help," he said with that low, sexy voice that made it sound as if he was talking about far less mundane things than where supplies were kept. "But you're right. I'm looking for very much more than soap. I'm looking for someone who's willing to begin an adventure and make a difference in people's lives."

Meg shook her head. "You're obviously way more misinformed than I thought you were, Mr. Gavard, if you think I'm capable of any of those things, and…" She blew out her breath in a slight sigh.

He waited as she chose her words. Or at least she thought he was waiting. "Why don't you want to come back?" he asked suddenly.

She chose the easiest answer. "I have a new job, you know. I've been there for a year, ever since I left Fieldman's."

"Edie said you worked in the office of a local fruit and vegetable market."

"And I fill in at the store sometimes, as well," she admitted. "I like it. Fieldman's is in my past. Gina's

Fruits and Vegetables is my present. I like stocking the bins. It's a useful task."

She stared at him defiantly, hoping she sounded convincing and that he would simply go. But he didn't budge. Instead he stared at her with a serious, solemn, contemplative expression. Those long-lashed silver-blue eyes studied her as if analyzing each part of her, and Meg did her best not to squirm. She knew what he was seeing: an overly tall, plump and squarely-built, very plain woman with hips and a mouth that were both too wide and a host of other scars, visible and otherwise. She'd been examined and found wanting all of her life, but Etienne didn't seem to be examining her in quite the same way as she was used to, and in the end, after his perusal, it was her hands that he brought his gaze back to.

She forced herself not to clench them, knowing that the nails were broken from opening cartons and from mishaps with the bins. Meg wasn't a vain person at all, but if she had ever had a body part that she might have been proud of, it was her hands. The rest of her was awkward, but her hands could be graceful. Now, of course, they looked hideous, but Etienne Gavard was studying them so intently that her fingertips started to tingle.

"So, this is your present," he finally said. "I see. You want a useful job. That's understandable. But you don't think it would be…useful to go out on a limb and try to help me save your former colleagues' jobs and keep them from losing all they have?"

Meg froze, her own concerns set aside. "Is that what's going to happen?" She could barely whisper the words.

He held out his hands. "I've seen the work that

Fieldman's used to do. I know of Mary Fieldman. She was a powerhouse and a woman with talent and she also had an eye for talent in others. Her company did very good work right up until the day she died."

"I know." Meg couldn't quite keep the pride and affection out of her voice. She missed Mary…every day.

"Edie said that Mary was…attached to you, that you had been there since you were sixteen and you were her favorite employee, that Mary consulted with you on decisions."

Meg shook her head. "That Edie," she said.

"It's not true?"

She shrugged. "Yes, it's true, but Mary didn't really need my input. She always knew exactly what she wanted for Fieldman's. She wanted quality, to sell a product that exuded exquisite class. She wanted the name Fieldman's to mean something extraordinary to potential customers."

"Have you seen what Fieldman's has been selling— or trying to sell—lately?"

She hadn't. "Edie mentioned that there had been a few changes, but no, I haven't personally seen the product. She and I don't discuss Fieldman's, as a rule."

Etienne reached in the pocket of his black suit jacket and pulled out a glossy brochure. He held it out to her.

Meg took it and flipped it open. Both eyebrows raised and she flipped another page. "Is this real? Are those actually wide-eyed urchins on that upholstery? Koala bears? Puppies with pink bows around their necks?"

The pained look on Etienne Gavard's face said it all. "I understand that Alan Fieldman had his own ideas.

He wanted to go in a different direction, capture a younger audience."

Yes, well, Alan had always wanted to rebel against his mother. He'd fought hard and used people like Meg to make sure his mother had placed the company in his hands and not his brother's. And he hadn't known very much about young people even when he'd been a young person.

"Help me bring back the company, Meg," Etienne Gavard said.

She looked up into his eyes and they were so blue, so compelling that she almost leaned forward.

"You don't understand," she said, forcing herself to take a step back instead of forward.

"Make me understand."

"I didn't walk away from Fieldman's. I was fired for insubordination. It was a major scene. I made a lot of noise when I went. I fought. I yelled. I didn't go quietly. Everyone was there."

"I see."

No, how could he see? He hadn't been there to witness how ugly and demeaning it had been. How reminiscent of an earlier period of her life she had tried so hard to fight free of.

"So you see why I wouldn't be a good candidate for the job you're trying to fill."

He slowly shook his head. "You said you fought. I need a fighter, Meg. I want one."

Her throat began to close.

"I don't think you understand what you're saying or what I'm saying. I think I might have even thrown something at Alan."

Was that a smile on the dratted man's face? "Okay, we'll work on that. No throwing things."

"I…"

Suddenly it was all too much. Too soon. The plan she had tried to stick by, to move forward by living quietly and closing off a lot of doors, was going awry. Emotion, a desire for things she had set aside as unrealistic dreams, was trying to push at her. Meg blinked, trying to compose herself.

"Why are you doing this?" she asked suddenly. "I mean…look at you. You're obviously well dressed, cultured, rich if you could afford to come all the way here and buy an entire company. Why would you do that? Why would you come all the way to America and throw your money away on what might well be a losing venture?"

It was a bold and nosy question for a potential employee to ask, but there was too much at stake here. She'd had doors slammed in her face too many times just when she'd seemed to be nearing her goal, and Etienne Gavard's offer had come out of the blue and seemed too good to be true. She needed facts, truth, a sense that she wasn't going to walk blindly into an incredibly stupid situation the way she had before.

So despite the rudeness and total impropriety of her question, she stood her ground. She watched as a fleeting look of pain darkened Etienne Gavard's eyes before a mask came down and he shook his head. "I came here because… Let's just say that money isn't the issue. At least not for me. Salvaging companies is what I do. It's a challenge, an occupation, and I'm good at it. I usually win."

"But not always."

"No, not always, Meg. And I'll be honest. Even with your help, there's a good chance I'll lose this time."

And Edie and all the others would lose their jobs, the little bit of security they had in their lives. That was so unfair, so totally, entirely wrong and frightening. And…there was another truth that she hadn't dared to face.

If the company was going down because Alan had been running it—

She, like it or not, willingly or not, had been instrumental in Alan ending up as CEO. The thought was like a blow. She wanted to close her eyes, but that would be cowardly. *Fieldman's was failing. Good, innocent people would suffer if it failed.*

Meg wanted to keep that tragedy from happening. If there was any chance at all that she could do something to help…but was that even possible? *Could* she help?

How could she *not* try to help? Edie was her best friend.

"How can you be sure I can make a difference?"

He shook his head. "I can't. There are no guarantees in life. Ever." Again, that fleeting look of pain crossed his face. He looked away and then back.

"But if we do nothing, I can tell you that Fieldman's will most likely go under. We have to try to reverse things," he told her. "People's livelihoods really are at stake. So, what would it take to convince you? What is it that you want?"

By now, Meg knew she had no choice. She had to help if she could, but… She studied Etienne Gavard. He was a successful man, a powerful man, one who never would have ended up in the situation she had ended up in at Fieldman's. He knew things and he oozed confidence, success, knowledge, stability. She had questioned his methods, but in truth, there was something about him that made a person think he was bound to succeed. Etienne Gavard was a man to be reckoned with.

Meg thought about that, about all the things she'd locked away in her soul and decided were undoable. Now here was a task and an opportunity she couldn't turn away from. The truth was that what she really wanted most in life was a home brimming with love and children, the kind she'd never had and probably never would have, but this man couldn't give her that. No one could, and she was grown-up enough to have made peace with that knowledge, so…

"I'd like… What I want is security, a place that's all my own and I want to build a position in the business world that can't easily be taken away from me on someone else's whim. I want to be not just good behind the scenes but also out in the open, a force to be reckoned with, the kind of person that people want to do business with, one they respect. Can you do that for me? Can you teach me to be a success? Tutor me? Teach me what you know and show me the ropes while we do our best to save Fieldman's?"

He didn't even hesitate even though she was pretty sure he wouldn't have expected a request like this. "If that's what you want, then I'll do my best to turn you into a stellar businesswoman."

"What happens when this is over?"

"That would be up to you. If you suited and you

wished to stay once the company was on its feet and I returned to France, that would be your choice. And if you only wished to stay as long as necessary to help me get the company back on its feet, I would pay you well and then let you go…wherever you wanted to go. I'd make sure you had a good leadership position, of course, if your training proceeds as both of us hope it will."

Meg let that sink in. This was all proceeding so darn fast. "Do I have to give you my answer now?" Having been given the whole story about Fieldman's, Meg now felt the urge to rush ahead and say yes, but it was that very urge to rush that stopped her. Rushing in had never worked out well for her. A smart woman would at least mull over the situation for a few hours to make sure she had covered all the bases and knew the whole story.

He smiled.

"What?"

"'Do I have to give you my answer now?' is a much better response than the one you were giving me a few minutes ago."

"You're a rather persuasive man." Which might be dangerous under other conditions, but there was no way a man like Etienne Gavard would be thinking of her in any physical or romantic way, so she was safe. Knowing she wouldn't be his type could be rather freeing, she supposed. She wouldn't have to warn herself about thinking of him as anything other than an employer. "But you haven't answered my question. How much time do I have before you need to know?"

"Let's say tomorrow. The sooner the better."

"Because the company is sinking."

"Yes. Rather quickly."

"Oh, heck." Meg blew out a breath, closed her eyes and did the very thing that had cost her so much in the past. She plunged in. "I'm *not*—I just can't walk away when Edie and the others are at risk if there's even a whisper of a chance that I can help. And…I don't know how in the world anything I do might help save them, but I'll try. I'll do my part."

"So, we have a deal." He held out his hand. His very large, long-fingered masculine hand.

She hesitated, but only for a second. What was the risk, after all? She wouldn't be foolish enough to start having romantic dreams about Etienne Gavard.

Meg placed her hand in his. The jolt she felt was expected. The extreme intensity of it was not. An unanticipated thrill ran down her arm, through her body and all the way to her toes. Every inch of her being felt as if it was humming. Were all French males this potent?

"I'll see you in the morning, Meg," he said. "I'll pick you up at eight."

"I know the way to Fieldman's, Mr. Gavard."

"Etienne. Call me Etienne. We're partners in this venture, Meg. And we'll be working side by side around the clock…on the Fieldman project and on your project as well. I'll pick you up."

He glanced down then, and Meg realized that Lightning had come out of the apartment onto the landing.

"You have a cat?" Etienne asked.

She laughed. "I'm not sure that I have a cat. Lightning has an attitude. Sometimes it's more like she has a human than the other way around."

"Lightning?" he asked. "She looks a bit lethargic."

Meg shrugged. Lightning usually *was* lethargic, but knowing her cat's moods, that wasn't the term she would have used in this instance. Lightning was slowly, very slowly curling herself around Etienne's leg in what could only be called an affectionate manner. "She doesn't usually like men."

"Ah. Then maybe you've simply been hanging around with a poor class of men."

Meg couldn't help herself then. She laughed.

"Did I say something amusing, Meg?"

"A little." He'd also said something truthful. Besides Alan, Meg had experienced several other catastrophes with the opposite sex; men who flitted away when the next new and better woman came along. So…no more. She'd sworn off men. Fortunately Etienne was her boss. Despite her no men policy, bosses didn't count. They were allowed.

"Someday I'll ask you to explain why you laughed. I'll see you tomorrow," Etienne told her as he left.

When he was gone, the hall felt suddenly empty, bereft of those broad shoulders and all that overwhelmingly male anatomy. The right type of male if her cat was to be believed. Lightning sat on the top stair as if waiting for him to return.

"Forget it," Meg told her cat. "He's not for us. Not ever. And we'd better both keep that in mind. In just a few months he'll be wooing women across the ocean. Gone forever. This is strictly business, I am not his type and you and I are not to allow ourselves to get attached in any way. Period." So why did she feel as if she wanted to join Lightning and sit there waiting for tomorrow when Etienne would return?

Etienne lay back on the bed of his penthouse suite and tried not to think about a pair of worried caramel eyes. Why was he doing this? It was obvious that Meg Leighton wasn't exactly thrilled about going back to Fieldman's, and who could blame her? Her departure from the company had clearly been less than pleasant. Given what little he'd been able to glean about the Fieldman family, at least the sons, they had been users lacking not only business sense but also consciences.

He wondered why Alan Fieldman had fired Meg.

Not that it mattered. He could tell, just from their brief conversation and just by looking past her to her wildly decorated but thoughtful apartment and at the array of books on her shelves, that she had a brain and a desire to learn. The topics ranged from history to philosophy to various how-to books.

She obviously had gumption. She'd tried to keep him from steamrolling her. He felt a twinge of guilt at having used her friends' financial situation to convince her and wondered for a second if he was any better than Alan Fieldman.

Probably not. He knew his flaws and his shortcomings all too well. But he was different. He was going to do everything in his power to keep Meg and her friends from getting hurt. And he was going to do his very best to fulfill the promise he'd made to Meg to help her carve out her own place in the business community. When he left in a few months—and his whole goal was to do his work and move on to the next job—she and her friends would, he hoped, be happy and smiling.

At the word smiling, he thought of Meg's lips. She was a plain woman but her eyes and her lips were amazing. Just a slight twitch of those lips spoke volumes and called up unexpected heat in his body.

"Enough," he told himself. "You know the rules. You never get to stay. You never get to take anything away other than a brief respite from the pain and a sufficient amount of money to move on to the next project." Socializing with the subjects wasn't allowed. Ever.

CHAPTER TWO

"WHERE is everyone?" Meg asked as they entered Fieldman's Furnishings the next day.

Etienne looked around the big, empty office with weak sunlight filtering in through the streaked and dusty windows high overhead. It shone on the mottled blue carpeting that was worn thin in places. There was a crack in one of the walls, and despite the fact that people still worked here, the place smelled of neglect. "I gave them the day off," he said.

"Excuse me? You did what?" Meg turned to him, her brown eyes open wide. She was wearing some wild red and white thing that hid a lot of her body, but wasn't camouflage enough to hide the fact that she was shapely and generously curved.

He frowned at her reaction. "I sent them home. With pay," he clarified. "Don't worry, Meg. I didn't turn your friends out without compensating them."

Meg shook her head. "I didn't mean that. I wasn't accusing you of cheating Edie and the others. And I *know* this is *so* out of line, but I was just… The company is dying and you sent the workers home? Why would—

I'm sorry for asking, but I just don't understand why you would do that."

He smiled suddenly. "Meg, see what a great help you're going to be. Look, you're already questioning my methods."

Instantly she looked contrite. A lovely pink crept up from the neckline of her white blouse. "Don't," he said suddenly. "There's no need to be embarrassed about the fact that you're questioning me. It's a good thing."

She frowned. "I'm not embarrassed."

"You're blushing."

"I never blush."

But she was. And in a very pretty way. The bloom continued to spread, the faint rose accenting the full curve of her cheeks. Etienne raised one brow. "Yes. You're blushing. If we're going to work together, we need truth between us."

Almost as if she couldn't help herself, Meg reached up and touched her face. The pale, almost indiscernible scar that ran three inches from the corner of her lip toward her ear was now the only part of her face that wasn't a delightful pink. There was something very… erotic about that small white scar, something that made a man think about placing his lips against that thin line and moving outward, kiss after kiss.

Etienne caught himself again and stopped that train of thought as quickly as he could. What on earth was wrong with him? The woman…Meg wasn't wearing anything vaguely suggestive. In fact, her clothing looked somewhat sacklike. Her shoes were made for comfort rather than to accentuate her legs. And yet he had been thinking…well never mind what he had been thinking. Or why. He didn't even want to know about the why. Instead he cleared his throat and flipped on a computer in the still, empty room. The sound of the machine booting up filled the silence. He looked at Meg.

"I *wasn't* lying or trying to be coy," she insisted. "I've never been a blusher."

"Good, then. It's something new in your life. These next few months are going to be all about new things. Unlike these out-of-date computers."

"You have a time frame?"

"I have a *goal*. Not only to bring back your business in the United States but to expand beyond your shores. There's a small business expo in Paris two months from now. Make an impression there and international business will flow in. That's our target date to be up and running again full speed."

"You're serious, aren't you? Two months seems so short. Not that I'm doubting you can do it. You're the genius of La Défense."

Etienne snapped to attention at Meg's mention of Paris's business district. "The genius of La Défense? And you surmised that how?"

"Um…you told me?" She looked up at him without guile, those big brown eyes as innocent as a newborn lamb's, even though he knew he had never told her the nickname given to him by the French press.

"Meg…" he drawled.

An instant expression of guilt shadowed her countenance. "All right, I looked you up on the Internet. I'm sorry if I intruded. I just… I don't really know you and I wanted to know if you were for real."

He wanted to smile at her forlorn tone. He felt very *real* staring at her right now, but…the Internet?

The urge to smile disappeared. He was from an old, well-known family. There had been articles written about Louisa's death. But that wasn't something he felt he could discuss. Despite the three years that had passed, the pain, the guilt was still like a flame inside him. "And what did you discover?" he asked, careful to keep his tone casual.

"I discovered that…you *are* real," she said simply, which said so much and so little at the same time. She hesitated. Then she took a deep breath. "So, can even a genius like you pull Fieldman's together in only two months? What can we accomplish in such a short time?"

Etienne felt a huge sense of relief. He wouldn't be asked to discuss Louisa. He wouldn't have to give evasive answers to mask his pain. If Meg had chanced upon that story, and she most likely had, she wasn't saying anything. For several long seconds he studied her carefully. She gazed back at him directly, unflinchingly. Only the way her fingers fidgeted with the cloth of her dress gave away even a hint of discomfort. All right, she probably knew his history. But she was ignoring it. He would, too, and he would be grateful. In other circumstances, he would be kissing her feet.

Which called up an image of something he knew he could never pursue.

"What can we do?" he asked, skirting all the issues except the only one he would allow himself. "Many things. When a company begins to fail, it's not enough to simply go back to the old ways. And yes, better accounting practices will help, but they won't get Fieldman's the attention we need to pique customers' curiosity. What we need are some quick, very visible, highly touted changes. We want a spark to intrigue the customers and fire up the employees. We want something to attract publicity."

He caught a smile on her face. "What?"

"I assume your changes won't be like the ones Alan made," she said.

Etienne laughed. "Well, I *was* thinking bunny rabbits. With carrots. Very eye-catching."

"Ah, I see you really *do* need me, after all," she said. "No bunny rabbits."

He tried to look wounded. "What do you suggest, then?"

For half a second, she looked self-conscious. Those pretty caramel eyes flew open wide. "All right, you don't want to go back to what Fieldman's was doing when Mary was in charge."

He slowly shook his head. "The world moves on. We have to move with it." It was a good reminder and more for himself than for Meg. He was a man constantly on the move, and he needed to be that way. There was no way to change the past. All he could do was move away from it.

"Your job takes you all around the world, doesn't it?"

"I never stop moving. It helps that I'm not married or likely to be. It wouldn't be fair to ask a woman to put up with a man like me who is never around."

Which was far more direct than he felt comfortable being, but he had learned that being direct was the only way.

Meg didn't even blink. In fact she smiled slightly. "I'm not a family woman, either, or likely to get married."

Which meant something bad had to have happened to her at some point.

"Someday I'll want children, but since I don't have them yet, I'm free to spend as much time on the job as necessary."

Children. Etienne's heart started thudding. He had once wanted a child.

He didn't speak. Memories rushed at him. A conversation with his wife. She hadn't wanted the baby. He had. But she was the one who lost her life due to the rigors of pregnancy and an undetected heart defect.

And he was obviously not hiding his reaction to her declaration well. Meg was looking at him with what could only be called concern in her expression. Etienne shook off the past. It was done. It was over. And he was making Meg nervous. That wasn't acceptable.

"But we don't need to spend time talking about my plans," she said quickly. "We need to discuss the company and…I understand what you said, but we don't want to toss out what worked completely, do we?" she asked. "That is, isn't my knowledge of what was working part of why you hired me?"

She licked her lips nervously. Etienne's pulse jumped. His body reacted…the way any man's body would react. And suddenly, standing here staring at those berry lips, he wondered for a second why he *had* hired Meg. She wasn't pretty in the common way at all—some might even call her plain—but there was something…some light in her eyes, something very full about those lips that made her very tempting, and temptation was never allowed to be a part of his dying business reclamation projects. Yet, here he was examining Meg as if he intended to do something that was out of the question.

He nearly swore. No doubt he'd simply been depriving himself of female companionship for too long. He was clearly going to have to watch himself around

Meg Leighton. And she was still waiting for an answer to her question.

"Yes, you have the keys to what made Fieldman's work before. Let's take that and give it a twist."

"Something classic but fresh," she said.

"Fresh and enticing," he agreed.

"Maybe…" Her whole face lit up.

"What?" He watched her, but she suddenly looked self-conscious.

"No. Maybe I'd better let that idea sink in and think it through a bit, let it play out and mature before I share it. I have an awful and long-standing tendency to jump in and do things without waiting for common sense to kick in, to react or speak without thinking. Bad habit."

"Not always."

She gave him a look that said he was clearly wrong. "For me it is. That's part of what I want you to help me with. How to think on my feet without saying or doing something tremendously terrible or embarrassing."

"What kinds of things have you said and done?"

She shook her head. "No. I am so *not* sharing my most embarrassing moments. It's bad enough that they happened in the first place. I've taken numerous classes to improve myself. I've tried to learn how to ski, how to skate, how to enter a room, and I know the basic concepts. I've even been taught how to fall gracefully several times, but when it comes down to the wire, I'm still the person who steps on the banana peel and ends up in an embarrassing heap with absolutely no grace. Or the one who yells something loud and embarrassing just as everyone in the room stops talking. I live in fear that someone will catch me on a camera phone and I'll end up on the Internet as one of those 'most watched videos.'" She threw out one hand in a gesture of remorse. "You don't happen to carry a camera phone around with you, do you?"

Etienne couldn't stop himself from chuckling. "Yes, I do, but I would never use it against you, Meg. That would be *trop*…I mean *too* unfeeling of me."

She gave him another look. "Ah, so you're a gentleman. Not the type of man I meet every day." Which made him wonder what her experiences with men had been. "So…about that idea for the company… How do you feel about leather?"

Etienne nearly choked. Ah, her so-called habit of saying something without thinking about how her audience would hear it…now he understood a little bit. Still, in this case, it was a charming addition to her personality. This woman was a delight, was all he could think of. Despite her original reluctance to work with him, she had clearly jumped in with both feet now that she'd made up her mind to commit. "Leather?" he asked, reminding himself that she was talking about furniture, not something kinky. "I like leather. What man doesn't?"

"All right. I'll keep that in mind. Tomorrow I'll bring you ten ideas."

"Of ways to use leather creatively."

They had been moving deeper into the office, but now she stopped and faced him. Though her eyes only met his chin, she tipped her head back and gave him the kind of look a woman gave to an errant schoolboy. "Are you making fun of me, Etienne?"

No. He was enjoying her. Immensely. In a quite improper way that he knew darn well he was going to regret. Later. "I might be," he conceded. "But I mean it only in the very best way. I think you're unique. I like the way your thought process works." And that, he suddenly realized was the key to Fieldman's future success. There was always a key. Finding it was the challenge. And here she was, standing right beside him. The woman who was going to make the difference in a way that hadn't occurred to him earlier.

"What?" she said. "Why are you looking at me that way?"

"What way?"

"I don't know. As if… I don't know. You're smiling. A lot. And I know I didn't even say anything remotely funny or weird. At least not this time. Did I—have I torn something again?" She looked down at her blouse, fussing with the material, clearly embarrassed.

Oh, yes, Meg was definitely it. But he didn't want to frighten her or to make her think that he was looking at her in a suggestive way. That wasn't fair. He was very careful not to even hint that he was offering things he wasn't offering or that he wanted things he couldn't be allowed to want.

"It's nothing overt you've done. I've just come up with a new part of our plan, the most important part."

"Wonderful. What is it?"

"You."

She shook her head. "I don't understand. I'm already here."

"No, not like this. Fieldman's needs to be fresh, different, exciting. You asked me yesterday to take you on as a student of sorts. So, let's do that. In a major way. Let's make you the new face of Fieldman's."

If he had taken her to a horror movie, Etienne could not have surprised a more shocked and terrified look on

Meg's face. "That is so not going to happen," she said. "That would be such a mistake."

"No. It's not a mistake. Meg, look at me."

She looked, and those big beautiful, terrified eyes nearly tore his heart out.

"I'm not going to hurt you," he said, but she looked as if she didn't believe him. "I wouldn't do that. Believe me, I've hurt people in my life and it's not the kind of thing I want to repeat. Ever."

"You don't know what you're asking me. You want me to stand up in front of people."

"I do. I want you to be the new symbol for the company."

"I can't do that. I have 'being the center of attention' issues."

Somehow he refrained from smiling. She really was frightened.

"Any other kinds of issues?"

"Trust."

"I have trust issues, too."

"You do?"

"Yes. I try not to ask people to trust me, and I'm not going to do that now, but I will tell you this. I won't send you out to speak or have your picture taken unless I'm right there with you. I'll be there to guide you and to shield you. And if anything happens that you don't like, I'll whisk you right out of there."

"Even if it hurts Fieldman's?"

"Even then."

She took a deep breath. "And you think this will help the company."

"There aren't any guarantees, Meg, but I know this much. A personality always gets more attention than a piece of furniture ever will. Mary was, I understand, a personality, and half the reason people bought from Fieldman's. We need someone to take her place, and you fit the bill perfectly, especially since you were Mary's protégée. If Fieldman's is going to rise again and to succeed, you're the best bet we have."

She hesitated, but only for a second. "All right, if you think it will help the people here, I'm in. I'll consider it my duty."

Etienne nearly groaned at her choice of words. "Don't do it for duty. That's something you do because you feel you have to. It robs you of your control and your joy and in the end may leave you with nothing." Which he knew better than anyone.

And which was obviously saying too much. Meg Leighton was studying him carefully, possibly seeing damaged parts of his soul that he didn't want exposed.

"Consider your spokesperson role to be part of our agreement. On the job training," he suggested.

She blew out a breath. "Okay, all right. Yes. So…what do we do now?"

"We get started."

"On me?"

Such guileless eyes. No wonder she had trust issues. Some wolf could waltz right past her defenses and hurt her. But it wouldn't be him.

"Let's start with the building first," he said. "Show me everything you know."

If he concentrated on the building, he would be less distracted by the woman. It was a solid theory. But as he walked behind her, the soft sound of her voice, the sway of her hips, even the gentle line of her arm as she pointed out the details of their surroundings…mesmerized him.

Etienne frowned, angry at his completely inappropriate reaction. He reminded himself of why he had come here and what the rules were. No attachments, no touching.

Suddenly Meg stopped. She turned and sighed. "The state of this place, the books... Saving the company is going to be a challenge, isn't it?" she asked, those big brown eyes worried.

"Don't worry, I can handle it," he said, the promise as much about his reaction to the woman as it was to the company. He was *not* going to get close enough to risk hurting her.

"You're very confident, aren't you?" she asked with a smile that sent pleasure arcing through him.

"No. I'm determined," he said. Determined to do what he had come to do and then leave. And that meant ignoring the fact that what he wanted right this minute was to see her smile again. No, if he was truly honest with himself, he wanted more. He wanted to taste her.

And for the first time he realized just how difficult it was going to be, working with Meg. Her smile, her lips... The woman was going to be a major distraction.

CHAPTER THREE

IT HAD been a long day. Meg and Etienne had covered every inch of the building. They'd pored over paperwork, gone through the computer files, sifted through the desk drawers that Alan Fieldman had left behind. There was a photo of Meg in there that she had given him. There was also a photo of Paula Avery, the stunningly attractive but uninformed woman Alan had hired and then promoted over Meg three weeks later. And even photos of two other women, one somewhat scantily clad.

Meg had discovered these while Etienne was busy elsewhere, and now she quickly shoved all the photos deep in the drawer and closed it. She had been fooled by Alan. He had seen that she had been his mother's favorite and had used her to make points with Mary. The fact that Meg had fallen for his act, had allowed her defenses to fall that much…it was a pathetic chapter in her life she wanted to remain closed. And she was wiser now. She would not allow herself to be weak again.

Especially not with Etienne. That thought dropped in out of nowhere but she didn't turn away. He had made a point of mentioning that he wasn't in the market for romantic entanglements. Some women might be offended, but Meg was glad for the gentle warning. The truth might sting, but it was always better than a lie. And she had learned the dangers of lying to herself. Etienne was not and never would be for her.

"All right, we know the lay of the land now, Meg," Etienne was saying, causing her to start.

She pulled herself back into the here and now and the business at hand. "The situation at Fieldman's looks pretty desperate," she said.

"Getting cold feet?"

She was. The thought of holding people's lives in her hands filled her with dread. She'd spoken with Edie at lunchtime, and her friend was so scared she was practically in tears.

"I don't want my friends to suffer," she said. "Edie's husband got laid off from his job last year and he hasn't been able to find another one. This place is all she has. She's not the only one, either. The people here…they're good people."

"They didn't stand up to Alan when he fired you."

"They have children, dependents. I don't. And I don't blame them. What could they have said that would have made a difference? And anyway, my problems with Alan were of my own making."

Etienne swore at that. At least she assumed he was swearing. "I don't know those words," she told him.

"Good. And you're not going to, either, *ma chère*."

Meg felt a jolt, a warmth, go through her at the French phrase. All right, she'd had high school French, enough to realize that he meant it just as a friendly term, but coming from Etienne's lips…oh darn, Etienne could say the words peanut butter and a woman would go all gooey inside.

Except me, she thought. I just declared my intent to be strong not two minutes ago. And it's true. It's got to be true. I have to make it true. Etienne's not available. I'm not available and I don't want to be available. From now on I'm immune to Etienne. Please let me be immune. Don't let me do or say something stupid.

"This Alan…he was the one in the wrong. You shouldn't let a man like that dictate your life," Etienne told her. "Your worth should never be dependent on one person." He said the words angrily with a slash of his hand.

"I don't let my worth depend on the opinion of others," she assured him. "I won't." But she had. Once upon a time she had tried to break past her parents' conviction that her birth had intruded on their plans and ruined their lives, but she hadn't been able to do that, and now that no longer mattered. She had a goal and a purpose and none of what had happened in her past could stop her.

"Good. I'm glad to hear that," Etienne said with a smile that lit up those sexy, silvery-blue eyes. "We'll save your friends together, Meg. This won't be all on your head. I wouldn't allow you to carry that burden or to ever feel that you were solely responsible for saving another person. I would never have asked you to go through anything like that alone." He broke off abruptly and she wondered what his experience with burdens or trying to save people had been, but she'd read the online articles about him losing his wife and baby and she was sure he knew about the depths of despair and the fear of not being able to save someone. He had good reason to travel the world alone and keep his heart intact.

Meg's eyes felt suddenly misty. She blinked. "Thank you."

"Still," he said in that low, deep voice of his, "I have to express my admiration. You were amazingly adept at deciphering those ledgers. They were gibberish to me, and I've looked at more than my share of ledgers."

She shrugged. "Mary had her own system. In retrospect, it probably wasn't a great idea."

"So, the ledgers are translated. That's one bridge crossed," he said. "Now, on to the next."

She blinked. They had already been here for ten hours. "What's next?"

"You," he said.

"Me?" Her heartbeat went into overdrive.

"I made you a promise yesterday. We had a deal."

"Oh. Me. You're going to transform me. And you're going to make me into a worthy spokesperson."

"You're already worthy and you don't need transforming. You need polish."

"Lots of polish."

He frowned, but she ignored that. "What are you going to teach me first?"

She looked up at him and was surprised to see a look of intense heat in his eyes. "First I'm going to dress you."

Meg swallowed hard. Even though, she reminded herself, there was no reason to be self-conscious. Dressing a woman was a lot different from undressing her. But her appearance was the last thing she had envisioned when she'd asked Etienne to help make her a success. This was unsettling, unnerving. The very thought… She felt ridiculously frivolous, but somehow she was sure that Etienne had encountered any number of successful women in his life. He knew the right ingredients.

"All right," she said slowly. "I suppose you could do that. I was never very fond of this dress, anyway."

"That dress should be destroyed so that no one can ever wear it again."

He sounded so offended that she just had to smile. "That's going a bit far, isn't it?"

"Not nearly far enough, Meg. You have…curves. You should show them."

"Curves?" she said with a laugh and a shake of her head. "Well, thank you for putting it that way instead of simply saying that I weigh too much."

"You do not weigh too much. You have shape. Here," he said, motioning toward her breast. He didn't touch her at all, but she felt as if she had been touched. "And here," he continued, curving his palm near her hip.

With great effort, Meg continued to breathe.

"Shape is a good thing," Etienne said. *"N'est ce pas? Isn't it?"*

It had never been a good thing for her before, but…

"You know a lot about women and what makes them…noticeable, don't you? That is, noticeable in a good way, not in a bad way."

"Has someone been making you feel bad about your looks?"

Okay, that was a subject she was not going to discuss.

Doing so would only make her look as if she felt sorry for herself, and she refused to be that kind of whining woman. "No. Not at all," she said brightly.

He smiled, and she knew that he probably suspected she was lying. "Good, because you should be proud of your looks. You have…"

He was hesitating. In her Meg plow-ahead way, she wanted to help, but discussing her physical attributes was virgin territory for her and also incredibly danger-ous to her peace of mind, she thought, remembering that curving-his-hands-near-her-body exploration that had made her ache and want to squirm closer. "Etienne, I'm not some fragile flower. You don't have to be so careful with me. I'm comfortable with who I am and I want you to know that I can do a pretty decent job of camouflaging this scar with makeup when I take the time to do that if it will help my image," she offered, ges-turing toward her mouth.

"Yes. I noticed that enchanting scar, Meg," he said. And somehow the way he said it, he made it sound as if every woman on earth should only *wish* they had such a scar. "How did you get it?"

But that was another topic she didn't care to discuss in great depth. "It was just a little fall. Not a big deal," she said, though of course it had felt like a very big deal when she was growing up. Her mother had constantly urged her to cover it up and had bemoaned the fact that Meg would never be half as beautiful as her sister, Ann. Ann being the grown daughter Leslie Leighton and her husband had actually planned and wanted and cher-ished, not the daughter who had been a major mistake, who had come along late in their lives and who had trapped them into staying in a marriage they wanted to rid themselves of. "And anyway, it happened so long ago that the details no longer matter."

And with this gorgeous, exotic, successful man gazing at her face as if he would like to touch her, Meg couldn't stay focused on the details, anyway.

She struggled to clear her head and concentrate on what they had been talking about before this disconcerting discussion of her scar began. "Since you're new to the area, you probably don't know any shops we can go to, so I'll help," she said and she offered up a few of the ones she frequented: inexpensive little out-of-the-way shops.

"I was thinking more…classic with maybe a hint of sass thrown in." He rattled off the names of several upscale stores and boutiques in the area.

Meg raised her brows in astonishment. "You live in Paris. So, how do you know these things? Where women buy their clothes and what the best places are?" she asked.

"It's part of the job."

"You dress women often?"

"Sometimes out-of-town clients have emergencies. It's a good rule of thumb, wherever you are, to always know a few good restaurants, a few good theaters and places where both women and men can pick up emergency supplies. It shows your clients that you're prepared to go the extra mile to help them. Presentation is important."

"I'll remember that, but…"

He waited.

"I can't afford to shop at those places."

"Yes, you can. I'm paying you very well." He threw out a figure that made Meg's breath catch in her throat.

"That's far too much. I assumed you were going to pay me what Alan's former assistant was making, or at least something in the ballpark."

He smiled. Okay, she was being pushy and outspoken again, but still…

"It's not too much," he said. "And you're going to earn every penny. You're now Fieldman's. When people see Fieldman's Furnishings, what they're really going to see is Meg Leighton. Here and abroad."

Her courage nearly faltered at that. Having people staring at her had always been difficult. But she had asked for his help and he was going to help her. She had agreed to be the spokesperson only hours ago. She couldn't turn craven on him now. "And as the actual owner of Fieldman's, you'll be in the spotlight, too."

"Yes, but I'm used to it. I've lived in that kind of spotlight all my life. You haven't. That means you need ways to conquer stage fright, should it rear its ugly head. You need the right clothes and you need to be able to make an instant impression. Consider it part of your job description."

"All right. But when I said that I wanted you to help me be a success, I wasn't even thinking that you would clothe me."

"What were you thinking I would do?"

"Teach me."

"I will."

"Guide me," she said, her voice coming out a little whispery and very unlike herself.

"I promise I'll do that and more."

Meg didn't even want to try to imagine what the *and more* part meant. Instead she followed Etienne out into the sunlight, into his sleek, expensive car and, eventually, into a very expensive boutique that she had only ever seen from the outside.

"We need a wardrobe," he told the woman. "Only items that complement Meg's complexion and her figure. Nothing gaudy, but…think…"

He studied Meg. "Nothing drab, either. Meg likes bright colors."

"How do you know that?" Meg asked.

"I peeked in your doorway while we were talking yesterday. Your living room is quite out of the ordinary."

She laughed. "You're being quite polite by describing it that way. Even Edie tells me I went too far with the aqua and tangerine and yellow."

"Maybe, but it suits you. And all those colors complement your eyes."

"My eyes are plain brown."

He did that wicked eyebrow raising thing again. "You, *mademoiselle*, don't even know what color your eyes are. There's nothing plain about them."

While he was talking he was looking into her eyes just as if they were alone. But they weren't, and Meg felt suddenly self-conscious. The saleswoman probably thought that Meg was paying Etienne for his services or something. He could certainly spend his time with someone totally beautiful if he wanted to.

"Okay, my eyes are gorgeous," she lied. "What should I buy?"

"This," he said, pointing out a stunning camel colored suit and adding a melon silk blouse. "For starters."

And he meant what he said. For the next hour, Meg tried on outfit after outfit. Etienne nixed many of them. "That doesn't do justice to her legs," he'd say, just as if Meg's legs had ever been the kind of thing anyone admired. And yet…in the camel suit or in the knee skimming navy sheath with subtle red trim, wearing red pumps that were slightly higher than she was used to, her legs did look different. Thinner.

"You have an eye," the saleswoman said to Etienne, and Meg knew that the woman was wishing that she was the woman Etienne was with.

It's just business, Meg wanted to tell her. We're not romantic people. We're just on this outing as part of the deal we made and because we need to make an impression at the expo. Still, the woman was right. Etienne had obviously dressed many women before, and those women had undoubtedly had more polish than the average female. It was a good thing to keep in mind. Even if he had the time and inclination to get involved with someone during his stay in Chicago, he was not for someone like Meg Leighton.

"Not this," Meg said when Etienne handed her a slender black strapless dress. "I'm all about business. I won't need anything this formal."

"Oh, yes," he said. "There will be at least one event either here or in Paris where you'll need this. I'm sure of it."

Suddenly fear took hold of her. What was she doing? She, plain, always awkward Meg Leighton, the girl whose mother had accidentally scarred her, then reminded Meg again and again over the years that she would never go far if she didn't cover up her deformity, lose weight, stand up taller, remake herself into a completely different person, was here trying on a cocktail dress just as if she was actually going to wear it.

She frowned and started to put it back.

Etienne gave the saleswoman a look, sending her scurrying away. He placed a hand on Meg's arm, and sensation jolted through her. Heat suffused her body.

"Please, Meg, do this," Etienne said, leaning closer to her so that she nearly had to close her eyes from the sheer sensation of feeling the warmth of his body. "You need to do this. Alan was an idiot."

Her eyes flew open at that. "What?"

"Don't you think that I know that that…that fool sapped your confidence in yourself when he let you go?"

"I never had that kind of total confidence in myself. Well, other than my brains. I knew I had those, but this…my…person…"

His eyes opened wide. "You should have confidence here, too. Look at you, Meg," he said, turning her so that they both faced the mirror. "Look at your cheekbones." Standing behind her, he raised his arms, framing her body so that his fingertips skimmed her skin.

Her heart nearly flipped over. "I—I have that scar," she reminded him.

"Yes, and I explained how adorable and sexy that was."

"I think you're blind."

"I have twenty-twenty vision."

If she hadn't been so overwhelmed by his nearness,

she might have laughed at how seriously he had taken her comment. As it was, she could barely breathe.

"Think of you in this dress," he said. "With your hair up like this." He reached down and gently lifted her long hair, so that her neck was exposed.

And then he simply stared.

"What?" she asked. "What's wrong?" She tried to twist.

"You have a beautiful neck. Has anyone ever told you that?"

And then the sheer incongruity of the situation hit Meg. The nervous laughter bubbled up out of her.

"I said something funny?" he asked.

"You said something wonderful. Not true, but wonderful. I definitely have to start hanging around with a whole lot more Frenchmen. Are they all like you?"

She looked in the mirror, and saw that his eyes were dark and not at all happy. "A few compliments. *True* compliments," he insisted. "And you want to start meeting all the men in Paris. And…how *am* I?"

Meg frowned, confused.

"You asked if they were all like me. What did you mean?"

"Only that you were full of pretty talk."

"*Pretty* talk?"

"You know, that thing about my neck. As if my neck is any different from any other woman's neck."

"You," he said. "Need more than just business lessons. You need to be introduced to the right kind of men. Obviously someone was negligent in your upbringing if no one has told you these things."

She shook her head, sadly. "My parents were…not

nice parents, but they weren't the only ones. Fat little girls with scars on their faces do not get compliments on anything other than their brains. And even then, pretty girls with brains still win."

"Well, this time you'll be the one to win. And you are pretty," he told her, clearly more than a bit angry.

"Please send all these things here," Etienne told the saleswoman as he gave her his credit card and a slip of paper with Meg's address on it. "And she'll need underthings. Lots of them. Silky, pretty stuff. Meg…"

But Meg was suddenly blushing horribly and by now even she knew that she was blushing for real. "You're not buying me lingerie," she said. "I'm not that kind of woman."

"What kind is that? Do you mean you don't wear underwear, Meg?"

Meg heard the woman make a choking sound and she wasn't sure if the lady was trying to hold back a laugh or just as startled as Meg was.

Meg looked at Etienne and there was no question that he was laughing. He was trying to cow her into buying something she truly didn't need.

"Sometimes I don't," she said, blustering in and lifting her chin defiantly even though it was a lie. She didn't care. All this talk of how pretty she was… How could she have forgotten her rotten luck with men? Alan had told her all kinds of lies and she had believed them. They hadn't been nearly as preposterous as the things Etienne had been saying.

But she took one look at Etienne and knew that she had stepped over a line. His eyes were dark and heated, and the look on his face was…territorial, sensual, utterly male.

There was no way she knew anything at all about handling that kind of reaction. She'd never elicited that kind of reaction from any man. She was definitely in over her head.

"But I'll probably need some things for the times I do wear underwear," she said quickly. "I'll tell you my size," she told the woman, scrambling for a scrap of paper. She was so not going to say her bra size out loud. Especially not in Etienne's presence.

She handed the woman the paper and began a march toward the door. Every step she took was agony. She felt as if the eyes of the world were on her, and that she was alone. It was a feeling she knew all too well.

But within seconds Etienne was beside her. He took her arm and curled his hand around hers. "I'm sorry," he said.

"For what?"

"I embarrassed you."

And she realized something. "You weren't laughing at me, were you?"

"I was teasing you. Because we're… Because I like you. That's a very different thing from laughing at someone."

Warmth stole through Meg. He was right, so right, but she had never had that. That closeness. At least not with a man.

"That *was* pretty clever and amusing," she conceded. "At least after I get over my initial surprise. Did you see that poor woman's face? We must have shocked her."

"She thinks we're sleeping together," he said. "Or at

least she did until you told me that you don't wear underwear. A man who was sleeping with a woman would know that."

Her delight in their closeness dimmed a bit. She and Etienne would be friends but despite the way he affected her, they could and would never be more.

Still, she'd known that from the start. She had no right at all to complain. As it was, his comment reminded her of why they had been arguing. "Etienne, why *do* I need special underwear? No one but me will ever see it."

"A shame," he said, "if that's true. But, even so, you need to feel beautiful all the way to your skin. In fact, Meg, I've learned a few things about you today. Your instruction has to be far more thorough than I had originally planned. We're not only going to resurrect Fieldman's Furnishings in the next two months, but by the time you and I are through, you're going to know that you're an attractive woman right down to the cellular level. Men will fall at your feet. Women will admire and envy you."

She laughed at his ridiculously optimistic comments, but later when he was seeing her off at her door, Meg had to face reality. Etienne had come into her life like a shooting star. He was all fire and enthusiasm and confidence, but she wasn't that way.

Picking up Lightning, who uncharacteristically allowed herself the indignity, Meg looked up at Etienne. "Do you always have this much passion about everything?"

"What do you mean?"

"I mean…me. I know I asked for help, and I know I need to look right if I'm supposed to be a spokesperson, but you've jumped in and taken me on as a kind of project, one where you're determined to get the blue ribbon by turning me into the best jam at the county fair. You're so sure, so enthusiastic, so determined. Don't you ever doubt? Or question?"

He reached out one hand, and Lightning coyly batted his finger with her paw. "I question many things," he said solemnly. "More than you'll ever know. I make lots of mistakes and I hate that. I've done things I regret and even things I can't live with. I question myself every day about those things and I always will, but I don't question truth when it stares me in the face, Meg. You are an amazing, striking woman."

"And you know this how?"

He smiled gently and tucked one finger under her chin. Lightning made her escape. "I know this because you came back to the business, you did something you hated the thought of doing just to save your friends. And I know this because I'm a man, and I have eyes in my head."

And without another word, he leaned over and placed his lips on hers. Gently but firmly, he kissed her. And then he left.

Meg felt as if her knees had turned to noodles. She swayed on her feet, but she didn't move.

"I'll see you in the morning, Meg," Etienne called to her as he exited the building. "Tomorrow we pick up the pace."

But as she lay in her bed that night Meg wondered if she could take a faster pace with Etienne. Already, she was short of breath and not thinking clearly. Another day like this and she wouldn't be able to survive.

Her mind was playing dangerous tricks on her. Her lips were tingling, and she was most certainly wanting things that she could never, ever have.

Drat the man! Why couldn't he have stayed in France?

Because Edie would be destroyed. He had to come save Edie. And Meg had to help.

But, Meg wondered, who would save *her* when Etienne had gone back to France and all she had were aching lips and arms and memories. She was just going to have to be stronger and more resilient tomorrow. She was definitely going to have to stop acting like a total idiot and wondering what it would be like if Etienne kissed her again.

CHAPTER FOUR

ETIENNE filed past the row of people at their desks. He had opened the doors to the employees today, and they were all waiting for him to say something. The expressions on their faces were a mixture of fervent hope and something less than pleasant. Suspicion. Well, that was to be expected. They didn't know him. Their fates were in his hands.

But when Meg strolled in a few minutes behind him, there were no conflicting emotions flickering across people's faces. Everyone was smiling. Tiny, wiry little Edie went to Meg and hugged her. "Welcome home," the older woman said.

And then there was a round of applause as others joined in, calling out greetings. Meg waved to her friends and the room went unexpectedly quiet. In the second immediately afterward, Etienne heard a man in the back of the room mutter something about how he hoped the new owner wouldn't lie to Meg like Alan had, followed by someone else's quick shushing sound.

Meg looked momentarily nonplussed, and Edie, with a wide, obviously hastily pasted on and slightly nervous smile, turned to Etienne. "We're very glad you bought the place, Mr. Gavard. I'm sure you'll be a good employer and treat all of us well." She looked toward the corner where the comment had come from and where an older man was looking decidedly uncomfortable and trying to pretend that he was fiddling with the copy machine. Etienne would have wanted to laugh except for the fact that the word "lie" had been used. He'd been told that Alan had fired Meg. Lying was something else entirely.

"I'm going to do my best by *all* of you," Etienne told the group. "And…um…no lying."

Meg rolled her eyes.

"Don't let them push you around," she told him.

Now everyone looked shocked. Etienne couldn't help it. One corner of his mouth lifted, even though he fought the urge.

"She's giving him orders," someone whispered.

"I'm just… Oh, never mind," Meg said and she headed back toward the inner office where she and Etienne had been working yesterday. Etienne noticed that she was wearing a navy-blue suit that fit her body, emphasizing the gentle sway of her hips as she moved.

Heat—and admiration for what she'd tried to do for him—filtered into his consciousness. He remembered how soft her lips had been and how her eyes had widened in shock when he'd kissed her. She had said nothing then, but today she'd found her voice again. Good.

"Meg's quite a sassy one, isn't she?" Etienne remarked half to himself. It seemed he liked sass.

"But very nice," the old man in the corner said.

"I've noticed," Etienne agreed.

The man looked mollified.

"Do you need anything special of us, Mr. Gavard?" Edie asked. "We know the company is in very bad shape. Mr. Fieldman wouldn't have run if that weren't the case, because he wanted this place badly enough to do whatever it took to get his mother to leave it to him."

She frowned, and Etienne began to suspect just how deep the problem with Alan had gone. Besides the man's general ignorance of good business, his blindness to his employees' talents and his lack of common sense, Alan Fieldman must have done something to Meg beyond firing her. No wonder the man in the corner was concerned.

Etienne looked at Edie's aging face and the fervent, anxious expression in her eyes. "I want you all to trust me. I know that's asking a lot. This is your work, your identity, your livelihood. But I want you to know that I don't take that lightly. My sole aim in coming here is to turn this place around."

"To make it profitable," Edie said.

"Yes." Even though he had little interest in his own profit in this case. He didn't really need the money. He needed the sanity and the peace of mind.

"If I don't do that, I will have failed, and I don't like failure. So, for now, what I want is for you to have faith, to keep doing your jobs as well as you can, to follow whatever instructions Meg and I give you and above all to squelch any rumors that Fieldman's is failing. That can be disastrous in the business world. From this moment on, we're on the path to success, and we want the world to know that."

"So…we're not failing?" an older woman asked. She was standing next to a desk that had a nameplate that read Marie. The nearly worshipful naked hope on Marie's expression almost buckled Etienne's knees. His life had nearly been ruined by people expecting too much of him, he had unwittingly but callously sacrificed his wife to the expectations of his family, his name and position, and here he was *intentionally* seeking out those who had no choice but to put their lives in his hands. So why did he choose to do this in his work?

Because I have to, he reminded himself. He had to be able to live with himself. A little, at least.

"From now on we're a team, and this team is going to survive," he told them. "I'll need all of your help. I may be asking you to do things that haven't been asked of you before. Legal things," he said at the look of alarm in one man's eyes. "But we're cutting corners to make things profitable and we may all have to pitch in and do double duty at times when people are sick or have emergencies. No temporary workers to step in, no outsiders handling maintenance. This is all going to be…us. Our methods may be a bit unconventional, but from here on out you have a vested interest in making sure this company succeeds. If it does, it's going to be yours someday. This will become an employee-owned company."

A buzzing began through the room. One person stepped forward. "Does that mean we can fire you if we don't like what you're doing?"

Etienne did laugh then. "Not yet. Besides, you won't have to fire me. When things are back in shape here, I'll be gone. Until then, you're going to be my prime concern, and I'll expect complete cooperation. This isn't going to be easy."

"What about Meg?" someone asked. "Where will she be when we're going full tilt again?"

Etienne didn't know. For some reason that bothered him even though it shouldn't. Meg was charming, but she was temporary, as was everyone in his life. Holding people at a distance was how he had maintained his sanity these past few years. "Meg will be wherever she wishes," he said. But he couldn't help wondering where that would be.

Meg bent over the desk beside Etienne. They were discussing changes to the line, how positions in the firm would have to be altered to accommodate the current financial situation and all the details of what they needed to do to bring life back to the business.

"I especially like this one," he said, pointing to one of her ideas for a new line of sofas. "I've contacted a textile firm in the east that's willing to cut their price if we give their firm prominent billing in our presentations and ads. As soon as we have some mockups and photos, we're going to schedule you with the photographer and visit some trade fairs. We'll speak to the local press."

Meg froze. Her heart began to thud wildly. She looked directly into his eyes. He gazed back at her, reached out and tilted her chin up gently.

"I once knew a woman who was totally dependent on a man for her identity and for her…everything. That won't be you. You'll have no need of a man if you don't want one, because you'll have you. You'll have this," he said, gesturing toward the room. "I can help you get from here to there. I want to. Let me."

His voice was like a caress. Meg almost felt herself

sway toward him, but that would be a mistake, one neither of them wanted.

She nodded. "Thank you," she said softly. "I made the rounds and have started to draft some revised job descriptions so we can take up the slack in areas where we've been lacking due to letting our outside services go."

"Good. But I want everyone to know that they'll be paid extra," Etienne said. "I'm not a poor man and I've set aside funds for the restructuring of Fieldman's."

"Thank you. Some of them have been here most of their careers. This is a second home for them." And for some like me, she thought, it was more than a home. It was a haven. Or at least it had been, before the incident with Alan.

"They love you," he said simply, and she glanced up into his eyes.

"They know me."

"It's more than that."

Meg shrugged. "I tend to get a little territorial and protective about people I care about. They know that."

"Sounds like they reciprocate. Some of them are very concerned about how I'm going to treat you."

She took a deep breath and reached for a jar that held pencils. Cupping her hands around it she pondered how much she wanted to divulge.

"I'll talk to them about that," she said. "They shouldn't be speaking to you that way."

He reached out and placed his hand on her arm. Sensation shot through her, awareness of the man beside her nearly overwhelmed her, warmth and something more made her feel flushed and awkward and needy and...

She lost her grip on the cup, and pens and pencils tumbled out, rolling off the desk.

She lurched to grab them, but Etienne's grip was gentle but firm. "Leave them, Meg. And...don't speak to the others about how you want them to treat me. I have to form my own relationship with them. I'm capable of doing that. What I'm not capable of is reading minds. I think I need to know more of what happened here before you left. As it is, I seem to be the only one in the dark."

"It doesn't matter."

"It does. It affects how everyone thinks of you and me. It affects how you approach your work."

"I wouldn't cheat you of my time or effort, not after we made a deal!"

"I know that, but you might be too careful, too controlled."

"That's not such a bad thing. I've been meaning to work on that self-control all my life."

He smiled then. "Self-control has its time and place. Not yelling at your employer is a good example of self-control."

"I haven't yelled at you."

"You've lectured me," he teased. "You told me not to let the employees talk to me in a disrespectful manner, and right in front of them, too."

"That was bad," she agreed, but she couldn't seem to keep from smiling.

"It was," he said, but he chuckled when he said it.

"Okay, reminding myself not to try to protect you from Raymond, the man at the copier, is a good example of self-control. What's a *bad* example of self-control?" she asked.

"Not voicing your opinions or offering your ideas because you think they might be seen as too wild and crazy or that others might criticize you or make fun of you."

She grew solemn then. "That's a tough one. I'll have to think about it."

"Did Alan criticize your ideas?"

So…they *were* going to discuss Alan.

"Why do you say that?"

"Your friends… They're worried about you because of Alan. I can understand that, because you told me that he fired you. But, what I can't understand is why."

Oh, no. She so didn't want to do this.

"He wanted me gone."

"Obviously." Etienne waited.

Meg stubbornly decided to dig in her heels. "These things happen."

"No." Etienne slowly shook his head. "I've run many companies, had thousands of employees, but…look at your work," he said, gesturing to the mock-ups she'd made in the middle of the night last night. "You told me you would come up with ten good ideas and you did it in a matter of hours. They're good ideas, and you mapped out the pros and cons of each one. You suggested possible options for changes. You circulated among the employees and thought up new ways to make things run more efficiently. You understand Mary's obscure accounting procedures. You know this company inside and out. You should be the last person standing if this company should go down, not the one who gets kicked out. What happened here, Meg? I can't be in the dark."

"Is that the only reason you need to know?"

"No, it's not. I don't like seeing people mistreated. I also don't like asking this of you, and ordinarily I wouldn't pry, but you were the brains of this company and Alan was the owner. You were asked to leave. I'm trying to piece this company back together, and if there are secrets or undercurrents that are still in place, then…"

"There aren't any undercurrents. They ended the day Alan asked me to leave." Meg closed her eyes. Tightly. "But yes, there were undercurrents prior to that. Alan and his brother had nothing to do with Fieldman's when they were younger, but three years ago, after they had both been out in the world for a while, they came back and joined the company. Alan was more outgoing, more take charge. He…he paid attention to me and eventually we became involved. He gave me a ring, but we didn't set a date even though we'd been engaged for a long time. Then Mary died and she left the company to him. His brother left immediately. And soon after that, Alan hired a new woman, promoted her over me and fired me. I had served my purpose."

"You're saying he pursued you only because Mary loved you."

"Yes. Because I was Mary's favorite employee, marrying me became his ticket to the CEO position. But I hadn't realized that he was simply using me to beat out his brother for the position. I had no idea there was a contest going on."

Etienne swore in French and then he swore some more. "No wonder your friends warned me. I'm surprised they didn't do more. Had I been in their shoes I would have."

"You're not to blame for my ignorance."

Etienne swore again.

"Stop swearing," she told him.

"I wasn't."

"It doesn't matter. I don't know French, so you could have been saying 'Pass the pretzels' for all I know, but it *sounded* very much like swearing, so it's the same difference."

"Then I apologize, but, Meg…you have to know that you weren't the one at fault here. The man was and is an ass. He didn't deserve you."

"Nonetheless I was going to marry him and now I'm not. End of story. It's over. It's ancient history. I'm completely fine now."

Except of course she wasn't completely fine. A woman like her, one who had faced rejection and untrustworthy people all her childhood and who had thought she had finally managed to make a place for herself using only her wits, didn't easily get over the shock of knowing she'd fallen victim to a con man. She had given Alan her heart and her trust and had been made to look like a naive fool.

"I hope when we're done here that you'll be able to tell Alan Fieldman that you've won. Sometimes men aren't to be trusted."

She blinked at that.

"You?"

"I'm no saint, Meg. I may not lie to you the way Alan did or make promises I don't intend to keep, but don't fall into the trap of believing that I'm better than I am. The one good thing I *can* say for myself is that I never make promises I can't keep to women anymore."

"Not even about this business?"

He gave her a grim smile. "I have high hopes for this business, but there are no guarantees. Mistakes are sometimes made that can't be called back."

Meg was pretty sure that he was thinking of his wife then, but she had no right to ask. She appreciated the gentle warning, however. Maybe he *had* just been trying to tell her that he wouldn't be like Alan, but she had needed a reminder that it would be dangerous to get too close to Etienne. And there was no secret about that. She already knew that he was a man who would only be in her life for a short while. His world and hers would not intersect once he returned to France.

"I should get back to work," she said.

He looked down at her then. "When I made that comment about women and promises, I hope you know that I wasn't implying anything, Meg. I didn't mean that you might be thinking of me romantically. I wouldn't be so arrogant as to presume that."

He ran one hand back through his hair and Meg couldn't help laughing.

"What?"

"You," she said. "Since we met two days ago, you always seem so self-possessed, so in control and calm and cool. Now you're flustered because you're worried I might have thought you were warning me not to fall in love with you."

"I never thought you might be."

Which only made her laugh again. "Etienne, have *you* looked in the mirror lately? Half the women in the office, old and young, are smoothing their hair and re-applying their lipstick when they hear the office door open. I'll bet they're all horribly disappointed when it's me and not you who appears."

"But you're their friend."

"Yes, but I don't have a Y chromosome, broad male shoulders and a French accent. I don't think you need to apologize for warning women away if there's no chance you're going to fall for them. It's only fair to let them know you're not available."

He shook his head. "Yes, but it still feels arrogant to say so."

"Better than letting them think you might be interested."

"Should I wear a sign saying that I'm not available?"

She grinned. "That would be interesting, but I don't think it's necessary. In an office this size word gets around quickly."

"Ah, the rumor mill. Who starts these rumors, I wonder."

"In this case," she said, with a mock curtsy, "I will."

"Meg Leighton, spreading rumors?"

"Spreading the truth," she corrected. "It's a tough job but hey, someone has to volunteer to do it." And she sighed.

"You are a very admirable woman," he said.

"Ah, more pretty compliments. I love them," she teased. Where had this man been all her life? And where would he be in two months?

Gone. The answer came in a flash. She'd be wise not to forget it.

CHAPTER FIVE

THE next few days went by in a blur of work, work and more work. The entire company had to be inspected, taken apart and put back together, and Etienne marveled at the enthusiasm with which Meg and her team tackled every task. He might be the planner and the one with the experience, but once he had made a decision, Meg led her troops full steam ahead into whatever he asked them to do.

What's more, she was a creative genius, so when he suggested that, besides updating their product, they needed to make the building suggest the appearance of a thriving concern, she drew up some ideas.

Now, here she was beside him, looking a bit uncertain. "Problems?" he asked.

"I… It's the paint for the office." She fidgeted with the poppy-red scarf at her waist. Meg's penchant for color wouldn't quite let her go the monochromatic route, Etienne had noted, and red was her favorite. It was a charming habit.

"There's a problem with…paint?"

She sighed. "I'm sure that you wouldn't find it a

problem, but…see, I feel perfectly comfortable handling the books or the employees or the orders, but as for choosing paint… I'd really, really appreciate your input. I have this teensy little habit of fixating on colors that are overly bright."

She did. He adored that, but for this, she was right. The office needed to have the right look for the brochure they were making.

"All right, let's go buy paint."

Meg shook her head. "Oh, there's no need. I stopped by the store and picked up some color cards yesterday. I narrowed it down, picked out a few and got some samples to try on the wall. I just want you to tell me what you think of the results. I found a corner of the room where I painted a few squares. All you have to do is tell me which square is the right one."

She led him into the main room and over to the spot she had indicated. There were four large colored squares painted on the chalk-white wall. There was a very pale almost invisible blue, a classic colonial-blue, a bold darkish blue and the last, a dazzling electric-blue.

"That last one looked better on the card," Meg explained, clearly embarrassed. "I just… I need to see things, but even I can tell that one won't do. It's a bit shocking, isn't it?"

Just then, a man stepped up to the water cooler not ten feet away. He stared at the squares, pretending to shield his eyes.

"Whoa, Meg, did you do this? Take it easy, will you? You're going to blind me with that bright blue."

Meg smiled self-consciously…and noticed that Etienne had moved to her side.

"What does that man—Jeff?—what job is he involved in?" Etienne asked, his voice low.

"Excuse me?" she said, lowering her voice to match his own.

"What task in particular is he working on?"

"He's… I believe he's working on the payroll statements."

"All right. Good. Ask him when you can expect them on your desk. Say it calmly but firmly," Etienne instructed.

"Is there a reason you need to know? He's right there."

"And you're right here, too." Etienne said. "A woman who wants to establish her place in the business world and wants to know how to do it."

She looked at him for several seconds, then took a visible deep breath and turned with a curt nod despite the concern in her expression. The other man was almost ready to leave the water cooler. "Jeff, excuse me, but could you tell me how far along you are on those payroll statements? I'd like them on my desk sometime today. It's not something I can wait on."

The uncertain woman had been replaced by a cool, confident one. The man did a double take. He looked at Etienne with a question in his eyes, but Etienne ignored him, so the man turned back to Meg.

"Today?"

For a moment Etienne saw Meg hesitate. She didn't want to push the issue.

"I know you can do it," she said softly. "I have faith in your abilities, Jeff."

The man gave her a shaky and grateful smile. "Thank you. And getting them to you today won't be a problem, Meg... I mean, Ms. Leighton," he said.

Her answering smile was glorious and if the man had looked as if he'd been hit with a rock before, now he took on the expression of a man who had been hit by Cupid himself. "Thank you so much, Jeff. Your expertise and promptness is making things run so much more smoothly."

"In an hour, Ms. Leighton," Jeff said. "You'll have them in an hour." He smiled at her again as he moved away.

Etienne waited for him to be gone. Then he turned to Meg.

"Well, *ma chère*, what do you need me for? You're a complete natural," he said. "I only meant for you to start making the switch from being his colleague to being his employer, but you moved him directly from employee to willing slave status."

"He was only being truthful about the bright blue," she said, wrinkling her nose at the vivid color.

"Maybe so, but he has to depend on you now. You outrank him and he needs to know that when he has a problem, you can help. If you don't maintain that employer-employee status, your friends and colleagues will have no one to direct them when I'm gone," he said.

Meg looked at him with those big, bright solemn eyes. Etienne worried that she, who had faced far too much criticism over the years, might be hurt by his comments, but she nodded. "I'll work on that, but I'll probably stumble now and then."

"You have an affinity for the job. You'll do fine."

"You're a good instructor," she said. "But we still have a problem." She looked toward the room.

"Ah, the color. Let's go with the dark blue with ivory trim. When it comes in…we paint."

"Us?" she asked with a smile.

"All of us," he said, indicating the room.

"Oh," she said, and he wondered if she was going to tell him that painting was beneath her dignity or that it wasn't what she'd had in mind when she'd told him she wanted to be a successful businesswoman.

Suddenly Meg grinned and wrinkled her nose in such a cute way that Etienne's heart flipped around a bit. "Don't look at me that way. I happen to love painting," she said. "The chance to slap stuff on a pristine wall with no repercussions? What's not to love?"

And for some reason, Etienne believed her. There was just something irresistible about watching Meg when she was enthused about something.

The painting had gone faster than she had anticipated, Meg thought several days later when most of the employees had gone home and she and Etienne were the only ones left.

"Everything looks good, doesn't it?" she asked, staring around the room. The paint had made such a difference.

"It does. It looks amazing," Etienne agreed and she looked up to see him looking at her.

She suddenly felt self-conscious in her baggy jeans and white T-shirt with a tear at the shoulder. She had lots of paint on her, especially on the part of her shirt right over her left breast, where she had accidentally brushed against the wall. She was a mess, but Etienne… That man could do wonderful things to a black T-shirt and a pair of white painter's pants. Today was the first day she had seen him wearing something other than a white shirt and tie. He was mouthwatering in business attire but the T-shirt revealed tanned muscled biceps that made her want to stare.

She forced herself to look away. "I'm glad we did the painting ourselves," she said, trying to change the subject quickly so that he wouldn't notice her staring. "It was fun. I love having the chance to relax and just get messy."

"I love watching you get messy," he said suddenly, affection deepening his voice.

Her breath caught in her throat. "I…"

"You're shocked that I said that about you. Frankly, so am I," he said, his voice washing over her. She couldn't turn around. She was too afraid that the naked desire in her eyes would be visible.

"You're right about the satisfaction involved in doing this ourselves," he said. "I could have paid to have someone paint, but it's a task everyone here could take part in. And when I'm gone, I want to leave you in charge, but as I've mentioned, I want the employees to own the company. When people own something, they fight for it. Painting the office was a start to staking their claim. By their own hands they've improved it."

Then Meg couldn't stay turned away from him anymore. "You are going to be missed."

"I'm still here for a number of weeks," he said. "And we're not even close to done yet. Even today…"

"A new lesson for me?" she asked.

"Not quite." He reached out and lifted a long strand of her hair. "You have golden lights in your hair," he said. No one had ever said anything like that to her, especially not with that appreciative tone of voice. Meg swallowed hard. "You also have paint in your hair. I'm taking you to a stylist."

"You're going to cut my hair?" She almost whispered the words. Why did the thought alarm her? She had no reason to be vain about her hair. It was just plain brown hair.

"I wouldn't think of it, unless, of course, that was what *you* wanted. It's your hair and a very personal part of you, Meg. I'm just suggesting that we shape it and cut out the paint. Would that be all right?"

He was asking her to trust him, though he hadn't said the words. She wanted to say yes. Unlike painting, styling her hair was one of those things she wasn't good at. Her father had disliked any reminders that he had produced a second, unwanted daughter and watching Meg fuss with her hair had always made him snarl. So she hadn't developed the skill. As for trusting Etienne, hadn't trusting people been what got her into so much trouble over the years? She wanted Etienne's help but she also needed to retain some pieces of herself.

"I'd like to talk to the stylist myself," she ventured.

He nodded. "Of course. Do you have a favorite one?"

"I don't have one at all."

"All right. I can take care of that."

In no time at all, they were in a shop where the chairs

were more luxurious than her furniture at home. The stylist, Daniel, asked her what she had in mind.

Panic ensued, and Meg sighed. She turned to Etienne. "I have no clue, but…" she maintained. "At least I got to say that much."

Etienne chuckled. "You did. You took charge, and if at any time during this procedure you're alarmed at how it's going we can stop."

"No," Daniel said. "I'm an artist. I don't do things halfway."

"I respect that," Etienne said. "But Meg is a person, and I don't want her to have any regrets."

"She won't."

Etienne gave Meg a look. She knew that she had to be wearing that total panic mode expression.

"Long," Etienne said in a tone that brooked no argument. "Just clean it up, shape it. Take as little off the length as possible."

And just like that, knowing that Etienne wasn't going to let her turn into a disaster zone, Meg relaxed. "About two inches shorter than what it is, I think," she said. "Shoulder length."

"Good," Daniel said. "You'd look good with some layers framing your face. Just a bit for softness. And bangs. Not everyone can carry off bangs, even though most people think they can. You can."

"Daniel thinks I can wear bangs," she said to Etienne. "What do you think about that?" All these compliments might have gone to her head if she wasn't so thoroughly grounded in reality.

"I think Daniel is an artist," Etienne said with a smile.

"You know how you feel about painting? Well, I'd say that Daniel feels that way about hair."

She looked up at the tall, bony man who was waiting a bit impatiently. "Sorry for all the discussion and nail biting. It's a life changing issue. But…okay. You're the artist. Give me bangs."

He did, and they were full and bouncy and Meg loved them. The soft tendrils that swept across her cheekbones made her feel feminine. When they left the shop she glanced in the window outside to see her dim and wavy reflection.

"It still looks as good as it did in the shop," Etienne told her.

"Thank you," she said.

"It was all Daniel," Etienne told her.

But it hadn't been. No one else had ever even seemed to care what her hair looked like. Of course, this was just all part of the deal she had struck with Etienne, but he could have simply given her a few tips on how to go on in the business world. Although she had used the word transformation, she hadn't expected to feel so different and free and…aware of herself as a woman.

"Then thank you for taking me to Daniel," she insisted. "You are a great person."

But her comment didn't elicit Etienne's customary charming, dimpled smile. She missed it.

CHAPTER SIX

ETIENNE knew he had to be careful with Meg. She had been so joyful, even grateful after Daniel had turned her already pretty hair beautiful. And she was starting to think that Etienne was better than he was.

That would be disastrous. With his annual anniversary date drawing nearer, dread was starting to creep in now and then. He was far too aware of who and what he was. If Meg saw him as a good guy, and he ended up disappointing her... If her faith in him led to him harming her in any way...

It wasn't going to happen.

For the next week he threw himself into work, trying to map out every angle, to figure out all the ways to make Fieldman's come back to life. He and Meg oversaw the day-to-day operations, the cleanup of the building. He bought new computers, had the outside of the building sandblasted and had the new sign installed.

A photographer came and took photos of the interior, the exterior and of the three sample pieces of furniture Don Handry had managed to complete in record time.

Not trusting himself to spend too much time alone

with Meg, Etienne drove himself, but the day came when there was no getting around what came next. He had a feeling Meg was going to…what was the term? Freak out just a little.

After everyone went home, he walked over to the open door of her office and peeked inside. She was bent over her desk, her soft, pretty hair swaying softly. As she worked, she ran those pretty long fingers over the keys of the keyboard gracefully, her eyes intent on the screen. She had no idea that he was there.

Etienne cleared his throat, and she jumped. One hand fluttered at her throat. She was wearing a plain white blouse and a navy skirt today. Very prim, except for the three red bracelets that clanked on her wrists and the red toes of her navy pumps. Meg certainly loved red. And red loved Meg, he couldn't help noticing. It looked good against her pale skin. Which was as far as he was going to allow himself to take that train of thought.

"I'm sorry that I startled you, but I had something I needed to speak to you about," he said.

"Of course," she said, rising as he entered the room.

"I have to apologize to you," he said.

"For what?"

"We have an appointment with some of the smaller local newspapers in—" he looked at his watch "—about forty-five minutes."

Meg's eyes widened. "Etienne, I'm— You know I'm not ready for this." Her voice cracked and then it rose.

"You are. You know every plan we've made, every step we've taken. When I leave here, you'll be the one in charge if you opt to stay. You're the voice. You're the face. You can do this, Meg. I'll be with you," he said. "Every step of the way."

"I don't know enough to do this."

"You know you do. Already, you're overseeing a lot of the operations."

"But that's different. People here are people I know. Some of them were here when I got here. They don't mind when I trip with these new shoes and end up slamming into a desk. They just smile and go on. And when I laugh too loud or wear colors that clash, they don't mind. It doesn't matter. They don't write it in a newspaper so everyone can read about it with their morning coffee."

Etienne stepped closer. He took her hands in his own. "Meg, look at me."

She did, and he was shocked to see that her eyes were glistening.

"You're— Meg, you're… Tears? I— Dammit, I didn't tell you ahead of time because I didn't want you to make yourself sick worrying. Now I've frightened you so much that you're going to cry." If ever a man wanted to kick himself, it was him right now, Etienne thought. "Meg… I'm… Forgive me, but…"

"No. I am *not* going to cry just because I'm a little scared," she said, shaking her head vigorously. "It's embarrassing and silly and unacceptable and juvenile and…I just won't. I never do. Not for years."

His heart split right there and then. She hadn't cried for years and he was the jerk who had brought her to the verge. But he could see that she was going to be as good as her word. She was fighting her fear with every ounce of strength she possessed.

"Ah, Meg, I'm so sorry," he said, pulling her to him, his arms going around her. "I thought that I could easily convince you of the truth, that you'll be just fine. I won't let you fall. I won't sacrifice you."

He wanted to look into her pretty brown eyes so that she could see that he meant every word. But Meg had hidden her face against his chest. She was probably embarrassed.

"Fine independent businesswoman I'm turning out to be. I ask for your help and then at the first hint of anything stressful, I'm running away and squawking. Etienne, I'm truly ashamed for carrying on this way," she said, confirming his assumptions. "I should know better. It's just… I'm not very good yet at being a public person with strangers. I haven't learned enough yet."

"You're very good with *me*."

"You're different."

"How?"

"You're…you."

He smiled as the muffled word echoed through his skin against his heart. He started to tighten his hold. She felt good against him, but suddenly she pulled back and looked directly up at him, straight into his eyes, her caramel eyes glistening, although no tears had fallen.

"I really am sorry for being such an idiot," she said. "I… The only very bad explanation I can give is that…my parents had me when they were older. They had a grown daughter by then and they didn't want another. In fact, they had been planning to divorce, but then I came along and they felt they had to stay married. My father might have been okay with me if I had been a son, my mother might have been okay if I had been pretty like Ann, but I wasn't either of those things. I was…not what they had signed on for, and then, one of those rare days when my mother was happy, she swung me in a circle, playing, but I was too big and we fell. I cut my cheek. After that, she not only wished I was pretty like Ann, she wished she could wipe away the scar she felt she had caused. To her I was a reminder of the mistakes she and my father had made. After that, they more or less ignored me.

"I read a lot, camped out in front of the television and gained weight. My reticence, my awkwardness and my height made me stand out at school, and not in a good way, either. So, I kept to myself and I never learned how to interact with people the way most women do. Except for here where Mary protected me."

"Meg, don't criticize yourself," Etienne said, stroking her hair.

She shook her head. "I didn't tell you this so that you would feel sorry for me."

"I don't. You're unique and I mean that in the best way."

"It's just… I'm sorry that I made such a fuss. It's hard for me to be a public person. It's what I want to be able to do. It's why I asked you to help me, and all right, I'm past my little fit. I'll be better in a few minutes."

Etienne saw red. He absolutely shouldn't have done this without telling her. What's more, he should have known all this about her background. Many people, maybe even most suffered from stage fright, but Meg had been forced to apologize for her appearance and for her very existence to the two people who should have pledged themselves to nurture and love her. And here he had gone and made things difficult for her and she was actually trying to apologize to him!

He gazed down into her eyes, those earnest, lovely eyes. Her lips were parted and he just knew she was going to try to reassure him some more and tell him that she would be fine, that he was not to worry that he had ambushed her.

It was too much. Etienne gave a small tug and pulled her deeper into his arms. He took her mouth with his own and swallowed her soft gasp of surprise.

Her body molded to his and for several seconds she was still as he tasted her, breathed her in and worshipped her lips. She was soft and very sweet and...

Meg shifted against him. She looped her arms around his neck and tilted her head. Her lips slid beneath his own, and flame shot through him.

A small moan escaped her, driving him insane to have more of her. He deepened the kiss, took more of her. He plunged his hands into those soft curls to hold her still.

But she wouldn't be still. Her body slid over his as she returned his kiss, and the heat climbed higher within him.

He wanted her. All of her. Right here. In this room. Right now. He wanted her for hours. For days. And to hell if anyone returned to the office who would wonder what was going on, who would remember how she had been taken advantage of by a man before...

Etienne groaned and stilled.

Meg froze.

"I'm sorry," he said, as they disentangled themselves.

"Please don't say that."

"I have to."

"No. Don't apologize. If you have to be sorry, don't tell me so."

And Etienne realized just what she meant. She had almost moved away completely, but he gently tried to pull her back.

Meg resisted.

"If you think I meant that I was sorry for wanting you, then you're very wrong." Even though he *was* sorry for that. Wanting her complicated things when he wasn't going to stay.

"It's all right."

"No. It isn't. I'm not Alan, Meg."

How did the Americans say it? Bingo. Her eyes came to rest on him, and he saw the truth.

"When you and I touch, there's nothing pretend about it for me," he told her. "I desire you, very much. If I'm sorry, it's not because the kiss was a lie but because it wasn't. You and I…touching or…doing more… I can't stay, Meg. I won't lie to you about that. That's why I'm sorry. I shouldn't start something I can't follow through on."

She smiled then. Actually smiled when his body was screaming with the need to pull her to him. And then a sad little look came on her face. "All that moving around you do… I… It's none of my business, I have no right to even ask why, but…"

"Her name was Louisa," he said. "I'd known her forever. She was shy but not with me. Our families knew each other and from the day Louisa and I were born, our parents joked about how Louisa and I would marry.

Only when my father died, it wasn't a joke anymore. I was the only remaining Gavard male, and my mother pinned all her hopes on me. I inherited the Gavard estate and all the responsibilities and commitments and history that that entailed. I was expected to do the right thing, marry the right woman, have the right child. So, I did all those things. Or I attempted to.

"I hated it, but it was my duty and my mother grew hysterical at the thought that I might fail the family name. So, I married Louisa and found out that she loved me. And also found out that I could break her heart because I was gone all the time on business. Fragile and afraid of my mother's intimidating ways, she stayed alone or in the Paris penthouse, and she was bitterly unhappy when I was gone."

Meg bit her lip. Her eyes were dark with concern. "Etienne, I shouldn't have pried. You don't have to tell me this."

"Maybe I need for you to know. I came here to save Fieldman's, but I don't ever want you to think that I'm better than I am. Do you understand?"

Slowly she nodded. "You want me to think that you're worse than you are."

If the next part wasn't so awful, he might have smiled. Instead he shook his head. "I used Louisa to achieve my goals. Marry a woman of good family? Check. I did that. Beget an heir?"

He paused. "She didn't even want children at first, but she felt that if she had the Gavard heir, I would stay home. And I wanted her to have it. But even when she was pregnant, even once she had explained why she agreed to get pregnant, I didn't slow down my business trips. I wasn't even there when the stress of pregnancy and an undetected congenital heart defect precipitated a heart attack that took her life and the life of our son." Anger at his inability to go back and change things, to take back all his mistakes, left him suddenly speechless.

Meg touched his hand. "How could you have known?" she said softly. "I know you would have prevented their deaths if there was any way you could have, Etienne."

But he couldn't respond. No matter the situation, no matter how much he wished he could reverse time and change the results of that day, he couldn't. He had failed Louisa long before the day of her death. He had broken her heart. And when, after Louisa's death, he'd told his mother that he was abdicating his place as the head of the family, dropping control of the family firm except for this small part he had started himself, and that he would not even consider ever starting another family, he'd broken her heart and failed her, too. Because after that, no matter how many times he apologized for his careless, thoughtless words, she felt responsible for pushing him into grief and she died feeling that way.

The truth was that he was hell on women. He disappointed and hurt them without trying. But, he promised himself, not this time. Please not this time.

He looked at Meg. She looked so sad, so chagrined. "I opened up old wounds by being nosy and speaking out of turn the way I always do. I— I'm so sorry I intruded."

Etienne shook his head. "No. It needed to be out in the open so that you understand completely, Meg. I've had reason in my life to regret how I've handled my associations with women, but that's not going to happen this time. I won't give you false promises of any kind," he told her, "but I won't disappoint you by failing to help you, either. Beyond business I have no right to get involved with anyone and you have the right to know that. Because when I go, I'm going to miss you. But I'm still going to have to go. I never stay. I can't."

She didn't blink, didn't flinch. Finally she took a step closer rather than a step farther away. "Then, if the clock is ticking, I'd better start learning how to be a totally independent woman and head of this company quickly, hadn't I? I'd better learn all the lessons you're willing to help me with, Etienne. I don't want you to have regrets. Instead I want to be a testament to your training, a worthy protégée. I'm going to do it. With your help, I'm going to go meet those newspaper people right now and be all that you intend for me to be."

She stood before him, tall and elegant and full of confidence, and he had never been so proud of her. But he had also never been so sad to think about the future. Never getting to see her again when his time here was up was going to be…difficult.

But it would happen, nonetheless. He couldn't even think about staying and taking the risk of seeing Meg hurt or growing to hate him.

CHAPTER SEVEN

THE room where the meeting was taking place was large with a conference table and cushy, big blue chairs. Ten of the twelve chairs were taken up by reporters, mostly female, all in black suits, and when Meg and Etienne walked in, Meg wanted to turn around and walk right back out again.

But she didn't. She didn't even look at Etienne even though she knew that if she did, he would be staring back at her, offering strength and encouragement. She wondered what he'd think if she told him that she was the girl who got poor grades on her oral presentations in school because she was so self-conscious that she stammered and forgot what she needed to say.

It didn't matter. She wasn't going to tell him. And she was going to do this right. Because Etienne was carrying too much guilt on his shoulders. She didn't want to be another weight, another woman he'd end up regretting. Besides, she might be the face of Fieldman's, but he was the actual owner, the one taking the biggest risk, and she wasn't going to fail him if she could help it. She prayed that she could come off looking reasonably competent. Or at least not incompetent.

Besides, hadn't she wanted to forge a place for herself in the world, to be a woman to be reckoned with, to become so self-sufficient that she didn't need to depend on a man for anything? Well, here was her chance. She needed to take it and she had to remember that wanting a man like Etienne would be self-destructive, a one-way ticket to doom and gloom and certain heartbreak. Anyone with any intelligence could see that.

Meg circled around to the open side of the table, facing the reporters. She tried to recall all the things she and Etienne had spoken about on the way over here, all his coaching, all the statistics and talking points she was supposed to spout, but the only thing she could really remember was his admonition to "be yourself. Just be Meg."

Meg looked at the group gathered there. She opened her mouth, uncertain of what she intended to say. It was school report day all over again, but then she looked at Etienne. His silver-blue eyes held no hint of concern. He was smiling at her. He believed in her.

"I have the most wonderful job in the world," Meg began, which was nothing like what she and Etienne had decided on. "Because I've been very lucky and because I've been blessed to be able to work with wonderful people.

"I got my start at Fieldman's when I was sixteen. I left a year ago and then was rehired a few weeks ago by Mr. Gavard," she said, nodding toward Etienne. "We're… partners and with the help of the other employees of

Fieldman's we intend to not only reenergize the company, but to make it the kind of place people will compete to work for. It's going to be a furniture friendly, consumer friendly, environmentally friendly and employee friendly company. We've already started. Let me show you."

She pulled out her portfolio of the new product line and some of the ideas she and Etienne had drawn up to make Fieldman's, small though it was, stand out from the crowd.

"Every drop of paint we use, every piece of technology we buy will be planet friendly. Our furniture is handmade out of materials that are certified chemical free for those people who have medical concerns."

"Isn't that expensive?"

"It is. That's why we're grateful that Mr. Gavard has taken over the company, although…he intends to eventually sell most of his shares to the employees."

"Mr. Gavard," one reporter said. "What do you say to all this?" The woman was eyeing Etienne as if he were a piece of man-size chocolate she wanted to bite into.

"This is not my show," he said. "I refer all questions to Ms. Leighton."

"Your…partner," the woman said. Then she turned suddenly to Meg.

"Is he really just your partner?"

Meg blinked. How to react? How not to overreact? Instructions flew through her head. Reactions begged to be spoken. She ignored them.

Then she smiled. "Ms. Banner," she said, reading the woman's badge. "Look at me. I'm a…decent-looking woman. I have my attributes, I rather like this new hairdo I have, don't you? But, I ask you…do I seriously look anything at all like the kind of woman Mr. Gavard would be entangled with? The man is absolutely gorgeous and he's got those great dimples and… Well, of course I like looking at him, but most of you here would make much more likely dating material for Mr. Gavard should he be looking for a date."

Every woman in the room turned to look at Etienne. Meg smiled and waved.

"He has dimples?" one woman asked.

"Oh, yeah," Meg said. "And when he doesn't believe something, he can do this great, sexy thing with his eyebrow. Show them the sexy eyebrow thing, Etienne."

He crossed his arms. "I think this press conference was supposed to be about Fieldman's, wasn't it, *partner*?"

"Oh, now he's going to get all professorial on us and give us a lecture. I probably won't be able to even drag him out to another one of these if you write something about him and not the furniture," Meg confided.

"Nice manipulative move, Ms. Leighton," one reporter said.

"Yes, and we'll bite," another one answered. "Usually we're just attending boring meetings. You bring Mr. Gavard back for us to drool over and we'll be right there."

"See if you can get him to take his shirt off next time," one woman teased.

"You just make sure you write something nice about Fieldman's and I might talk him into rolling up his shirt-sleeves," Meg promised.

The women laughed. Even the two men in the crowd looked amused. "You're totally cute," one said to Meg.

Meg's mouth fell open. "Well…thank you," she said.

"And I think your ideas for Fieldman's and your products are going to stir up a lot of attention at the local trade shows."

"Will you say that in your article?"

"Absolutely. It's what I do."

Meg smiled and nodded and fielded another question. When the meeting finally ended and the room had emptied, Etienne walked toward her. "That was the most unconventional press conference I've ever attended," he said.

Meg played with the buttons on her suit. "You've attended a lot, haven't you?"

"Thousands." He moved forward two feet.

"And none like this? Hmm."

"'Hmm' is right. I didn't see any statistics."

"I kind of forgot about those in the heat of the moment."

He took another step closer.

"No schedules."

"Forgot that, too."

"And no mention of your impending trip to Paris and the international arm of the company."

"I'm sure I'll remember to talk about that next time."

"And…what was that about my sexy dimples and how you were going to talk me into rolling my shirt-sleeves up?"

"But I totally saved you from having to take your shirt off. I didn't think you'd want to do that, even though it would've livened things up a bit."

And he took the last step toward her, slid his hands up her arms, walked her back three steps to the wall and gently pinned her against the wall.

He kissed her. Totally. Thoroughly. Completely. A kiss that was wet, hot and made her knees forget their job of holding her up.

She slid.

He caught her.

And kissed her again.

"This was not a press conference," he said. "This was major torture for me. I can't take having you look at me like you want to climb into bed with me, especially if you're doing it merely for the sake of theater. Now kiss me, Meg."

She did.

He smiled and did that amazing Etienne dimple move. "You were marvelous," he said. "Don't do it again."

"Don't kiss you?" she asked, teasing him even though her heart was beating wildly, her blood was rushing around her body and her entire being was hot and crazy and on fire for one more kiss, one more touch.

"Don't tease me while other people look on. Seriously. I can't take it, Meg. I was in danger of walking over there and pulling you down on the table right in front of everyone. That just wouldn't be right."

"No," she agreed. "Because then everyone would want some of that."

"You make me crazy," he told her.

"You make me crazier, but, Etienne?" Reality was returning. Her lips were burning. Reality was intruding and she was afraid. Really afraid. She hadn't even hesitated or protested or thought while he was kissing her. This man could break her, so easily.

"I know," he said, brushing her cheek with his thumb. "We can't do this, and I have no right to blame you, Meg. You were just working the crowd. You really were spectacular. They liked you, all of them. Especially the men."

He frowned.

"They were just being nice."

"No. You have what it takes to win people over. You just didn't know it before."

Because she'd just never had someone like Etienne telling her things like this before.

"You're going to be fine. You're going to be great. You're going to make it," he told her.

And she knew that he was thinking about all the things that would happen after he was gone. He had said that there were no guarantees in life, but she could tell that there was one. One day Etienne would board a plane. And then it would be just her. Without him. Forever.

She had to stop wanting him. Right now. The wisest thing to do would be to keep her distance from him.

But that just wasn't going to happen. At least not yet.

CHAPTER EIGHT

EVER since Meg had fallen into Etienne's arms like a ripe plum, she had been reminding herself that while she might be enjoying herself now, the time would come when it would just be her and Lightning and the occasional foster cats from the shelter. If she was very lucky, she might find some way to have the baby she wanted, but even then, she would be a single adult. It would be a total mistake to start thinking that having Etienne around could continue for more than a few weeks.

If she did, she was going to die a thousand emotional deaths. And that just couldn't happen. She needed to channel her fantasies into more productive avenues. No more waking up at three in the morning, dreaming of Etienne in her bed, his lips nuzzled against her neck.

Her dreams had gotten steadily more dangerous. Because of that, she did her best to foster normalcy at work, to plan for her future as a solo adult. So, she read the books Etienne gave her on management techniques. She signed up for some business classes for the fall at a local college. She watched her employees and concentrated on learning their work habits and tending to their needs not only as a friend but as a manager. And she tried not to notice Etienne, who seemed to be driving himself just as hard as she was.

He had been meeting with distributors, meeting with buyers, meeting with everyone but her, she couldn't help noticing. Not that she blamed him. That press conference had been totally outrageous, and possibly embarrassing to Etienne, even if it had spawned a lot of other meetings and a couple of great articles about the company.

Besides, she knew why Etienne was driving himself so hard. There was another reason. When she had pried into his personal life that day, he hadn't mentioned the date of his wife's death, but Meg knew it just the same. There had been rumors in those online articles she'd read about him that last year Etienne had closed himself up in a hotel room and not come out for two weeks. The date was approaching fast. He was obviously trying to work hard, either to punish himself or to forget. Either avenue wasn't healthy.

That just wasn't acceptable. Somehow she needed to be a better friend and partner.

Meg put down the papers she had been looking at and wandered out to find Etienne. She found him with Andy, a computer specialist who moonlighted as a graphic artist. Both men looked up when she came near.

"Look at this, Meg," Etienne said. "This is a mock-up of some ads I thought we might run locally. What do you think?"

She thought that no one other than Mary would have

ever asked her that kind of question in the past, but both men looked at her as if expecting her to make an intelligent contribution to the conversation. Warmth swirled through Meg.

"I think the ad and the graphics project have exactly the kind of new look we want for Fieldman's." She hesitated.

"But…" Etienne coached.

Meg looked at Andy.

"Give it to me, boss," he said. "Don't hold back."

"The font just seems a bit too…"

"I knew it," Andy said. "It's too cartoonish. I should have known."

Automatically Meg placed her hand on his shoulder. "No, the whole thing looks great, very visually appealing, and I think in other instances we might use this particular font. Maybe down the line once we've started winning people over. For now, do you have something…I don't know. Bold but still classic? Slightly edgier but not so much so that people will notice the font before the furniture?"

"Yes, that's the problem, isn't it?" he said. "I think… Yes, I've got just the thing. I'll change this and get it back to you asap. And, Ms. Leighton?"

She blinked. She still wasn't used to people calling her Ms. Leighton.

"Good eye," the man said. "Mr. Gavard and I knew that something was off just a bit, but we hadn't decided what." And he went back to his work as if nothing out of the ordinary had happened.

For Meg, however, it was an amazing moment.

"I know it's nothing," she told Etienne, "but I didn't really feel as if I was helping all that much until this moment. It felt as if I was playing at the job."

"You're joking, right? You've been running rings around all of us, Meg."

"Not you."

"Even me. You have a seemingly endless abundance of energy." And then he smiled. There were those intriguing sexy dimples again. Her breathing kicked in. She concentrated on taking slow, deep breaths so that he wouldn't see how he affected her.

"I just…when I'm worried, I tend to move faster, talk faster, do everything faster," she admitted.

"We're doing as much as we can. I don't want you to make yourself sick," he said.

"And I don't want you to make yourself sick, either." She raised her chin.

Etienne considered that. "I feel fine."

"You're driving yourself."

"Bad habit," he admitted.

"I don't think it's a good idea."

"Don't you, Meg?" he asked, and his words sounded like a caress. "Why not?"

"Because." She crossed her arms.

He grinned. "Good reason."

"I'm working on the reason. No, I know what the reason is, but you might think it's silly."

"There's nothing wrong with silly. Sometimes."

She considered that. "It's just…you've been in Chicago for weeks. Have you actually seen any of the city? That is, I know that you know a lot about it, but while you've been here you haven't had time to do anything except take care of Fieldman's and me."

"Ah, you're worrying. Don't worry, Meg. I like taking care of you."

Those words, that deep voice, the way he was looking at her... For a second, Meg wanted to purr like Lightning, to lean in to him. But this wasn't about her giving in to her foolish desires.

"Well..." she said. "That's...that's nice, but now I think it's time that I took care of you."

He raised that brow.

"Don't do that."

"Don't do what?"

"You know. That thing you do with your eyebrow. You're trying to distract me."

He looked mildly amused. "I didn't know it distracted you."

She gave him a "you've got to be kidding" look, but she had made the comment about his eyebrow without thinking and now her thoughts were catching up to her words...as usual. It was probably better not to pursue this topic any further. She didn't want to have to admit how susceptible to him she was.

"All this time you've been the one guiding me. I think...I *want* to be the one to do the guiding this time. Will you have some free time after work?"

"For...?"

"Sightseeing. Playtime. You actually taking a breather from work and getting out into the city for something other than baby-sitting all of us. Me, being the guide for a change."

"You're going to take me out, Meg?"

Okay, she was blushing. She knew she was. Why had she ever thought that she wasn't a blusher? Or, more to the point, why did she only seem to react this way with Etienne? She didn't want to know.

"Is there something wrong with a friend taking a friend out to see the town?" she asked, tilting her chin high.

He grinned. "Not a thing, and yes, I'd be delighted to have you as my tour guide."

They smiled at each other. The phone rang and Meg started to leave. Behind her, Etienne picked up the phone.

"I'm afraid that won't be possible. When you sold the business to me, I made it clear that you were selling everything."

Meg stopped in her tracks as Etienne's voice broke the silence.

"You know that you have absolutely no claim to the Fieldman's name," he said. "And I'm not interested in allowing you to buy back in to the company in any way. Your association with the company and with everyone in it has ended. Don't approach me or anyone here again. Don't call."

Meg's heart started to pound. Hard. She turned back toward Etienne. Her eyes must look huge. She probably even looked a little scared, but she couldn't help it. And she couldn't help noticing that while Etienne's voice had been as cool as ice, his jaw was tight and his hands were curled into fists.

"Has he called you before?" Her voice came out much too softly.

"Once. I barely managed not to ask him to meet me in a dark alley. After the way he treated you, it was what I wanted to do, and it would have made me feel a hell of a lot better to hit him. But getting into a physical altercation with Alan would only hurt you. He's the kind who likes to bring very public lawsuits. But, Meg…"

She waited.

"He can't hurt you. Or anyone here. I've made sure of that. I have an airtight contract. He has no legal recourse. Still, if he ever calls here or approaches you in any way, I want you to call me. I don't think he'd be that stupid, but still… As much faith as I have in your abilities, I don't want you to have to be the one to deal with him."

Her heart stopped pounding. It melted. She barely managed a nod. "Thank you," she said.

Etienne shook his head and gave her a crooked smile. "It's just the way business goes," he said, even though she knew that wasn't true. "Now, weren't we on the verge of going out to have fun?"

"I think I might have promised you something like that."

That was how, just a few hours later, Meg found herself standing under The Bean in Millennium Park.

"It's an odd nickname for something with a name as beautiful as Cloud Gate," Etienne conceded of the highly reflective steel sculpture that did bear a striking resemblance to a bean. "But it's a very beautiful and imposing structure. Look at us, Meg. Look what all that work is doing to our bodies," he teased, as they stared at their distorted images in the sculpture.

She bopped him on the arm. "Etienne, you promised

to transform me into a gorgeous woman, not this hideous creature I see here. What have you done to me, you evil man?" she teased.

A group of teenage tourists standing nearby gave the two of them a strange look, and Etienne held out his hands in mock surrender. "She's been working much too hard," he told them, and Meg couldn't help laughing. "Her mind is going."

"Maybe she's a little crazy, but your woman has some fine legs," a boy in the group said.

Etienne chuckled. "I couldn't agree with you more," he said.

"They think we're strange," Meg told him as the two of them moved on through the park.

"And involved," Etienne pointed out.

Instantly Meg sobered. She didn't want him to think that she was growing too attached to him. She didn't want to grow too attached to him. "Well, at least *we* know that we're just business partners."

"And friends," he reminded her.

"Yes. And this friend still has more to show you." It was Thursday and there would be a concert at the Pritzker Pavilion later, but it hadn't started yet, so they walked over to the Crown Fountain, two huge structures connected by a reflecting pool and projecting the ever-changing images of over one thousand Chicago residents. "The kids love it when an image opens its mouth and water flows out. It's pretty cool. Come on." And without another word, Meg took off her shoes, held them in one hand and walked out into the reflecting pool.

Etienne shook his head and followed suit. "When

you told me you were going to take me sightseeing, I was picturing something more dignified."

"Museums?"

"Maybe."

"Theater?"

"Of course."

"No dancing in the fountain?"

"Not a chance. That's not sightseeing."

"What is it?"

He laughed. "It's just plain fun, Meg. This was just what I needed. This letting loose."

The two of them joined in with the kids and a few other adults. Etienne took Meg's hand and led her into a romping polka, their feet kicking up water. "It's the only dance I do well," she explained. "It's wild and fast and I can lead and no one seems to notice."

A few minutes later, somewhere in the distance, the concert started up, the majestic and imposing strains of "Respighi's Pines of Rome" echoing throughout the park. The music was beautiful, but Meg's eyelids were beginning to droop.

Etienne led her out of the fountain, made her sit on a bench and reached out for her foot.

"What are you doing?" she asked, instantly awake.

"I'm putting your shoes on."

"I can do that."

"Too late. I already did," he said, deftly cupping her foot in his palm and sliding her shoe on. There was something so intimate about the gesture that Meg felt a tingling running from the sole of her foot all the way up through her body. And then he did it again, with the other shoe.

All traces of tiredness had fled by now.

"Come on, Meg," he said as he put his own shoes back on. "I'm taking you home."

"There were more things I wanted to show you," she said. "Navy Pier. The giant Ferris wheel. The cruises on the lake."

"Another day," he said. "You're tired."

But somehow she knew that there wouldn't be another day. She had started attending functions, talking up the company. Orders were starting to trickle in. The wheels of Fieldman's were picking up speed, and soon she and Etienne would be headed to Paris for one last push at an entirely different set of potential customers. And once the expo in Paris was over…Etienne was over, too.

"Another day," she agreed.

When she opened her apartment door, the phone was ringing. "Go ahead," Etienne said and she moved to answer it. When she returned he was standing in the middle of her apartment. Lightning was flirting with him shamelessly, standing on the couch next to him and rubbing up against him.

"I thought you had *a* cat," he said.

"I do."

"No. I can hear another meow from somewhere." He gestured with his head.

Meg shrugged. "The other cats are Pride and Prejudice." She nodded toward the other room. "They were supposed to simply be foster cats, but they're a pair and difficult to place. They're shy. Eventually, they'll come out." She went about the business of putting food out, talking soothingly to each cat as she fed them.

"And all three cats get along?" Etienne asked.

"They're my family. Family members do not fight other family members. If I can prevent it," she added.

Etienne chuckled. "Are there others?"

"For today, this is it. But it's an unpredictable family and is subject to unexpected growth at any time. The local shelter contacts me now and then when they need help saving an animal and they think I can be of use."

"And you once said that you wanted a child."

Despite the fact that it was Etienne himself who had dropped this conversational nugget in, the room felt as if the temperature had changed. Etienne had been playing along with Lightning and rubbing her head as she purred and leaned against him shamelessly. Now he stopped, his fingers stilling.

"You told me that you were unlikely to get married. How do you plan to get one? A child, I mean."

She looked directly into his eyes. "I don't know yet. I needed to have a stable position before I tried adopting...or maybe I'll go to a sperm bank."

"So...there won't be a father?"

"No. No father."

Because men had not treated her well, he was sure. In the silence that followed her announcement, the slow burn of anger slid through Etienne.

He still hadn't replied to her comment, and Meg picked up the small ginger colored cat that had wandered into the room, nuzzled it and began to pet the animal. "I'll be a good mother," she said, as if promising herself and him that. "I'll care."

"I have no doubt of that."

"You don't approve."

"It's not that at all. It isn't my business to approve or disapprove. I just… You should have help." Etienne studied her attention to the cat. He watched as her fingers threaded through the little cat's fur and then as the third cat, a small ball of black fur, demanded his turn.

"I'll manage," she said. And she could just as easily have added, I always do. But she didn't say those words.

"I suspect you'll do better than manage," he told her. He glanced at the cats. "Pride and Prejudice?" he asked as she put the little black cat down and soothingly spoke to the pair as they went on their way.

She shrugged. "It's my favorite book."

"I see. So, of course you'd name two cats after it just as you'd name a cat who never jumps and barely even blinks Lightning."

"Of course. I have a unique naming system. It's called the impulse system," she said with a small smile, but when she had bent over to release the cat, her hair had snagged on her lips. Without thought, Etienne stepped forward and brushed it away. His fingertips touched her mouth.

His gaze settled there.

He touched her again and lowered his head.

Their lips had barely met, he'd hardly gotten a taste of her, when he heard an enquiring purr and looked down to see Lightning gazing at them like a mother standing guard over her daughter.

"You have a bodyguard."

"No. She likes you."

Etienne had some crazy urge to ask Meg if she liked him, too. He wanted to know how much she liked him.

And that was unacceptable. A man didn't tell a woman he was leaving one day and the next day demand that she pledge her love and loyalty. Hadn't he already destroyed one woman in a relationship where she did all the giving?

"Even if she likes me, I have the feeling that Lightning would protect you if she felt I was up to no good." And kissing Meg couldn't be good even if it felt right.

"Were you up to no good?" Meg asked suddenly.

He leaned in and stole one quick kiss. "Yes. I like kissing you too much. And…I want to do more than kiss you. You make me want more. So, I should thank Lightning for breaking in. And I should go before I do something we'll both end up regretting. Besides, you need rest, and we have a lot to do tomorrow. Lessons," he warned.

"What kind of lessons?"

"Meg lessons. Food and wine. Table settings. Just mundane stuff, in case you ever get asked to one of those boring business dinners. And you will."

"That won't be mundane for me. I don't handle alcohol well at all."

"Well, then, this should be fun."

Then he was gone.

CHAPTER NINE

ETIENNE was not a happy man. It had nothing to do with the fact that during the previous day's lessons he had discovered that Meg and wine were not a pair and that she tended to fall asleep after a single glass. There was something rather endearing about watching her struggle not to yawn and then finally succumb, her head falling softly forward and then jerking up as she attempted to keep herself awake.

Now that he knew her weakness, he could head off trouble easily. She could simply drink water and forget the wine. But drinking wine wasn't the problem.

The problem was this matter of Meg and her family and her family-to-be, something that had been bothering him ever since the other day in her apartment. It was clear as anything that she was a nurturing woman. Just watching her interact with and talk about her cats, that was obvious. Just thinking about the fact that she had been so concerned about his welfare that she had insisted on taking him out for some playtime, or the fact that she had even agreed to come back to Fieldman's, he knew that she was a woman who cared about the welfare of others.

But it was also obvious to him that she had had some pretty brutal parents if they hadn't been able to see what a treasure that she was. And then there had been that complete imbecile Alan who had not recognized Meg for the talented gift of a woman she was. She'd spent too much time trying to please people who couldn't be pleased, but…her cats weren't judgmental. A good scratch behind the ears, a little food and shelter and a woman had a friend for life, one who wouldn't turn on her.

And now she was planning on raising a baby alone.

That wasn't right. Not that she didn't have the talent or the ability or enough love to go around. It was just…she shouldn't always have to be shouldering everything alone.

It burned him. And yet he could do nothing about it. He was, after all, no better than any of the others. He would spend time with her, accept her aid, enjoy her talent and her company and her warmhearted, friendly teasing ways. He had even several times broken his rule of maintaining his distance and she had ended up in his arms. He liked having her in his arms…too much. He wanted to have her in his bed…for hours. But that, all of it, was wrong, because in the end, he would leave her as everyone else had.

So why was he so angry at her parents and Alan? He had no right to be angry on her behalf if he was going to act no better than anyone else had. And maybe that was why he was so upset. Because he had no right. And he never would have.

The phone on his desk rang. When he picked it up, it was the receptionist, Dora, telling him that there was a woman to see him. A woman named Paula Avery. She said the name as if he should know who it was, and it did sound slightly familiar but not enough for him to figure out who the woman was.

And when Paula Avery walked into his office, he still didn't have a clue. It was only after she began talking, her voice fast and nervous as she kept looking over her shoulder, that Etienne began to understand.

He held up both hands. "What you're telling me is that you've worked here before."

"Yes. Recently."

"Who hired you?"

"Alan Fieldman did," she said.

Etienne automatically frowned. He couldn't seem to help it. It was difficult not to hold that against the woman even though it wasn't fair at all. "What was your position?" he continued, trying to soften his tone and set aside his prejudice.

"I was the office manager." And that was when Etienne's resolve flew out the window. He looked down at her application and saw that she had been hired not long before Meg left the company and that she had worked almost up until the time that Alan left. This was the woman Alan had hired instead of promoting Meg.

Anger as hot as a flame rolled over him, but he fought it. Meg had been a total hit with the reporters from the local newspapers and television and radio shows, and she was developing a bit of a fan club. Owning a Fieldman's piece of furniture was becoming trendy.

Everyone wanted to be like Meg. It was good for her to finally have some true adulation. She deserved so much more, and he didn't want her associated with anything negative. Following through on his inclination to yell at this woman would only harm Meg. Etienne fought for calm, for a sense of quiet purpose. Years of training kicked in, thank goodness, and he was able to modulate his voice. "I'm sorry, but I'm afraid we don't have anything here for you, Ms. Avery," he said.

"Are you sure? Please. I don't expect anything like the position I held before. But after Alan fired me, I couldn't find work. I... I have children," she said, just as Meg poked her head around the door.

Amazingly the look on Meg's face wasn't as shocked as Etienne would have expected. She was staring at Paula Avery intently and moving closer. He realized that the woman's voice would have carried out into the hallway and that Meg might have recognized it.

"You're applying for a job," she said to the woman.

The woman turned as white as schoolroom paste. "I—I guess I didn't think. That is, I just thought...with Alan gone... I'm sorry. I'll go. Right now."

Her hands shook, her shoulders slumped and she rose to leave.

"Paula, stop. I heard you before," Meg said gently. "You need work."

The woman looked at Meg with suspicion and fear, and her eyes were dark and haunted. "I've tried other places, but my record isn't too great. Alan wouldn't give me a reference. He blamed me for the fact that the company wasn't doing well."

"Why here?" Etienne said suddenly. "Why would you return to a company where you got fired?"

As if he'd just realized what he'd said, as if he'd forgotten that he had begged Meg to do the very same thing, he looked up and his gaze locked with Meg's. Was she all right? She looked tired and sad, but there was a softness about her, a sense of resignation and…acceptance. She didn't look as tense as he might have expected.

"I know it sounds crazy, but…you were hiring. I heard that and…I need to make a living somehow. I'm willing to take whatever you can offer me. Whatever you're willing to give me to do."

Etienne knew as well as he knew anything that Meg's soft heart was going to lead her to offer this woman a job. What he wasn't prepared for what Meg suggested next. "We're acting as a distributor right now for a couple of companies who design for us, but we'd also like to start an experimental in-house line. If I remember correctly you had a background in design. There might be room for an entry level position on the design team if you're interested," Meg said.

The woman murmured a quiet yes. She looked as if she wanted to drop to the ground and hug Meg's legs. "You should hate me," the woman said, clearly confused.

Meg sighed. "You weren't the one who fired me. Part of my job is to hire good people. If you're competent and you do your job, that's all I care about. Come back tomorrow, ready to work."

The woman nodded and gathered her things. After she had gone, Meg looked at Etienne. "She needed a job," was all that Meg said.

He studied her for long, silent moments. She looked at him, then looked away to the side. He noticed that she was fidgeting with the red leather band of her watch. Meg clearly wasn't as calm as she appeared to be.

"You needed to prove you were better than him, didn't you?" Etienne asked.

Now, she turned back to him in a rush. Her eyes flashed fire. "I *am* better than him," she said.

Etienne laughed. "Meg. Amazing, surprising Meg. You're not going to get a single argument from me. There's no question in my mind that you're miles better than Alan is, was or ever could be. The question is…are you really going to be able to take working with the woman who was given your job the last time around? Without attempting to bring her down, I mean?" he asked gently. "Not that you'd do it consciously. I'm sure you'd be appalled by that, but…subconsciously, her presence has to sting a little."

"A little," Meg admitted. "But not as much as I might have once thought. After all, she and I have something in common. By rights we should actually bond over our dislike of Alan."

"Is that going to happen?"

"Probably not. I won't hold what happened against her, but the truth is that it was a dark day for me. She's a reminder of that. Bonding isn't going to take place."

"Still, you've just established yourself as a woman who knows how to be magnanimous and walks the walk. I'm betting that the people in the outer office are going to have an awful lot of questions."

"Yes, I know. I can hear the buzz already and…why not? I'd certainly be buzzing if I were in their shoes."

She walked out the door and prepared to meet the barrage of questions.

And as she moved, Etienne realized one thing. By giving Meg this job, he had sentenced her to a somewhat lonely existence. Before, she had been a part of the masses. Now she was the one who handled all the decisions. At least she would handle all of them, alone, once he had gone. But being alone had been her curse all her life, and now he had sealed her fate. He *knew* what that place at the top could be like. It could make good people do bad things. It could doom a person to a loveless life.

Etienne swore softly in French. But that didn't change things. Meg was and might always be alone.

Except for her pets.

Except for her child.

Except for any man who might—finally—win her over, a man who would stay and be there for her, night and day. She said she didn't want a man. Would she ever change her mind? And what man would ever be good enough for her?

No man, Etienne thought. Not one. Lightning might turn out to be the perfect companion for Meg, after all. But no man as a husband didn't mean that there would never be a man in Meg's bed.

Etienne frowned. Where had that thought come from?

He didn't know. He didn't want to know. And he darn well wasn't going to pursue that line of thought, because the only thing he did know was that he wouldn't be the man in Meg's life.

A woman had loved him once. Her whole life she had loved him, but in the end, he had failed her.

He wouldn't do that to Meg, too.

So, what would he do?

Keep working for her, keep trying to save this place and these people she loved. Keep trying to make a difference in her life so that when he left she and her child and her world would be better off.

What was the next step?

Touch her, taste her. The thought leaped right in there. Meg Leighton was doing serious damage to his sanity. He wanted what Alan had thrown away. If he had needed any more proof that Alan had been a fool, that was it. Alan had walked away from the woman who made Etienne break out in night sweats.

What had she done, Meg wondered a few hours later. Paula Avery was young, blond, curvy and petite. A total cutie pie. The woman Alan Fieldman had chosen when he had gone looking for a hot, attractive, intelligent woman. The woman he had thrown Meg over for.

And Paula would be right there in front of Etienne every day of the week. He said he didn't want a woman, couldn't have one, but there was no way a man like Etienne was celibate. His kisses were too hot and demanding. He was most definitely a man who enjoyed women. And Meg had just hired a tasty dessert of a single woman who would be in the office every day.

Maybe she was doing it to punish herself for wanting him. "And maybe the stress of constantly striving to do better, to be better, to be different is starting to get to me," she muttered to herself.

Still, one thing was certain. Etienne had said he would

leave. Other women had surely tried to get him to stay, and all of them had failed.

So, please, get Etienne out of your thoughts, she told herself. Don't even dare to remember his kisses.

But she woke in the middle of the night, remembering. She was going to have to do more to bring this relationship back into the realm of business partners and friends.

What could she do?

Something drastic.

CHAPTER TEN

"WHAT are you doing, Meg?" Etienne asked the next day.

Meg looked up at him. He was eyeing the green canvas bag she was carrying with curiosity.

"I'm planning something," she said, not hesitating lest she lose her nerve. "The thing is that everyone has been a bit stressed lately. With the way things are taking off with Fieldman's, it's kind of like watching an airplane trying to take off over a mountain range. You hope it will make it, but you're not completely sure that it can clear the upper peaks."

He grinned.

"Okay, I know why you're looking at me like that. The mountain analogy didn't quite cut it, but what I'm saying is still true in its own way, isn't it?"

"*Absolument*, Meg. *C'est vrai.* Of course. You're right."

Meg's breathing kicked up and she wanted to groan. She hated when he spoke French even though he was always careful to translate for her. *No, that was so wrong. She totally loved it when he spoke French, but it made her shake and burn inside so much that it scared her. French should be illegal or it should at least come with a warning label.*

"But I still don't understand," he said, nodding toward the bag.

"It's simple," she explained, dropping her bag of objects with a clatter. "Everyone is tense. We're beginning to snap at each other."

"I haven't heard you snapping at anyone."

She blushed. Okay, she was lying just a little. And she might even lie a little more. "On the inside I was snapping," she explained, and she quickly raised one hand. "Do *not*, under any circumstances, raise that eyebrow."

So, he didn't. He grinned, with those darn dimples that made her shiver.

"All right, Meg. What were you snapping about *on the inside*?"

She thought. Long. Hard. Trying to come up with a plausible answer. "I can't think of what it was right now, but there was something, and anyway, the whys and wherefores are beside the point. The point is that we're all under a lot of pressure. The expo is coming up in just two weeks and we need some way to let off steam. Hence, this."

She gestured toward the canvas bag she had been carrying.

"I see," he said. "And what is *this*?"

Meg pulled out a bat. "We're going to do something to help us get back to bonding and away from snapping. Something we can all do together as…as friends, but also as business partners. I understand that lots of businesses have teams of one sort or another and since there's a big field right outside our door, I thought that tomorrow at lunchtime, we could have a very short game of…of baseball."

"Of course. Do you play a lot of baseball, Meg?"

"Not a lot, no." In fact she had been horrible at all sports in school, but at least she knew the basics of baseball. And the equipment was simple, the field was there and she'd heard Jeff and some of the other men discussing the sport. This could be a good thing. It could take some of the edge she'd been feeling around Etienne off and bring her thoughts back to mere friendship. She hoped. "I thought you might captain one team and I would captain the other. I checked on the Internet and I know this isn't a very popular game in France but they do play it, don't they? There were eight major league baseball players in America who were born there, although…not for a while and not all even in the twentieth century. I would have chosen something else, like soccer…I mean your football…except I thought it would be best to have a low contact sport so that everyone could feel comfortable and not self-conscious. Not much touching in baseball, is there?" Oh, would someone please shut her up already?

"Except for the tagging part," he said. "That would be touching."

"But the baseball glove or at least having to have a ball in your hand when you tag a person would make it okay," she reasoned. "I was hoping this might be fun." Did she really sound wistful, hopeful, nervous? This had seemed like such a good idea when she'd thought of it, but now… She was terrible at sports. She'd been doing so well here, otherwise. This wasn't a good idea at all, was it?

"It's an excellent idea," Etienne said as if he'd been reading her mind. "And yes, people are getting a little tense. Let's do it."

"All right, I'll announce it today. That way everyone can bring casual clothes. Shall we shorten the game to either three innings or an hour, whichever comes first?" She was beginning to feel better now. Organization was something she understood. Meg smiled and started to leave the room to make the announcement over the intercom.

"Meg, it *is* a great idea. And I think this might help with Paula, too."

She didn't even ask what he meant. No matter how much Meg had asked the people at Fieldman's to try and accept Paula, the woman was having a rough time of it. "I know. I think people are afraid that if they show her any kindness that they'll be disloyal to me."

"I can understand why they feel that way."

"I know. They think she hurt me and that I might still be hurting. I'll be putting her on my team to try to dispel that notion, if that's okay with you."

And Meg realized that while she wasn't heartbroken over Alan anymore, Paula did make her nervous in one very unacceptable way. Paula's eyes followed Etienne everywhere. She clearly had a crush...or more, and Paula was just as cute and tiny and as much of a showstopper as she had been before. Meg hated that she even noticed that. Jealousy was not in her plans. She had no right to notice anything that went on between Etienne and Paula, so yes, Paula was going to be on her team, and she and Paula were going to work together.

"She's yours," Etienne said. "And Meg?"

"Yes?"

"Thank you. I've never played baseball before, but I have a feeling that this is going to be an unforgettable experience."

Meg had the feeling that it was, too. Had she really thought this through? Of course not, but heck, she had set it up and now she was going through with it. And she was going to make sure that Etienne enjoyed his first experience with baseball.

After all, what could really go wrong?

Etienne's team was in danger of losing, not because he didn't get the game. It was fairly simple, after all. And not because he was so inept. He'd discovered that he had a natural aptitude for hitting the ball with the bat, pitching and catching.

No, the problem was that he was worried about Meg. She seemed so determined to make sure that everyone had a good time, especially him, that she was running herself ragged. And also…she was just so very cute in her blue jeans and red T-shirt, with her inability to do anything that remotely resembled playing the game. She couldn't hit, throw or catch, but she was still making such a valiant effort that it was all but impossible not to want her to win.

He could tell that he wasn't the only one, either. Jeff was pitching now and while he was doing his best to give Meg easy pitches, she wasn't getting anywhere near the ball when she swung. Etienne looked at Jeff and the man seemed to be perspiring heavily.

"Jeff, don't look so worried. This is just a game," Meg said, propping her bat on the ground. But Etienne knew that Jeff didn't have any fear that Meg would fire him. She was the only person who hadn't managed to make contact with the ball today and the man just wanted it for her so badly.

"Now," Etienne said, hoping that his low tone would carry to Jeff but not to Meg.

Apparently it worked. "Are you sure, Meg?" Jeff asked, but as he did, he threw the ball…straight toward her now stationary bat. It hit the wood and bounced back slightly into the field. A fair, playable ball.

"Run, Ms. Leighton!" Paula screeched.

Meg's eyes went wide. No one dove for the ball even though Lily, the catcher, could have easily reached it.

Meg glanced at her bat, at the ball, at the bat. She ran. Fast. Around first base, around second, nearing third as her team members jumped up and down and yelled and as the members of Etienne's team smiled and didn't do much of anything. But Etienne knew this deal wasn't completed yet. If Lily didn't go for the ball soon, Meg would be coming around third base and heading toward home plate with the ball lying not three feet away, right where it had fallen when it thudded off the bat. And while Jeff might have managed to surprise Meg with that hit, and while she hadn't yet noticed the opposition's inactivity, she was a highly intelligent woman. Eventually she would figure it out if no one made any effort at all. And Meg was not the kind of woman you let win. She would take it personally.

But what to do? Lily could still pick it up but Etienne wasn't sure that she would without some coaxing. As for him, he was playing short stop, not that close to the home plate. Still, he sprinted toward the base. Not too fast since he didn't want to beat her there, but not so slow that she would suspect.

As he moved, he looked at Meg. She was running, running, her pretty hair flying out behind her. Etienne was approaching the ball, but at this pace Meg would make it over the plate first. He could tag her just after the fact just as he wanted to and she would have scored for her team. He took his time when he scooped up the ball.

But Lily was standing near the plate, yelling Meg on and encouraging her. Suddenly Meg, fearing she would hit Lily, veered aside. She collided with Etienne, a bundle of soft skin and hair and elbows, one of which caught him in the side. Caught totally off guard, he took the hit full force and winced. Then, seeing she was falling down, he ignored his pain and reached for her. Too late. He missed. Meg fell to the ground, her body sliding on the dirt.

Etienne swore, in French, in English, even in Spanish.

"Meg! *Ma chère*, are you hurt?" Immediately he dropped to his knees and started examining her, running his hands over her. Her leg was bent slightly crooked and he couldn't tell if anything was broken or damaged. "Meg, talk to me. Say something. Say anything, all right?"

She gazed up into his eyes, blinking. "I… I ran into you. I didn't see you. Did I hurt you?"

Etienne closed his eyes. He let out a breath of relief. Then he opened his eyes and gazed down at her. He smiled. "Never."

Now her eyes were starting to clear. She was focusing. "Then…did I make it?"

No, she hadn't. Her arm was over her head, but the base was half an inch beyond, and he had touched her while holding the ball. By now he knew the rules of the game and that meant that she was out and hadn't scored for her team. Out of the corner of his eye, he saw Paula and Lily exchange a look.

Then Paula suddenly rushed forward and fell to her knees. "I… Years ago I started nursing school and I've had CPR training. Now I know that you think you feel all right, Ms. Leighton, but it just never hurts to make sure. Let me ask you a few questions just to be on the safe side. How many fingers am I holding up? What's your name? And what day is it?"

As she spoke, Etienne saw Lily stick her foot out and give a tiny kick.

"You seem okay," Paula said, "but that certainly gave me a scare. You could have hit your head."

When Paula rose and moved out of his way, Etienne saw that Meg's hand was now resting on the plate. He resisted the urge to smile.

"You made it," he whispered.

Meg suddenly sat up on her elbows and turned slightly, looking at the plate. When she turned back, there was a funny, crooked grin on her face. "Nice," she said.

And then she stared straight into his eyes. He was still kneeling beside her. One hand was still on her right leg. Both of them looked down to where their bodies were joined, and now it became something more than him trying to make sure she wasn't injured. The palm of his hand felt…warm. When she looked at him, her eyes looked languorous.

Someone—maybe Jeff—coughed, and Etienne slowly withdrew his hand. He helped Meg to her feet.

"I think game time is over," she said. "But it's been fun."

"You don't mean that."

She smiled, a smile that Etienne felt down to the soles of his shoes. "Yes, I do. I've always hated sports, but not today. I loved every minute."

"But, Meg," Edie said. "You can't give up now. Your team is still behind by one run."

Meg looked at Paula. "It's okay, isn't it?" She turned to the other members of her team, who seemed uncertain what to do. "It's not so much that we want to win," one of them said. "We just want *you* to win. No disrespect to you, Mr. Gavard."

"None taken," he said.

Meg's smile grew. "But I'm happy. I did win. In my own way, I did."

"Yeah," Paula said. "She made a run. That's winning."

And everyone took up the cry. Meg looked over her shoulder at Etienne. "Thank you," she said.

"For what?"

Meg shrugged. "You'd never even played baseball, but you went along with this impetuous plan of mine."

"I told you it was a great plan." And it had been. She had been right. There had been some sniping and tension during the past week, but here on this field where everyone wanted Meg to have her day in the sun, they had all joined together. Even Paula seemed to be taken into the fold.

"You are a man of many talents," Meg told him before joining Paula and Edie.

"I want you to know that I see how it is," he heard Paula saying. "And I wouldn't ever do anything that idiotic and cruel again. Not with you, that's for sure. He's yours free and clear."

And, even though they were farther away now, Etienne was almost certain that she heard Meg say. "Not mine."

He stared down at the baseball in his hand. Then he dropped it to the ground with a frown.

"Hey, at least we won," Jeff said.

But he hadn't, and he had no reason to complain. No reason at all. His relationship with Meg was what it was. There had been no hope for it from the start.

CHAPTER ELEVEN

THREE hours after the baseball game had concluded and a good two hours before the end of the workday, Meg looked up to see Etienne standing in the door of her office.

"Come on," he said. "Come with me."

"Where?"

"Home. And then out."

"Home? Now?"

"Yes. To change clothes."

"And then out? Do we have a meeting with anyone that I didn't hear about? A presentation? A dinner?"

"Yes, I'm taking you to an early dinner. Just us."

She tilted her head. "Is something wrong, Etienne?"

"No. Yes. You got hurt today, and I noticed that you're still limping even though you said you were fine. I'd simply try to send you home to bed but I understand that several people have already attempted that, and you've resisted. I suppose I could order you home, but…"

"You don't want to do that, because I'm in training to take over when you're gone, so you don't want to take my power away. Is that it?"

"Something like that."

"So you're taking me out to dinner."

"Yes, and then I thought I'd whisk you back home early and by…oh…seven o'clock you'd be in bed asleep."

She smiled. "That was very clever and conniving of you."

"It was, wasn't it," he said with a grin. "Too bad I'm not capable of lying to you."

"That's not such a bad thing, you know."

He shrugged. "Will you come with me, Meg?" And when he held out his hand to her that way, how could she say no?

She placed her hand in his. Why was it that every time he touched her, she felt it a little deeper and the longing got a little stronger? The pain when he finally left was going to be excruciating, but she didn't want to think about that. He was still here, right by her side. For now.

"I'm yours," she said.

Those gorgeous eyes turned dark and fierce. "Figuratively speaking," she added, trying not to blush. That had been a stupid, impetuous thing to say.

"Of course."

Of course. And in no time, he had her home. She changed into a white dress, an unusually colorless choice for her, but there was something serious about Etienne tonight, and she didn't want him to feel that he had to tease her about her bright colors the way he usually did.

What was wrong? Was it the upcoming anniversary of his wife's death? Or had she, Meg, failed to digest all that Etienne felt she needed to know?

In the weeks since they'd met, they had spent an

hour or two of each day together while he coached her on all the aspects of business he felt she would need to know. And he had been amazingly well versed in the American system. He possessed an abundance of knowledge about business law and labor and trade laws here. He taught her about stocks and bonds and retirement plans and employee insurance plans, about taxes and safety considerations and…everything, it had seemed. She had tried to digest as much as she could; she had taken books and files home every night, but her time had been limited and…she was worried and…

"Something's bothering you," she said. "Tell me." Just as if she had a right to invade his privacy.

But he didn't seem to notice that she had overstepped a boundary. "I let you get hurt today. I wasn't paying enough attention. If you had hit your head on the ground…if I had fallen on you and crushed you or caused you to break something vital, I…"

He turned to her and took her hands in his own. "I've pushed you too hard, Meg. You've been trying to be all things to all people, to prove that you can do it all, but you don't have to do it all. You shouldn't be forced to play a sport just to make everyone feel good. That day I came and lured you back here, I was pushy. I set a pace that was too driving. I've sapped your energy. You're limping."

His tone was angry, but she could see now that he wasn't angry at her but at himself. Still, she knew that the tragedy of his wife was at the heart of this. How could it not be? How did any man get past the guilt that she knew gnawed at him?

So what could she do? Meg rose up on her toes,

wrapped her arms around his neck and kissed him. Solemnly. Slowly. And with fervor.

When she pulled back, she saw that Etienne looked dazed and stunned…and heated.

"Yes, I'd say I'm perfectly healthy," she said, a bit breathlessly. "My heart started pounding just as it does whenever we kiss."

"Meg," he warned. "Don't do this. I don't have much self-control tonight."

"I don't, either," she said weakly, "so no, I won't do that again, but I just wanted you to know that I'm fine, Etienne. Really. And nothing is going to happen to me. You don't have to save me."

She looked away as she said that because yes, it was a bold and daring thing to say even though she was pretty sure that it was true. She finally got it.

Etienne saved things. He saved people. He did for everyone else what he hadn't been able to do for his wife.

That was why he was always so concerned about her. Oh, sure, he desired her, but then she was pretty sure that Etienne had a lot of experience desiring women. The concern thing clearly had its roots in his personal tragedy. It was up to her to free him from that. From now on, that was going to be her goal, to disentangle Etienne from her life so that if some little something ever did happen to her, he wouldn't blame himself.

That meant she needed to be less concerned about things. Publicly, that is.

"What?" she asked, realizing that she had missed his words while she'd been plotting.

"Here. Come inside, or would you rather sit on the

patio? It's overcast, but I think we're safe from the rain for now," he said as he stopped walking. Meg looked up to see that they had walked to the entrance of Bistro Campagne.

Meg chose the patio. It was full of chatter and interesting people. The restaurant was a charming place, one she had never been to and the food was *magnifique*, as Etienne said, but Meg was concentrating so hard on being bright and cheery and convincing Etienne that she was now the strongest, most learned, most accomplished, least likely person to ever suffer a tragedy or setback or even so much as a paper cut, that she missed most of the meal.

When they left the restaurant and began walking down the street, Etienne gave her a sideways smile. "You are an intriguing and infuriating woman, Meg Leighton."

That certainly got her attention. "Infuriating? In what way? I thought I was being rather pleasant tonight."

"*Exactement*. You're being the brightest, most falsely cheerful person ever. It is an act a man who didn't even know you could see right through. And I happen to know you. Well," he said in a way that made her feel that he knew intimate things about her. She felt the tingle rip slowly through her body.

"I was that obvious, was I?"

"Well, maybe not that obvious, but as I said, I know you."

He did, but…not everything. He certainly couldn't know just how much his words, his accent, his dimples, the way he looked at her or touched her affected her. She was totally incapable of managing her feelings when Etienne was near.

"You were trying to distract me so that I wouldn't worry," he accused. "Weren't you?"

She couldn't lie to him. Much. "Maybe a little," she admitted. "But what about you?" she said. "I happen to know you, too, and I know very well that I did not score a run today."

Etienne looked as if she had taken that baseball bat and physically walloped him with it. "Meg…" he began.

"Etienne," she said, turning to face him and standing her ground. "You know you won't lie to me."

"I won't."

"What was Lily doing behind me when Paula was asking me all those questions? I heard a sound, and later when we went inside I saw that things looked a bit…disturbed around the base."

"You don't seriously think I would say something bad about Lily, do you?"

"It wouldn't be a bad thing. Don't you think I know that everyone felt sorry for me because I was such a stinker at the game and that they all wanted me to at least have one drop of success? That's true, isn't it?"

He reached out and brushed her cheek, and sensation shot through her. "If it's true, it was a good thing, Meg. They love you."

"But it was cheating."

He laughed. "Not when both teams are rooting for the same person. Besides, it broke the ice for Paula. In the end, I'd say several good things happened there. Everyone worked together, they all went away happy and now people are speaking to Paula so she can concentrate on her work more."

"If she wasn't concentrating on her work before, it was because she has a crush on you."

"That's just because she's lonely. It will pass."

"Etienne?"

"Yes?"

"Thank you for trying to make me believe that I don't suck at baseball. I knew it wasn't true, but it was nice to be forced to pretend for a while."

"So you'll let them continue to believe you believe?"

"If it will keep everyone happy, I will. And…when I said that I won today, well, I did. Maybe I didn't break my long running record of never scoring a run, but the fact that people cared enough to make me want to believe that I had…that was winning for me. So no, I won't say anything."

"You're going to be so good at this, Meg. You have the love and loyalty of the people who work for you. I didn't teach you that."

She smiled. "But you are responsible for this." She looked down at herself. "Daniel sent someone to my house to teach me how to apply makeup and do my nails. A woman showed up and gave me all kinds of instructions on the best clothing to, quote, accent my physical features. She even showed me how to walk with more confidence so that I would 'wear my clothes well' and they wouldn't wear me. I know that was all your doing."

"Window dressing," he said. "Polish. So…since we're discussing clothing, I notice that you, Meg Leighton, are dressed all in white tonight. No other color. Meg?"

She shrugged. "It seemed to fit the mood."

Etienne frowned. "But it's not you. Don't try to change yourself in order to accommodate someone else's mood." He turned the corner. It wasn't the way to his car.

"Where are we going?"

"Somewhere… I know there was a man the other day when I was out this way… Here," Etienne said, satisfaction coloring that rich, deep voice of his. He stopped before a flower vendor, picked out a nosegay of wine-red roses and handed them to Meg.

When she took them, Etienne moved back two steps. "Yes. All's right with the world now. Red. It's you. Passionate. Colorful. Exciting."

She laughed. "Is there another woman standing behind me that you're talking about? No one has ever said that I was exciting."

"Well, now they have. I have. And you know that I don't lie to you."

They had backtracked and were on their way back to the car when the threat of rain became a reality. A light mist began to fall and quickly became harder.

Automatically it seemed, Etienne put his arm around Meg and pulled her under the shelter of an awning.

"Wait here," he told her as he rushed back out into the rain, which was coming down harder now.

"Etienne, you're getting soaked," she yelled, but he paid her no mind. Instead he ducked into a nearby hotel. Through the glass doors, she could see him speaking to the doorman, gesturing to the man. Then he reached into his pocket and pulled out his wallet. Within seconds he was running back to her carrying a large black umbrella. He flipped it open and when he reached the awning, he took her hand and pulled her under the umbrella with him.

"The man sold you one of the hotel's guest umbrellas?" she asked, laughing as Etienne wrapped one arm around her waist to hold her close and keep her out of the rain. "I'll bet he's not supposed to do that. Did you have to give him half your fortune?"

"Meg," Etienne lectured. "Are you making fun of me for trying to keep you from getting soaked?"

Suddenly she stopped. She turned in his arms and faced him. "Not at all. I like the way you identify a problem and then immediately identify a solution. You're a magic man, *mon cher.* Is that how you say it?"

But he was still holding her against him, the flowers crushed between their bodies. "That's how you say it, my Meg. And no, I'm not a magic man. Just a man. A man who has to do this. Right now."

His mouth came down on hers. He pulled her closer still. She dragged her arm, flowers and all, free and looped it around his neck, trying to get closer to him.

The rain came down, and Etienne's kisses became deeper, more demanding.

Meg tilted her head and gave and gave. And took and took. She tasted him, she savored him, she wished this moment would never end, that they could stay beneath this cocoon of an umbrella in the rain forever. Alone. Just the two of them. With nothing else to come between them.

But in the distance a car horn honked. People yelled

at each other, they laughed. More traffic noises intruded, and the streetlights came on.

The real world returned, and in the real world Etienne was a man who might want kisses but didn't want more. He could have any woman he wanted, but he wanted none. At least not for more than this.

And Meg realized how unprotected her heart was. She was in grave danger of doing something very unhealthy to herself. Something she had sworn not to do again. Fall for a man who would, ultimately, break her heart. Etienne might not want to do that to her, but it would be done nonetheless.

And when it happened, he would know. It would send him to a very bad place, emotionally. She needed to keep that from happening. Somehow she needed to be a woman who dealt in solutions. Emotional solutions.

Gently, carefully, reluctantly, Meg eased herself away. "That was…very nice. You're exceptionally good at that. But I suppose you know that. It was…a very effective lesson."

He frowned. He growled. "You know that was no lesson."

"I know you didn't mean it to be one, but nevertheless it was. If I'm going to be doing business with the big boys, I have to know how to go one-on-one with them. I'm assuming that now and then there might be temptation. I need to know how to…to walk away from it, don't I?"

For several seconds Etienne didn't answer. He was looking angry, angrier than she had ever seen him. "You definitely need to know how to walk away from temptation. Especially temptation that is bad for you."

She just couldn't do it. No matter the need, even to save Etienne in the end, she just couldn't pretend in this way. Instead she touched him on the sleeve. "I didn't mean it. You're not bad for me. You know how much you've done for me, but...this...this part of the two of us...it's only going to hurt us both in the end. I don't want to hurt you."

"Dammit, Meg, I'm the one who's supposed to say that. I pulled you into this. I get to be the protector."

She placed her palm across his lips and slowly shook her head. "You can't be my protector, Etienne. You can't save me. In the long run we both know that that job can't be yours. And I don't want you to regret it. I want you to enjoy your time with me."

"I do," he promised. "I am. I will."

"For now," she whispered. "We still have some time left. And we have rain and red flowers and a beautiful umbrella. Let's walk in the rain."

"Impetuous," he said and the word was a caress. "But your leg. I've walked you too far already."

"I don't even feel it anymore," she promised. And it was true. For now all she felt was the need to walk with this man who had changed her life so much. For this one moment she would not worry about tomorrow and just enjoy this man and this simple pleasure. Who knew what tomorrow would bring?

CHAPTER TWELVE

ETIENNE knew that he was losing control where Meg was concerned. There was just something about her that made him forget all the things he needed to remember. Yes, he was a successful businessman, but he had failed in his personal life and had hurt those he should have taken better care of. He just could not risk failing or hurting anyone else, especially not Meg.

Bright, beautiful Meg who deserved that loving, secure home surrounded by children that she desired. The thought of interfering with those dreams of hers in any way just wasn't something he could face. He'd hate *himself* if he caused her any pain. So he had to stop thinking about her all the time, stop spending so much time with her before he did any irreversible harm to her.

How was he going to do that?

Keep it low-key, Gavard, he told himself. *Keep it all business.* The way Meg wanted things. Couldn't he do that much for her?

With that as his goal, he pressed himself to concentrate on the company and drove himself around the clock. He almost thought that he was making progress when he had gone a whole week without touching Meg. Yes, it had been a hellish week. He missed Meg so much that he felt crazy and hot, so much so that he hadn't even been paying attention to the calendar and that hated day looming before him. He wanted nothing more than to go slamming into Meg's office and just…look at her, be near her. But somehow he managed to stay away. With a gargantuan effort he kept his distance. He was even beginning to think that he might have himself under control a bit.

Until he looked up one day and found her standing in the doorway to his office. Her brown eyes were bright and fierce.

Immediately, as if he couldn't help himself, he rose and went to her. "Meg, what's wrong?" He reached out and took her hands.

She hesitated.

"Meg? Tell me."

She shook her head. "It's you."

"Me? What did I do?"

"You're just doing too much for us. You're pushing yourself too hard. You've been here day and night and you're looking tired. It's occurred to me that there's a lot more at stake here than just Fieldman's and all of us who work here."

Etienne frowned at that. "What do you mean?"

"I mean you. Your reputation. You've been working so hard for us, but…what about you? You've been very nice about not pointing out to all of us that you have a reputation to uphold. Whether we…*I*, do a good job and cut a good image could affect you. And you haven't even said anything. Is that why you've been so upset lately?"

It almost broke Etienne's heart that Meg was worrying about him. "I haven't been upset, *ma chère*."

She crossed her arms. "You promised me truth."

"All right, the truth is that I've given no thought whatsoever to my reputation." He offered up a smile.

Meg frowned harder. "Then the reason you've been upset—"

"I didn't say I was upset."

"Etienne, did I ever tell you that I'm a very visual person? I need to see things in order to get them straight, but once I see them, everything falls into place. You've been preoccupied and you've been frowning a lot. Your eyes…"

"My eyes?"

She glanced up then and blushed. "Well, never mind your eyes, but something is wrong. I know it."

What to say? He was not going to bring up his concerns about hurting or disappointing her. He had promised that they would be friends and all business. The fact that he was having trouble sticking to the script was his problem and not hers.

"Is it… Etienne, I know this is nosy. And it's none of my business but…I mentioned earlier that I read about you and your life on the Internet. I'm sure this is a difficult time of the year for you. I don't want to be insensitive. If you'd like… If you need time away, Edie and Jeff and the rest of us won't let the place collapse while you're gone and I can promise you that we…

Etienne, you've made things easier for us. I wish I could make this easier for you somehow…"

Her voice faltered and Etienne realized that she was all but ripping off the button on her skirt, twisting it nervously.

Carefully he covered her hand with his own, stilling her.

"I don't want you worrying about me," he said.

"But…"

"Meg, my problems aren't yours. And don't worry. I'm used to dealing with problems. It's what I do."

She got that stubborn look in her eyes. "Maybe, but you're still human. When July 18 rolls around, I'll expect you to take the day off."

The fact that she had the day right hit him in the solar plexus. The fact that she hadn't backed down and was still insisting that he tend to his needs…amazed him.

"Are you giving me orders, Meg?"

She pushed her chin up. "No, I'm not. I'm just being your friend. You had a wife. You had a child on the way. You get to be human and take time out to mourn them."

But he never really had. He reached out suddenly, took Meg's hands and pulled her to him. "It's not that simple, Meg. I wasn't a good husband to Louisa. The child was a duty for her, another accomplishment to be checked off the list for me. Had I been paying any attention to her at all, we might have discovered her condition and avoided the pregnancy, but I wasn't even thinking about her. And later, when I made that statement to my mother, I didn't even think about the fact that I was, intentionally or not, placing some of the blame for Louisa's and our son's death on her. I failed my wife, my child and my family, so no, I don't allow myself to mourn. If I didn't do the right things while they were with me it's too late to do them now. There's no need to worry about me, though, Meg. Work may have been what killed my marriage, but it's also what keeps me sane now."

He looked up and saw that Meg's eyes were wet. Two thick tears hung on her lashes.

"I thought that you never cried."

"I don't," she said, dashing the tears away. "I'm not crying. I'm angry."

"At what?"

"At you. Why do you expect yourself to be so…perfect, so responsible for everyone and everything? That's wrong. People should be responsible for their *own* happiness, but… No, I'm not going to say any more. It's totally wrong for me to be telling you all this when I have no idea what it's like to live in your shoes. I never can keep my mouth shut."

"I've never asked you to."

She shook her head. "I know that. I'm trying to learn to do that myself, but I'm still a work in progress."

He smiled sadly. "Don't worry about me, Meg. My distance lately hasn't been because I'm morose but because…well, you know that I desire you. I don't want to leave here with regrets."

"You're still worried that you'll hurt me? Well, I still say that my emotional state is my own problem. You can't be responsible because I won't allow it. Our deal was that you should teach me, not that you should wrap me up in tissue paper and put me in a box so I won't get broken."

"Do you feel that I've fallen down on the job? Have I failed to teach you something you think you need to know? You already know most of what's necessary to keep this company running."

"I don't know. What more *do* I need to learn?"

Not much, Etienne conceded, but the fact that he'd been upsetting Meg with his attempt to protect her from himself was unacceptable. She had enough on her plate. He didn't want her worrying about him.

"Perhaps…we need to take a stab at some dance lessons?"

Her eyes widened. "You're kidding, right? I need to know how to dance, too?"

"You told me that you only knew how to do the polka."

"And I don't even do that right, if you remember correctly. I was leading you the whole time. Plus, remember all those classes I told you that I took? You're talking about a woman who couldn't even master the basics of how to fall gracefully."

Etienne grinned. "I'm not going to let you fall, Meg."

She smiled back at him. "Okay, but I can't imagine why this would be an essential skill. Will we be dancing in France?"

He didn't want to lie to her. "Definitely." He would make very sure of that. Especially since what was needed right now was some dancing, some levity, a release of the tension they'd all been subjected to.

"Where should we go?"

He grinned. "The outer office."

"In front of everyone?"

"They can dance, too."

She put her head back and laughed at that. "Oh, they're going to love that. Somehow I don't think that I can simply tell everyone that we're expanding their job descriptions again."

"Don't worry, Meg," Etienne whispered. "Just tell them that we're having recess. Tell them that it will help you. They'll do anything you ask."

"They'll do anything you ask, too."

He raised a brow.

"Really," she said. "You may not have noticed but they've latched on to you as one of their own. They trust you now."

Which made Etienne more than a little nervous. No matter what Meg said, he *was* responsible for this company, for her and for what happened at that expo. Betray Meg or fail the company and he would be destroying lives. Again.

"So, you think they won't report me to the labor union if I ask them to tango?"

"As long as you remove the thorns from the roses they hold in their teeth, I think they'll be amused by the diversion."

But, of course, it wasn't that simple.

"We need music," Meg said, "and something to play it on."

After an announcement and a quick search, it just so happened that Jeff had a portable MP3 player in his car with some tiny speakers that would plug into it.

"Sometimes I like to go to the park at lunch," he explained. "You may not like my taste in music, though."

Jeff's taste in music ranged from hip hop to jazz with

a little rock thrown in. Trying to find something that a person could ballroom dance to was a challenge, but Harold managed to locate some slow love songs. "Ooh, this one sounds hot!" Harold said, which made Jeff's ears turn red.

"I don't know how that got there," he said.

Etienne chuckled. "Just keep repeating that, my friend," he said. "Not that anyone will believe it."

"Jeff, it's a really nice song," Meg argued. "You play that when you have a woman with you and I guarantee she'll melt."

Which made Etienne sit up and take notice. He wanted Meg to melt for him.

But, of course, that wasn't what he was supposed to be thinking about. "Let's get some space," he directed. Together everyone pushed the desks out of the way.

Then he turned to see a small sea of expectant faces turned his way. "Partner up," he directed. "Grab the person next to you, no matter what sex. We'll switch for the next song."

There was some giggling as people paired up with colleagues.

"We'll begin with a simple waltz. If you haven't done much of this before, then this is how the dance proceeds. You place your hand on her, or his, waist like this," Etienne said, and he slowly slid his palm around Meg's waist.

Immediately he was aware of her softness, how she fit him and how his heart pounded when he stared down into her eyes. "She places her hand on your shoulder. And then you take her hand in yours," he said, his voice thick in his own ears.

As he called out instructions, Jeff started the music and the group began to move, but Etienne was only aware of Meg, of looking into her eyes, of twirling with her around the floor.

"You're very good," she said, her voice so soft he nearly had to lean close to hear.

"Years of practice. It's second nature." But it wasn't. Not with her. The waltz had never seemed so exhilarating, so meaningful, so short.

The music ended. "Switch," Jeff said, and he headed straight toward Meg.

Etienne's hand tightened on hers for a second, but then he released her, ceding his place to the other man. The one who would stay. Etienne hadn't failed to notice Jeff's interest in Meg. She might find happiness with him.

But not yet. Not today.

Etienne led them through a series of mini lessons in various ballroom dances, but when they came to the tango he claimed Meg as his own again.

"Last one," he said. "And for this one, Meg is mine."

He looked up into Jeff's stubborn eyes and felt a twinge of sympathy for the man. Also a trace of guilt. He had seniority here and it wasn't fair to pull rank.

But he did it anyway. "There might be dancing in Paris," he explained to the man, even though he was pretty sure that there wouldn't be an opportunity for anything quite like this. He just wanted the chance to dance with her, to be with her.

He pulled her into his arms, swirled her into the dance.

Meg was obviously new to the dance; she was awkward, very self-conscious and totally charming. "If

I step on your feet you'll forgive me, won't you?" she asked. "And not yell out too loud?"

"I'll swallow the pain," he promised. "And love every minute."

Which, of course, made her chuckle in that low, husky way she had that made his nerves sing.

They moved through the dance, circling each other, twirling, gazes connected, not paying attention to anyone else in the room until the music reached its crescendo. "Now dip," Etienne directed, and he lowered Meg into his arms, ending up only a breath from her lips.

"And up," he whispered, pulling her back into his arms as the music died away.

By then everyone was laughing and breathing heavily. "Do you do this kind of thing at every company you reclaim?" Edie asked.

"This was Meg," he said. "All Meg."

So no, he would never do this again. The sands of time were running out. In just over a week, she would walk out of his life.

And he would have to take it. There was no other way.

CHAPTER THIRTEEN

THE days were spinning by, the expo was almost here, Meg and Etienne were leaving the next day and the company was developing a slow, quiet hum of efficiency rather than the awkward thump, thump of a car driving along minus one wheel.

Still, with the prospect of speaking before an international audience, Meg should have been petrified. That had been her modus operandi for most of her life. Stay out of the spotlight. Don't attract attention. Hide your defects. But, that just wasn't happening this time. The scar, the weight, the awkwardness and tendency to speak her mind too freely…those things just weren't bothering her. Etienne had worked his magic and made her feel unique. Whether it was true or not, she felt it and that was really all that mattered.

He'd changed her life, and she was grateful, but…

"What are you going to do when he's gone?" Edie asked her one day.

Meg froze. "I don't know what you mean."

"Meg, this is Edie. I've known you forever. You

follow him with your eyes. You watch for him when he's not here. You're falling in love with him."

Meg opened her mouth to deny it, but this *was* Edie. No point in trying to pretend.

"It doesn't matter. He's not a staying kind of guy. He doesn't want children. I'm not even sure he could deal with the cats, but mostly it's just…he's not a man a woman should allow herself to fall in love with."

"And yet you have."

"Not yet. Not completely," Meg said. "I've known he was off-limits from the start, so I've been careful." Or as careful as she was capable of being. "But I *will* miss him." Desperately.

And more than that, she would worry about him. For all he had done for them, for all that she knew he would move on and do the same for another company, maybe hitch up with another woman such as herself, he was essentially alone. He had built himself an emotional prison of constant movement where he wasn't allowed to make lasting connections.

Still, it was what he wanted, and maybe, Meg realized, it was the first time in his life he was able to have what he wanted. From what he'd said, it sounded as if his younger years had been lived according to the family plan. His marriage had been expected, an heir had been expected, and trying to twist himself into a pretzel to do the expected things had hurt a lot of people. One of the people most damaged had been Etienne, though he would never admit that.

But Meg did. She also admitted that his choice to live his life alone was one she had to respect. It wasn't the kind of thing she would choose—she did want those babies—but if being alone and always on the move in his bid to help failing companies brought Etienne peace and made him happy… She *so* wanted him to be happy.

So, she pasted on a smile and ignored the pain in her heart. She still had him for a few more days before she had to give him up.

Etienne looked on in amusement as Meg squirmed in her seat on the plane. "Can you believe that you and I are going to France?" she asked.

He smiled. "I think I can."

"Okay," she said with a grin. "I suppose that was a silly question. *You* jet around all the time, but I've never been anywhere, least of all France."

"I hope you like it."

She gave him a tap on the arm. "As if I couldn't. I'm going to love it." She squirmed some more.

"Are you worried?" he asked. "Meg, you're not worried, are you? Because I've explained that you're going to be fantastic, haven't I?"

"Yes, you have."

"And…"

"And, has it ever occurred to you that you may be a tiny bit biased? I'm your creation, after all."

Etienne frowned and turned in his seat. "You're no one's creation. You're one of a kind."

She laughed. "Let's hope that's a good thing."

It was. A very good thing. And everyone would recognize that at the expo. Etienne had put more effort into Fieldman's than he had ever put into any company and he knew it was because he wanted to make sure that Meg was set up with her heart's desire when he left. That company was her home, and he wanted it to thrive and grow, for her sake. He wanted her to have everything she wanted out of life.

Including those children. Meg, he knew, would never choose to have a child simply out of some misguided sense of duty the way he had. Like some task that had to be accomplished.

Regret hit him, but he ignored it. This wasn't about him. It was about Meg and her happiness.

"You're going to shine," he assured her.

"I will," she promised, and he felt a twinge of concern. She wasn't just doing this for him, was she?

"Where's Lightning?"

"I left her with Edie. And Jeff took Pride and Prejudice, although he agrees with you. He said that they were both guys and they needed more manly names. I expect to come back and find that he's teaching them how to pick up felines."

Etienne laughed. "Jeff's a good man. He'd make sure that everyone ended up happy, I'll bet." He had the feeling that Jeff might be looking for a mate for more than the cats, too, a fact that sent an arrow straight into Etienne's heart. But he had no business going there. Jeff *was* a good man, one who wouldn't destroy a woman's self-esteem and lose her love by leaving her alone all the time. Or by valuing her child more for what it meant to the family name rather than for the joy a child could bring.

Meg had said she wanted to raise a family alone, but that didn't mean there wouldn't be men in her life. She might even change her mind if the right man came along. And if Jeff was the man who could make Meg happy, then he would do his utmost to be happy that the man was there for her, Etienne promised himself.

But for now, Meg was still with him, and he was going to savor every moment he had left with her.

So, the next morning, after she'd had time to rest up from the flight, he was at her door.

She opened it wearing some sort of slender, red dress that emphasized her shape and showed her pretty knees.

"I don't remember that dress," he told her.

She gave him a brilliant smile that made him want to lean close. "I bought this myself. I wanted to do some shopping while you were still around to tell me whether I had made a mistake...or not."

He tucked a finger beneath the long, slender deep-cut collar, sliding his way down the length of the cloth. "Very definitely an *or not*. No question. It suits you, very much."

"Well, there you go," she said as Etienne came into her room and she began to comb her hair. "My day just started off right. Edie told me it worked, but Edie is always nice about what I wear and she doesn't have much better taste than I do. You, however, are an expert."

"On some things," he agreed, watching the hypnotic movement of her arm as she stroked the comb through her curls. "Not on everything."

"What things don't you know enough about?" she wondered, turning to face him.

"Cats?" he suggested.

"Okay, cats. I take it you never had any growing up. How about a dog?"

"Not a dog, either."

"No pets?" she asked. Etienne noticed that there was a stray curl that Meg had missed. It lay partially across her cheek. He wanted to brush it aside with his fingertips.

"No pets," he said, continuing to study that curl and the one next to it that swirled down, just touching the hollow of her throat. That very sexy little hollow made for a man's lips.

"None?" Meg asked with that sad voice that told him she was moving directly into her "I want to fix things, I want to help you" mode.

He cleared his throat, tried to ignore the need to touch her and managed a smile to reassure her. "Don't look so sad. I had no clue I was missing anything. My mother simply feared animals, and she didn't like having their fur on her clothing or the furniture at Mont Gavard."

"Wow. Your home is on a mountain?"

"Sounds grand doesn't it?" he asked with a laugh. "But the mountain is really just a small hill. It's a pretentious name, but a beautiful estate nonetheless."

"You must miss it when you're away."

Those beautiful eyes of hers looked suddenly sad.

"I'm not a puppy or a kitten, Meg. You can't save me. And anyway, I don't need saving. There's no reason to be sad about the ancestral home because I'm away from it so much. The truth is that it's far too big for one person, so I've only been there once or twice since my mother died."

"How long ago was that?"

"Almost two years. There's a skeleton crew that takes care of the grounds and keeps things running smoothly."

"It sounds like a lovely place."

"I could show it to you if you'd like."

"Would you do that? I mean…I wouldn't want to ask you to do something you didn't feel like doing. You don't have to play the host if it makes you sad or brings back unhappy memories."

He thought about that. He *had* been sad the last time he was there. His mother had loved Mont Gavard, and the place had seemed to be missing an essential element without her, but…

"I didn't live there with Louisa. The vastness of the estate intimidated her, and my mother was never happier than when people were admiring her home. I think she'd be happy that someone was showing an interest. But…"

"See, there is a problem. I shouldn't have asked."

Etienne brushed a finger across her nose. "Stop it. There isn't a problem in the way you're thinking. I just… We only have two days before the expo. If you go to Mont Gavard, that will only leave you one day to see Paris."

She looked at him with that clear, direct gaze of hers. "There's only one Paris, and I might never get the chance again, but lots of people see Paris. How many see Mont Gavard? I'll see what I can of Paris in a day. I'd like to see where you grew up."

"Why?"

She hesitated. "You're an interesting man. Your home must be an interesting place."

"Flattery will get you there, sweet Meg. I would love to show you my home," he said. "Come on." He took her hand. And then, because he couldn't seem to help himself, he stopped and smoothed that curl back behind her ear.

She shivered, and his self-control wavered even more. With the greatest of difficulty he managed not to kiss her. He had a feeling that these next few days were going to be very difficult, very wonderful and far too short. He hoped that when they ended their time together he would handle things right. He wanted Meg to be happy when he had gone, with no regrets.

Visiting Mont Gavard was probably a very good idea, after all. Despite the way things had been between him and his mother at the end, he had always loved the place. There was a serenity about it that reminded him of the way Meg made him feel when she was smiling.

That was a good thing, because while most of the time Meg seemed to be blessed with bravado, there were those moments such as the one when she asked him about her dress, when he realized how much she disliked being on display. How nervous and self-conscious she still was when she had to face strangers.

At the expo, he would be the only familiar face in the crowd. And for the two days they were there, she would be very much on display. A day at Mont Gavard might be just the thing to help her relax before all the madness to come.

He was going to make it a priority to help her relax, second only to his priority to keep his hands and his lips off her.

That would be a tough one, because every time Meg opened her mouth…or smiled…or laughed…or just existed, he wanted to kiss her.

* * *

Meg was thinking fast. Tomorrow was the anniversary of the day Etienne had lost his wife and child three years ago. She probably shouldn't have asked to see his home. No matter what he had said, there had to be some residual melancholy lingering about the place, memories of things gone by that could never come again because the key players were gone.

When she had first discovered that he was going to be running Fieldman's she had done an Internet search on his background and discovered that his reclamation business had grown much more intense after the tragedy of his wife and child. Even though he hadn't said so, she had seen firsthand how Etienne threw himself into work when something was bothering him. She also knew that he had arranged this two day lull before the demands of the expo so she would have time to rest up after the flight and have time to relax and prep herself.

But what was good for her was probably the exact opposite of what was good for Etienne at this moment. He needed activity, something to take his mind off things, a distraction.

"Well, I've certainly been called that more than once in my lifetime," Meg muttered to herself. And not necessarily in a good way, either, but for the first time ever, she was glad of that.

For the next two days she was going to devote herself to making sure that Etienne had no time to dwell on his sorrows, no time even to think, and no reason at all to regret that he had taken Meg on as a project.

She was going to do her darnedest to distract the man and to keep him busy, even if he ended up sorry that he had ever met her. She was pretty darn sure that he would spend at least some of the next two days beating up on himself if he had time to think about the past, so she was just going to have to deal with the fact that a sacrifice was needed here. There was no one around to care about Etienne's state of mind but her, and…she cared. A great deal.

So, that night, Meg sat down and made a list of places she intended to drag Etienne to, things she intended to ask him to show her, questions she intended to ask him, even general points of conversation to pursue should she need a desperation move.

She was a woman on a mission.

CHAPTER FOURTEEN

ETIENNE had chosen not to drive today. Instead he'd had Carl bring the limo to the hotel, so he and Meg were seated next to each other when they came over the rise and first caught a glimpse of Mont Gavard.

It had been a long time since he'd seen it, and the familiar rolling lush green fields, followed by the double rows of trees forming a canopy over the long driveway had him sitting up straighter. When the limo emerged from the tunnel of trees, the familiar pink brick of the L-shaped three story house with its white stone trim and cupola was revealed.

"It's… Oh, my, it's beautiful and so much larger than I had envisioned it," Meg said. "And…did you say that there was a skeleton crew taking care of the place? Because those shrubberies are perfect, there's not a weed in sight, and the flower beds, what I can see of them, are spectacular."

"It's an excellent crew," Etienne conceded with a smile.

"I can tell. Can I meet them? And…will you show me the rest of the gardens? And…"

She glanced down at something in her hand. "And

isn't there a pond? I looked up Mont Gavard on the Internet and it said there was a pond."

Without a thought, Etienne reached over and took the piece of paper from her.

"Don't," she said.

But it was too late. He had already looked. "Meg," he said gently. "Don't you trust me to show you everything?"

She nodded. "Yes, yes I do."

"Then why the list?"

That adorable chin rose just a touch. He could tell she was going to get stubborn on him. "I just…like lists."

"Nothing wrong with lists," he agreed, "but this one seems incredibly long. I'm pretty sure that even if we had a month we wouldn't be able to do everything on it."

"Not everything on the list is a thing to do. Some of them are talking points."

He laughed out loud. "Meg, have you and I ever run out of things to say to each other?" No, they hadn't, he thought. "Don't you think I'm capable of carrying on an intelligent conversation with you? Especially about the place where I lived for most of my life?"

Her brown eyes opened wide. "Of course. I would never insult you by insinuating that you couldn't carry on a conversation with me. I love talking with you."

Warmth slipped right through him. "Then, Meg…"

"I just want to keep you busy today. And tomorrow," she said. "To distract you. That's all."

"Ah, I see."

"You weren't supposed to see. I was supposed to be talkative and demanding."

"Oh, I like that," he said. "Especially the demanding

part. Go ahead. Demand something of me, Meg," he coaxed.

And suddenly, his talkative Meg seemed to have nothing to say. She simply…looked at him. "I can't. I can't…even think."

He slid his hand beneath her hair, curling his palm around her neck. "Then don't think," he said. "I know what day it is, but don't try to distract me. Don't feel you have to be my keeper today. Let's just be. The two of us. We'll take it slow. I'll show you my favorite places. We'll talk when we like and we won't talk when we don't want to. You don't have to worry about me, Meg. I like spending time with you. You're already distraction enough. Come on, we're here. Walk with me."

She nodded. When they left the limo, she took his hand, and he led her around this place where he had spent so many years. Meg, his boisterous, talkative, sometimes outrageous Meg was very quiet.

"Are you all right?" he asked.

She frowned. "That was supposed to be my job. Asking you that…or *not* asking you that. I didn't want to remind you, and look at this… I had barely arrived when you got me to blurt out the whole truth. I'm hopeless where you're concerned."

Something about that very fact and the way she said it turned Etienne warm inside.

"You're not hopeless. You're adorable."

"You have so got to be kidding."

"I have so *not* got to be kidding, Meg." He kissed her nose, only allowing himself that much. "Adorable. Now, come on, I want to show you what I used to do when I needed to be alone."

He took her hand and led her down the path, past the patio where his parents had first told him that his father wasn't going to live much longer and all that would be expected of him. This was the place where he had dashed his mother's hopes of him ever fulfilling the Gavard legacy. His chest tightened as he thought of those times, but he concentrated on Meg. He squeezed her hand and she looked up at him with a smile that made him forget everything but her. Had the woman really had some plan to keep him so busy that he wouldn't have time to think about Louisa and his child? That was so…so very Meg.

She was so giving, amazing, vulnerable. If he hurt her…ever…

He wouldn't. It wasn't allowed.

Instead he led her to the water and a small boat that was kept there. "It's a shallow pond," he told her. "Are you game?"

"Is Paris in France?" she asked, climbing into the boat. She had worn slacks and a vivid red blouse. Now, perched in the small boat, she was like a brilliant, beautiful poppy that had been cast on the water.

He rowed around to the back side of the small island in the middle of the pond. Willow trees lined the shore here, their fronds trailing in the water. It was peaceful, quiet, secluded.

"I liked this place because no one ever looked for me here. Despite having a pond, my parents weren't fond of water. Now," he said. "You were going to distract me. Tell me all the things you were going to do."

She gave him a look. "I'm not ashamed of any of them."

"Good. You shouldn't be. I'm moved that you would make such an effort for me."

Meg shook her head. "You've certainly gone out of your way for me. That means so much to me."

Her voice dropped and he wanted nothing more than to lean forward and kiss her. Instead he tried to distract himself.

"So what was on the list?"

"I was going to ask you to give me a tour of the house and a tour of the grounds. If necessary, I was going to have you ask your cook to give me a list of your favorite recipes. I thought that might take a while. If necessary, I would have had you introduce me to all the staff here, take me to the nearest town, introduce me to the townspeople, and if worse came to worse, I was willing to go so far as to ask to see your stable of cars. I hear there's a very well stocked garage here."

"You have an interest in cars?"

"Not a bit, but if you do, that's all that matters."

"And I stopped you from doing all those things. That's probably a good thing, especially because you're not even interested in cars," he teased. "Meg?"

She looked up, waiting.

"This," he said, gesturing to the boat. "You wouldn't have lied to me and expressed an interest in going out on the boat with me if you really had no interest, would you?"

She took a deep breath. "Ordinarily, no, but today I would have done pretty much anything."

"So, you don't like boats much, do you?"

"I don't swim very well, but I like *this* boat."

"What makes this boat different?"

Without even seeming to think, she looked straight up in his eyes. "You're in this boat."

And that was all it took. "I'm sorry, Meg," Etienne said, "but I just have to kiss you now." And bracing his hands on the sides of the boat, bracketing her body with his hands, Etienne leaned forward and laid his lips on Meg's.

She was sweet, ripe, and twisting to meet him, totally involved in the kiss, so much so that Etienne's heart began to pound, his hands began to sweat, his body ached with the need to do more.

But they were in a small boat and she didn't swim well.

He would die before he would let her fall out, but there was just no denying that this wasn't a very good place to kiss a woman.

Which was a good thing, his head told him. But his body told him something different.

Slowly he leaned back. He smiled at her. "Meg?"

"Yes?" Her voice was low and soft, her eyes were languorous.

"That was a wonderful distraction. Let's do it again. Somewhere else next time."

His comment had been meant to break the tension and make Meg laugh. Only no one was laughing.

And now all he was thinking about was how many more hours he had with her. And how he would manage to keep his mind off of her when she went home.

It had been a mistake, after all, to touch her again. Now he wanted her even more, but touching her... An honorable man didn't love a woman like Meg and then send her away. If he couldn't keep her—and he couldn't—he shouldn't even consider touching her.

But all he could think about when he looked at Meg was how much he wanted to hold her in his arms.

The time was slipping away and she was letting it happen, Meg thought the next morning. Ever since Etienne had kissed her and made that comment in the boat, the minutes and the march toward goodbye had seemed to fly faster and faster.

He'd shown her the rest of Mont Gavard, they'd dined beneath the stars at Le Pre Catelan. Now there was just one last day before the expo and her return home.

"I want this to be memorable for you," Etienne said when he picked her up outside her door at the hotel where the expo would be held.

Meg laughed. "Etienne, it's Paris. It's memorable just by definition. It's the trip of a lifetime."

"All right, then, let's fit a lifetime into one day," he said.

They tried. They strolled along the Seine and the Champs-Elysées. They visited Sainte-Chapelle, Montmartre, the Arc de Triomphe and the Jardin des Tuileries.

Meg was usually the one who talked a mile a minute, but today it was Etienne, trying to fit as much into her day as possible. But the day was coming to a close. Standing by the water next to the pyramid at the Louvre, the sun began to sink as it always did. The sky put on a master performance and decked itself out in silver and red and gold and purple. There was a family nearby, a father playing with his two children, the mother looking on. The whole scene of Paris, the sunset, this gorgeous setting, the family was just…beautiful. Meg looked at the family lost in their own world and their own happiness and her throat closed up. She thought, that could be us.

But it couldn't be.

She looked up into Etienne's eyes. "Thank you. For showing me all this and for Mont Gavard," she said.

"I wish there had been more time. It wasn't enough."

She raised her hand and allowed herself the pleasure of touching his cheek. She ran her palm over his jaw. "It was more than I ever expected. I wasn't on the path to Paris when I met you."

He slowly pulled her close and gathered her in his arms. He kissed her hair. "Don't try to make it sound as if I'm the one who made this happen. I've never brought anyone else to Paris."

She pulled back and looked at him. "Why not?"

"Because you're special. Don't make me say it again."

She didn't. Instead she rose on her toes and kissed him on the nose. He tilted his head and returned the kiss…on the lips, on that little scarred spot. Etienne groaned and kissed her there again, then dipped his head and kissed her throat.

Meg nearly fainted with pleasure.

A child coughed. Meg froze. "There are children nearby," she whispered.

Immediately Etienne released her. He took her hand. "I'll take you back," he said.

But when they made it to her hotel room door and she had the door open, Meg turned and faced Etienne. "There are *no* children nearby now," she said.

He laughed. He covered her mouth with his and tasted her. His hands went to her waist and climbed higher.

Heat flashed through Meg's body. She plunged her hands into his hair and gave kiss for kiss. "Come inside."

Etienne stopped kissing her. "Meg," he said. "I want you, but I don't want to be like Alan. I don't want to use you." His eyes were sad. He was like a piece of granite, unmoving when she tugged.

She stopped. Doubts assailed her. She had thought—

"You don't want me?"

Etienne's eyes opened wide, a shocked expression deepening their silver-blue. "I'm afraid of hurting you, but I'm not completely insane, Meg. I want you so much that it's killing me to stand here."

Meg stopped tugging. "You could never be like Alan, Etienne. Alan wouldn't have cared about hurting me. But you're right. I don't want to hurt you, either. I don't want to force you. I don't want this to end on an unhappy note or ask you to do something you'll regret later. I don't want you to feel obligated to entertain me beyond the normal sightseeing or think that I expect kisses or more or—"

But she had barely got the last word out when Etienne scooped her up, carried her inside, kicked the door shut and dropped her on the bed. He came down on top of her, his arms braced so that his body wasn't touching hers. Much.

"Are you trying to manipulate me, Meg?"

She looked up into those glittering, gorgeous eyes, but she wasn't even vaguely afraid. Etienne might be frustrated but he would never intentionally hurt her.

Still, she had goaded him into this and as much as she wanted him…

"I… Yes," she answered. "That is…not exactly, but…yes. Maybe. I don't really know. I wasn't even thinking straight. I just…want you, but I don't want to use you, either. I want our last days together to be happy. I want you to make love to me, but I also want you willingly, and if that can't happen and you're only here on this bed with me because I manipulated you here, then I would like a do-over, please. I would like to change my mind."

She couldn't keep the sad, sorry note out of her voice, and she absolutely hated that. What a pathetic woman. She tried to sit up.

Etienne didn't budge. "Meg, this suggestion of yours for a do-over intrigues me. Does that mean you no longer want *me*, *mon petit lapin*?" he whispered, dipping his head to nuzzle her neck.

Flames shot through Meg's body. When Etienne stopped his nuzzling and looked into her eyes again, some part of her that had survived the inferno managed to register that he was waiting for an answer. "I don't know what *mon petit lapin* means," she whispered.

He smiled and kissed her nose. "It's an affectionate term that roughly translates to my little rabbit."

She smiled slowly. "Affectionate?"

"Of course. Would I curse a woman who makes me as crazy to touch her as you do?"

"One wouldn't think so, Etienne, but…my little rabbit? That doesn't sound very sexy at all." She reached up and began to unbutton his shirt. Slowly.

Etienne took a deep, visible breath, his nostrils flaring slightly. "The term doesn't have to be sexy," he said, his voice raspy. "Because *you* are. Incredibly." He ran his palms down her body. She arched against him.

"I've been wanting to do this for a very long time, Etienne," she said, continuing to release his buttons. "I want us to end on the right note. I don't want you to have any regrets, and I don't want to have any regrets, either, so I'm getting you out of my system—completely—tonight. All right?"

He paused and gazed down into her eyes. "Promise me," he said. "Promise me that after I'm gone, you won't be sorry you let me touch you."

"I couldn't be sorry," she promised.

"Good. Because if you couldn't tell me that, I would have to stop, and…Meg…"

She placed her hands on his bare chest and whisked his shirt down his arms. "What, Etienne?" she whispered.

He shrugged out of his shirt and in only seconds had slid down the zipper that ran down the front of her dress, sliding the garment down and off her body. For long seconds he simply stared at her, his gaze moving slowly from her head down the length of her.

"Etienne?" Her voice came out on a choked gasp.

"That comment I made about stopping, Meg?"

"Yes?"

His eyes met hers. While he gazed at her he finished undressing her. "I'm not going to. Unless you ask me to. And I'm hoping that you won't ask."

"I'm asking you to make love with me, Etienne," she answered.

He smiled and shrugged out of his clothes, then took her in his arms. "You are the most amazing woman, Meg."

She pressed herself to him and took a deep, shuddering breath as his skin met hers. "And you are the most amazing man, Etienne. Please…amaze me."

But he did so much more than that. He kissed her, he caressed her.

She nipped at him and smoothed her palms over the chest she'd been wanting to touch.

He lifted her hair and made love to the nape of her neck. He made shivers run down her whole body, then followed with kisses that made her burn.

And then, he did something even more wonderful. He joined his body to hers. He turned her world to bliss. He made her forget everything but him.

Afterward, as they lay there half asleep, he held her and whispered in her ear, "Don't miss me when I'm gone, Meg," he said.

She kissed his hand. "Don't worry about me when I'm gone," she said.

But when morning came and he had returned to his room, Meg realized that neither of them had answered the other, and with good reason. She *was* going to miss him, and he *was* going to worry.

There was nothing she could do about the first. No matter what happened, she would miss him. How could she not when she loved him so much?

But as for the worrying about her, that couldn't be allowed to happen. Worrying that he had failed one woman, his wife, by walking away from her and leaving her on her own had nearly destroyed Etienne. That wasn't going to happen here. She was no fragile flower; she could take care of herself and she was darned sure going to show Etienne Gavard that he had absolutely nothing to worry about where Meg Leighton was concerned. She was totally capable of surviving completely on her own. He could leave her with a totally clean conscience.

He never needed to know that her heart was broken.

CHAPTER FIFTEEN

ETIENNE was worried. Ever since he and Meg had made love, she had been avoiding him. And when she hadn't been avoiding him, she'd been running full tilt. His concern wasn't because she looked unhappy. On the contrary, she was always smiling and cheerful. Extremely cheerful. More cheerful than any one person would ever be for that length of time. She even, occasionally, stopped and gave him one of those little pats on the cheek he had often seen her give her friends at Fieldman's. As if she was trying to reassure him. As if she was concerned for *him*. As if she was worried about *his* well-being.

When she knew very well that he had been the head of the Gavard family with all its lands, money, businesses and obligations for years. She knew things about his personal life, too. Above all, Meg knew that his Achilles' heel was vulnerable women.

All of which led him to believe that something wasn't right here. Because besides the fact that Meg was treating him as if he was merely a friend, she had not said one word about making love with him. Not a sound of regret, of joy, of anything. That just wasn't Meg. She was an emotional, involved, complex woman, and he was totally positive that she didn't take making love lightly.

Etienne fretted. He weighed the evidence...and decided that there could be only one likely conclusion. Meg was afraid that *he* would think she was falling in love with him and she was trying to protect him from beating up on himself.

That was exactly like Meg. And that really did make him worry. He didn't think she was falling in love with him. She'd made it clear from the beginning that long-term relationships with men held no appeal for her. She didn't even want to have a father hanging around when she finally had those babies she longed for. If he'd thought there was even a remote chance she might fall in love with him, he would... How *would* he feel?

For a minute his heart soared...and then fell. What did it matter how he felt? The truth was that he was all wrong for Meg. She wanted children; she needed a man who would stay in one place and be there for her. He was exactly the wrong kind of man for her. He was the kind who would end up hurting her even if he didn't want to. The fact that she was worrying about him was proof enough that her association with him was already taking its toll.

Especially since right now she had too much on her plate. She still had speeches to give at the expo, she had to fly home alone and then she had a company to run. From here on out, she would be shepherding her flock at Fieldman's alone. She didn't need to add "trying to make sure Etienne doesn't have any concerns" to her list of things to do.

What could he do? Tell her that she could stop putting on an act for him? Tell her that he wasn't worried about her?

Well…he *was* worried about her, because…

Because I love her, he thought. The truth stared him in the face. He *loved* Meg. He would always worry about her, but those were the last things she needed to hear.

Her career was taking off. She was in demand. She was right where she had told him she wanted to be on that first day they met. A man like him…he'd merely been her springboard. Now he needed to get out of her way and let her do and be the things she wanted to do and be.

Etienne blew out a shaky breath. He resigned himself to letting Meg continue this charade. But he hated it. He didn't want her gentle pats on the cheek and her affectionate little smiles. What he wanted was all of her. Forever.

But he would *not* tell her that. It would just make her sad. And he would sacrifice anything if he could prevent Meg from suffering any more heartache in her life.

Meg never quite knew what happened on the last day of the expo. Everything had been going as planned. She had been meeting and greeting people, smiling, laughing, pasting on the "Face of Fieldman's" for the world to see. She had given some presentations. Orders had started pouring in, Jeff told her in a conference call.

But mostly she had been trying not to let Etienne know in any way that her heart was crumpling and cracking and that she was generally a mess inside whenever she thought about the fact that she would never see him again.

Still, she continued on. The hours were passing and she almost looked forward to the time when she could get on the plane and fly home, because then she could finally stop smiling and let herself cry.

She only had two more things to do before that could happen. First, she had to give one more presentation. And then, she had to kiss Etienne goodbye.

The second thing was the important one. No matter how much she had been avoiding him, she couldn't leave without being in his arms just once more. Just once. That would have to last her forever.

She was rushing to the presentation area and thinking about kissing Etienne, about where and when to do it and how long she could press her lips to his without him suspecting that she was totally in love with him, when she started to climb the five stairs to the makeshift stage, and the heel of her red stilettos clipped the last rung.

Most people would have been surprised by how quickly a person could go from standing upright at the top of a set of stairs to hitting the ground beneath, but Meg had taken all those classes she'd told Etienne about. In an attempt to garner some small measure of grace, she had been taught how to fall time and time again and had experienced the "upright to ground" phenomenon many times before, but in the past she had been concentrating so hard on trying to master the fall that she had inevitably failed.

Now, however, her first thought was that Etienne would witness her mishap and be either scared out of his wits or concerned that she still couldn't manage a simple walk across a room. In fact, she was sure she heard him cry out her name as she went down.

Consequently, somehow, Meg managed to gracefully roll and rise to her feet, brushing off her clothing and trying to simultaneously smile, rearrange her hair, pick up the papers she'd dropped, ignore the pain shooting through her body in various places and still be ready to turn and face Etienne as if nothing untoward had happened.

Too late. She was still disheveled, still missing papers when he vaulted over a table in his path and ran up beside her.

"Meg, *ma belle*, are you all right? What am I saying? Of course, you're not all right. You fell down the stairs. You must be damaged, Meg," he said in a rush as he reached for a chair, drew her to it and demanded that she sit down. Right then.

"Meg, *mon petit lapin*, look at me. Is that a bruise on your jaw?" His fingers gently brushed.

Meg melted. She leaned forward…and saw a world of worry in his eyes.

Slowly, she shook her head. She found a small smile. She touched his face. "Etienne, don't worry. Really. I'm fine. I did it. I finally learned how to execute a fall and live to tell the tale." She even laughed a little.

He wasn't laughing. His eyes looked stricken, scared. "Meg, you were wonderful, but…my heart may never be the same again. I was too far away, you were falling too fast. I was afraid you were going to hit your head, break something, worse. Meg, Meg…"

She couldn't help it. She framed his face with her hands and kissed him. "Etienne, I—"

"I can't leave you," he said suddenly. "It's too... You're too... Meg, I want you to marry me. Now."

Meg wasn't sure which one of them was more surprised to hear the words falling from his mouth. Etienne's gaze was fierce and intense and slightly shocked as if he wondered who had spoken, and Meg... For two seconds her heart overflowed with love and joy and...

No. She was totally sure that this proposal had been an impetuous decision on his part, wrenched from him by his concern for her. He'd been teaching her and working with her for weeks and he was naturally concerned for her welfare, worried that he would fail her in some way the way all teachers did. Then he'd seen her fall and he had thought of Louisa, of how he'd failed his wife. In some small way, not being able to be at Meg's side when she'd fallen was reliving his past. This time they'd shared had made him feel responsible for her, and his suggestion that they marry was simply an attempt to protect her and save her from future harm.

It was as she'd already admitted to herself. Etienne saved people. But who saved Etienne from himself?

She would.

Meg slowly shook her head, she cupped his jaw, she bent and kissed him. "Thank you, but I can't marry you," she whispered. "It would be...so wrong."

Then she got up and stumbled out of the expo. She didn't give her presentation. She didn't stop to sign out. She just left.

The flight home was a blur. She vaguely remembered calling Edie and blurting out...something. She sort of recalled Edie meeting her at the airport and how she had sobbed in her tiny friend's arms.

After that, nothing much mattered or made sense or sank in. There was a lot of sleeping, a lot of tears, a few attempts to work and then more tears. She mindlessly watched television. She sat for hours staring at nothing.

And then one day a few days later, the phone rang.

Meg stared at it, but didn't answer. Two minutes later it rang again, and she picked it up, meaning to hang up again.

Edie's panicked voice rang out. "Don't hang up, Meg. Come quick. Alan is back, and he's threatening everyone in the office. He's making Paula cry."

Meg snapped to attention. "I'm on my way," was all she said before she hung up the phone and started to scramble for clothing.

Her heart was still raw, but that couldn't matter. She had neglected her friends and colleagues and there was no Etienne to save them. She had to put to use all that he'd taught her. She had to be the one.

The last time she and Alan had had a confrontation she had pushed back, but she'd had no real ammunition. Now she did. Etienne had given her what she needed.

Her heart lifted at the thought, and for the first time in a week she managed to smile.

Etienne probably broke every speeding law in the book on his way to Fieldman's after receiving Jeff's call. That jerk was terrorizing the employees and Jeff said that

Edie had apparently gotten through to Meg after not being able to for most of the week.

Etienne thanked the stars above that he had returned to Chicago to begin the process of setting up the sale of the company to the employees. He only hoped he could reach Fieldman's before Meg did. *If that poor excuse for a man, Alan, does one thing to hurt her, I'll...*

You'll what? he asked himself. Already, he had made several wrong turns with Meg. That proposal... She'd been so proud of how she'd handled that fall and had he praised her? Well, maybe a little, but mostly he'd tried to corral her into marrying him. When he'd known that Meg had a strong need to be independent.

Nonetheless, he couldn't let Alan destroy her again. It was damned hard being a man in love, Etienne decided, as he slid into the parking lot at Fieldman's. Dammit. Meg's car was already here, parked crookedly across three spaces as if she'd arrived in a hurry.

Etienne's pulse began to thunder in his ears. She was in there with the man who had almost destroyed her. Swearing beneath his breath, Etienne started for the front door, then thought better of it and went around the back.

Everyone in the office was clustered up against the private offices as if they'd been herded there like cattle. Alan's voice rang out. "The contract has changed, because Gavard is selling it to you. That means you now have control, and I think you'll find that what I'm offering you is extremely generous. It could make a bundle for everyone here."

If steam could come out of a person's ears, it would be coming out of Etienne's now. He started to charge ahead, but then he saw Meg's face through the crowd. She was turned toward him and the man she faced had his back toward Etienne. The man was advancing and Etienne started to surge, but the expression on Meg's face wasn't one of fear. He saw determination and concentration and… Suddenly she lifted one eyebrow in a perfect expression of disbelief and condescension.

Etienne stopped moving forward. He noticed that Jeff and Edie had sidled up next to him. "Did you see that, my friend?" he whispered to Jeff. "What a wonderful woman!"

"Yeah, I was afraid that after she stayed holed up in her place all week that she was going to come out looking insane, but she's beautiful," Jeff whispered back.

A jolt went through Etienne. She was, indeed, beautiful, but…

"My Meg was locked up in her house?"

"Yes, what did you do to her?" Edie whispered. "I couldn't understand what she was telling me when she got off the plane, she was crying so hard."

Another jolt. "I proposed," he said.

"Oh. Did you say that you loved her?"

No, he hadn't. He shook his head.

Edie glared at him. "Well, that explains it, then," she replied. "If you didn't love her, you should never have proposed. Meg kept saying something about how you wanted to protect her and save her and she couldn't let you do that after what had happened to your wife and how you would always consider her a burden and a responsibility. The rest was hard to hear. She was pretty broken up."

Ah, he'd botched things badly. How had he done that to his lovely Meg? But he couldn't ask any more questions now. He was straining to listen to Meg. After her eyebrow-raising, Alan had gone off on some rambling attempt to make his case. Now, she was crossing her arms and stepping forward.

Alan took a step backward, closer to the rabble behind him. It was a bit like the French revolution revisited. Etienne wanted nothing more than to beat the man senseless for daring to even speak to Meg, but after Edie's comments, he saw where he had gone wrong. Meg needed to be strong, to earn her place in life. People had always forced her into a weak position. They'd made her feel that her strengths were weaknesses, but a man who loved her would never do that. He wouldn't insist on saving her. He'd let her fight...unless she asked for his help.

"I believe you were told that you weren't to approach anyone in this company," Meg was saying. "I think it's more than safe to say that you have stepped over the line, Alan."

"I believe that if this company is employee-owned, then you don't get to make all the decisions, Meg. This sounds like you're just upset because I scorned you and dumped you."

Etienne jumped forward a little before Edie and Jeff grabbed him and before he got control of himself. He swore...in French. Too loudly. Alan apparently was too worked up to hear, but Meg's head immediately came up. She looked straight into Etienne's eyes.

Then she smiled.

"I could see where you might think something like that, Alan, and I probably can't change your mind. You always did think a lot more of yourself than anyone else did. But the truth is that I've…um…been involved with men that are far better, more admirable, and ten times more handsome than you'll ever be, so no, the woman scorned thing just isn't doing it for me. Try something else."

"How about this?" Alan turned to the crowd. "I'll pay you a lot more than Meg will ever make for you."

A murmur went through the crowd. "Wow, is that true, Meg?" Paula asked.

"I don't know. Maybe," Meg said. "But do you really want to ever work for a jerk like this?"

"Hmm, no, but I *would* like to throw a bottle at his head," Paula said.

"Or worse," someone yelled. "He hurt Meg. We don't want to have anything to do with someone like that no matter how much money he offers. What can we do to make him leave?"

Meg looked up into Etienne's eyes. "I believe that this might be a question for my advisor," she said, nodding to Etienne.

Jeff let go of Etienne's arm and he moved forward, making a beeline for Meg. "There are various possibilities here," Etienne offered. "He's been warned to stay away, so we might consider him a trespasser."

"Hah! That'll never stick," Alan said.

"I believe I was talking to Meg," Etienne said. "And yes, it probably wouldn't stick…yet," he told her. "But we could establish a precedent, file a complaint and eventually manage to bar him from the property. After that he could be arrested."

Meg nodded solemnly. "I like that idea. Not as much as the hitting him with the bottle, but it does have the appeal of being legal."

"Or we could have his car towed. Right now. It's an unauthorized vehicle in the parking lot, isn't it?"

A cry went up from the rabble. "Yeah, he's got a really expensive car. I'd love to see that on the back of a tow truck. Let's go call right now and we'll stand guard so he can't drive it away," someone said.

Alan swore.

"Alan, shame on you. Such language," Meg said. "I don't like swearing in the office…unless it's in French. Yes, let's definitely tow his car."

Alan swore again. And then he ran for the door.

A round of applause went up from the rabble standing behind Etienne. He walked forward and pulled Meg into his arms. "I know this is unprofessional, but I just have to do it," he said. "You were *magnifique*, *mon coeur*." When his lips met hers, Etienne's heart began to pound. She was all he wanted and needed, but he had to let her go.

CHAPTER SIXTEEN

ETIENNE turned to leave, and Meg's heart skipped. She held out her hand. "Thank you," she said. "But…" It was going to be so hard to ask this. It was opening a conversation that might end so badly, so awkwardly, so heartbreakingly. "You know I don't know much French. What did you call me just then?"

His smile was sad. "My heart. It's an affectionate term."

"Like my little rabbit?"

Now his eyes were sad, too. "A bit, but…more."

Her throat felt so full she could barely speak, but…he was going to leave. If he left…

"I never thanked you," she said. "So…thank you."

"For this? This was all you," he answered.

"For the proposal."

"Meg, I'm so sorry for that. It wasn't meant to be an insult."

"I know. You were worried about me. You wanted to protect me."

"And yet, today you didn't need protecting."

Her heart was aching, and yet she laughed. "It felt like I needed protecting at times. I was afraid and angry and not thinking all that clearly at first, but yes, I managed, because I remembered things you had told me. You gave me courage. You made me realize that I could be me, and that being Meg Leighton was a good thing."

"It's a wonderful thing."

"I wondered… You didn't even try to step in with Alan today. That's so…not like you."

A pale imitation of that wonderful grin appeared, and pale as it was, her heart still leaped. "I wanted to. For a few seconds, Jeff and Edie were holding on to me so that I couldn't rush forward, but mostly I held back because I realized that you didn't need my help. At all. You didn't need saving. Meg, I have to be honest… You have to know that I'll always want to save you and protect you. Always. Forever. I can't seem to help it. You do that to me, but I also want you to know that I wouldn't, unless you asked. That proposal…"

She tried to shrug and to look as if she didn't care. "It was an impulsive thing, I know. You felt you had to do it."

The pale grin was gone. Etienne's eyes burned fire. "Meg, look at me. I love you. It might have been out of the blue, but it wasn't remotely impulsive. It was because I couldn't do anything else. When a man feels about a woman the way I feel about you… I love you, Meg. You've turned my world around and I just can't help loving you."

A tear slipped off her lashes and fell.

"Meg, *mon coeur*, I've made you cry," he whispered in wonder. "You never cry."

"I know."

"Why? Have I hurt you?"

She shook her head vigorously. "Do you think... I'm sure I hurt your pride when I told you I couldn't marry you, but do you think... I mean... I do love you, Etienne. So very much. I hated telling you no when I wanted to say yes and..."

He pulled her into his arms right then and there. "While I was here, I bought a piece of property. At the time I didn't know what I would do with it, but now... I'm thinking of a second Mont Gavard. I'd build a house, maybe get a cat and... If I asked you to marry me, again, Meg, would I hurt you again?"

She turned in his arms. She pressed her lips to his. When she pulled away, she stared directly into his eyes. "I don't know if that was a hypothetical question, Etienne, but please ask me again. I know your work takes you far away, and much as I'll miss you when you're gone, I'm strong. I can handle your absences...or I'll travel with you. You don't have to build the house or get a cat or...anything but...just love me."

"I love you now. I'll love you forever. I'm asking you again. And I'll ask as many times as it takes. Marry me, Meg. Love me. And yes, we *are* building the house. You may be strong enough for the separations, but I couldn't be apart from you that long. We'll delegate, bring new people into the business. We'll make a family, Meg."

"And we'll travel back and forth between France and here?"

"Whatever you want, love. Wherever you are is home to me."

Meg smiled through her tears. "I'm so glad Alan

dumped me and fired me. If he hadn't, you wouldn't be here."

Etienne laughed. "What an amazing way of thinking you have, love. And yes, I agree with you. I'm grateful for anything that brought us to this moment, but don't expect me to send the man a thank you card. And Meg?"

She looked up and waited.

"The eyebrow thing?"

She blushed. "Lots of practice. I'm very good at practicing."

"You're very good at lots of things, and I intend to learn about every single one of them, my love, my heart, my everything, my Meg."

"Mon petit lapin," she whispered to him. *"Mon coeur."*

"Look at that. Meg's speaking French," someone whispered.

"And our bosses are kissing. This is the best place in the world to work." That was Paula's voice.

Etienne and Meg chuckled. He whispered in Meg's ear. She whispered back. Then she turned to the group.

"Etienne and I would like to declare this a paid holiday for all of you," she said. "Beginning right this minute."

A cheer went up.

"Best ever place to work!" someone else agreed. "Kiss her again, Etienne."

"Oh, I intend to," he said. "Many times. Kissing Meg will be the greatest joy in my life. It's going to be at the top of my to do list every day, at the bottom, and lots of places in between." He twirled Meg into his arms and against his heart. She was a perfect fit.

"Now, about that list," she said.

He smiled. "It's written on my heart, but this is how it begins." He kissed her.

"And this is how *my* list continues," she whispered, returning his kiss.

He smiled against her lips. "I like the way you think, my love. I always have."

"Show me," she said.

"*Toujours, always,*" he said. Then he kissed her again.

HIS L.A. CINDERELLA

BY
TRISH WYLIE

Trish Wylie tried various careers before eventually fulfilling her dream of writing. Years spent working in the music industry, in promotions, and teaching little kids about ponies gave her plenty of opportunity to study life and the people around her. Which, in Trish's opinion, is a pretty good study course for writing! Living in Ireland, Trish balances her time between writing and horses. If you get to spend your days doing things you love, then she thinks that's not doing too badly. You can contact Trish at www.trishwylie.com.

For my new friend Lisa from Warner Bros.
Studios for the behind the scenes tour.

CHAPTER ONE

THERE he was: the infamous Will Ryan.

Pathetically, her palms felt clammy. Though that could just have been the horrible cold she'd picked up on her way to California, she supposed…

But, truthfully, Cassidy Malone couldn't remember the last time she'd felt so nervous or self-conscious. Or so completely incapable of fooling people into thinking she was more self-confident than she actually was. She really needed the latter if she was going to stand a chance of pulling off the deception of a lifetime. And if she couldn't do it in the land of make-believe, then where could she? If she just didn't have this stupid cold to add to everything else. Who flew halfway across the planet to a place twenty degrees warmer than home and ended up with a cold? She felt awful. So much for the theory that she would feel more confident away from home, where nobody knew her…

But therein lay her immediate problem. Because the man making his way across the beautiful lobby of the Beverly Wilshire knew her all too well. A decade ago he'd known every inch of her body intimately, and had held her heart in the palm of his large hand—the same heart that now jumped in joyous recognition and then twisted in regret at how comfortable *he* looked in their surroundings.

Cassidy was incredibly jealous of that.

Will didn't so much as bat an eyelid at the white marble, the large chandelier, the carved wooden elevator doors or the polished brass and black accents. *I belong here*, his confident stride said silently. But then Cassidy couldn't remember a time when there'd ever been a place he *hadn't* had that air of self-assurance. He'd always had a way of carrying himself that practically dared people to say he was somewhere he didn't belong.

That confidence, and the hint of potential danger if pushed, had added to his potent sexuality from the very beginning as far as Cassidy was concerned. Add boyish good-looks and a smile that could genuinely melt female knees... He'd been the flame and she the moth. But to see him so at home in a place where she felt so very lost... Well, it just widened the already cavernous gap between them, didn't it?

Ridiculously, it hurt. When it really shouldn't have. Not after so long...

His bright green gaze sought her out and brushed nonchalantly from her head to her toes and back up again, forcing her to suck in her stomach and silently pray that he couldn't see any sign of the foundation underwear she'd struggled her way into. Like every woman Cassidy knew, every inch counted in times of crisis—even though she had absolutely no idea where those missing inches had been relocated *to*. With any luck Will would keep their meetings to places where there was air-conditioning, so she stood a better chance of not passing out in the California heat and the thin air of Los Angeles. Restricted circulation plus bunged-up nose didn't exactly give her a head start...

Mentally she crossed her fingers.

'Cass.'

He held out a ridiculously large hand when he got to her, and for a second Cassidy looked down at it with an arched brow, as if confused by what she was supposed to do with it. They were *shaking hands*? Like complete strangers? *Really?*

Okay, then.

Surreptitiously swiping a clammy palm on her hip, she placed it in his; the heat of long fingers curled around her cooler ones, sending another jolt of recognition through her veins to her heart. Good to know her body hadn't forgotten him either. She tried to think professional thoughts. It wasn't easy. But she had to *work* with this man.

Will let go of her hand somewhat abruptly. 'Recovered from your flight?'

'Yes. Thank you. I think it's easier this way than going back.'

'Happy with the hotel?'

'How could I not be?' She glanced around, but couldn't stop her gaze from shifting back to study him. Still boyish. He hadn't aged a day. How was that fair?

Will nodded, and glanced around him the way she had. 'It has a history firmly tied up in Hollywood. Dashiell Hammet wrote *The Thin Man* here. Elvis lived here while making movies at Paramount, and they've had everyone from members of the British royal family to the Dalai Lama stay at one time or another.'

'That's nice.' Inwardly she rolled her eyes as the words slipped off the tip of her tongue. Eloquent, Cassidy. Way to go. But, however foolish she felt, it was nothing in comparison to how stunned she was by his coolness. It was like talking to a tour guide. An uninvolved, unattached and in fairness disgustingly good-looking tour guide. But nevertheless…

'I thought you might appreciate it.'

Cassidy lifted a brow again. Meaning what? That she should be thanking her lucky stars she was here in the first place? True. But she didn't need to be made to feel as if she'd been invited to Tinsel Town by some miraculous accident. Some *timely* miraculous accident, she corrected. Because she couldn't have needed a break more if she'd tried.

He was right, though. She'd been as thrilled by the hotel as she had by her first glimpse of the Hollywood sign on the hill. Located only a few steps away from the glittering shops of Rodeo Drive, she knew the famous hotel's ornate European façade, with its distinctly rounded awnings and rows of sculpted trees, was straight out of the pages of Hollywood history—not to mention being the site of one of her favourite films of all time. It was just a shame she wasn't going to be there at Christmas, when they reportedly did an outstanding job of decorating, transforming its exterior into a dazzling display of twinkling lights.

By then she'd probably have been discovered as a fraud and sent home with her tail between her legs—back to eating rice and pasta like she had in her student days, while she'd waited for her grant money to arrive. Only this time she'd be waiting for meager pay-cheques that couldn't support the debts she had after caring for her father before he died. Well, now, *there* was something to look forward to.

'Ready?'

She nodded as Will swung a long arm in invitation and allowed her to step ahead of him. Squinting at the bright light outside, she took her sunglasses off the top of her head moments after Will donned his. A California necessity, she'd discovered since she'd landed. And as much of a status symbol as everything else, judging by the designer wear everyone but her had shading their eyes.

Silently, they turned right—Will matching his longer stride to hers—then right again at a major light, until they approached a strip of nice-looking semi-casual restaurants. Will's choice was an ivy-covered courtyard, where the *maître d'* greeted him by name and held out chairs for them before unfurling linen napkins onto their laps and handing them leather-bound menus with a flourish and a small bow.

Cassidy fought the need to giggle like a schoolgirl. At the grand old age of thirty, she should be more mature. 'Well, this beats cheese sandwiches in the park.'

Thick dark lashes flickered upwards from their study of the menu. They brushed his deeply tanned skin once, twice, and then he quirked his brows a minuscule amount and continued reading. 'That was a long time ago.'

Seeing him again, it felt like yesterday to her. But she didn't say that. Instead she allowed herself a moment to surreptitiously examine him while he made a decision on what to eat. Had he got sexier as he'd got older? Yes, she decided, he had. Darn it. Men were known to do that. Wasn't the fact he was more successful than her, richer than her and plainly more confident than her enough? At least one of them had got it right. Small consolation, though.

It was tough not to be as mesmerised by the sight of him as she had been at twenty. And twenty-one. And twenty-two. From the thick dark hair that curled disobediently outwards at his nape, all the way down the lean six foot three of his body, he was one of those guys blessed with the ability to mesmerise woman. Who could have blamed her for the crush she'd had from a distance for over a year? Or for how shy she'd been when he'd first talked to her during a group project in their screenwriting class? Or how…?

'Do you know what you want?' Will asked, in a low rumble that sent a sudden shiver up her spine.

The spine she straightened a little in her chair. Because, yes, actually—she did know what she wanted. She had a list, as it happened. High up on it was the ability to make the most of an opportunity when it came e-mailing her way, without blowing it by drooling all over the man who had long since left her behind. So now he'd given her an opening, it seemed as good a time as any to ask:

'A better idea of what the studio expects from me would be nice.' She even managed to tack on a smile when he looked at her again. See—she could do confident if she tried.

Will took a breath and closed the menu, calmly setting it down on his side-plate as he glanced around at the lunch-time crowd. 'They expect what they paid us that hefty advance for back in the day. We both knew what we were doing when we signed on the dotted line.'

Did *we?* If she'd known the heartache signing that contract would bring her way she wasn't so sure she would go back in time and sign it again. But Cassidy let it slide. 'So, after all this time they suddenly want script three? Just like that? When movie number two pretty much fell flat on its face…'

'At the box office. But thanks to a rabid internet fan base

it made money on long-term residuals. You'd know that from the fact we still get royalty cheques. This time we have the opportunity to be one of those sleepers that might well prove an accidental tent pole, with a good script and the right budget.'

Cassidy blinked at him for a moment, and then confessed, 'I have no idea what you just said.'

He almost smiled. 'Hollywood speak.'

'Is there a dictionary?'

'Not that I'm aware of.'

'Pity.' She tried another smile to see if it had any effect. 'You'll have to translate for me, then.'

'Bottom line?'

Oh, please, yes. 'That might help.'

Something resembling amusement glittered across his amazing eyes. 'They want a script yesterday, and as you and I own the rights jointly to the original copyright we've both got to do it. We're joined at the hip till it's done and they're happy…'

'No pressure, then.'

The wide shoulders beneath his expensive dark jacket lifted and fell in a brief nonchalant shrug. 'We did it before, Cass. We can do it again.'

The tiny word 'we' seemed to tug on a ragged corner of her heart every time he said it in his deep rumble of a voice. Not that it meant anything any more. He probably didn't feel the pressure she did. Why would he? He'd been writing scripts ever since he left—had success after success to his name: award nominations, contracts and his own production company. Whereas she, his former writing partner…?

Well, she had a knack for getting seven-year-olds to

stay quiet, but that was about it. The closest she'd got to writing was putting her lessons on a blackboard…

Automatically she reached for iced water the second a waiter poured it, swallowing a large gulp to dampen her dry mouth. A cold dew of perspiration broke out on her skin while she wondered when was a good time to confess how long it had been since she last written a single original word. Maybe just as well she hadn't unpacked properly yet.

The waiter smiled at her as if he felt her pain. So she smiled back.

Will's voice deepened. 'Have you done much writing?'

Oh, come on! How could he still read her mind when it had been so long since he'd seen her? It was the perfect opening for honesty; yes. But since she already had a shovel in her hand it seemed a shame not to use it.

'Not much scriptwriting. I've dabbled with other stuff.' In that she'd read instructional books—lots of them—to no avail. 'You know how it is. Use it or—'

'Lose it.' He nodded, the corners of his wide mouth tugging in a way that suggested he was fighting off one of the smiles that would addle her thoughts. 'This shouldn't take long, then. If you were rusty it might have taken a while to get you back up to speed.'

Cassidy swallowed more water to stop a confession from slipping free. Had it got warmer all of a sudden? She suddenly felt a little light-headed.

Out of nowhere he added, 'We made a good team once.'

She almost choked, her eyes watering a little as she looked at him and he finally let *that* smile loose. Oh, that was just unfair. She instantly hated him for it. With the white-hot intensity of a million burning suns she hated him for the fact *that* smile could still knock her on her ear. But even more than that she hated him because she'd been *waiting* for it to appear and knock her on her ear. She'd *known*! Had known from the second his name appeared in her In-box that he would have the capability to do damage to her self-control all over again.

But then being attracted to him had never been a problem. It had been his complete lack of availability to commit that had. She wasn't ending up the fool twice. She darn well *wasn't*!

Lifting her chin an inch, she set her glass safely on the white tablecloth and dampened her lips in preparation for saying the right words to make it plain to him it was strictly business between them this time round. After all, if she wanted to be made to look a fool she could do it all by herself. She didn't actually *need* any help.

But her resolve faltered in the sight of *that* smile. Light twinkled in his eyes, fine laughter lines fanned out from their edges, the grooves in his cheeks deepened, and his lips slid back over even teeth that looked even whiter than she remembered when contrasted with the golden hue of his Californian tan.

Put all those things together and it was infectious. Cassidy could even feel the reciprocal upward tug of her own mouth. No, no, *no*—she mustn't smile back. That was how it had started last time.

Will's deep voice added words husky with appreciation. 'You look beautiful—as always…'

The woman inside her so lacking in self-confidence blossomed under the simple, if unfounded praise. She could feel her skin warming, could feel her heart racing—could feel her smile breaking loose…

Then a sultry female voice sounded above her head. 'As always flattery will get you everywhere, Irish boy…'

Whipping her head round, Cassidy found herself staring up at a face she recognised from movie billboards and TV screens. The woman wasn't just beautiful, she was perfection. Even without airbrushing.

When Will pushed his chair back, the actress stepped over to him and kissed each of his cheeks, European-style. 'I heard you got a green light for your pet project. Bravo, you!'

'You know what I had for breakfast this morning too?'

'Not in a long time.' She aimed a wink at Cassidy, who smiled weakly in return. 'Not that you haven't been invited often enough…'

Will remembered his manners. 'Angie—this is Cassidy Malone. Cass, this is—'

'Angelique Warden. Yes, I know.' Cassidy made the smile more genuine as she stood up and stretched a hand across the table. 'It's nice to meet you. I loved your last movie.'

'Shame the box office didn't feel the same way. But thank you.' Her eyes narrowed momentarily. 'Wait a second. You're not Cassidy Malone as in *Ryan* and Malone?'

Cassidy's gaze slid briefly to Will and then back. 'A long time ago…'

'Then the rumour is true? They picked up the option?'

Will nodded, and glanced around him as if it was a state secret. He even lowered his voice. 'It's not been announced yet, so—'

'Oh, you don't have to tell me, you idiot. *How exciting!*'

Suddenly Cassidy was much more interesting to her than

before, and a matching set of European cheek kisses were bestowed on her before Cassidy could warn her of her cold.

'So nice to meet you. Make him bring you to dinner. I have a million and one questions to ask about the Ryan and Malone years. Will thinks being enigmatic makes him more interesting.'

'Not everyone likes their every move reported in the dailies.'

Still blinking in stunned amazement at having been kissed by one of the highest paid actresses on the globe, Cassidy found her attention caught by the drawl of Will's newfound American twang. The words made her scowl in recrimination. He'd been many things back in the day, but cruel had never been one of them. The famous Angelique Warden had hardly had an easy time with the press in the last year.

But Angelique laughed huskily and batted his upper arm with her designer purse, pouting and rolling her eyes. 'Yes, but it's such a joy for the rest of us. Dinner. Saturday. Bring your partner. I'm going to learn all your darkest secrets.'

'No, you're not.'

'I'll ply her with alcohol if I have to.' She winked at Cassidy for the second time and Cassidy was immediately charmed by her.

In fairness, if she plied the only Irish native on the planet who couldn't hold her drink with alcohol then she would get everything she'd probably never wanted to hear. Half a glass of wine and Cassidy's tongue tended to take on a life of its own.

'No, you won't. I need her lucid for the next few weeks.'

'Was he always so serious?'

Cassidy looked at Will, found him staring at her with a

disconcertingly unreadable expression, and her answer kind of popped out. 'No. He wasn't.'

He stared at her until she could feel her toes curling in her shoes.

So she bravely lifted her chin in challenge.

After what felt like a very long time, Angelique laughed musically. 'Okay, then. Well, you two kids have fun. I can highly recommend the scallops. Saturday, Irish boy—you hear me?'

'I hear you.'

He waved an arm to indicate Cassidy should sit back down, and she was glad of it. She really was starting to feel light-headed. Maybe she should have dragged herself out of bed for breakfast after all?

'I'll call on Saturday and tell her we can't make it.' He re-opened his menu. 'I think we should start brainstorming tomorrow and get something down on paper over the weekend.'

That fast? Great. Now she felt nauseous as well.

Hiding partially behind her auburn hair as she lowered her chin to scan the menu, she cleared her throat and asked, 'You have any ideas?'

'A few.'

It was like pulling teeth. 'Any you'd care to share?'

When she glanced at him she saw the slight upward pull on the corners of his mouth before he answered. 'Not here, no.'

Cassidy's gaze moved from side to side and she lowered her voice to a stage whisper. 'Are they watching?'

'They?' His gaze rose, curiosity lifting his brows.

'The script gremlins…'

There was a second of silence, and then a brief rumble of low laughter broke free. 'Haven't changed, have you?'

Oh, how little he knew.

They managed small talk after that. The latest movies Will's company had produced, the differences in living in California compared to Ireland... They even segued from there to the *weather.* But she couldn't help missing the ease they'd once had with each other. Angelique was right— Will *had* got serious with age. It made Cassidy feel like even more of an idiot. She couldn't seem to manage a conversation without a wisecrack or teasing him the way she'd used to, and it added to her feeling of awkwardness. Then she hit rock bottom in the embarrassment stakes when he walked her back to the hotel.

The air really was thinner in California. And it really was incredibly warm. Food hadn't got rid of her light-headedness. Her nose felt more blocked than ever, her throat hurt, and her voice was beginning to fade...

Then, back in the foyer of the beautiful hotel, surrounded by beautiful people in expensive clothes, Will turned to say goodbye and the world began to spin. The edges of her vision blurred—she swayed. And, as she had figuratively speaking so many years ago, Cassidy fell at his feet.

She came to with her head resting against Will's hard chest, his warmth surrounding her. He must have sat her up. He had his arm around her. Blinking the world into focus, her eyes immediately sought his.

He was frowning. 'What happened?'

'If I had to guess, I'd say I fell down,' she informed him dryly.

'Are you sick?'

'Bit of a cold. I spent the morning in bed.'

His mouth narrowed into a thin line as he held a glass of water to her lips. 'You should have said something.'

Allowing the water to wash the dryness from her mouth and throat, she glanced around at the sea of interested by-standers and immediately felt colour rising in her cheeks. Great. The never-ending humiliation continued. It reminded her of that time in high school, before she'd had laser surgery, when she'd forgotten her glasses and got into the wrong car outside the school gates. She'd held a five-minute conversation with a complete stranger before she'd realised what she'd done…

Irritation sounding in her voice, she tried to push up on to her feet. 'I'm good now, Will. Thanks. Let me up.'

But he held her in place. 'Give it a minute.'

When he held the glass back to her mouth, her sense of mortification was raised several notches. She pushed his hand away. 'Stop that. I can do it. I don't need a minute.'

Taking the glass from him, she struggled anything but gracefully to her feet, splashing water onto her hand and the floor. Once she was upright, she swayed precariously. Will stepped forward—one hand removing the glass, one arm circling her waist as he calmly informed her, 'That went well.'

Cassidy scowled at the grumbled words as he handed the glass to a hovering concierge before demanding, 'Key card.'

'What?'

'Give me your key card.' Lifting his free hand in front of her body, he waggled long fingers. 'Hand it over. You're going back to bed.'

'I don't think—'

'Good. Run with that. *Key card.*'

While her brain tried to think up an argument against the new and not necessarily improved attitude he seemed to have acquired with age, her traitorous hand reached into her bag for the card. Apparently the best she could come up with in reply was, 'I don't remember you being this bossy.'

'Comes with the territory in my job.' His fingers closed around the card.

'Can we get anything for the lady?'

Will nodded at the concierge's question. 'You could send up some chilled orange juice to room…?'

When he lifted his brows at Cassidy, she sighed. 'Ten-twenty-eight.'

'And send out to the nearest pharmacy for cold medicine of some kind.'

The concierge nodded. 'Of course, sir.'

Completely out of nowhere, Will did the last thing she'd expected and bent at the waist, scooping her into his arms like some kind of caped superhero. The man would put his back out! She was a good twenty pounds over the weight she'd been the last time he'd pulled that stunt.

A part of her curled up and died even as her arm automatically circled his neck. 'Put me down, Will. I can walk.'

As she whispered the words her gaze met that of several fascinated observers, and a couple of women who looked distinctly as if they were swooning. Now her cheeks were on fire. 'Will, I'm serious! I'm too heavy.'

'No, you're not. Shut up, Cass.'

She wriggled, and felt her lunch rearrange itself inside her stomach, drawing a low moan from her lips. If she threw up in public she was taking the next plane home. It would serve Will Ryan right if she threw up over *him!*

He walked through the remainder of the foyer as if she weighed nothing, and then turned to hit the elevator button with his elbow. Adding even further to her nightmare, he then moved the hand at her waist and dropped his chin to frown at her body. 'What *are* you wearing under that blouse?'

Oh. Dear. *God.*

'I think you'll find we're eight years too late for a conversation about my underwear.'

When he looked at her, she summoned a smirk.

His green gaze travelling over her face, he took in her flushed cheeks and the way she was chewing on her lower lip before he looked back into her eyes. 'Wearing something so tight that it restricts your breathing is hardly going to help any, is it?'

'It's not like I *planned* on falling at your feet.' Oh, she just didn't know when to stop, did she?

Amusement danced across his eyes. Before he could say anything the elevator doors opened, so he turned sideways and guided her inside. 'Push the button, Cass.'

She did. Then Will took a step back and lifted his chin to watch the numbers as they lit up above the doors.

'You can put me down now. Seriously.'

'That's not happening.'

Cassidy sighed heavily. His stubborn streak, she remembered. When Will had dug his heels in over something he'd been an immovable object. It had led to more than one heated debate when they were writing, but back then they'd had one heck of a good time making up afterwards. Naturally now she'd thought about *that* her body reacted.

So she tried to think of the names of all of the seven dwarfs to distract herself—there was always one she couldn't remember; now, which one was it? Scrunching her nose up while she concentrated didn't help. Nope still couldn't get him. Elusive seventh dwarf! She sighed again.

'Huff all you want, Cass. I'm not putting you down.'

The elevator pinged and the doors slid open while she informed him, 'You'll have to put me down eventually. It'll make it a tad difficult to do the basics, lugging me around like a sack of spuds all day.'

When he turned from side to side to search for the plates on the wall that would indicate where her room was, she waved a limp arm. 'That way.'

'Why didn't you call and say you weren't feeling well?'

Because a part of her had been looking forward to seeing him again, that was why. Her curiosity had been getting the better of her ever since his e-mail had arrived. Only natural considering their history, she'd told herself. What girl *wasn't* fascinated by how her first love looked years after the last time she saw him? It was one of those things that never completely went away. Along with the associated paranoia of wondering whether time had built her memories of him into some kind of magical figure he couldn't possibly live up to, or whether he would have aged much better than she had.

In the face of further humiliation, she lied, 'I felt better when I got up.'

'Liar.'

Cassidy sighed louder than before. 'I *hate* that you can still do that. Fine, then—I wanted to know why I was here.'

'Yes, obviously. Because I didn't explain it in the e-mails I sent you…'

Was he fishing? She lifted her chin and frowned up at his profile at the exact moment he chose to lower his dense lashes and look down at her. It made her breath catch in her lungs. One man should *not* look that good! It took every ounce of strength she had not to drop her gaze to his mouth. Then she had to dig deeper to make herself breathe normally again.

She should never have made the trip over. 'It wasn't like you picked up a phone to discuss it.'

Broad shoulders shrugged before he slotted her key card into the door. 'Different time zones. And my schedule has been crazy.'

Cassidy lifted a brow. 'Liar.'

'Nope.' He shouldered the door open. 'You're seven hours behind over there. I've been dealing with a movie that's running over budget every second. Any time I had to call you would have been during school hours your end. Plus, if you were worried about making the trip and *wanted* me to call you, you'd have said so in your e-mails—wouldn't you?'

She hated it when he used reasoning on her. And when she couldn't read him the way he did her. Back in the good old days the former had been useful mid-debate, and the latter had been endearing as heck—especially when he'd told her what she was thinking in a husky voice, with his mouth hovering above hers. But now? Now it just kept on making her feel like even more of an idiot than she already did for not realising the physical attraction she'd had for him would be as uncontrollable as it had been before. There was no fighting chemistry. When the pheromones said it worked, it worked. It was up to the brain to list the reasons why it couldn't.

Setting her gently on her feet by the giant bed, he leaned over to drag the covers back before standing tall and letting a small smile loose. 'Take it off.'

'Excuse me?'

He jerked his chin. 'That industrial-strength whatever-it-is you're wearing. What is it with women and those boned things, anyway?'

A squeak of outrage sounded in the base of her sore throat. 'You're unbelievable. Go away.'

'I'll go when you're all tucked up in bed. Anything happens to you within twenty-four hours of hitting L.A. I might feel guilty for bringing you here...'

Somewhere in the growing red mist of her anger came a question that temporarily made her gape at him. *'You* brought me here? I thought the studio brought me here? Are you telling me *you* paid for all of this—the flights and the limo pick-up and the fancy room and everything?'

Say no!

'Yes.'

Uh-oh. Room swaying again. But when his hands grasped her elbows she tugged them away and managed to turn round before she flumped down onto the mattress. Automatically toeing her shoes off her feet, she shook her head and blinked into the middle distance. 'I thought the studio paid for it.'

'They paid for a script. We took the money. Now we have to deliver.'

What had she got herself into? She couldn't be beholden to him. It wasn't as if she had the money to pay him back—not until they were paid the balance of their advance for the last script. Even then. Every cent was precious. There was no guarantee she could start writing again without Will and make money at it. Not that she'd tried the last time…

A crooked forefinger arrived under her chin and lifted it to force her gaze upwards. Then he examined her eyes for the most maddening amount of time while she held her breath. 'You need to sleep. I'll come back later and check up on how you're feeling.'

'You don't have to.'

'Go take that ridiculous thing off while I'm here—in case you pass out again.'

'I won't pass—'

'Humour me.'

Pursing her lips, she reached for her pyjamas from under the soft pillows, pushed to her feet and scowled at him on her way to the bathroom, 'I don't know that I can work with this new bossy Will.' She lifted her chin. 'I don't like him.'

Closing the door with a satisfyingly loud click, she took a second to lean against the wood until the world stopped spinning again. For a long time she'd told herself her life was a mess, but it was a glorious kind of mess. Now she felt very much like dropping the 'glorious' part…

She had to sit on the edge of the bathtub to struggle her way out of everything without another dizzy spell. Then she hid the offending underwear under a pile of towels, in case he decided to use the bathroom before he left. Stupid cold! That was what she got for working in a room full of children—she must have incubated the germs on the plane. So much for being considerate and taking the time to see the children through the last term, postponing her trip by a couple of weeks until the summer holidays. They'd repaid her in germs. Bless them.

'You okay in there?' He sounded as if he was standing right by the door.

When she yanked it open, he was.

'You can go away now.'

Will blocked her exit and took his sweet time looking her over from head to toe and back up again, for the second time in as many hours. Only this time it left her skin tingling with more than the cold sweat from her cold. Just one comment about her two-sizes-too-big pyjamas and he was a dead man.

Then his gaze clashed with hers and her eyes widened. What was *that*?

He stepped back. 'Bed.'

Cassidy made a big deal about making sure she patted the covers down the full length of her legs when she was between the cool cotton sheets. The room was wonderfully cool too. Had he turned on the air-conditioning for her? Then she saw the glass of water on the bedside table, alongside the remote control for the television, a box of tissues and the large folder with all the hotel's numbers in it. He'd thought of everything. It was amazingly considerate, actually. It tempered the sharpness brought on by her humiliation, and her voice was calmer as she snuggled down against the large pile of cushions.

'There. Happy now?'

When she chanced another look at him he had the edges of his dark jacket pushed back and his large hands deep in the pockets of his jeans. He seemed so much larger than she remembered—as if he filled the room. And yet still with those boyishly devastating good looks and that thick head of dark hair, with its upward curls at his nape, and the sharply intelligent eyes that studied her so intensely she felt a need to run and hide…

Half of her silently pleaded with him to go away.

The other half probably wished he'd never left to begin with.

'I'll be back later.'

'You don't need to. Call in the morning if you like. I'll sleep.'

The green of his eyes flashed with determination. 'I'll be back later.'

The balance of power within Cassidy swayed towards 'go away'. 'I won't open the door Will.'

'I know.' He took his hands out of his pockets and backed towards the door, his long legs making the journey in three steps. Then he lifted a hand and casually turned something over between his long fingers like a baton, 'That's why I'm keeping your key card.'

Cassidy could have growled at him. But instead she rolled her eyes as she turned away and punched the pillows into shape, hearing the door click quietly shut behind her. After counting to ten, just to be sure, she fought the need to cry. Oh, how much easier it would be if she could hate him…

He was way out of her league now. *Way out.*

She wanted to go home.

CHAPTER TWO

THE dream was feverish. In the no man's land between deep sleep and consciousness came vivid images that were a mixture of the past, the present and some imaginary point in time real only in her mind. The sheets knotted around her legs felt cumbersome, still heavy, even though she'd long since kicked the blanket to one side and damp strands of her auburn hair were stuck to her cheeks and her forehead.

She felt awful.

But she was old enough and wise enough to know she was at the sweating-it-out stage. She just had to let it run its course and her body would fight it off. It might mean she was looking at a few days holed up in the hotel room, but it wasn't as if it was the worst hotel in the world, was it?

The low light from her bedside lamp shone irritatingly through the backs of her eyelids, and voices sounded from the television she had on low volume to help lull her to sleep. She'd never been particularly good with silence. But then neither was she accustomed to the noises of a busy American hotel. So keeping the TV on had seemed like a plan—especially when she'd discovered a channel that showed the familiar programmes she was used to watching

at home. That was why it took a moment for her to drag
her mind out of its half-slumber into a cognitive state. The
door had to have been knocked on several times by then,
she figured—with increasing levels of volume…

'Cass?' It was Will.

She groaned and croaked back at him. 'Go away, Will.'

Please go away. Don't make it worse. Let me die in
peace. Then if he wanted to he could come and take her
body away and donate it to medical science. She was
beyond caring any more.

'I'm coming in.'

The man had no idea when to take a hint! The next
thing she knew the door was open and he was walking in,
with a large paper bag in his hand. So she did the mature
thing and grabbed a pillow to hold over her face with both
hands. Maybe she could suffocate herself…

'How's the patient?'

'Not in the mood for company,' she mumbled from
under the pillow.

'You have a pillow over your face, so I couldn't quite
hear that. Here, let me help you.' He pried her fingers loose
and removed the pillow. Then he waited for her to squint
up at him through narrowed eyes. 'Hello there.'

Cassidy silently called him a really bad name. 'Please
go away Will.'

Setting the pillow on the other side of her head, he laid
the backs of his fingers against her forehead and frowned.
'When's the last time you took tablets?'

'I don't know—half an hour after you left…maybe…'

'Time for more.'

Struggling her way into a sitting position, she accepted

the tablets he dropped into her palm and washed them down with what was left of the glass of juice on her side table. Then she set the glass back down and lifted her heavy arms to try and tidy her hair before looking up at him from under her lashes.

'I appreciate what you're doing, Will. I do. *And* whatever it is you've brought me in the paper bag. But I just need to sleep it out. It'll be some kind of freaky twenty-four-hour thing, that's all. I've taken my tablets and had some juice, and now I'm going back to sleep. If you leave a number I'll call you when I wake up. I'm not that bad. Really.'

She then ruined the effect by sneezing with enough force to make it feel as if she'd just blown the top off her aching head. She moaned. Someone should just shoot her.

Will calmly handed her a tissue.

She decided to disgust him to get him to leave, blowing her nose loud enough to alert all shipping routes of an incoming fog.

Will had the gall to look vaguely amused. 'You need to eat something. I brought you chicken noodle soup.'

How *could* he? As he reached a large hand into the bag memory slammed into her frontal lobe and ricocheted down her closing throat, wrapping around her heart so tight it made it difficult to breathe. Because he'd done this before, hadn't he? Only she'd had flu that time. They'd been in the tiny bedsit they'd shared for a while instead of living in halls of residence. As well as bringing her everything she'd needed to feel better, and heating endless pans of chicken noodle soup, he had sat up with her, watched television with her, held her in his arms, smoothed her hair until she fell asleep…

It wasn't that she'd forgotten. It was just that the memory hadn't been so vivid in a long time. There had been so many different memories to overshadow it. Heartbreak had a tendency to do that—taking the best of memories and tingeing them with a hint of painful regret for the fact there wouldn't be more memories made in the future. But right now he *was* adding a new one. One that was surrounded in bittersweetness because it wasn't one she could hold onto the same way as the first.

It hurt.

Removing the lid of the soup carton, he wrapped it in a napkin and handed it to her along with a plastic spoon. 'Here…'

Dampening her lips, she hesitated briefly before reaching for the carton. She had no choice but to slide her fingers over his during the exchange, and a jolt of electricity shot up her arm. Her chest was aching when he slid his fingers away. It would have been easier if he'd just set the carton down. Darn it.

Purposefully she took the spoon from him by grasping the opposite end from his fingers, croaking a low, 'Thank you.'

'You're welcome.' He inclined his head.

When she blew too hard on the soup, and splattered just enough hot liquid on the back of her hand to make her frown, she glanced up at him and found amusement dancing in his eyes again. He truly was the most irritating man in the world.

Then he sat on the edge of the bed and turned towards her. 'If you're not better tomorrow I'll get a doctor to come see you.'

'I don't need a doctor; it's a cold—not bubonic plague.'

'And they say *men* make lousy patients…'

Cassidy shook her head. Then leaned in and blew more gently on her soup to cool it. When she looked up, Will was studying her intently—almost as if he'd never seen her before. It made her sigh for the hundredth time that day. 'What now?'

'You changed your hair.'

The words surprised her, but as usual her sarcasm kicked in. 'Yeah. Women tend to do that a couple of times in eight years. We're fickle that way.'

'Still have a smart mouth, though.'

Which apparently gave him leave to drop his gaze and look at it as she formed another pouting 'O' to blow air on the soup. She immediately pursed her lips in response. When his thick lashes lifted she scowled at him. 'Your good deed is done for the day now. You can go and do whatever it is you normally do at this time of night. Wherever you do it and with whomever you do it.'

'Whomever?' The corners of his mouth tugged again. 'Nice use of the English language. Fishing for details, Cass?'

Cassidy had never wanted to scream so much in all her born days. 'Writers are supposed to have a good grasp of the language. Not that you'd understand that. I spent half our time together correcting your spelling mistakes…'

She really had. It wasn't that he couldn't spell, it was just that sometimes his mind worked faster than his typing fingers.

Then she addressed his cockiness. 'And I'm not fishing. It's none of my business.'

'You could try asking me.'

'I'm sorry. Wasn't "it's none of my business" clear enough?'

'Not the littlest bit curious?'

'Why would I be?'

The beginning of one of *those* smiles started in his eyes. And if it started in his eyes first it was devastating when it made it to his mouth. She *knew*. So she stopped it happening by throwing out somewhat desperate words. 'Even if you're free as a bird it doesn't make any difference. You and me? We're workmates. Business partners, if you like. Barely platonic ones. We're like two people stranded on a desert island who have to make the best of it till the next rescue boat arrives—as good as strangers. You don't know any more about who I am now than I know about—'

'You're babbling. You always babble when you're nervous. Why are you nervous, Cass?'

Screwing up her face, she set the soup carton onto the side table and slid down under the covers, lifting them and tucking them over her head. 'I hate you. Would you *go away*? I'm not up to this. You're still the most annoying man I've ever known.'

'Makes me memorable…'

Cassidy growled, and promptly ended up coughing when the vibration hurt her raw throat. Somewhere mid-cough she heard what sounded like a low chuckle of laughter. She peeked over the edge of the covers ready to scowl at him and found him lifting his brows in a question, a completely unreadable expression on his face. It made her narrow her eyes.

'You know we need to get on better than this to work together, don't you?'

She did, and immediately felt like a fool again. 'Can we try and get on better when I don't feel like the hotel fell on me?'

'When you're weak is probably the best time to talk this through.'

'That's evil.'

Will had more difficulty stifling his smile than he had so far. 'True.'

He wasn't apologising for it, though, was he? The rat. Cassidy tried hard not to be charmed by it; she did. But a small sparkle-eyed smile was apparently nearly as effective as a killer one, and before she knew it she was smiling back at him. Then she shook her head. 'I hate you.'

'Mmm.' He leaned forward, his large body distractingly close to hers and his familiar scent somehow making it through her blocked nose. 'You said.'

When he lifted the soup carton Cassidy lifted her gaze to his hair. He had great hair. The colour of dark chocolate, thick enough to tempt a woman's fingertips, and distinctly male to the touch when she touched it, but soft enough to encourage her to slide her fingers deep... She wished she didn't remember so much...

Will leaned back. 'You need to eat.'

'Bossing me again, Ryan?'

'Necessary, Malone.'

Without comment she went ahead and sipped at the soup, her gaze flickering to his often enough for her to know he was still watching her. Not that she needed to look to confirm it. She'd always known when Will was looking at her. In the same way she could feel the newfound tension lying between them.

Thick lashes blinked lazily at even intervals, and then he asked, 'Good?'

'Mmm-hmm.' She nodded. *'Good.'*

Looking around the room for a moment, Will folded his dark brows in thought before he took a deep breath and focused on her again. 'I think you should stay at my place while you're in L.A.'

Cassidy almost choked on her soup. He had a knack of doing that to her. But he couldn't be serious! There was no way she could go and stay at his place—be under the same roof with him twenty-four-seven. They were barely managing to make civil conversation between his short sentences and her loose tongue. And now he wanted them somewhere they couldn't escape from each other? Oh, yeah. That would help.

Then she thought about the fact he was paying for the hotel room she was in and felt guilty. Maybe if she found a computer and checked her meager bank account she could discover somewhere cheap and cheerful to stay? It didn't need to be fancy: a bed, a door that locked, a shower, a minimal number of cockroaches...

Will continued while she blinked at him, 'We need to spitball ideas and get to work. And we never used to stick to a nine to five, so if we're working through the night it makes sense to be somewhere we can do that. I'll come get you in the morning.'

Cassidy wondered if there was ever going to be a point where she got to make decisions on her own. 'Don't you have an office?'

'I have one we can work in at home, yes.'

Not what she'd meant, and he knew it. 'In the city. You can't run an entire production company from home.'

'I probably could. But, yes, I do have offices in the city. Still the same problem there—this makes more sense.'

It didn't matter if it made sense. Surely he remembered that about her? But before she could even string together a thought, never mind form the words to argue it out, he was pushing to his feet. 'While you're not feeling well you can take a break to sleep any time you need to. I'll come get you at nine.'

Cassidy watched him get halfway to the door before she managed to open her mouth. 'I'm not comfortable with the idea of living in your house—or apartment—or whatever it is you have.'

'You'll forget that when you've been there a few days.'

'Damn it, Will!' She frowned at him when he turned round. 'You can't keep riding roughshod over me like this. If I don't want to stay in your house I don't have to. And if it's because you're paying for this hotel then I can find somewhere—'

Lowering his chin, he lifted his brows with amused disbelief. 'You think paying for this room is a problem for me?'

'That's not the point. Whether or not you can afford—'

Will shook his head, smiling incredulously. 'It's got nothing to do with money. It's got to do with practicality. *Man.* I'd forgotten how stubborn you can be.'

Swallowing down another pang of hurt that he'd forgotten *anything* about her when she remembered everything about him, Cassidy arched a brow. 'Pot, meet kettle. Regardless of whether or not you can afford to pay for this room, the simple fact is you shouldn't be. I'll pay you back whatever you've already forked out. I don't want to owe you anything. This is business and we both know it. Whatever we once had doesn't matter any more. We're not even friends now.'

'And blunt. That part I hadn't forgotten.' He lifted his chin and frowned at a random point in the air while taking a deep breath that expanded his wide chest. Then he dropped his chin and looked her straight in the eye. 'You're right. It *is* business. You have a job back home. I have a job here. So the sooner we get this done the sooner we can get back to work. If we dig in, and eat, drink and sleep this script for the next few weeks, we can nail it.'

It was all about the script; of course it was.

Will quirked his brows. 'Well?'

'It's business.'

'Exactly.'

'Right.' She didn't have the energy to keep fighting with him. 'Fine, then.'

With his mouth drawn into a thin line and a frown darkening his face, Will swung round and tugged on the door. 'Nine o'clock.'

When the door closed behind him Cassidy blinked at it. For a brief second he'd almost looked angry. How on earth were they supposed to communicate well enough to write a script if they couldn't even hold a conversation? She flumped further down on the pillows and put what was left of her soup on the nightstand before tugging the covers up over her shoulders. She felt cold again, she was shivery— and suddenly she had an incredible sense of loneliness to add to her feeling homesick.

Her first trip to Hollywood should be a fairytale experience. It was a dream she'd had since childhood, when the magic of movies had sucked her into the kind of imaginary worlds that had enthralled her for most of her life. Everything about it had fascinated her as she got older: the sets, the effects, the lighting, the locations, where the words the actors and actresses spoke came from. The latter had then become something she wanted to do—she wanted to put those words there. To watch a movie on a big screen and hear words she had written on a flat page spoken by an actor or actress who could add depths and nuances she might never even have thought of.

When she'd got her dream the world had become the most amazing place to her. And she'd got to share that magic with the man she loved. It had been perfect. She had been so happy.

But there was no such thing as perfect happiness. Life had taught her that. Failure had taken the sparkly-eyed wonder from her eyes. Then she'd had to give up her dreams, her confidence shattered, her heart broken, because Will had gone and she'd had no choice but to watch him walk away. The last time she had seen him was indelibly imprinted on her brain, and in the empty part of her heart that had died that day…

Cassidy had felt as if all the magic had been sucked out of her life. And she'd never got it back. Just small pockets of happiness ever since. But then that was everyone's life, she had told herself. She just needed to get on with it. One day after another.

Even if for a very, very brief moment on her flight over she'd allowed herself to dream again. Not so much of Will, but of the other great love she'd lost. She'd foolishly allowed herself to think about what might happen if she rediscovered her muse and decided to take a chance in Hollywood for a while. But this script was simply something to get out of the way. Then she would go home. End of story. No pun intended.

Then she would have to decide what she wanted to do with the rest of her life.

At nine she'd been in the foyer for ten minutes, glad of the concierge to help her with her bags and glad at how easy checking out proved to be. Still a little light headed, she found a plump cushioned chair and waited…

Will was outside at the stroke of nine. Something else that was new about him. He'd once been the worst time-keeper she'd ever known.

'You'll be late for your own funeral,' she would tell him.

'Ah, now, that's the one time I can guarantee I'll be on time,' he would tease back with a smile.

Cassidy missed that Will.

The new Will was frowning behind his designer sun-glasses the second he got out of his lowslung silver sports car. He said something to the uniformed man in charge of valet parking as he slipped him a folded bill, then pushed through the doors and removed his sunglasses before seeking her out. Four steps later he had his hand on the handle of her case.

'Did you check out?'

'Yes.'

'Any problems?'

'No. They said it was taken care of.'

With a nod he stepped back, watching her rise. 'Feeling any better?'

It was said with just enough softness in his deep voice to make it sound as if he cared, which made Cassidy feel the need to sigh again. Instead she managed a small smile as she stood. 'Yes. Thank you.'

Somewhere in the wee small hours of the night she had decided the best way not to be so physically aware of Will's presence was to avoid looking at him whenever possible. So she didn't make eye contact as she waited for him to load her case into the boot of his car. Instead she smiled at the liveried valet as he opened the passenger door for her— though she did almost embarrass herself again by trying to get in the wrong side of the car...

When Will got into the driver's seat and buckled up she looked out of the side window to watch Rodeo Drive starting to think about coming to life. But they had barely pulled away from the hotel before he took advantage of the fact she was trapped.

'Want to tell me what's *really* bothering you about staying at my place?'

Not so much. No. She puffed her cheeks out for a second and controlled her errant tongue before answering. 'We don't know each other that well any more. It's going be like spending time in a stranger's house.'

There was a brief silence, then; 'I disagree.'

Well, now, there was a surprise. They worked their way through intersections and filtered into traffic while Cassidy noticed all the differences that indicated she was in a different country from home. Larger cars, palm trees, billboards advertising things she'd never heard of before, different shaped traffic lights...

Will kept going. 'We're not strangers. People don't change that much.'

She begged to differ. And if she hadn't had living proof

in herself then she had it in the man sitting so close to her in the confined space of what she now knew was a Mustang something-or-other—she'd seen a little tag somewhere. Not that she was going to turn her head to look for it again, if it meant she might end up catching a glimpse of him from her peripheral vision. Just being so close to him, so aware of every breath he took and every movement of his large hands or long legs, was enough for her to deal with, thanks very much.

'Yes, they do. Life changes them. Experiences change them…' She had a sudden brainwave. 'It's exactly the kind of problem Nick and Rachel will have when they meet again.'

The mention of their fictional characters momentarily silenced Will. Then she heard him take a breath and let it out. 'That's true.'

So it was true for their fictional characters but not for them? How did *that* work? It was enough to make her turn her head and aim a suspicious sideways glance at his general gorgeousness. 'It's not like they're going to trust each other either.'

'Well, she did steal the artifact from him.'

'No—she took it to give it back to its rightful owners. There's a difference. He'd have sold it on the open market for whatever he could get.'

'She lived off the money they made doing the same thing in the past. You can't use that as an argument against him.'

'Oh? Now we're saying there has to be moral equivalency?'

Will shot her a quick yet intense gaze as they waited in traffic, his deep voice somehow more intense within the car's interior. 'It's not the best plan to alienate everyone to the hero and heroine before we even get started, is it? There are always two sides to every story. You want to make him into a bad boy then you have to make the audience understand why his morals are lower than hers.'

'Bad heroes sell. You can't tell me they don't. Bad heroines are universally hated.' Cassidy lifted her chin, but she could feel the smile forming on her face. It was like one of their debates of old. 'Unless you're thinking of turning her evil—which, incidentally, you'll do over my dead body. The audience needs to empathise with her. That'll sell.'

'Actually, I can tell you exactly what sells these days. Right now its superheroes and family-friendly.' His long fingers flexed against the steering wheel. 'The real money can be found in family-oriented movies, where good is good and bad is bad. It's black and white. Moral equivalency needn't apply. Last year seven films with a G or PG rating earned more than one hundred million at the domestic box office, and three PG-rated films were among the year's top ten earners. Only one R-rated film was in the ten top grossing films—and there was no moral equivalency in that movie, I can assure you.'

The smile on her face faded and was replaced with blinking surprise as he recited it all in an even tone, negotiating increasing traffic at the same time. It seemed everyone in Los Angeles had a car.

He knew his stuff, didn't he? Who was she to argue? Not that it stopped her. 'Correct me if I'm wrong, but haven't you just proved my point on moral equivalency?'

Silence. Then to her utter astonishment a burst of laughter—deep, rumbling, oh-so-very-male laughter—

then a wry smile and a shake of his head. 'It's been a long time since anyone spoke to me the way you do.'

Cassidy blinked some more. 'Maybe people should do it more often.'

'If they did they'd get fired more often.'

The corners of her mouth tugged upwards. 'Wow. Who knew you were a tyrant in the making, back in the day?'

'I'm not a tyrant.' He seemed surprised she thought he was.

'No?' Turning a little more towards him, she leaned her back against the passenger door and angled her head in question. 'What are you, then?'

'The boss.'

'So no one can correct you when you're wrong?'

'They can put forward a different point of view, if that's what you mean.' He was forced to break eye contact with her to concentrate on where they were going. 'No one ever does it the way you do, though.'

Cassidy couldn't help but allow the chuckle of laugher forming in her chest to widen her smile. 'So no one actually looks you in the eye and tells you you're wrong?'

'Not in so many words, no.'

No wonder he'd got so arrogant over the years. If no one ever stood up to him, or gave as good as they got, it would be a breeding ground for arrogance. Irrationally, it made her feel sorry for him. Everyone needed someone who cared enough about them to be brutally honest when it was needed. No one was ever right one hundred percent of the time, after all. Being blunt on the odd occasion to demonstrate another point of view showed you cared enough about them to try and save them from the kind of mistakes arrogance might make. To Cassidy,

knowing no one did that for Will made him seem very...
alone...

'She'll probably feel awkward when she sees him again.'

Huh? Oh, he meant Rachel, didn't he? Right—script
stuff. Stay with the flow of conversation, Cassidy. 'I doubt
she'd have sought him out voluntarily.'

'So we need something that brings them together.'

Cassidy arched a brow. 'You're going to want him to
rescue her, aren't you?'

The one corner of his full mouth she could see hitched
upwards. 'Who doesn't like it when the hero swoops in to
rescue the heroine?'

'*Sexist.* Why can't the heroine rescue the hero? Or
rescue herself? Or just be in the same place as him searching for something when they *both* get in trouble and have
to work *together* to get out of it...?'

Will shot a brief, sparkle eyed glance her way. 'Okay,
then. He has to rescue her from something when they end
up in the same place hunting for something.'

Cassidy rolled her eyes. 'Fine. But I'm fighting for a
later scene when *she* has to rescue *him* right back.'

'We're not making Nick look weak.'

'Vulnerable—not weak. Women find vulnerability sexy
in a strong male. You should try it some time. Might get
you a girlfriend...' The reappearance of her errant tongue
made her groan inwardly and avoid his gaze when he
looked her way again.

'You don't know I don't have a girlfriend.'

'I told you, it's none of my—'

'I don't have one right now. But all you had to do was ask.'

Oh, for crying out loud. Not only had she just caused a

self-inflicted wound at the idea of him with another woman, but now he'd managed to slip that little piece of unwanted information into the conversation it was only a matter of time before—

'What about you?'

Yep. There it was. Well, if he thought for one single, solitary second she was discussing the disastrous attempts she had eventually made at having a love life—long, *long* after he'd left—then he had another think coming. Not that it would be a long conversation.

Lifting her chin, she smiled sweetly. 'I don't have a girlfriend either.'

Will chuckled for the second time.

The sound was ridiculously distracting to her. How did it do that? It wasn't as if she hadn't heard him laugh before; she'd heard him chuckle, laugh softly, laugh out loud—had felt the rumble in his chest and been in his arms when his body had shaken with the reverberations. She knew how the light would dance in his eyes, how he would smile the amazingly infectious smile that gave everyone around him no choice but to smile along with him. For a long time Cassidy had believed she'd fallen for his laughter first. Yes, his boyish looks, height, gorgeous hair, etc., etc. might have been what had initially caught her eye. But it had been the sound of his laughter and the first glimpse of *that* smile that had drawn her heart to him.

Since she'd got to Los Angeles she'd wondered if she'd imagined the effect his laughter had on her. As if her memories were tangled up on some mythical pedestal she might have elevated him to over the years. But it was having exactly the same effect on her as before: skin tingling, chest warming—as if the sound had somehow reached out and physically touched her…

Forcing her gaze away, she turned forward in the seat to look out through the windscreen, and was surprised to see the ocean beside them. 'Where are we?'

'Pacific Coast Highway. It's the equivalent of Malibu's main street.'

'Malibu?'

'It's where I live.'

It was? Malibu? Where the rich and famous lived? She knew he'd done well since he came to California, but that he'd done well enough to be able to afford—

'It was originally part of the territory of the Chumash Nation of Native Americans. They called it Humaliwo— or "the surf sounds loudly". The current name derives from that. but the "Hu" syllable isn't stressed…' When she gaped at him he looked away from the highway long enough to raise his brows at her. 'What?'

'Who *are* you?'

The question was out before she could stop it, her words low and filled with incredulity. It was just the more he said the less she felt she knew him; it was as if he had somehow morphed into a completely different person when he'd moved halfway across the planet—and it was just so at odds with the many things that were familiar to her that it left her feeling a little…*lost*…

Will checked the road again, then looked back at her. 'You know me, Cass.'

His saying it in a low rumble that made goosebumps break out on her skin and her heart do a kind of weird twisting move in her chest only made her study him even more intently. 'How do you know all this stuff?'

'About Malibu?'

'It's like you've swallowed an encyclopaedia since you got here. Hollywood-speak, movie industry stats, local history…'

What looked almost like confusion flickered across the green of his eyes before he turned his head to watch the road again. 'Hollywood speak is everyday language here. Movie stats I study as part of my job, and Malibu I just happen to like—it's why I moved here the minute I could afford it. I hate the city.'

Actually, the last part she understood. Home of Disneyland and movie stars, Beverly Hills and Hollywood, she knew Los Angeles had long lured people into its glittering fantasy world, with its endless sunshine, palm trees, shopping malls and beautiful people. The city was like no place she'd ever been before. But after so many years dreaming about it, she'd known in less than twenty-four hours that she couldn't live there. Not in the city anyway. Too many people, too many cars, too much smog. No one saying hello to their fellow human beings in the street unless they were dressed as iconic movie figures and demanding money in exchange for a photograph with them. Cassidy had taken one afternoon to wander along Hollywood Boulevard, and as fascinating as it had been, reading the iconic stars beneath her feet, it hadn't made her feel at home. And now she'd discovered Will possibly felt that way too…

Well, it gave them some common ground, didn't it? A stretch maybe, but she would take what she could get…

Despite the danger, Cassidy wanted to know more. Her dilemma became whether or not to actually *ask* any more. If she did she would be getting a window into his life—

would have new Will Ryan memories to add to the cornucopia of old ones she already carried around with her. If somewhere along the way the new version of him proved as addictive as the old? Well, then she was in big, *big* trouble…

Who was she kidding? Cassidy had always been one of those people that needed to know. Christmas presents—she shook them. Books—she read the last pages before she got halfway through them. Favourite TV shows—she trawled the internet looking for spoilers for a new series before the episodes made it to the screen. There was about as much chance of her not asking as—

'So tell me more about Malibu.'

'What do you want to know?'

'Whatever you decide to tell me…'

She looked out through the windscreen at the glittering aquamarine blue of the Pacific Ocean, the thrill of seeing it for the first time bringing a soft smile to her mouth. She had always loved the ocean. Not surprising, really, when she lived on a tiny island surrounded by it. But there was just something about the ebb and flow of the tide…as if it was the subliminal heartbeat of the planet. Every time she saw the sea it made her smile. Seeing the Pacific for the first time was like meeting a new friend.

'That's the Pacific. Beautiful, isn't she?'

'She is.' Cassidy allowed herself to wonder why anything associated with the sea was always a 'she'. Probably something to do with moods and unpredictability and seduction, she supposed. From that point of view it was easy to see why seafaring men of old would have chosen the feminine to describe her.

'Malibu hugs the Pacific north of Santa Monica. It

has over twenty miles of coastline. Surfing is the big thing, obviously—endless opportunities for catching the perfect wave…'

The smile she could hear in his voice made her turn to look at his strong profile; the flicker of his thick dark lashes as he watched the traffic was unbelievably hypnotic to her. 'You surf?'

The corner of his mouth tugged. 'Used to. Don't have as much time now…'

A sudden visual image of Will walking out of the surf, glistening with water and shaking his head to loosen silvery droplets from his thick hair while he smiled *that* smile, did all sorts of delicious things to Cassidy's libido and left her mouth unbearably dry. There were times her active imagination took on a life of its own—useful in writerly terms, but not so useful when she was supposed to be thinking in terms of Will as a business partner. There could be no thinking of him bare-chested. Or towelling his hair for him. Or lying down on a large blanket beside him on warm sand.

Goodness, it was hot all of a sudden…

'It's part of the reason I bought a house on the beach.'

Suddenly staying at his house was looking more attractive to her. But… 'You bought a house on the beach so you could surf more, and then quit surfing? That makes perfect sense.'

He shrugged. 'Just the way it worked out.'

The house they pulled up in front of looked small and cosy. The sound of the ocean filled her ears as she stepped outside into warm salty air that made her breathe deep and appreciate the difference in air quality after the lack of oxygen in Los Angeles. But when Will unlocked the front door and stepped back to allow her to go ahead of him her eyes widened. Okay, it wasn't small and cosy. Will's house was… Well, it was amazing…

The deceptive frontage on the road made it look like it was just the one storey, and not all that big, when in fact it was split level and stretched for miles, with its lower level suspended above golden sands outside so that the huge picture windows made it look as if the entire house was floating above the waves. Open-plan, rich wooden floors, sparse furniture that didn't take anything from the views. It was very male, very modern, but stunningly beautiful.

It yelled *money* from every corner.

When Cassidy hovered at the top of the stairs, Will closed the front door and stepped over beside her. 'The view sold it.'

'Well, it would, wouldn't it?'

'Kitchen, living room, gym, home cinema and office are all on the lower level. Your room is over here to the left.' He took her case in that direction while she continued staring out of the windows.

Now she knew why Lizzie had fallen for Pemberley before she fell for Darcy. Because the part of Cassidy's soul that loved the ocean could live happily ever after in a house like Will's. Give or take a few feminine touches. If *she* lived there she would have bright comfy cushions on the large sofas, flowers in vases, books on the almost empty shelves where pieces of modern art were displayed. She could picture it in her mind's eye. She could practically hear music playing from an invisible stereo, laughter echoing off the walls, and the sound of small, running bare feet coming in from the beach. It made her heart hurt. How dared he have the house of her dreams? It was as if he'd purposely gone out and stolen every dream she'd ever had and held it from her, to add to breaking her heart the way he had.

She genuinely hated him for that.

With a deep breath she turned on her heel and followed Will along the hall that skirted the floor below, rolling her eyes when she got to the open doorway and looked in at the bedroom she would be staying in. Of course it had the same ocean view. And naturally Will was sliding open the glass windows so the sea breeze caught the light curtains. Was there ever any doubt it would have its own balcony, with comfy lounge chairs just waiting to be occupied so she could watch the sunset at the end of the day?

Stepping into a little corner of heaven, she plunked down on the end of the large bed and allowed herself to bounce just once on the deep mattress while she fought the need to cry. It really wasn't fair. How *could* he? What had she ever done to him to deserve this kind of torture?

Will turned from the windows and pushed his hands deep into the pockets of his dark jeans as he studied her. 'Tired?'

Weary would have been a better word, she felt. 'A little. Coffee would probably help. And I should take some tablets again, just in case.'

'Okay.' He nodded. 'Did you have breakfast?'

'No.'

'Yeah, that'll help you get better. Will bagels and lox do?'

'Depends.' Cassidy lifted her chin, stifled a wry smile and arched a brow. 'What is lox, exactly?'

His eyes sparkled. 'It's smoked salmon. Bagels with cream cheese and smoked salmon.'

'Ahh.'

'Is that "Yes, Will"?'

A more genuine smile broke free as she inclined her head. 'Yes, Will. Thank you. Bagels and lox sounds lovely.'

As if to emphasise her approval her stomach growled softly, making Will's mouth twitch as he left the room. 'Come down when you're ready. Feed a cold and all that…'

She wished he would stop being nice. Annoying Will her heart could cope with. But if he started adding Nice Will to the house she'd fallen in love with at first sight she would be in even bigger trouble than she had been twenty-four hours ago.

Lying back on the bed, she turned her head and closed her eyes, breathing as deep as her aching chest would allow while she compared Will's life to the one she had. It wasn't hard to see who had fared better. If her self-confidence had been low before she'd stepped on the plane in Dublin, it was pretty much sitting at the bottom of a dark pit of despair now. She really needed to do something that would make her feel like herself again. But that was just it. Since Will, she'd never really discovered who Cassidy Malone was without him. Maybe it was time to find out?

After all, she was in the house of her dreams in California, a stone's throw away from the industry she still found completely absorbing—even from the periphery, as a viewer of the art form. It was a step in the right direction, wasn't it? Nothing ventured, nothing gained?

She slapped her palms against the cool covers and sat upright, reaching into her bag for her tablets and taking them with her as she left the room. Coffee, bagels and lox, tablets—and then she was going to start work and see if she still re-membered how to write. That was somewhere to start…

CHAPTER THREE

'THAT'S the most ridiculous thing I've ever heard.'

'How is it?'

'How is it *not*?' She blinked incredulously at him, then continued looking around the large glass desk for the pen she knew she'd had five minutes ago. 'You want them to find a hidden nuclear warhead in the middle of an archaeological dig?'

Will allowed a pen to twirl between his thumb and forefinger, as if teasing her with it because she couldn't find her own. 'We need explosions.'

'A nuclear warhead is a little more than a simple explosion. And how on earth did the terrorist group get the thing down there, when we've already said that no one has discovered the site after centuries of searching?' Cassidy shook her head, lifting discarded scene cards in her search.

'We can change that. It's one line.' His pen stilled and his deep voice informed her, 'Behind your ear.'

'What?' She scowled at him, her pulse hitching when she realised how intensely he was staring at her as he lounged in his chair and swung it from side to side. That chair had been driving her crazy. It had a squeak. She'd have thought a man of Will's means could afford a can of oil to fix something that irritating, but *no*. He just kept swinging and squeaking, and swinging and squeaking, until she thought she might have to kill him.

He jerked his chin at her. 'Your pen. It's behind your ear.'

When she reached up her hand she sighed; of course it was.

Retrieving the pen from behind her ear, she reached for the last card he'd scrawled notes on and scribbled through half of it forcefully. 'Rachel wouldn't be seen dead wearing *that* either. You're turning her into a sex object.'

The chair squeaked back and forth. 'Bad boy hero, sexy heroine, explosions, treasure hunt, hint of romance—all the ingredients of a blockbuster, trust me…'

'The box office is all that matters to you, is it?' Cassidy began rhythmically tapping the end of her pen on the glass tabletop. 'Forget telling a story, or little things such as character arc and continuity.'

'We're still at the brainstorming stage. We're miles away from character arc and continuity. This is the fun part.'

Really? Because Cassidy hadn't noticed the 'fun part' so much. It was almost as if Will was determined to get her to argue with him. Surely a man with his experience in the business knew better than to fall into the usual traps of cliché and plot device? If she didn't know better she might say he was playing with her on purpose…

While she considered the possibility of that with narrowed eyes, she tapped her pen harder and faster against the glass. Will continued to add to the ambient noise with the squeaking of his chair.

Then his mouth twitched and he nodded at her pen. 'That could get irritating after a while…'

'You think?' She lifted her brows and tapped the pen harder. 'Like the squeaking of your chair, perhaps?'

When she pouted there was a split second of silence as the tapping and the squeaking stopped. Then, out of no-where, they both laughed at the same time. Cassidy tossed the pen down, running her palms over her face as she groaned loudly. The man was making her *insane*!

Residual laughter sounded in the deep rumble of Will's voice. 'Time for a break.'

It only occurred to her that his voice sounded closer when warm hands closed over hers to lift them from her face, and she found herself tilting her chin up to look into the green of his gaze. He was gorgeous. Take-a-girl's-breath-away gorgeous. Her heart thundered against her breastbone loud enough for her to hear it in her ears as he smiled a small smile that darkened his eyes a shade, then lowered her hands before stepping back and gently tugging her upright.

'I need food.'

'Again? We ate less than an hour ago.' There had been sandwiches. Cassidy definitely remembered there being sandwiches.

'Five hours ago.'

It was? She looked out of the windows as Will turned, keeping hold of one of her wrists to draw her towards the door. Sure enough, outside the light was changing, the tide was turning and people were beginning to—

Hang on a minute. *Why* did Will still have hold of her wrist?

Turning her head, she dropped her chin and frowned down at the human handcuff. Long fingers were lightly hooked over her pulse-point, but they were hooked never-theless, and he was walking them through the living area towards the kitchen. She couldn't take a chance on him re-alising what he did to her pulse. So she gently twisted her wrist and reclaimed it, frowning all the harder at the fact her skin still tingled where he had touched.

Will glanced briefly over his shoulder, then walked to the giant refrigerator and looked inside. 'Steaks okay with you? We can flame-grill them on the deck.'

'Sounds more than fine with me.' She stopped at the end of the narrow breakfast bar and rested her palms on the granite surface. 'What can I do to help?'

'Chop some salad, if you like. Use whatever you fancy out of the fridge.'

Cassidy forgot herself and smiled as he reappeared, tossed the steaks down on the counter and reached into a drawer for barbecue utensils. 'You have the weirdest ac-cent now, you know. Tang of American, but still using Irish phrases.'

A brief sideways glance of sparkle-eyed amusement was aimed her way. 'You can take the boy out of Ireland…'

She rolled her eyes.

Will jerked his dark brows as he unwrapped the steaks. 'Everyone does it. You spend time in a certain environ-ment, surrounded by people who talk a certain way, and you absorb some of it. It's probably a subliminal need for acceptance.'

The idea that a man like Will would feel the need for acceptance anywhere momentarily baffled Cassidy. Maybe she was reading too much into it? She was known to do that. A lot of women were. She stepped towards the fridge to have a poke around for salad ingredients. 'Was it weird at first? Living here, I mean?'

'In Malibu or in California?'

When he reached past her for a bottle of sauce Cassidy's breathing hitched. He'd bent his upper body over hers, had reached his arm over her shoulder and brushed his finger-tips against her hair on the way past, surrounding her for a fleeting moment with an intensely male body heat that contrasted so very sharply with the cold air from the re-frigerator's interior. It had an immediate visceral reaction on her. Goosebumps broke out on her skin, her abdomen tensed, her breasts grew heavy. She even had to swallow hard to dampen her dry mouth and close her eyes to stifle a low moan.

For crying out loud—she knew it had been a long time since she'd last made love, but it was really no excuse for the compulsive need she suddenly felt to turn round and launch herself at him, so they could spend several hours seeing if they still remembered how to play each other's bodies like fine instruments…

One, two, three breaths of cool, refrigerated air—then she reappeared from behind the door with an iceberg lettuce, tomatoes, a cucumber, and two different bottles of salad dressing. When she chanced a sideways glance at Will she found him on the other side of the breakfast bar, studying her intently.

'Malibu or California?'

'What?'

'You asked was it weird living here. I asked Malibu or California.'

Oh, yes, that was right. She had done that. 'California.'

'Yes.'

She set her things on the counter and lifted a brow. 'Malibu?'

'No.'

When light danced across his eyes she knew he was messing with her, so she shook her head. 'A bowl for this stuff?'

'Second cupboard on the left, underneath you.'

'So why was California weird?' She opened the cupboard and hunched down to look inside.

'Why don't you hit me with *your* first impressions and I'll tell you if I felt the same way when I got here…' The sound of doors sliding told her he had moved towards the deck.

By the time she came back up, with a large wooden bowl in hand, he was firing up the outdoor grill. So she found a knife and a chopping board all on her own, while raising her voice to continue the conversation. 'Way more people, nobody smiles and says hello the way they do at home, hotter, brighter—drier. Nothing as green as you'd see in Ireland. Food's different, television is different, the cars people drive are different… Some things are familiar, but the vast majority of differences outshadow them…'

Will was smiling yet another small smile as he came back in, the sea breeze outside having created unruly waves in his dark hair that made him look even more boyish than he already did in his simple white T-shirt and blue jeans combo. No one would ever look at the man and put him in his early thirties. Good genetics, Cassidy supposed. His kids would inherit that anti-ageing gene, and the boys would all look like him, wouldn't they? With dark hair that

even when tamed would rebel, with that outward flick at
the nape, and green eyes that sparkled with amusement, and
the charm of the devil when they wanted something, and—

Cassidy couldn't believe she was standing in his beautiful house and picturing dozens of mini-Wills standing
between them. She'd be naming them next. Maybe her
biological clock was kicking in?

'In other words weird…'

She smiled as she chopped. 'Okay. Point taken. So why
is Malibu different?'

'It's not so crowded here. The air's better.' He shrugged
his shoulders as he turned bottles of wine on a rack to read
the labels. 'Quieter. More private. I'd lived in California
long enough by the time I bought this place that it wasn't
so alien to me any more. But this was the first place I felt
I could call home.'

'You don't see Ireland as home any more?'

'I see it as where I come from, and a part of who I am,
but I have my life in California now.'

Cassidy had known that for a long time. But hearing him
say it didn't make it any easier. It was another thing that
highlighted how different they were. Somehow she knew
she would always see Ireland as home. She had thirty
years' worth of memories there—not all of them good,
granted. But it was the good and the bad that made her who
she was—for better or worse. A part of her would always
ache for the green, green grass of home if she left it behind.
The fact Will had left *everything* behind without any
apparent sense of poignancy made her wonder if he remembered their time together the same way she did. Or remembered that he had said he loved her.

Maybe the harsh truth was he hadn't. Not the way she had loved him. If he had he would never have left her, would he?

The sound of a cork popping brought her gaze back to him as he set a bottle of red wine on the counter to breathe. But when he reached for deep bowled glasses and she opened her mouth to remind him of the dangers of her errant tongue and alcohol, he surprised her.

'Why teaching?' he asked.

She frowned in confusion. 'What?'

'Why teaching?' He turned around and leaned back against the counter, folding his arms across his chest and studying her with hooded eyes. 'I don't remember you ever showing an interest in it when I knew you before.'

Well, no, because when he'd known her she'd still had dreams that felt as if they were within her grasp. Then she'd been given a harsh reality check. She shrugged and tossed the chopped-up salad ingredients in the bowl. 'Necessity to start with, I guess. I needed a job with a regular wage. If I was going to spend a good portion of my life working, it made sense to me to be doing something I might enjoy…'

'Do you?'

'Do I what?'

'Enjoy it?'

'I'd enjoy it more if I was better paid.' She shot him a brief smile, then concentrated on reading the labels on the salad dressings. 'I like little kids. They think in straight lines. They still believe in magic. Adults get the magic knocked out of them with age. Every day when I spend time with a classroom full of kids, and they do or say or discover something that makes me smile, I get a little of that magic back for a minute.'

When he remained silent, curiosity made her turn her head so she could try and read his expression. He was still staring at her, thick lashes still at half-mast so she couldn't see his eyes properly. It was disconcerting.

Then he tugged on a ragged corner of her heart with a low, rumbled comment. 'You used to believe in magic more than anyone I'd ever met…'

Cassidy felt a hard lump forming in her throat, and immediately felt the need to turn her face away, dropping her chin and hiding behind a strand of hair that had escaped from her up-do as she tried to open the lid of the salad dressing. 'Like I said. It gets knocked out of you with age.'

Was this lid cemented on? She pursed her lips and felt the cap digging into her palm as she tried twisting it with a little more force, shifting her shoulder so she was literally putting her back into it, while forcing words out through tight lips at the same time.

'Just part—of life—that's all. Nobody's fault. Or any—'

A large hand settled lightly over her fingers and Cassidy's chin snapped up. He gently removed the bottle from her hand and opened it with one deft twist of his wrist. Then he held it out for her, warmth shining from his eyes and the corners of his mouth tugging upwards. 'Borderline babbling again, Malone.'

Sighing heavily, she reached for the bottle. 'You're the one in charge of the magic these days—industry of dreams and all that. Maybe I handed on the baton.'

Will's head lowered closer to hers, his voice dropping an octave. 'You're saying I couldn't make magic back in the day?' Apparently it was enough to bring one of *those* smiles her way. 'I think my ego might be bruised.'

That wasn't the kind of magic she'd meant. But before she could form a coherent sentence he turned away, lifting the steaks from the counter-top and walking out onto the deck. Leaving Cassidy staring through the glass at him and feeling distinctly confused. Her inability to read him was really starting to bug her.

Once the steaks were on the fancy stainless steel grill he had on the deck, Will closed the lid and came back to the open door, leaning on the frame and studying her before he took a deep breath and asked, 'How are you feeling?'

'Better.' She smiled before turning to put away everything she hadn't used. 'I've stayed upright for more than twenty-four hours now—go me.'

'How do you feel about a trip tomorrow?'

Cassidy's eyes narrowed with suspicion. 'Where to?'

'Magic land…'

Leaning forward in her seat on the golf cart, Cassidy couldn't help but grin like an idiot at her surroundings. It was better than Christmas as far as she was concerned.

'You want to stop and take a look around?'

Yes! She turned to nod enthusiastically at Will. *'Please.'*

It might have seemed like an ordinary street to some people, but to Cassidy it really was magic land. From the second they'd pulled up at the studio's parking lot it had been nigh on impossible to keep the smile off her face. She'd dreamed about places like this for most of her life—but to actually be there…

To Will, visiting the back lots of a studio was probably like taking a busman's holiday, but there wasn't a single thing that Cassidy didn't find fascinating, with an almost child-like glee. Every large warehouse structure they passed was the cover of a storybook waiting to be opened; every extra in full costume was someone she wanted to talk to; every truck full of props was an adventure playground. And the streets of the back lot, with houses and storefronts and windows and open doorways, were just calling out for fictional characters to live there and tell their stories. Cassidy could practically *see* them walking around, hear their voices as they spoke.

She even found her imagination filling in the words…

With her short lap belt undone, she turned in her seat and found Will standing beside the open-sided cart. He held out a large hand to help her down, and in her excitement Cassidy forgot all the reasons why she shouldn't let him hold on to the hand she slipped into his as he led her down the deserted pseudo-New York street.

After a few steps he asked, 'You want to see inside?'

Nodding, she threw another smile his way.

So Will took them to the nearest open doorway and stepped back, setting her hand free to allow her to go ahead of him. 'Some have a room like this they can dress to be any kind of store they want, but most of the buildings only go back a couple of feet from the frontage.'

Cassidy turned a circle in the empty space, tilting her head back to look up at the skeletal structure of wood and ladders. Her nostrils were filled with the scent of that same wood warmed by the Californian heat outside, and it was all too easy to see why there were so many fire extinguishers around. The danger of fire would always be a worry for a studio. The whole place would go up like a tinderbox, wouldn't it?

'When they dress the room they put in a false ceiling and leave space to hang the lighting. If you look outside you'll see there aren't any door handles or streetlights; they get changed by the props department according to the era of the shoot…'

Drinking in every word, she felt her chest fill with what felt distinctly like joy. It had been such a long time since she'd felt that way. She could have wept with how wonderful everything was. To some it might have seemed false and empty, a charade—but not to her. To her it was a world full of possibilities…

Will's deep voice lowered until it was barely above a whisper, making Cassidy wonder for a moment if he'd even realised he'd spoken out loud. 'Yeah, I had a feeling you'd love this.'

Lowering her chin, she caught her breath when she realised how close he was to her. There was the beginning of a smile in the green of his eyes, and the accompanying warmth she could see seemed to reach out and wrap around her like a blanket on a winter's night. Then his gaze studied each of her eyes in turn, thick lashes flickering.

The intensity forced Cassidy to silently clear her throat before she could speak. 'I do. It's amazing. Thank you for bringing me here.'

Will studied her for another long moment that made her feel as if time stood still. Then he took a breath and looked around, shrugging wide shoulders beneath the pale blue shirt he wore loose over his jeans. 'Sometimes seeing where movies are made can help with the writing process. Anything that can be filmed on a back lot or on a stage saves money on the budget. Studios like that.'

It all came down to business for him, didn't it? He saw everything in terms of the bottom dollar. Another thing that was different. Yes, Cassidy knew it was part of his job—but it was yet another reminder that he wasn't the same Will Ryan she had known. In the last twenty-four hours she had actually convinced herself she'd seen brief glimpses of the old Will she had loved. But every time she thought she saw something in him that might help rebuild the merest shadow of the relationship they once had—and would therefore make it easier to remember how well they could work together—it was as if a switch flipped inside him. Then the Will she didn't know and couldn't read was back.

It was both disconcerting and frustrating. For a second she even wanted to grasp hold of his wide shoulders and shake him, demand that he let out the Will she knew from behind the impenetrable wall he seemed to have built around himself.

'I guess you have to worry more about that kind of stuff these days?'

'I do.' He wandered around the empty room, glancing briefly out through the windows clouded almost opaque with dust. 'It's one thing letting your imagination run riot in a script, but it's another producing something all the way through onto the screen.'

Cassidy nodded, her gaze following him around the room. He was practically prowling. Almost restless, silently alert, his steps taking him in a wide circle around her. His gaze slid unerringly to tangle with hers at regular intervals, and it felt as if he was assessing her, trying to decide what to say and what not to. It felt vaguely predatory to her. But that was ridiculous…

Finding her mouth dry again, she swallowed, and then dampened her lips before asking, 'So tell me what your company does.'

Pushing his hands into his pockets—a move Cassidy noticed he made a lot—Will continued circling her. 'We're responsible for the development and physical production of films and television shows. Sometimes we're directly responsible for the raising of funding for a production—sometimes we do it through an intermediary. Then we sell the end product to the big studios when it's done.'

'You script some of them yourself?'

'Some, yes.'

'Is it easier to sell your scripts if you can produce them?'

'Not always.' The corners of his mouth tugged wryly.

He was so guarded. Had Hollywood taught him to be that way? she wondered. It was a tough industry, after all. The fact he'd been successful in it meant he'd had to learn to play hard ball at some point. But then Will had always been driven. He'd had a rougher upbringing than most. To go from fostercare kid, handed from home to home, to end up rich and successful in Hollywood was one heck of an achievement. Surely he knew that?

As jealous as she was of his success, in practically every corner of his life in comparison to how very ordinarily hers had turned out, Cassidy was incredibly proud of him. She just wished she could tell him. Not that he wanted or needed to hear it.

'One of our productions is filming on one of the sound stages here. You want to go watch for a while?'

It was enough to put the smile back on her face. 'Can we?'

Will looked amused by her enthusiasm. 'Wouldn't have offered if we couldn't, would I?'

Oh, he could try and make her feel like a child for being so excited by everything he was showing her, but it wasn't going to stop her feeling that way. She rushed to the door and yanked it open to walk into the bright sunshine, jerking her head and grinning at him. 'Hurry up, then. We might miss some of the good stuff.'

An hour later she was sitting on a high folding chair, with her hands over the headphones on her ears, watching the small screen in front of her and listening to the dialogue from the actors mere feet from her. She wasn't even distracted by the fact Will was in a similar chair close beside her—or that every time she glanced at him he was watching her with silent amusement glowing in his eyes. In fact the only thing that took some of the excitement away was when she foolishly allowed reality to seep in around the edges of the experience.

It was a one-off experience for her—and no matter how much joy she felt, it was tainted by the fact it was another fleeting glance of what could have been. Had she been brave enough or selfish enough to leave Ireland behind her, follow the man she loved to California, her life could have been as wrapped up in the world of make-believe as Will's was. With luck, hard work and Will by her side, maybe she'd have made a go of it too. She could have been so happy. Maybe there would even have been a couple of those miniature Wills she kept seeing in her mind's eye running around that beachfront house of his by now...

The thought made her heart twist painfully in her chest.

When the director yelled 'Cut!' she removed the headphones and swallowed away the lump in her throat as she handed them back to the sound engineer. 'Thank you.'

'No problem.' He smiled at her before moving away.

Will's low voice rumbled at her shoulder. 'What's wrong?'

'Nothing's wrong. Thanks again for this, Will—it's been amazing.' She flashed him a smile.

But he could still read her too well, and his eyes narrowed almost imperceptibly. 'Feeling sick again?'

Actually, she'd pretty much forgotten the tail-end of her cold as the day progressed, so she could answer that one with conviction. 'No. I'm feeling much better, as it happens—haven't even needed tablets.'

He continued studying her eyes. 'Then what is it?'

If she lied and said she was tired there was the chance he might suggest they leave—if he didn't see right through her the way he usually did when she lied—and she wasn't ready to leave yet. It wasn't as if she could tell him the truth, was it? How was she supposed to look him in the eye and tell him her active imagination had painted a picture of a life that wasn't hers so vividly that it made her feel the loss of it like a bereavement?

So she avoided his gaze and changed the subject. 'Is this a new show?'

'End of the first season. It's done well in the ratings. Already been renewed.' He waited for her to glance at him again before he added, 'We'll go take a look at the editing department next. Special effects are done somewhere else.'

Cassidy found herself mesmerised by the softness in his deep voice. And her errant tongue couldn't help but ask, 'Why are you doing this?'

Dark brows lifted in question.

'I thought you were mad keen to get the script done.'

He shrugged. 'Thought it might help.'

When he continued looking her straight in the eye, Cassidy had a moment of fear that he might know how much of a fraud she was. Was that what this whole behind-the-scenes day trip was? A way to try and get her creative juices flowing again? In fairness, it was a pretty great plan if that *had* been his aim. But if it had how, exactly, had he known? Had she been so transparent? Had the scenes she'd worked on with him been so dreadful in Hollywood terms? If they had, why hadn't he said so? If he knew what a phoney she was why hadn't he said something? Bringing her all the way across the world to allow her to make a fool of herself when in all probability he could more than likely have just bought her out of the contract...

'You were always as fascinated by this stuff as I was.' He stared into her eyes for another long moment, then looked away, turning his profile to her as he got to his feet. 'Seeing it should keep it real in your mind while we work on the script. And if we can cut a few corners by filming some scenes here instead of on location then we can free up some of the budget for better effects.'

Ah. Right. *Business*. That made more sense to her than him doing it because he knew how much she would love it. It put her mind at ease that he hadn't seen right through her charade. She didn't feel any better, though—it would have been nice if he'd cared enough to do it just because he knew the pleasure she would get from it.

But then Will Ryan had long since ceased to think of

Cassidy in terms of anything remotely resembling the word 'pleasure'—physically or otherwise…

She nodded firmly and edged off the seat. 'Editing department it is, then.'

CHAPTER FOUR

THEY'D spent most of the day at the studio, so it meant they had to spend the next few days digging in. To Cassidy's amazement it was going pretty well, all things considered.

Will's guided tour had indeed given her an extra dimension of insight to the logistics of each scene they came up with, and—even though she knew he hadn't intended it—it had also got her creative juices flowing. When they started getting words down on paper she felt as if she was getting a part of herself back again. It was exhilarating, and it boosted her self-confidence no end. Heck, she was even starting to have *fun*.

That would be the reason she would cite later for not having seen the danger coming her way before it arrived. Because if she'd been paying more attention…

When they couldn't agree on what should happen at the end of an action scene, Will came up with the idea that they read the lines aloud. Nothing unusual about that, she had thought at the time. It wasn't anything new, after all. When they had worked on the first of Nick Fortune's adventures they'd often acted out a scene before they'd even put words down, and sometimes they'd become so absorbed in the roles they were playing that it had added a dimension to the fictional characters they might never have thought of otherwise.

But back then they'd had a very different relationship. And it never occurred to Cassidy to take that into consideration when they got to their feet with their matching sheets of script in hand, hot from the printer.

Nick and Rachel had got themselves into trouble, and had been arguing about whose fault it was they were in the mess they were. They were minutes away from being tossed off the edge of a cliff by armed terrorists…

'"I suppose you're going to kill us now?" *That's* what you asked them? Why didn't you just offer to shoot us too?' said Will as Nick.

'Ooooohhh,' laughed Cassidy as Rachel. 'Believe me if I had a gun right now I'd be more than happy to shoot you!'

She grinned when Will changed his voice to read one of the terrorists' lines. 'Would you two shut up? You've got about five minutes to make your peace.' He threw her an all too brief smile before jerking his chin at her to indicate it was her line.

Cassidy lifted her sheet and tried to find where they were. 'Just make sure *he* goes first. He's the one that got us into this mess.'

'*Me*? I'm not the one who screamed and gave away our position!'

'That spider was the size of Moby Dick!' Cassidy couldn't help but laugh again at the line. She *loved* that line. It was her line; she'd thought of it. She was *back*! What had made her think she couldn't do this again?

Will became Will again. 'Which brings us to the part under debate…'

The original idea had been to have Nick and Rachel fight their way out of the situation by distracting the terrorists with increased arguing. Cassidy had wanted it to be Rachel's idea; funnily enough Will had wanted it to be Nick's. Will suggested Nick should wink at Rachel, to let her know what he was doing. Cassidy said Rachel was too mad at him to play along with anything he came up with.

Suddenly Will looked at her, with a gaze that made her heart jump out of rhythm.

'What?' she asked a little breathlessly.

'I have an idea.' He stepped closer. 'Play along.'

Cassidy turned her head and eyed him with suspicion. 'What are you doing?'

'They get to the edge of the cliff. They're still arguing. Guns at their backs.'

'Uh-huh… And then…?'

Something dangerous shimmered across Will's eyes as he closed the gap between them, his deep voice lowering to a husky-edged rumble. 'Then, just before they're pushed over the edge, Nick asks for a last request for a dying man…'

'And that request would be…?'

Will smiled *that* smile and knocked her on her ear again. 'He asks to kiss Rachel.'

Cassidy's eyes widened. 'He *what*?'

'Just for the record, her face looks exactly like yours does right now…'

Somewhere in the foggy haze of her completely distracted brain Cassidy knew it would ramp up the scene to a new level, but that wasn't what made her heart thunder loudly in her ears and her body temperature rise. *No*. It was the fact that Will was staring down at her with a darkening gaze.

He wasn't seriously going to—?

Thick dark lashes lowered slowly as he took the last step to bring his body within inches of hers. And as she swayed a little on her feet he angled his head, his gaze lowering to focus on her mouth. Oh, God. *He was*. But why? He couldn't—

Cassidy's lips reached for his of their own volition when he was less than an inch away, like a flower lifting towards the sun. His mouth was full and firm and hotter than she remembered from the hundreds of times she'd kissed him before, but no less familiar. When his large hands framed her face, she took a deep breath through her nose. When he leaned into her she exhaled against his lips, her heavy eyelids closing…

If anyone had told her a month ago that some time in the very near future Will Ryan would be kissing her again, and she would be feeling it in every cell in her body, she'd have laughed out loud at the ridiculousness of the notion. But he was—and she did.

It was surreal. And at the same time it was like coming home.

Long fingers slid down her cheeks, around her neck and into her hair. The taste of him was on her lips and the heady scent of clean laundry and pure Will was surrounding her. Cassidy forgot about the script, forgot about the fact they were playing the part of Nick and Rachel, forgot about the danger in what they were doing. She forgot all those things.

Instead she dropped her sheet of paper and reached for handfuls of the shirt above his lean waist, while he slipped a hand up to cradle the back of her head, his fingers threading into her hair as Cassidy drowned in the sensations flooding her body.

She'd missed kissing him. *How she'd missed it.* It was as if her body had been asleep like Snow White's, and only now, with the right man, was she being kissed back into life. But then no one had ever kissed her like Will kissed her. He could make the world tilt on its axis beneath her feet. *Always.* From the very first time he'd kissed her. He'd caught her similarly off-guard as they'd walked over the O'Connell Street Bridge in Dublin, after taking photographs of possible locations for a short film they'd been working on for their class. With no warning he had taken her hand, tugged her to him and kissed her. *Because he had to*, he had told her afterwards. As if it had been as vital to him as breathing or drinking water, or any of the other things a person had to do to survive…

When he slowly drew his lips from hers, her mouth followed his back for the inch she'd closed, her eyes opening wide and searching his with a combination of wonder and fear.

After a brief moment of studying her with a dark unreadable gaze, Will rested his cheek against hers, whispering into her ear in a husky voice, 'Then Nick says, "You take the one on the left".'

Cassidy's heart plummeted to the soles of her feet.

Will released her and stepped back, turning abruptly and informing her in a flat, businesslike voice, 'That works better. So, we'll add that in and jump straight to the fight and the chase scene…'

'Right.' Cassidy nodded dumbly while she tried to get her breathing under control. The script. Nick and Rachel. Not Will and Cassidy. That was what the kiss had been about. He hadn't kissed her because he'd wanted to. He'd just forgotten they didn't have the same relationship now they'd had before when they would have played out similar Nick and Rachel scenes—*apparently*.

Bending down to retrieve the sheets of paper on the floor, she took a deep breath and puffed out her cheeks as she exhaled. She could only pray he wasn't planning on acting out the love scene they had planned for Scene Three…

She didn't think she could survive Will Ryan breaking her heart twice in one lifetime. She wasn't entirely sure she'd got over the first time.

The kiss changed things. At least it did for Cassidy. She tried not to let it, but she couldn't stop it—partly because she couldn't seem to get it out of her head…

What she needed to do was focus on what they were doing. Heck, at this point she would even take a stab at re-building some kind of platonic friendship with Will. After all, she had to work across a desk from him every day. How was she supposed to do any of those things if every time she looked at him she was thinking about how it had felt to be kissed by him and to kiss him back? Why was she so obsessed by it anyway? It wasn't as if she'd kissed him back because she'd wanted to—at least she told herself it wasn't. She'd been playing a part, the same way he had, thinking on her feet, reacting to what he'd done—that was all. It didn't *mean* anything.

Darn it, he was looking at her again. She could *feel it*. Every time he did it the hair on the back of her neck tingled.

'Stir crazy?'

She kept pacing around the room, the same way she had for most of the two days since they'd kissed. 'I'm fine.'

'Well, I'm not,' his voice rumbled back. 'All that pacing is making *me* crazy.' Will sighed heavily. 'You're not used to sharing space with someone these days, are you? I never pictured you as that much of a loner…'

Cassidy stopped dead in her tracks and angled her head. 'Excuse me?'

'Lived with someone else after me, did you?'

Her jaw dropped. What business was it of his who she had or hadn't lived with? She could have lived with twenty men. Not that she *had* lived with anyone else, barring the time she'd lived in her father's house while he was ill. But that wasn't the point.

A few times over the years she'd considered advertising for a flatmate, but by then she'd got used to having her own space. Living on her own, she didn't have to worry about someone else's opinions on things like what TV channel to watch, or how loud she could play music, or any of a dozen other compromises a person made when they shared living space.

'Compromises…'

Cassidy frowned when he said the very thing she'd just thought—as if he'd somehow stepped inside her head. 'What?'

'I said living with someone involves compromises.'

'It does.' She nodded. 'And forced intimacy…'

'Shared responsibilities…'

When he looked up at her she turned away and began pacing again, the words quietly slipping off the tip of her tongue. 'Never being alone.'

She frowned sideways at him when she said it, confusion clouding her vision as he studied her with a curious expression that almost said he suspected why she'd been so uneasy with him of late. She hoped he didn't! But while he continued staring at her there was an inexplicably heavy tension in the room.

Her chin lifted. 'Okay. Fine. You're right—all are things I suck royally at. Barring the last one. I excel at being alone these days—it's what I do best.'

'Cass…' He kept his voice low. 'Living with someone is nothing like what we're doing now. You know that. And being alone isn't—'

'Of course it's nothing like this. This is artificial. And temporary.' Cassidy tried to figure out why that felt so bad and couldn't seem to find an answer. Maybe being alone for so long had affected her more than she'd realized? She started pacing again. 'This isn't sharing space. It's temporary. A charade.'

'A charade?' he repeated dryly.

She glanced sideways at him again as she changed direction. 'Oh, come on. It's miraculous enough that we've managed to work together this last while…'

'We shared space before and it was never this much of a problem…' Will reached for his mug and frowned when he discovered it was empty. 'You want coffee?'

He didn't wait for an answer, reaching across the large desk for her empty mug and pushing his squeaky chair back. 'I don't think this has anything to do with sharing space with me. I think trying to keep me at arm's length is starting to take its toll on you.'

When he left the room her feet immediately followed him. 'And what exactly is *that* supposed to mean?'

'I think you know what it means.'

How dared he assume he knew her every thought? Just because nine times out of ten he was in the ballpark area, it didn't mean he could read her damn mind.

She followed him across the living room. 'So if I'm not throwing myself at you it means I'm fighting some inner battle, does it? How do you get that head of yours through doors?'

Setting their mugs down on the breakfast bar, Will went about refilling the coffee-maker, replacing the filter and spooning in coffee granules. 'Doesn't have anything to do with throwing yourself at me. You're determined not to allow yourself to even be friends with me again. It's childish, frankly. We're both adults.'

Placing her hands on her hips, she stopped dead at one end of the breakfast bar, speechless.

With the coffee set to percolate, Will turned around, leaning nonchalantly against the counter-top on the opposite side of the kitchen from her and calmly folding his arms across the studio logo on his T-shirt. 'You're different. The Cass I met in the Beverly Wilshire just over a week ago isn't the girl I knew in Dublin. The girl I knew in Dublin was open-minded and honest to the point of bluntness, and she would never have let something brood in her the way you have since you got here. So let's just clear the air and get it over with, shall we?'

Cassidy opened her mouth to tell him to go straight to—

But he looked her in the eye and knocked the air out of her lungs by saying, 'You blame me for our break-up, don't you?'

He wasn't done, either. Not content with opening the can of worms, he then twisted the knife she felt she had in her chest by adding, 'Maybe you should just take a minute and remember who it was that did the breaking up before I left…'

The sharp gasp of air hurt her already raw throat.

Then a muted doorbell sounded, and the door at the top of the stairs was flung open. 'Hello? Anybody home? Time to put down the keyboard!'

Cassidy had a brief glimpse of the frown on Will's face before she snapped her head around to watch with wide eyes as Angelique appeared. If it wasn't surprise enough finding out that the woman had a key to Will's house, there was then a thundering of footsteps and a small blonde-haired ball of energy ran down the stairs, across the wooden floor, and launched itself into Will's waiting arms.

'Uncle Will!'

Uncle Will? Cassidy couldn't help it; her jaw dropped. Not just at the sight of the little girl throwing her small arms around the column of his neck. What really amazed her was Will's expression as he held her. He was transformed. Gone was the intense, unreadable, pain-in-the-rear Will, and in his place was a man who looked as if he'd just shed five years. Light danced in his eyes, he grinned broadly, and there was the sound of deep, rumbling, happy laughter before he made an exaggerated groan and leaned his head back to look down at her.

'Hey, munchkin.'

'We brought a picnic!'

'Did you, now?' He lifted his dark brows as he looked in Angelique's direction, 'Did I know we were having a picnic?'

'It's a surprise, silly!' the little girl informed him.

'Indeed it is,' he answered dryly.

Angelique had made it to Cassidy's side. 'This is what

happens when you two stand me up for dinner. Script or no script, you still have to eat.'

Will looked up as he bent to set the child on her feet. 'We have managed to feed ourselves on our own. Ever hear of a little thing called a phone, Angie?'

'Ah, but if we'd phoned ahead it wouldn't be a surprise, would it?'

'Remind me to ask for my key back some time.'

Cassidy was rapidly putting two and two together. She even found her gaze sliding across to the little girl who was tugging on Will's jeans to see if she could see any similarities between them. Having had such vivid images of miniature Wills in her mind since she'd arrived in his gorgeous house, she felt the ragged edges of her heart grate painfully at the thought of finding any. She didn't *want* Will to have any children she might be forced to look at. The thought of him having them with any woman who wasn't her was apparently painful enough.

Which made no sense whatsoever, considering how much she currently disliked him and how close they had been to a major argument not five minutes earlier.

'Uncle Will?'

He hunched down to look the little girl in the eye; the thoughtfulness of the simple act made Cassidy's heart hurt all over again. 'Yes, munchkin, what can I do for you?'

'The picnic's for the beach.'

'Is it indeed?'

She nodded enthusiastically. 'And I brought my swimsuit and my bodyboard.'

'Ah.' Will pursed his mouth into a thin line and frowned almost comically at her, before taking a deep breath through his nose. 'We'd better go check the sea is still there, then, hadn't we?'

The little girl giggled, and Cassidy found herself smiling at them as Angelique linked their arms at the elbow and lowered her voice conspiratorially. 'Sometimes I wonder who has who wrapped around their little finger. I hope you've brought a bikini with you?'

The thought of publicly displaying her body on a Malibu beach next to the goddess that was Angelique Warden made Cassidy want to curl up in a ball and die. That was not happening in this lifetime. Not that she owned a bikini to begin with, but still…

'Will could give you a surfing lesson while he's helping Lily bodyboard.'

Cassidy's gaze shifted sharply and crashed into Will's as he stood to his full height. Then her troublesome imagination revisited the image she'd had of him emerging from the surf and she swallowed hard. For a moment she even thought she could hear herself making a gulping noise.

Thick lashes blinked while he stared at her. The intensity returning to his gaze was even fiercer than before. Oh, please, *please* don't let now be one of the times when he can read my mind, she silently pleaded. There was only so much humiliation she could take.

Then he nodded. 'You'll need sunscreen. Beach towels are in the laundry room. Angie knows where everything is.'

Before Cassidy could protest, he turned his attention to Lily. 'Right, then. While Cass and I get changed, you and your mom can go get this picnic we've been promised. Are there cookies?'

'*Duh*, Uncle Will.'

* * *

Despite many, many, *many* carefully worded protests, Cassidy found herself on the beach—thankfully in a swimsuit rather than a bikini. Even that was covered by a thigh-length light shirt. Smothered in the highest factor sunscreen she'd packed, she also had the large-brimmed straw hat Angelique had left behind on her last visit to Will's house on her head. She had the prerequisite sunglasses on, and had bent one knee as artfully as she could manage as she sat on the large blanket beside the bikini-clad Angelique. If people squinted Cassidy reckoned they might look like nineteen-fifties movie star next to modern-day goddess. Hopefully. After all, women had been adored for their hourglass figures back then—which meant, as always, her timing was severely off. Not that it made her feel any more comfortable in her own skin.

Watching Will playing in the surf with Lily was the worst form of water torture she'd ever been submitted to. It was just plain *wrong* to be drooling at the sight of him in long swim shorts—bare chest, toned, tanned, gorgeous enough to die for—while he played with a small child. Especially if he was that small child's father, and she was sitting chatting to the woman he'd made that child with. Cassidy had never had a worse case of the green-eyed monster in all her life.

'Lily adores him.' Angelique was smiling at them when Cassidy looked her way. 'He'll make a great father some day.'

Cassidy exhaled with relief as quietly as she could manage it. 'She's gorgeous.'

'Obviously I think so. But then I'm a tad biased. Do you have kids, Cass?'

'Thirty of them.' She smiled at Angelique's expression. 'I'm a schoolteacher.'

'Ahh. You scared me for a minute.'

Despite a lingering modicum of jealousy over her relationship with Will, Cassidy found herself warming to Angie. She wasn't at all the way the tabloids portrayed her. And seeing her obvious love for her daughter humanised her.

Turning onto her stomach, Angie swung her feet back and forth in the air and studied Cassidy from behind her sunglasses. 'Did you and Will ever talk about having kids when you were together?'

It was a very personal question, but by asking it she'd already shown she knew there had been more to their relationship than being scriptwriting duo Ryan and Malone. The thing was, talking about their relationship with someone who might well be in, or have been in, a similar relationship with Will made Cassidy uncomfortable.

So she sought a simple answer. 'We were young.'

The fact she'd said it with a shrug of her shoulders didn't seem to fool Angie. 'Ever since I've known Will he's been reluctant to talk about you. It took us to get him drunk one night before he would even talk about growing up in Ireland…'

He'd talked about his childhood? Wow. Cassidy wondered if Angie knew what a big deal that was for Will. She'd been dating him for nearly a year before she'd got the full story—though in fairness she hadn't had to get him drunk.

But her brain had latched onto one seemingly insignificant word. *'Us?'*

Angie examined the perfectly manicured fingernails on one hand. 'Lily's father—my on-again off-again partner Eric—is one of Will's best friends. It's how I got to know Will. And why he's Lily's godfather.'

Immediately Cassidy's gaze sought them out again in the sea. Will was swinging the little girl round and round in circles, while she squealed in delight and he grinned boyishly at her. 'Oh.'

She'd got that one completely wrong, then, hadn't she?

There was a chuckle of laughter. 'Yes, I wondered if you'd thought that. You're delightfully easy to read, aren't you? I can't tell you how refreshing that is in Hollywood.'

Heat built on Cassidy's cheeks that had absolutely nothing to do with the sun.

'Can I ask you a question, Cass?'

A sense of dread made her cringe as she looked down at the woman she had a sneaking suspicion was about to ask the one question she didn't want to answer. 'Depends on what it is.'

Angelique smiled. 'I've wondered why Will didn't bring you with him.'

'When he moved here from Ireland?'

'Yes. You were quite the writing team, on top of the relationship you had.'

Okay, not the question she'd been waiting for. Maybe that was why she answered it honestly, her chin dropping and her voice lowering even though there wasn't any chance he could hear her from where he was. 'I couldn't leave.'

'So he did ask?'

'Yes.' It was a simplistic answer to a situation that had been very complicated.

There was a moment of silence, then, 'Do you regret it?'

Cassidy smiled sadly. 'That's not an easy one to answer. It's not a case of regretting; it's more of a case of what was right and what was wrong at the time, and what was meant to be and what wasn't. And I have *no idea* why I'm telling you this…'

'Maybe you need a friend?' Angelique waited until Cassidy looked at her, and then she nodded sharply and beamed. 'I've decided I like you, Cass. I think we'll be great friends. You don't treat me like a movie star, and that's a huge bonus.'

Cassidy lowered her voice to a conspiratorial whisper. 'You *are* a movie star.'

Angie lowered her voice to a similar level, 'Shh. Somebody might hear you.'

They were laughing when the sun was suddenly blocked out, forcing Cassidy to shade her eyes with a hand as she looked up at the dark silhouette surrounded by bright light.

'Ready for your surfing lesson?'

CHAPTER FIVE

'I DON'T actually want a surfing lesson. Honestly.'

'Don't knock it till you've tried it.' Will turned round and took the two steps required to get to where she'd been dragging her heels. Reaching out, he captured her wrist in long fingers and tugged her along behind him. 'You might like it.'

'I'll sink like a whale,' she grumbled.

'Whales don't sink; they swim. So will you.' He threw a frown over his shoulder as he continued tugging her along the sand, 'Stop being paranoid about your weight, Cass. Women are supposed to curve. I'm sick to death of being surrounded by stick-thin women counting the calories in a bottle of water.'

Trying to free her wrist was getting her nowhere. 'Bullying me again, Ryan?'

'Nope. Forcing you to have a good time. It's for your own good. You seem to have forgotten how.'

'Said by the man who doesn't have time to go surfing, having bought a house by the ocean for that very purpose? I think you'll find that falls into the category of *I will when you will*,' she retorted.

He stopped so suddenly she careened into the wall of

his back, and grunted in a very unladylike manner before scowling up at his face.

The sight of his face leaning closer to hers made her eyes widen. That was before he lowered his voice and rumbled a meaningful, 'Oh, I know how to have *fun*, Cass. Don't you worry…'

Judging by the glint in his eyes, he wasn't talking about surfing fun either.

Standing back a little, he frowned at her body. 'That's got to go.'

When he released her wrist, she lifted both hands to grip hold of her shirt as if he might try to remove it at any second. 'The shirt *stays*.'

Will folded his arms across the sculpted chest she was trying very hard not to look at. 'You *do* know it's going to be transparent in the water, don't you?'

Actually, that thought hadn't occurred to her. But now he'd pointed it out she was even less likely to participate in a surfing lesson than she had been sixty seconds ago…

She started backing away. 'Well, I don't know about you, but I'm famished. I've heard a rumour there's a picnic on the go, so I think we should just—'

There was a short chuckle of deep male laughter, and then he leaned over and captured her wrist again, shaking his head as he tugged her forward. 'Down on your stomach on the board…'

Huh? Her gaze dropped and discovered a surfboard on the sand. She scowled at his words. 'On my stomach? On the board?'

He ducked down a little to get her attention, his nose mere inches from hers. 'Surfing lesson—remember?'

'I thought it would be in the water.' How was she supposed to think straight when he was so close?

Will's gaze dropped briefly to her mouth when she dampened her lips, then lifted to tangle with hers for equally as brief a moment before he leaned back and looked down at the board. 'Basics on dry land. *Then* we go in the water.'

Well, how was she supposed to know that? Okay, on her stomach—with Will standing over her, looking down at her rear. Cassidy silently prayed for a tidal wave…

'Why am I getting on my stomach?'

'Because that's what you do to paddle the board out far enough to catch an incoming wave…'

Right. Except that statement presupposed she actually *wanted* to catch a wave—which frankly she didn't. Waves shouldn't be caught. Cassidy believed they should be allowed to roam the earth in freedom, with all their other wave friends. She might even start a campaign of some kind: *Save the Wave*. Catchy, she thought.

She sighed heavily, focused her mind on another method of stalling Will, and came up with, 'Maybe you should demonstrate first?'

With a shake of his head that indicated he was fully aware of what she was doing, Will dropped onto the board, leaving her staring down at him in the same way she'd feared he would stare at her. Somehow she had the feeling her view was much better than his would be. Then he started to move his arms, and she became fascinated with the play of muscles on his tanned back. Was he working out nowadays? She didn't remember him being so…*toned*…

'Paddle evenly with both arms, and then turn and watch

for a wave. Try to time it so you jump to your feet as it hits your board.' He demonstrated by jumping lithely to his feet and reaching his arms out to his sides for balance. 'Then use your feet to steer the board. If you shift your weight to your toes you'll go one way; rock back onto your heels and you go the other.'

He made it sound so easy. But his description of brain surgery would probably consist of *Pop skull open, move jelly stuff around and put lid back on*. Whereas Cassidy suspected *her* version of surfing would involve less of the standing up and more of the getting wet and spluttering as she tried to get salt water out of her lungs.

'Your turn.' Will stepped off the board and quirked his brows when she hesitated, his voice lowering and his eyes sparkling. '*Chicken*. Whatever happened to the hunger to learn and the spirit of adventure you used to have?'

Cassidy threw another scowl at him, pursed her lips and lowered herself cautiously onto the board. 'I really do hate you, you know.'

'No, you don't.' He hunched down beside her.

When she was on her stomach, she looked up at him in time to see his gaze rise from studying her body. It made her laugh. 'Oh, yes, I do.'

The first time she attempted jumping up to her feet she fell over, but managed to get a hand on the hot sand to help right herself. Will encouraged her with a low, 'Try again.'

The second time she fell on her rear, and frowned hard at his obvious amusement. He cleared his throat and held out a hand to help her up. 'Again.'

Cassidy growled at him. 'When does it start to be fun, exactly?'

The third time was the charm. She not only fell over, she fell on Will, and toppled him backwards onto the sand, creating a tangle of legs and forcing him to wrap her body in his arms. Yup—her run of incredible luck had continued. Because when she puffed air at the loose strand of hair that had got in her eyes and looked down her face was inches away from his. And he was smiling one of *those* smiles.

Someone, somewhere really had it in for her.

The heat from his bare chest seeped through the thin material of her shirt and made every cell of her body unbearably aware of where she was fitted against him. It was like being set on fire. She felt the lack of oxygen to her brain making her dizzy, felt the ache of physical awareness so keenly it almost snapped her in two. Then one large hand lifted, and impossibly gentle fingertips brushed her hair back and tucked the strand behind her ear.

Cassidy felt her heart beating so hard against her sensitised breasts that she was certain Will must feel the erratic rhythm too. She needed to say something funny to break the tension—needed to move as far away from him as possible before he realised how damn turned on she was—needed—

She saw his throat convulse before he took a deep breath that crushed her breasts tighter to the wall of his chest. 'We should try again.'

What? Her eyes widened at the words. He couldn't possibly mean—

Will studied her eyes, then rolled her to the side. 'You need to pick a point in front of you to focus on as you jump onto your feet. That'll make it easier to balance…'

Struggling awkwardly to her feet while she felt her cheeks burning, Cassidy avoided his gaze and frowned at her foolishness—or her wishful thinking, or whatever it was that had made her heart leap the way it had. 'If I can't do this on dry land I don't see how I stand a bat's chance of doing it on moving water.'

While she bent over to swipe the sand off her legs, Will's deep voice sounded above her head. 'Don't give up so easy, Cass. Some things are worth the effort.'

Her gaze shot up to tangle with his and he shrugged. 'You love the ocean. Always did. Makes sense that anything that allows you to appreciate it more you'll end up enjoying.'

Several hours later she discovered he was right. The fact he'd been just the right degree of persuasive, determined and patient at varying stages to get her to that point had not gone unnoticed either. Any more than she'd failed to notice when he saw his theory on the transparency of her shirt when wet had been right too.

It was her last attempt. She managed to stay upright long enough to ride the wave for several feet, and the exhilaration of achievement burst forth from her lips in joyous laughter at the same time as Will let out a victory yell. When she inevitably fell off and surfaced from the water, lifting her hands to smooth her wet hair back from her face as she grinned like an idiot, she looked up—and her grin faltered. He had hold of the board as he waded towards her, waist deep in water the same way she was. But then he lifted his chin, his gaze travelling across the foaming surface and sliding up her body oh-so-very-slowly.

When he looked into her eyes the heat she could see both robbed her of her ability to breathe and slammed into her midriff with such force that the next wave almost made her lose her footing in the shifting sands.

For the longest time they stared at each other. The ebb and flow of the tide dragging her abdomen back and forth was all too evocative, considering the ferocity of her physical desire, and eliciting a low moan from the base of her throat that the wind thankfully dragged away. Then Will frowned—hard—turning his head and looking out to sea so that Cassidy caught sight of a muscle moving in his clenched jaw.

Almost in slow motion she saw him exerting control over himself. It was heartbreaking. Especially considering the fact that she was faced with the very image of him she'd conjured in her imagination when he had first told her he surfed. Standing there, with silvery rivulets of water running off his body, shining silvery in the bright sunshine, droplets of the same shimmering water falling from wet tendrils of the dark hair that clung to his forehead and the column of his neck. *He was glorious.* More than that, even. He was the most sensationally sexy man she had ever laid eyes on. And she had never wanted him as much as she did at that moment—while he'd taken a deep breath and got his self-control back in the blink of an eye.

When he looked at her again the small smile on his full mouth didn't make it all the way up into his eyes. 'Told you you'd get it. Well done.'

But Cassidy couldn't let it go that easily. And the very fact he had so obviously been affected by her gave her enough of a subliminal confidence boost to take a step towards him. 'Will—'

His eyes narrowed at the husky edge of her voice. 'I'm going to catch a few waves of my own. Be back in a while.'

With that he turned away, got on the board, paddled further out to sea—and the moment was gone. He'd made it plain that whatever moment of remembered desire from the past he'd just experienced could be dismissed in a heartbeat. Men were supposed to think about sex at ridiculously regular intervals, so they said. Cassidy was merely a woman in the nearest equivalent of a wet T-shirt. She got that.

But the rejection hurt. It hurt *bad*.

Setting a sheet of the first draft of their script to one side after she'd proofread it, Cassidy reached for another. Even though they worked in silence for the following fifteen minutes, she could still feel him studying her. He'd been doing it for days. And it was getting to her big-time.

'What, Will?'

'I'm just thinking of going to the kitchen to get a knife.'

'To do what?' She didn't look at him. He might have been studying her like some kind of bug under a microscope, but since the beach she'd been able to look at him for no longer than a few seconds before she had to avert her gaze. Apparently his rejection still hurt. And looking at him made it worse.

'To cut the atmosphere in this room…'

She sighed heavily. 'Will—'

'Right.' He pushed to his feet and lifted the sheets from her hand, setting them to one side. Then he grabbed hold of her hands and tugged. 'Time for a change of scenery. And lunch.'

It was beginning to feel as if she'd been trapped in the house with Will for years on end. People didn't get jail sentences as long. Every hour felt as if it was dragging. Plus, if Will kept feeding her the way he was she was going to go home weighing more than when she'd arrived.

The second she was on her feet he let go of her hands, turned, and headed into the next room. Cassidy automatically fell into step behind him, somehow unable to drag her disobedient gaze from the errant curls of dark hair brushing the collar of his cream shirt. It was easier looking at him when he didn't know she was, she supposed…

'We'll eat on the deck,' he announced as he glanced over his shoulder. 'The ocean is supposed to have a calming effect.'

Cass shook her head at his dry wit as they moved into the kitchen. 'You want me to take anything out?'

'Juice and glasses would be good.'

She opened a cupboard for glasses and the fridge for juice, feeling a pang of sadness at how they moved around each other as if they'd been doing it for years. It was like a choreographed dance. He reached an arm up to the cupboard door; she ducked under it. She turned for the fridge; he circled around her in one fluent step. She opened the refrigerator door to put away the juice; he reached inside for mayo and ham before he closed it again…

Cassidy had watched her parents doing a similar dance hundreds of times over the years during her childhood, and had never appreciated how much it demonstrated their ease with each other. But then they'd had decades to learn the moves; Cassidy and Will hadn't had all that long even when they were together.

Without thinking she casually handed him a chopping board on her way to opening the sliding doors. When he looked sideways at her, he frowned for a second before taking it.

'It's always beautiful out here,' she said from the doorway.

'I know,' Will answered, with a smile in his deep voice.

Stepping on to the deck, she set the glasses down on a small table and then moved towards the railing, where she breathed deep and smiled. It was the kind of place she would have allowed herself to relax and just 'be', under better circumstances. She wondered if Will ever felt that way. Pleasure in the simple things had never been the young Will's thing—not that he hadn't appreciated them; he'd just always been ambitious for more. But Cassidy had learned how precious and fragile life could be. It was important to take pleasure in the simple things, she felt.

But, looking at the ocean, she found her thoughts wandering inevitably to the same things. For the hundredth time since it had happened she found herself revisiting what had happened the day he'd taught her to surf—which in turn led her to revisiting the kiss during their 'rehearsal'. She had no idea why she was so obsessed by that kiss. Okay, admittedly the mature version of Will was oh-so-sexy—she would have to be blind not to have noticed. Under tall, dark and handsome in the dictionary it probably said *see Will Ryan*.

The sound of a plate being set on the table behind her gave her enough warning to get her thoughts under control before he appeared in her peripheral vision. Then they stood there for a while, side-by-side in silence, before Cassidy chanced a sideways glance at him just as Will turned his head to look at her.

He smiled a more genuine smile than he had in days, and she felt another shiver of awareness as he asked in his deliciously deep voice, 'Better?'

'I shook the cold a week ago.'

'That wasn't what I meant.'

Yes, she knew it wasn't what he'd meant. Since stalling never seemed to work with him any better than lying did, she took a deep breath and admitted, 'I'm sorry. I guess being cooped up in that room is starting to get to me…'

Will nodded his head, as if he'd already known the answer, his gaze shifting back to the ocean. After a few moments he said, 'Thank you.'

'For what?'

Turning around, he reached out and lifted a glass before smiling at her with a light sparkling in the green of his eyes. 'For helping with lunch.'

Cass smiled back at him. *Liar.* But she didn't call him on it; she appreciated that he hadn't pushed her any further on why she was feeling the way she was. Apparently a little honesty really did go a long way. Anyway, she had a sneaking suspicion he already knew, and was letting her off the hook by not saying it out loud. She should really thank him in return for that. But she didn't, because that would be bringing it up all over again. Instead she turned away from the railing and sat down in one of the comfortably padded wicker chairs on the deck, reaching for a sandwich as Will did the same and sank into a matching chair beside her.

They managed a whole ten minutes of companionable silence, but then he casually ruined it by asking, 'So… you want to tell me what else has been bugging you?'

The half-eaten sandwich froze halfway to her mouth, her appetite waning. Then she took a deep breath and went right ahead and took a bite, filling one side of her cheek as she chewed.

'Okay, then.' Will lifted another sandwich. 'I'll just ask

every half hour from here on in until you yell it at me in the middle of an argument. That usually works.'

Then he glanced at her from the corner of his eye and had the gall to add a wink. She forced herself to speak. 'Still got that pitbull quality to your personality, don't you?'

'Mmm-hmm.' He took a large bite of sandwich and grinned at her as he chewed.

'That wasn't actually meant as a compliment…'

He spoke with the food still in his mouth. 'I prefer to think of it as a dogged determination to get to the root of an issue before it becomes a bigger problem than it needs to be.' Ridiculously thick lashes brushed against his skin a couple of times while he considered her and swallowed his food. 'If my memory serves right—letting you work things through in your head for too long before you talk about them does that.'

'I've been stuck under a roof with someone I can barely hold a conversation with for two weeks. How is that *not* supposed to get to me? Maybe I have a *right* to be moody for a while under those circumstances?'

'No, you don't. Not if talking about it is all it takes to fix it.' He frowned, 'Who *likes* being moody anyway?'

Shrugging her shoulders, Cassidy focused her attention on her sandwich, mumbling under her breath, 'In my experience cute guys who think it adds to their feeble attempts at seeming mysterious…'

There was a very noticeable silence that drew her gaze back to his face, where a stunned expression was warring with amusement. She scowled at him. 'What now?'

'You think I'm *cute*?'

'I didn't say that.' Well, not on purpose she hadn't.

'It's okay. I'm fine with you thinking I'm cute. Though I should probably tell you it has a slightly different meaning over here than it does in Ireland…'

'I know what it means over here, and for the record it's not all that different to what it means back home. And I *don't* think that about you.'

Very visibly having to control his smile, Will leaned back and nodded. 'See, I was going to tell you what I really think is making you feel cooped up…and how I feel about the same thing… But now…? Now I think I'm just going to let you come to your own conclusions. That way I get to be both cute *and* mysterious…'

'That's not what I—' She fought the need to throw her sandwich at him as she felt heat rising on her neck. 'Don't edit my lines outside the office, Ryan.'

'You know,' he sighed dramatically, and let loose a killer one of *those* smiles, 'suddenly I'm in a much better mood than I was twenty minutes ago.'

Will had the gall to chuckle, looking at her from the corner of his sparkling eyes. Darn it. He was gloating, wasn't he? What had happened to the supposedly professional relationship they'd agreed to have? Flirting with her, using a combination of random winks, sparkling eyes and *that* smile, could hardly be considered *professional*.

Cassidy felt distinctly as if she was constantly waging a battle of some kind with him and…heaven help her…he was *winning*.

He was showing her that he could read her better than anyone ever had—get under her skin and bug her more than anyone ever had—get her hormones to scatter all rational thought to the wind and make her laugh when she really didn't want to by lifting his eyebrows ridiculously at her like he currently was…

With a shake of her head she dragged her gaze away from him, to look for some of the peace the ocean had briefly brought her way. 'You are still the most annoying man on the planet, you know.'

'Ahh…but I'm also *cute*.' He inhaled deeply through his nose, smug satisfaction oozing from the rumble of his voice. 'And *mysterious*…'

When she glanced sideways she saw him take another bite of his sandwich. Instead of saying anything smart in return she did the same thing. They sat for another ten minutes in what could almost have been misconstrued as a companionable silence, eating and looking out over the ocean. It was nice. Under further scrutiny Cassidy realised to her complete and utter astonishment it was better than nice. She almost felt…*content*…and it had been a long time since she'd felt that way…

'Do you think she'll ever forgive him?' Will asked.

Cassidy turned her head to look at his face. 'Rachel?'

He nodded, studying her eyes with the silent intensity she was now almost used to. 'She can be pretty bloody-minded when she digs her heels in.'

Cassidy shrugged one shoulder. 'It's self-preservation. Look where being up-front with him got her last time.'

'She knew how Nick felt about her.'

'No. She *thought* she knew how Nick felt about her. Then she convinced herself she was wrong…' A memory from real life wrapped itself around Cassidy's memories of their last script, making her turn her gaze away and frown at the ocean. 'The last argument they had was pretty heated.'

'Lots of things can get said in the heat of an argument that might not have been meant the way they sounded…'

'They can.'

'Maybe we should have them talk it through?'

Cassidy grimaced, then looked sideways at him. 'I think Rachel would rather have needles poked in her eyes.'

'So would Nick. *Hot ones.*'

It made her smile. 'They both need a smack upside the head.'

To her amazement, Will smiled back. 'That would make for a short script.'

'True.'

Dark lashes flickered as he searched her eyes, then Will nodded firmly—just the once—as if he'd made some kind of momentous decision. Swiping a palm against his thigh, he reached his large hand towards her. 'Will Ryan.'

Cassidy arched a brow, her smile still in place. 'What are you doing, you idiot?'

'Starting over.' He jerked his chin at his hand. 'The idea is that you now put your hand in mine and introduce yourself the way I just did. Give it a try. Take a deep breath if you need to. Go on. You can do it.'

'Uh-huh.' The smile grew. 'Patronising me is really going to help your cause.'

Will shook his head. 'Count to ten and swallow down the sarcasm. Otherwise it's going to get to the point where—when we're done with the script—only one of us is coming out of that room alive…'

'You were the one who suggested getting a knife.'

'*Malone.* Don't make me turn on the charm.'

It wasn't an empty threat. If Cassidy hadn't known that

from experience she'd have known it from the way his eyes darkened several shades and his voice lowered an octave to a deep grumble that spoke of tangled sheets and early morning pillow talk. The thought made her smile falter.

Dropping her chin so she could study his outstretched hand with caution, she weighed up the danger of keeping her distance versus taking a chance and ending up friends with him again without her heart wanting more. It was risky.

Long fingers waggled in the air between them, and his voice lowered another octave, sending a shimmer of sensual feminine awareness of nearby hot male across her body. 'Come on, Cass…'

She wondered how he managed to sound like temptation itself—and scary at the same time. Did he even know he was doing it? Or how dangerous a decision it was? Because, despite the intimation, they had never actually been 'friends' at any point of their relationship—there had always been something more.

Taking a deep breath, she swallowed hard and lifted her arm, her hand hesitating mere inches from his. It was Will who closed the gap this time, circling his fingers around hers and holding on—allowing the warmth of his touch to seep through her skin and travel into her veins, where it rushed up her arm towards her racing heart. He clasped more firmly and shook their joined hands up and down.

Then he repeated, in a voice laced with determination, 'Will Ryan. Known to be the most annoying man on the planet at times. Tendency towards occasional arrogance that I'm never going to learn to control. Strange obsession with peanut butter and jelly sandwiches at two in the morning…'

Cassidy smiled as her gaze travelled up his arm, past the

lock of errantly curled hair below his ear to the sparkling green of his eyes. Then she shook her head and swallowed down the need to giggle like a shy schoolgirl. 'Cassidy Malone. Known to be the woman with a natural knack for public humiliation. Tendency to over-think things to the point of complete randomness. Strong belief that peanut butter and jelly anywhere in the vicinity of a slice of bread is just *wrong*…'

'Hello, Cassidy Malone—can I call you Cass?'

'Somehow I doubt I'll be able to stop you.'

Will smiled *that* smile, then cocked his head as he ran the pad of his thumb back and forth over her knuckles. 'We could use this for Nick and Rachel, you know…'

Cassidy rolled her eyes and attempted to quietly extricate her hand from his. 'Just no escaping those two, is there?'

'You want to?' He held onto her hand.

'Do I want to what?'

'Escape them for a while?' The thumb kept brushing over her skin, distracting her from looking away from his mesmerising eyes.

It meant it took a second or two longer than normal for her to focus on what he'd said. 'Will, we can't keep taking breaks if you want to get this thing done. It's counter-productive. You know that.'

He studied her intently. 'You're hating every minute of this, aren't you?'

Not *every* minute, no. She loved rediscovering her muse, she loved it when their scenes started coming together, she loved staying in Will's beautiful house by the ocean, she'd even loved spending time with Angie and Lily on the beach—and she agreed that, given the chance, she probably could end up good friends with a world-famous actress…

But she couldn't allow herself to enjoy those moments. Not properly. Not when she was living in a fantasy world on borrowed time. One day soon she would have to walk away from Will's life and try to find one of her own. One more fulfilling than the one she'd been living. Because if she'd been happy in the life she had she wouldn't have been so quick to leave it behind, would she?

'Cass?' The thumb stilled, and the impossibly gentle use of her name made her realise she'd dropped her gaze to the beating pulse at the base of his neck.

She looked back up. 'Sorry. Drifted off for a minute. I've got a tendency to do that too.'

'I remember.' He said it with just enough softness in his voice to suggest he remembered it with a degree of affection. Darn it.

When she made another attempt at freeing her hand he let her. So she folded her fingers into her palm and let her arm drop to her side as he leaned back, his expression changing to the unreadable blankness she hated so much,

'It's okay, I've got my answer.' Lifting a glass of juice, he pushed to his feet and turned towards the open door. 'We'd better get back to it then.'

CHAPTER SIX

WITHOUT any idea why she felt compelled to correct his assumption, Cassidy found herself on her feet, matching glass in hand, and following him into the kitchen. 'Wait, Will. You're wrong. You didn't get an answer.'

Turning in the middle of the room, he lifted his chin and looked at her with hooded eyes.

Which left her squirming inwardly as she tried to find the words to explain it to him without giving too much away.

'I' m not… That is it's not that I'm not…' She puffed her cheeks out in exasperation, and avoided his gaze by glancing at random points around the room. 'I guess I just—' A deep breath and a grimace, and then she silently said to heck with it and took a run at it. 'I feel a bit—lost, I suppose. You and me? We're not the same. This living to-gether under the same roof—' One of her hands flailed in the air in front of her body, towards him. 'Well, we're not the *same*…'

'You already said that.'

Cassidy scowled at his calm tone, and the fact that her gaze shifted to meet his and discovered what looked like a glint of amusement only made her feel more stupid than she already did.

She sighed heavily. 'This is your life, Will, not mine. I'm just a visitor here. But this script…it's important…it means a lot. I don't want to mess it up.'

When there was silence it drew her gaze back to him again, then he took a shallow breath and asked, 'Why is it so important?'

Now, there was a question with a loaded answer.

Her hesitation brought him a step closer, his hand reaching out to set his glass on the nearest counter top. 'I get the not wanting to mess up part. Everyone feels that way when they work on a script. Or on any kind of a project that means something to them. There was a time you wanted to succeed in this business as much as I did…'

Cassidy smiled wryly. 'Apparently not *quite* as much as you did…'

The low words were enough to tug on the edges of his mouth. 'Okay. Fair enough. We had different motivations but the same goal—at least I thought we did. Maybe I was wrong about that?'

If she had, she'd have left everything behind to go with him to California. That was what he was intimating, wasn't it? Yes, Will had been driven for different reasons from Cassidy. But the goal *had* been a dream they'd shared. What had broken them apart had been Cassidy's starry-eyed romanticism over the life they would have together weighed against Will's need to be successful enough to prove to all those people who had thought him worthless that they'd been spectacularly wrong in their assessment. Cassidy had believed they would achieve their dreams together. Will had left her behind and done it on his own. But she'd let him go, hadn't she?

Will took another step closer. 'Why is it so important, Cass?'

She took a deep breath, while warily watching to see how close he planned on getting. 'We bombed last time, Will. You remember how bad that felt as well as I do…'

'Oh, sweetheart, I've bombed a few times since then—trust me. It's par for the course out here.'

The use of the drawled 'sweetheart' made her cock a re-criminating brow at him, but she let it slide when she saw the light in his eyes. 'But you're a success, Will. Look around you—this house, your company, the awards you've won—you've made it. I'm a *schoolteacher*. Not that there's anything wrong with that—it's one of the most honourable professions on the planet—but it wasn't something I'd planned on doing for the rest of my life.' Any more than living on her own had been. 'The last script I cowrote with you is the only thing I have on my movie-writing CV. The script for a movie that bombed at the box office and gave movie reviewers globally the excuse to ramp the venom volume up to high—remember? I ended on a failure. A very public failure. I don't want another one. Seriously, I don't think I could take it…and… And I'm babbling again, aren't I?'

'Like a brook.' He smiled indulgently.

Another step forward brought him to within reaching distance. But instead of offering her the kind of comfort-ing hug she desperately needed and dreaded at the same time, he lifted his hands and pushed them deep into the pockets of his jeans—meaning the only way a hug would happen was if *she* reached for *him*.

But that wasn't going to happen, was it? No matter how much she sorely needed to be held—just held—for long enough not to feel as if she had somehow detached herself from her fellow human beings. Now that she thought about it, it was probably the same fear that brought tears of emotion to her eyes when small arms would hug so tightly around her neck on the last day of term…

'It was a success in the long haul, Cass. Or we wouldn't be here. You need to remember that. Sometimes the road to success has its twists and turns. That's all.'

She managed a somewhat shaky smile and a roll of her eyes at her continuing inability to listen to reason or appreciate thoughtfulness without the need to cry. 'I'd just rather skip the hobnailed boots stomping all over my self-confidence this time round, if that's all right with you.'

The green of Will's eyes softened and warmed. 'Welcome to Hollywood.'

Cassidy laughed softly, then stared at him in wonder. 'How do you do it?'

'Thick skin.' He shrugged.

'Is there a store nearby where I can pick one of those up?'

''Fraid not. It's something you acquire over time. Wouldn't suit you, anyway.'

Sighing heavily, she nodded. 'I'd be willing to try it out for a while.'

Whether it was something he saw in her eyes, or something he knew instinctively she needed—as he so often had once upon a time—Will pulled his hands out of his pockets and closed the gap between them. He reached for her with a rumbled, 'Come here, Malone.'

Oh, great. Now she was welling up the way she did with the kids. Only this time it was bittersweet for different reasons. Even as Will drew her close to the wall of his chest and circled her with his arms, she felt the deep-seated sensation of coming home after a long, long time in exile. She hadn't realised how homesick she'd been for him until he was holding her and she had her arms around his lean waist. The scent of clean laundry and pure Will surrounded her, but she breathed it deeper anyway. When one of the large hands on her back gently rubbed to soothe her she had to fight the need to sob uncontrollably. But not just because it was a hug when she so desperately needed a hug. It was because it was *Will*. The Will she'd missed so very much that even while she was being held in his arms the fact she knew it might never happen again was enough to break another corner off her ragged-edged heart.

'You're doing great, Cass. Don't be so hard on yourself. There are days in that room I forget it's been so long since we worked together.'

She *had* been feeling better about her scriptwriting abilities, but hearing him say it meant a lot to her. 'Thank you.'

'You're welcome.' The smile sounded in his voice.

It made her smile too, as she tilted her head back to rest her chin on his shoulder. Then she took another deep breath and forced herself to step away from him. 'I guess I can stand to be cooped up in that room for another few hours if you can.'

'Good.' A devilish smile was backed up by another wink. 'We can talk about Rachel wearing that harem girl outfit again.'

Cassidy laughed. 'No. we can't. She's not doing the Dance of the Seven Veils for Nick...'

'She'd be very sexy doing it.'

'She'd feel like a complete idiot doing it.'

Will retrieved his glass and headed back towards the office. 'Okay, then. We'll play out the scene and see how it goes.'

Cassidy chuckled; he could go right ahead and hold his breath for that one. But she suddenly felt a lot better going back into his office with him. *Much better.*

Ryan and Malone were on top form when they pitched their script for the first time—even if it was technically just a trial run.

Will had driven them into Los Angeles, to his plush, if chaotic offices. making small talk on the journey that Cassidy knew was meant to distract her from her nervousness. It was yet another thoughtful gesture she both needed and feared at the same time. Between his thoughtfulness, his ability to read what she needed—sometimes before she realised it herself—and the amount of mild flirting he'd been doing since the day of their partial truce she was already walking a fine line. If she made the mistake of falling for him again…

Once they were in the conference room with selected members of Will's team, and they began the read-through, something clicked. Maybe it was because she let herself get lost in what they were doing. Maybe it was because, for the guts of an hour, reality was shut out. Maybe it was because they became Nick and Rachel again. Maybe it was the fact their audience laughed and sat forward in their seats with rapt expressions at the right times. Heck, maybe it was a combination of all those things. But whatever it was, it was magical. For the first time since she'd come to California it felt as if the old Will was completely back.

He laughed more, he smiled *that* smile at her when she

blushed as she skirted over any kisses or love scenes in the script, he even danced with her and dipped her the way the script directed—to the obvious amusement of their captive audience. He took her hand so they could both take a bow when that same audience applauded at the end…

Then they spent another hour talking with the team about special effects and storyboarding and locations—and Cassidy forgot she was with a group of complete strangers who worked for Will, and debated with him the way she usually did when they were alone.

After handing out work assignments, Will watched her shake the last hand at the open doorway, then leaned casually against the doorframe. 'Trying to start a revolution inside my production company, Malone?'

'Meaning?'

'You didn't see some of their faces when you debated with me?'

She had—and she might have been worried he was angry about it if she hadn't seen the sparkle of amusement in his eyes. 'I noticed the look on their faces when you conceded anything. I get the impression that doesn't happen too often…'

'It's rare.' He shrugged and cast a glance over the open-plan work area outside the conference room like some ruler surveying his kingdom. 'But not unheard-of.'

'Hmm.' Cassidy leaned against the other side of the frame, pursed her lips and then smiled when he looked at her. 'Might do you good if it happened more often, Ryan. Who knows what creativity you have here, hidden under too many layers of fear to speak up in front of the boss. You should thank me.'

'Or hire you.'

Her jaw dropped. But before she could figure out if he was being serious, he pushed off the door frame and jerked his head. 'Come on. I have something I want you to see while we're here…'

Of all the things she had expected to be shown—fancy office, great views over Los Angeles, other productions he might be working on—a room the size of a large stationery cupboard, filled with piles of paper and sacks of letters pretty much came at the bottom of the list. So when he turned the lights on and closed the door behind them, she turned round and lifted a brow.

'A mailroom? That's what you wanted to show me?' Her voice was flat.

Will blinked lazily at her. 'Pick a letter.'

She was obviously missing something. Frowning, she turned her head and examined the room more closely. Nope—it still looked like a mailroom to her. Not a particularly well-organised one either.

'Pick a letter. Or an e-mail—doesn't matter.' He stepped closer to her. 'Any one you want.'

Okay, she'd play. Glancing at him from the corner of her eye, she made a big deal out of waving her hand in circles before closing her eyes and feeling around for a random selection—not helping with any invisible filing system he might have.

When she opened her eyes and held it up in front of her face, the corners of Will's mouth were tugging upward. 'Read it.'

Dragging her gaze from his, she slipped the letter from the opened envelope and began to read, her eyes widening when she realized what it was. Lifting her chin, she stared at the rest of the papers—then at Will.

The green of his eyes radiated warmth, and his deep voice lowered as he told her, 'Pick another one.'

She did—and got an e-mail that made her throat tighten.

Will's voice was lower and closer when he spoke again. 'Keep going.'

'All of them?' Cassidy lifted her chin and silently cleared her throat, so her voice didn't sound so strangled. 'This whole room is fan mail for our movie?'

'Yes. The studio forwarded it here to begin with, but when it started increasing we changed the address on the website. We get mail from all over the world.' He searched her eyes and smiled. 'They call themselves the Fortune Hunters.'

For the first time in her life Cassidy was at a complete loss for words.

So Will kept going, his gaze locked on hers. 'It started with message boards. Then they launched their own site and it grew from there. There are role-playing games, conspiracy theories—some of them have all the lines memorised so when they have a screening they can join in. They even dress up as the characters at conventions…'

With her emotions threatening to overwhelm her, Cassidy forcibly dragged her gaze from his and reached for another letter. 'What's this one?'

Will held an edge so he could read it. 'California's Fortune Hunters. There are chapters all over the place now, but California was the first. They organise a yearly charity screening of the movie, and let us know when it is so we can send memorabilia to auction on the night.'

'I had no idea.'

'I didn't think you did.' He waited for her to look at him before he told her. 'The movie may have tanked at the box office, Cass, but it's been successful in ways no one could ever have predicted. It's brought people together—it's even been the catalyst for a few weddings. There's a community of amazing people out there who are making a difference to other people's lives with their charitable causes through it. Does that sound like a failure to you?'

Cassidy shook her head.

'No.' Will smiled one of *those* smiles as he reached up and tucked a strand of hair behind her ear. 'If you didn't get enough of a self-confidence boost from the reaction to the pitch we just did, then maybe this will do it.'

She still couldn't speak.

When Will's gaze dropped briefly to her mouth she held her breath, her heart thundering against her breastbone as she waited to see if he was going to kiss her…

But he dropped his hand and stepped back. 'Read through some of them while I make a few calls, if you like. There's a coffee machine down the hall. Then I'll come back and drive us home, so we can work on the changes we agreed in the meeting.'

She nodded. Then watched as he turned round and opened the door. The first tear slipped onto her lower lashes after he'd disappeared. It wasn't just because of what he'd shown her and told her, or the fact he had known how much she'd needed to see it. It was because he'd used the word 'home'.

As if it was *her* home too…

The thing was, somewhere along the way, his house *had* started to feel more like home than the one she had in Ireland. It would take strength to leave and close the door on their relationship for once and for all. She knew she'd be leaving even more of herself behind than he'd taken with him the first time.

They didn't go straight to work on the script revisions when they got back to Will's house. Cassidy couldn't allow herself to think of it as 'home'. She'd already allowed herself to get too comfortable in her surroundings as it was.

Unusually—since she'd arrived anyway—it was raining outside: hot, heavy, humid rain. So they had a take-away Moroccan dinner inside—plates of a half-dozen dishes she'd never tried before spread out on a coffee table in front of them while they sat on one of Will's large sofas.

'I'm curious about your life,' he said.

'Why?'

'I can't ask you a simple question?'

'Maybe I'm *curious* why you need to know.' Cassidy was fully aware of the verbal game of poker they were playing over dessert, but she wasn't backing down.

'I thought we'd decided we're friends again?'

She avoided his gaze, playing with the ice cream in her tub. 'Okay, we're friends.'

'Friends talk about stuff. Try me.'

It took a long while for her to make a decision, and Cassidy couldn't help but smile when he lifted dark brows in challenge. She knew *he* knew the reason she was reluctant to talk about her life was because it involved emotion. She knew *he* knew that *she knew* Will didn't talk about emotion. End of story. He'd rather chew off his own arm. So it was, therefore, a case of what was sauce for the goose…

But this change for the better in their relationship had allowed them to start getting to know each other again, and she was reluctant to put a dampener on that. Especially when they were both smiling more, and working together had got easier, and he'd been so thoughtful of late…

The ice cream took several violent digs before she sighed heavily. 'One hint of anything resembling sympathy, Will Ryan…'

When she glanced up he was continuing to smile his patented humouring smile at her.

She frowned. 'You're doing it already.'

'I'm not.' He pasted a serious expression on his face, folding his arms and jerking his chin at her. 'Go on. I'm listening.'

'I hate this. I tell you about my life and it's just going to sound pathetically ordinary compared to yours.'

'Not necessarily. Most of my life is more ordinary than people might think.'

Cassidy snorted softly in disbelief. 'Like what, for instance? Hanging out with movie stars? Working in the motion picture industry? The fact you attend the Oscars every year? The millionaire's beach house you live in?'

It took a second, then one of *those* smiles broke free, the green in his eyes glittering hypnotically. He shook his head before looking at a point over her left shoulder as he considered his answer. 'It's hard to find words.'

'Will, you work with words every day.' She kept her voice purposefully soft. 'Can't spell them—but you know how to use them…'

'Very funny.'

'Try. One ordinary thing about your life.'

'Just the one and you'll tell me about *your* life.' He looked as if he doubted that.

'Make it a truly mundane one and I'll fill in the blanks.' She lifted her spoon and made a cross in the air above her breasts. 'Cross my heart.'

The move apparently gave him an open invitation to drop his gaze and watch the increased rise and fall of her breasts as he looked at them. Then his thick lashes lifted and he chuckled at her look of accusation before informing her, 'I don't have a housekeeper. So I do all my own cleaning.'

'Oh, no—your obsession with neatness doesn't count.' It was something that had never ceased to astound her, but he'd always seemed to get pleasure from an organised environment. Whereas Cassidy had always lived in the kind of chaos that was reflective of her life in general. In the end she'd put his borderline obsession down to control—the same kind of control that he'd exerted over so many areas of his life.

Only in the bedroom had he ever fully lost that precious self-control. When he'd made love to her she'd never had any doubts about how he felt. But then neither had he about how *she* felt. They'd been stripped naked—emotionally as well as physically. Something Cassidy had never allowed herself to come close to experiencing with anyone else. Not that he would ever know that.

Will shrugged and stole a spoonful of her ice cream. 'Still counts as ordinary. Everyone does housework. It's a universal equaliser.'

Cassidy laughed. 'I've made a valiant effort to avoid it wherever possible, believe me.'

The corners of his mouth quirked. 'I believe you. Now I've lived up to my end of the bargain it's your turn. Tell me about this ordinary life of yours.'

It was on the tip of her tongue to ask again why he wanted to know, but instead she dropped her chin and played some more with the ice cream. 'I teach, so I work according to the school terms. In the summer I usually manage to find work at camps, or at places where working parents can leave their kids while they do their nine to fives. I have a flat. I have teacher friends I meet for lunches or coffees or whatever. I used to have a cat—'

'What happened to it?'

'It must have been about a hundred years old when I got it from the shelter, so it didn't last long.'

'Didn't get another one?'

'Nope.' She smiled wryly at her ice cream. 'Apparently I wasn't ready to deal with another loss after my dad. I cried for weeks over that dumb cat.'

When Will didn't say anything she stole an upward glance at him from underneath a wave of lose hair. He was studying her again. But instead of asking *What?* that way she usually did, she took the opportunity to say, 'Thank you. For the card and the flowers you sent.'

He knew she didn't mean after the cat had died. 'I got your note. You don't have to thank me again.'

Cassidy dampened her lips and took a breath. 'It meant

a lot. I didn't put that in the note. And I should have. That time is kind of a blur to me now.'

'Grief can be like that.' His gaze shifted to her loose hair, and Cassidy wondered if he was thinking of tucking it away again. 'You had a lot to do to wrap everything up as well. At least you had your family to help you.'

'I did.' Unlike the eight-year-old Will, who'd had no one when his mother had passed away; it still killed Cassidy that he'd been left so alone.

'You could have called me if you'd needed anything— you know that.'

She did. Even if he hadn't written it in the card he had sent. 'Wasn't that easy.'

Taking a deep breath, he reached forward for the remote control of his ridiculously large widescreen TV and handed it to her. 'I've decided we're taking the night off. Pick a movie.'

Cassidy blinked in surprise. 'I thought you wanted to get this thing done?'

'It'll wait.' He waved the remote in the air. 'Pick a movie.'

Setting the ice cream tub between her knees, Cassidy took the remote with one hand, leaning forward and resting the back of her other hand against his forehead. 'Are you feeling sick? Do you have a temperature? Maybe you caught my cold…'

He removed her hand. 'You can't spend an evening just sitting doing nothing with me, can you?'

'Yes, I can.' But she could feel her cheeks warming at the 'doing nothing with me' part. Because in the past sitting on a sofa watching a movie with him would have led to kissing. Kissing would have led to touching. Then—

'Prove it. Pick a movie.'

With an arched brow she lifted her chin and curled her legs underneath her, glaring sideways at him as she pointed the remote at the TV. 'You'll regret this.'

Will toed off his shoes and lifted his feet to rest them on the coffee table, settling back into the large cushions. 'No, I'm not.'

'Oh, yes you are.' She smirked as the screen jumped to life and she flicked through the channels to find what she was looking for. There it was. That would do, 'Because it is now officially chick-flick night...'

When the credits played at the end of the movie, Cassidy turned her head against the back of the sofa and found Will fast asleep, his face turned towards her. He was gorgeous. Strands of dark hair falling across his forehead, cheeks flushed with sleep, full lips parted as he breathed deep, even breaths. For a long while she just looked at him, drinking in the sight and memorising every detail. Then she gave in to temptation and brushed a single strand of rich hair off his forehead with her fingertips. Her voice was a whisper, as if she was reluctant to lose the stolen moment. 'Will?'

He didn't react, so she smiled and tried again with a slightly stronger voice. 'Will.'

'Hmm...?'

Still smiling, she watched as he slowly made his way into consciousness. How many times had she watched him waking up? Probably hundreds. Yet apparently, even after so many years, it was still one of her favourite things to do.

Will blinked her into focus with heavy lashes. 'Cass?'

Though obviously still caught between sleeping and

waking, he lifted a hand and gently brushed her hair back from her cheek. *'Cass...'*

Cassidy froze when he leaned towards her. What was he—?

Oh, no—no, no, no, no, no, *no!* This wasn't happening! Why had he—? What did he think he was—? Was he seriously—? He was *kissing her*! *Unscripted*! No, wait—it was worse than that. He was kissing her, and it was...it was—well, it was...

Oh, wow.

At first she was stunned at how fast her body responded. The heat built like a flashfire in dry scrubland, even though the kiss was soft and sweet and so tender it shredded yet another edge off Cassidy's already ragged heart. It seemed endless, as if the world turned more slowly, while her heart pounded heavily against her breasts. Nothing had *ever* felt as right in her entire life—not one single thing—and knowing that scared her to death. She *could not* fall in love with this man again. Oh, *please*. But what if she'd never fallen *out of love* with him?

Oh. God.

Now she was kissing him back. Stupid, *stupid* girl! What was she doing? It was Will Ryan—the man who broke her heart and changed her life for ever, ruining her for any other man who ever showed the vaguest little interest in her! What was she doing kissing him back? Had she lost her mind?

When the moan formed low in her chest she had the fight of her life to keep it there. She couldn't let the sound out. If she let it out he'd know. He'd know he was making her toes curl. He would know how little it would take to get her horizontal again. Who did that after eight years apart? What was it about him? Was she really so needy that she—?

Oh, it was *good*. She never wanted it to end.

But it had to. *It. Had. To.* So she dragged her mouth from his—then stared at him as she fought to control her breathing, while his eyes opened and his warm breath washed over her flushed cheeks. He stared back. Then frowned and opened his mouth…

CHAPTER SEVEN

SHE couldn't have him say anything. Not when she still felt as if she was drowning in sensation. From somewhere she found the strength to beat him to it.

'You fell asleep.'

Will looked at her as if she had two heads.

'That must have been one hell of a dream I interrupted…' It was the only thing that made any sense to her.

'It was,' he said with a husky-edged voice.

Oh, thank you, god. As much as it hurt, at least it was a way out. 'Thought so.'

Her half-hearted attempt at a smile was met with a narrowed, searching gaze. But before he could say anything else Cassidy pushed to her feet and gathered together their plates. 'I'll clear up down here. You should go and grab more sleep. Maybe you can pick up that dream where you left off?'

There was silence from the sofa as she walked across the room, then; 'What's going on, Cass?'

'I'm clearing up. I already told you that.'

She'd made it all the way into the kitchen, and had set the plates on the drainer, when two large hands settled on her shoulders and turned her around.

'You're the one who avoids housework, remember? So what's going on?' Will moved one hand, the backs of his fingertips tracing along her jawline and pushing into the hair at her nape. Then he unfurled his fingers and curled his palm around her neck—his thumb smoothing against her cheek.

If he kissed her again…

Dampening her lips, and almost moaning out loud when his gaze followed the movement, she lifted her hand to quietly remove his. 'If you kiss me I won't be able to think straight.'

Oh, dear! That tongue of hers just didn't know when to stop, did it?

The brief glow in his eyes told her how much the confession meant to him. But he dropped his arms and then shook his head.

'I know you're scared,' he said, in a low voice that made her stomach cramp.

Cassidy lifted her chin. 'I'm not scared.'

'No?'

'No.' She quirked her brows in warning, and then angled her head and answered his slow smile with one of her own. 'I'm…wary…'

When she purposefully took her time enunciating the word his smile grew. 'Wary is a good word.'

'I have more.'

'I don't doubt that.'

She nodded, letting her gaze examine a thick strand of his dark hair. 'Cautious would be another good one.'

'It would. Even if means the same thing as wary.'

'Forewarned, then…'

'Can't say I'm happy with that one…'

Drawing her lower lip between her teeth, she made the

mistake of glancing at his eyes and found him watching the movement. His gaze rose, locked with hers, and coherent thought left her brain at speed. How did he still *do* that to her?

His next words removed her ability to breathe. 'I'm wary too.'

In the absence of thinking or breathing, she asked him a silent question. And he must have read it in her face, the way he was so very good at, because he nodded, the warmth in his stunning green eyes sending her temperature up a notch.

'I knew what I was doing when I kissed you.'

Cassidy stared at him with wide eyes. He really was so much braver than she was. And because he'd laid it so tenderly on the line for her, she met him halfway, her voice one octave above a whisper as she asked, 'You did?'

'I did. I've been thinking about it ever since the day we rehearsed that scene.'

When he'd kissed her as Nick?

Will took a breath. 'But this was never the part we had a problem with—was it, Cass?'

Swallowing to dampen her dry mouth and take the sandpaper edge off her throat, Cassidy shook her head. 'No. It wasn't.'

Will laid his palms on the counter either side of her body, effectively boxing her in as he took a step closer. 'You kissed me back.'

'I know I did.' She was about thirty seconds away from having a heart attack, judging by her rapid heartbeat and her continued inability to breathe.

'I bet I can make you kiss me again.'

'Probably. But there wouldn't be any point to it—and you know that as well as I do.' She silently prayed he did.

'Why wouldn't there?'

'Because… Well, because it's not as if we're going to end up… Well…*you know*…'

His eyes sparkled dangerously. 'Aren't we? We always did before.'

'Well, we're not this time!' When she wriggled away from him it had the opposite effect she'd been aiming for. Instead it made her all too aware of everywhere his body had touched hers. While she was still catching her breath from that realisation he made his move—he had her hands in his and tugged her forward—then rearranged her hands behind her back so that he had both of them trapped at the wrists in one of his.

'What do you think you're doing?' she gasped.

With a glint in his eyes, and a killer one of *those* smiles, Will leaned her back over the counter. 'I'm not going to kiss you. Don't worry. I'm checking to see how your body feels about me touching you…'

Cassidy gasped, her eyes wide. 'Don't you *dare*—'

As he let his fingers skate across her midriff he watched the reaction in her eyes. 'Tell me you don't want me, Cass.'

'I don't want you.'

'*Liar.*'

She didn't want him to stop. And now his hand was moving higher…

When she trembled, he studied her eyes again. Then his gaze dropped to the rapid rise and fall of her breasts. But just when Cassidy was about to take the safer option and cave in to kissing him, his thumb moved. An involuntary giggle escaped.

'Ticklish…' He leaned into her, his voice a husky rumble above her ear. 'I remember that…'

'*No.*' Now her knees were giving out on her.

Will moved his thumb to prove his point, and chuckled above her ear when she squirmed. 'When are you going to learn you can't lie to me, Cass? You never could.'

He was killing her!

'You want me. And I want you.' He pressed a soft kiss to her throat—on the sensitive skin below her ear—before whispering, 'I remember what we were like together. How good we were. How many weekends we spent in bed…'

When he kissed his way to her collarbone Cassidy's head automatically dropped back to make room for him, while she gasped short, sharp breaths of air that tasted of Will's familiar scent.

He lifted his head, placed his cheek against hers and told her, 'But I'm not going to seduce you, Cass. You're going to come to *me*. That way I won't take the blame this time…'

When it fell apart—that was the part he left out. But that was what he meant. Meaning he didn't see it as anything lasting? Meaning this time it would be an affair? Cassidy wasn't sure she could do that. Not with Will.

Releasing her hands, he stepped back and looked down at her wide eyes, studying them each in turn. 'Think it over if you need to. But this isn't going away, Cass. You know that just as well as I do.'

She did. But it didn't make it any easier a decision.

There was an edge of warning to his deep voice when she continued staring at him. 'You need to go upstairs now.'

Or he would kiss her until she made her decision? Was that what he was saying?

'*Cass.*'

Practically running from the room, she made short work

of the stairs and of walking along the hall—only glancing back down at him when she had her hand on the door to her bedroom. He stood with his back to her, looking out at the reflection of the moon on the rolling ocean, tension radiating from every pore of his large body.

It would be so very easy to give in to how much she wanted him. *Too easy.* But, with a strength that surprised her, she pushed open the door and turned away. Shredding yet another edge off her heart along the way…

He was officially making her crazy. *Again.*

Her disobedient gaze flickered across to look at him for the twenty-eighth time that morning. Like the other twenty-seven times, he looked at her at the same time and smiled knowingly. It was infuriating. And Cassidy was deeply resentful that Will was so in control. She hadn't managed a single night's sleep in three.

She forced her gaze back to her screen and pursed her lips, narrowing her eyes and willing herself to read an entire sentence and get all the way to the end of it knowing what she'd read!

Her peripheral vision caught him moving a second before his chair began to squeak. That was another thing that was making her crazy. 'The *chair.*'

'Hmm?' He looked at her when she looked at him. 'Sorry?'

'Your chair. Don't you have a can of oil somewhere?'

'Oil?' He blinked at her.

Nice try, Mr Butter-Wouldn't-Melt. Her eyes narrowed.

He pushed his chair back and got up. Something else he'd been doing a lot of was leaving the room at regular intervals. But she didn't say anything. She just smiled sweetly when he glanced her way before turning to leave—and could tell from the small, incredibly satisfied frown on his face that he knew she'd been noticing the number of times he'd been wandering off during the day.

He was restless.

Will stopped, turned, and jerked a thumb over his shoulder. 'Thought I'd grab a sandwich. You hungry?'

'At eleven-thirty? Bit early for lunch, don't you think?'

Trying a new tactic, he smiled at her the way he'd taken to doing so much lately. 'I can't go and get something nice to surprise you with either, I suppose…?'

The word '*nice*' made her purse her lips again. If he did one more '*nice*' thing she thought she might scream. His campaign of *nice*—and thoughtful and considerate and caring and sweet and tender—was the worst form of torture she'd ever been subjected to in all her born days. Especially when coupled with his being effortlessly sexy. But, barring brushing her hair back from her face, and smiling *that* smile at her, he hadn't done one single thing to pick up where they'd left off in the kitchen the other day!

When she focused her gaze on his mouth she frowned harder, and felt her foot begin tapping in the air underneath the desk. 'I don't like surprises.'

'No—you don't like surprises you don't already know about. There's a difference. We discussed that many, many times in the past.' He stepped round to her side of the desk and rested one palm flat on the surface, while his other hand grasped the back of her chair and turned her to face him. 'So what do you want me to surprise you with?'

Cassidy's gaze shot upwards and locked with his.

Will smiled *that* smile in reply.

She scowled. 'Stop that.'

'Stop what?'

'*That.*' She felt a bubble of borderline manic laughter work its way up from the base of her throat as she pointed the tip of her pen at his face and made a circle. 'Don't think I don't know what you're doing, Ryan.'

'And what *am* I doing?'

'Trying to wear me down.' Leaning closer, she lowered her voice. 'So that if I say yes to you it'll seem like it's my decision. When in actuality *it's not*—you'll have backed me into a corner.'

'Oh, well, I'll stop, then—obviously.'

'This whole being nice to me thing can stop too. Nice *never* works on me. It just makes me suspicious. You *know* that.' She angled her head and lifted her chin.

Much to her annoyance, when he smiled again, she smiled back at him. How was this tactic *working on her*? In any relationship—including the one she'd been in *with him*—she couldn't remember there ever being the equivalent of a 'mating dance'. She hadn't a clue how it was supposed to work. It had her on tenterhooks. Her damn stomach even got butterflies when she woke up in the morning and knew she was going to see him! Then there was the whole smiling thing she was doing when he wasn't around…

At first she'd told herself every time he left her alone to go and tend to business elsewhere that she was glad of the break. Then she'd been annoyed with herself for noticing every time he was gone for more than five minutes—as if she was so addicted to the sight of him that she missed him when he wasn't within appreciation distance every time she needed a fix!

Which was pathetic—completely, totally and utterly *pathetic*.

When he left the room now she began tapping her pen and her foot again, only stilling when his voice yelled, 'We're getting low on provisions. Want to take a trip to the store with me? Or do you want to stay in there and spend the rest of the afternoon figuring out what dastardly plans I currently have on the go?'

She sighed heavily and tossed her pen down before yelling back, '*Store!*'

They were halfway around the giant supermarket when Will finally did what she'd wanted him to do for days— reached an arm out to hook it round her waist and pull her close so he could press a kiss to her lips.

Rocking forward onto the balls of her feet, Cassidy took a deep breath and looked up at him from beneath heavy lashes. 'What was that for?'

'You were pouting.'

'I was *not* pouting!'

'Kinda cute, actually…'

'Oh, my God.' She leaned back against his arm. 'Kill me now.'

Will chuckled as he released her and reached for avocados. 'See, when you called *me* cute I took it as a compliment…'

'Yes, but my head fits through doors…' When he looked at her she folded her arms. 'A woman ceases to be "cute" the second she leaves puberty and pigtails behind. Don't ever say I have a pretty face either—it means you think I'm fat.'

'I don't think you're fat,' he informed her dryly as he pushed their trolley down the aisle. 'And I don't remember you having this many body issues before.'

Well, *duh*. She'd been twenty pounds lighter before. Not that she hadn't noticed how Will's habit of feeding them little and often and disgustingly healthily had been having a positive effect on the tightness of her waistband, but even so…

Will stopped, waited for her to get to his side, and then asked, 'Is that why you're stalling the inevitable?'

'Excuse me?' Cassidy's eyes widened with disbelief. 'The *inevitable*?'

'Is it?'

'Inevitable? That ego of yours is the size of Europe.'

'That's not what I meant and you know it. It had better not be because of body issues, Cass. I'll be disappointed in you if it is.' He took a step closer that made her take a step back, but all it did was trap her between him and a large display of sweet potatoes. A fact that made his eyes sparkle with amusement. 'Just say the word and I'll show you exactly how far my appreciation for curves can go…'

She gaped at him. 'You're unbelievable.'

He stole another kiss before moving back. 'Takes two to flirt the way we have been of late—remember that.'

I-n-c-r-e-d-i-b-l-e. The man's arrogance knew no bounds. Angrily tossing sweet potatoes into a bag, she lifted a brow at him. 'And this is us flirting now, I suppose?'

'Nope.' He winked at her. 'This is our version of foreplay.'

Cassidy rolled her eyes.

But Will smiled, a hand lifting to brush her hair off her shoulder so he could set his fingertips against her neck—

the neck she immediately arched to the side, to allow him access. Despite her best efforts to fight it, he had a way of making her feel like the most sensual woman on the planet. The darkening of his eyes in reaction to her silent submission was as much an aphrodisiac as the feel of his fingertips on her sensitive skin.

Sliding those fingertips inside the collar of her blouse, he set his thumb against the beating pulse at the base of her neck and leaned his face closer to hers, lowering his voice to a husky rumble. 'Come to a film premiere with me on Friday. It's at the Chinese Theater.'

The words rocked her back on her heels, her eyes widening. 'A film premiere? You and me? Posh clothes, red carpet, movie stars, press photographers—all that stuff?'

He nodded firmly, moving back and releasing his hand to tangle their fingers and tug to get her to walk beside him. 'Yup. All that stuff.'

Oh, no. An affair was one thing—the equivalent of a date turned it into something else completely. Surely he knew that? What she was doing with him was already dangerous enough, never mind knocking her self-confidence again by demonstrating the fact she didn't fit in to the Hollywood set he mixed with.

'I don't have anything to wear.' It was an excuse as old as time itself. But it was the first thing that came to her mind under pressure.

'We can fix that.'

She glanced down at their joined hands and frowned at them. 'I don't think—'

Will stopped and reached past her for brie. 'Good. When you do think you have a tendency to make things more complicated than they need to be. We both know that. It's just another movie night, Cass—this time in a theatre, with fancy clothes.'

Quietly clearing her throat, Cassidy lifted her gaze to meet his. 'Oh, I think you'll find it's a little bit more than—'

'No, it's not. There's nothing to be nervous about.' He smiled almost affectionately at her. 'You'll have fun. Wait and see.'

But it didn't help. 'Will, taking me as your date to the equivalent of a Hollywood "see and be seen" is—well, it's ridiculous.'

'Why is it?'

'Because…' She floundered, giving him a wavering look that silently begged him to let her off the hook. When he stood firm she explained, 'We can't just go out in public…on a date…like normal Hollywood people…'

Will's brows rose. '*Normal* Hollywood people? There's no such thing.'

When he continued staring at her she chewed on her lower lip—and then the babbling began in earnest. 'It'll give the wrong impression. People might think…I mean, it's not like there won't be questions, is there? I know what happens with the pictures taken at these things…they end up beamed around the globe and on the internet and in magazines and… Well, it's not like we're a couple or this is anything permanent. And if anyone knows you they're going to ask who I am, and if they find out we were together before they're going to make assumptions—the *wrong kind* of assumptions. And then—'

'See? Over-thinking and making it more complicated—told you. No one will make assumptions. You're assuming they'll be far more interested in my private life than they actually are. I'm not a movie star—I'm a writer/producer. I'm nowhere near interesting to the press unless I appear somewhere with a movie star. The only time I've ever done that was when she was someone in a movie I'd written and produced. It was publicity for the movie. That's how Hollywood has worked since the golden age.'

'Will—'

The use of his name as a plea for understanding made him let go of her hand and frame her face in large warm palms; his head lowered so he could look deep into her eyes as he told her, 'Quit it, Cass. It's not that big a deal.' Her eyes widened as he angled his head and lowered it even further, his words a whisper over her lips. 'It's just a night out. We're taking this slow and easy…'

It would be so very easy to give in to the heat between them and forget everything else. But if she did then she'd be in exactly the same vulnerable position she'd been before. The very thought of it made her fight for control all over again. Because a very primal part of her DNA structure already knew he was indelibly printed on her body. Nobody else's touch would ever have the same effect on her. She was his, in that sense. Had been from the first time he'd made love to her—when she'd given him something she could never give to another man ever again.

The fact she knew all that held her back. Slow and steady, he'd said. But slow and steady suggested they were working towards something more than an affair. He'd never once mentioned the possibility of her staying once the script was approved by the studio. A brief affair was possibly a way of ending their relationship with the kind of closure they'd plainly never had, and she felt they both deserved that. It was foolish to hope for anything more.

'We'll get you something to wear for Friday night. Angie can take you shopping. She'll love that.'

Cassidy sighed dramatically. 'I'll *think* about it…'

When he tangled their fingers again she took a deep breath and looked sideways at him as they started to walk. 'But it's a maybe. Not a yes. Going shopping isn't an actual guarantee of *finding* something to wear.'

Will chuckled. 'It is if you go shopping with Angie; Eric says she's never once come home with anything remotely resembling an empty car…'

Pursing her lips as she considered the kind of shopping budget Angelique Warden had compared to her own, Cassidy glanced sideways at him again. 'I'm glad we're giving me time to think this over and make up my own mind.'

The sight of Angelique rounding a corner as if on cue made Cassidy frown and attempt to tug her hand free.

Will simply tightened his fingers. 'Hey, Angie—excellent timing for a change. We need your help.'

'You do?' She glanced down at their joined hands, her finely arched brows rising in interest as she looked from one of them to the other.

Cassidy pursed her lips and tugged again. Will smiled and held on.

Angie looked thoroughly amused. 'Am I sensing a problem?'

'No.' Will's smile grew. 'Nothing the United Nations couldn't negotiate.'

Without warning Cassidy gasped and pointed her free

hand at the windows. 'Oh, my God. Is that someone doing something to your car, Will?'

Instantly both her companions swung round to look where she pointed, Will releasing her hand and stepping forward. He frowned. 'Where?'

There was a burst of melodic laughter from behind him. Turning in slow motion, he sighed heavily at her smug expression while Cassidy lifted her chin high, linked her arm with Angie's and stepped light-footed around him. 'I swear. You make it too easy for me sometimes…'

Angie laughed loudly as they rounded a corner. 'He should never have let you go, my friend—you're one in a million.'

Managing a small smile as she set her arm free, Cassidy took a deep breath and plunged into deep water with both feet. 'I need your help finding a dress for a film premiere Friday night. I wouldn't ask if—'

'Oooohhh—is Will taking you?'

'Yes.'

'Like, on a date?'

Cassidy grimaced. 'It's not as simple as that.'

While people stopped in the aisle to surreptitiously photograph Angelique with their cellphones, she took a step back and eyed Cassidy from head to toe, as if oblivious to her fans. 'I feel a make-over coming on. We'll use my usual hairdresser and make-up artist. Then I'll take you to see the hottest designer right now—I've worn enough of his dresses to premieres for him to owe me. Stilettoes for your feet—*naturally*—and we'll need to borrow something sparkly and worth millions from a big-name jeweler, of course…'

'*Oh, no.*' Cassidy's stomach dropped several feet. 'Angie, I didn't mean—'

The most famous eyebrow on the planet arched again. 'Do you want to knock Will on his ear or not?'

Actually, a little return of that particular favour wouldn't go amiss, but… *'Well…'*

'Exactly.' She linked their arms again. 'Rodeo Drive, here we come!'

A cellphone magically appeared, and with the tip of one manicured nail pressed to a single key—assumedly speed dial—appointments were made…

Cassidy was actually starting to feel a sense of optimism. Until they rounded an aisle and found Will talking to a stunning brunette who had her hand on his chest.

Cassidy froze. Will's gaze lifted and found hers. He didn't even flinch.

Then Angie came to her rescue again. 'I'm stealing Cass, Irish boy.'

'When are you planning on bringing her back?' The man seemed oblivious to the fact there was a woman attached to his side. One who *still* had her hand on his chest!

Angie shrugged. 'Whenever.'

Cassidy officially loved Angie—especially when she looked the other woman up and down with obvious disdain before smiling and waggling her fingers. 'Bye-bye, now.'

Turning swiftly on her heel, she leaned her head closer to Cassidy's and stage-whispered, 'You're about to get the make-over of your life.'

CHAPTER EIGHT

TRY as she might to put it to the back of her mind, curiosity was eating her up. Sighing heavily, Cassidy stretched to loosen the tension in her spine. It was her own stupid fault they were sat on the floor, checking the continuity in their rewrites; she was the one who'd insisted they get back to work the second she returned from a marathon of appointments to confirm other appointments. It wasn't as if she could casually grill him about his relationship with a certain touchy brunette, not without him knowing why, so work had seemed like a good idea at the time.

'Hungry?' He didn't look up from the sheet he was reading.

'Getting there…' She leaned over and pulled the sheet she was looking for from a pile. Then her errant tongue worked loose. 'Not all of us popped out for a nice long lunch…'

When his mouth twitched she wanted to kill him. 'We can eat any time you're ready, Cass. I'm easy.'

A burst of laughter escaped her lips. 'You said it.'

Will calmly set his sheet to one side. 'You got something you want to ask me?'

'Me? No-o.' She took a deep breath, inwardly cursing

the fact she *knew* she was about to wade in regardless. 'Why? Have you got something *you* want to tell *me?*'

'If you want to ask me about Diana, then go ahead. It's not like you to be so behind the door about it.'

She shrugged and fiddled with her papers. 'This is different.'

'Different how?'

Darn it—she wasn't answering that! He could whistle.

When she wasn't forthcoming, he pushed. 'Are you jealous?'

'What? No, I'm not jealous.' She scowled at him. 'Whatever you do in your own time is…'

'Yes?' His smile grew.

So she quirked her brows and reached for a sheet of paper she didn't actually need. '*Whatever you do.*'

In the blink of an eye she found her wrist captured by one large hand. She frowned at it and tugged. He held on. She looked up at him and glared in warning. He continued smiling and still held on.

Then his deep voice lowered. 'There's nothing going on with me and Diana. You don't need to worry.'

Worry? She wasn't *worried!* Although it didn't explain why she suddenly felt better.

'Your sex life is nothing to do with me.' Oh, terrific— now she'd mentioned the word sex. Her gaze snapped upwards and crashed into his. And the heat she could see there made her breath catch painfully in her chest.

When his thumb moved against the beating pulse in her wrist she felt her stomach clench, and the need to close her eyes and moan was so strong it almost flattened her. Oh this was bad. This was bad in global proportions.

Frowning even harder, she closed her eyes and tugged on her hand. 'Let go.'

'Cass, look at me.'

She didn't want to look at him. But she forced herself to—and immediately regretted it. 'I'm not jealous. You should be so lucky. Now, give me my hand back.'

'No.'

'What do you mean *no*?'

'I don't want to.'

He smiled the smile that did something all too familiar to her pulse-rate, his thumb brushing back and forth over her wrist in a hypnotic rhythm. She wasn't crossing that invisible line with him.

She shook her head. 'I've made my decision. This isn't going to happen.'

Will continued smiling.

'I'm serious, Will. It's not.'

He blinked lazily, his ridiculously thick lashes still the most fascinating thing in the world to her.

'All right—so maybe, somewhere very deep inside me, there is an eensy-weensy possibility I feel some sort of completely unwanted attraction to you...' His thumb moved down into her palm and started to draw a small circle. Cassidy heard a strangled noise in the base of her own throat. 'But I'm telling you—this is *not* going to happen. Not this time round.'

When his gaze lowered to her mouth she automatically dampened her lips with the tip of her tongue. As if she was preparing herself to be kissed. She saw his throat convulse as he swallowed. She saw his wide chest rise and fall faster than before, as if he was having as much difficulty breathing as she was. Then his gaze rose again, and she felt the force of wanting him slam into her midriff like a punch.

Fighting what she wanted was one thing. Fighting Will's wants was still another. Cassidy knew she wouldn't recover this time round. Not when the image of him with another woman had sat in her stomach like acid for the whole afternoon.

The fear must have shown in her eyes. Because Will let go of her hand. Cassidy immediately drew her arm back to her side, folding her fingers into her palm to hold onto the remnants of his touch while she floundered in a frantic search for words to put them back to where they should be.

When he spoke his voice was rough-edged, and deeper than she remembered it ever sounding before, telling her he was just as affected by what had had happened between them as she was. 'So, how was your shopping trip?'

'I don't think we should go out on Friday night either.'

'You'll find a dress, Cass.'

'It's got nothing to do with finding a dress. We found a dress.' The most beautiful dress she'd ever tried on or probably ever would again, as it happened. But even if the idea of never getting to wear it in public took some of the magic away from seeing herself in it for the first time, she knew she was making the right decision.

'Then what's the problem?'

Sighing heavily, she unfolded her legs so she could get to her feet. 'I'm not going out with you. Things have changed since this afternoon.'

While she swiped her clothes for any dust she might have picked up off the floor, Will lifted his chin to look at her. 'A lot of things have changed.'

Cassidy froze, staring down at him and feeling the same tension between them there had been when he'd held her wrist. She even had to swallow to make her throat work again.

'I know.' There was no avoiding it. They had. But even if they hadn't she couldn't let it change her decision. 'I'm going to put a fresh pot of coffee on…'

She was at the door when his voice sounded again. 'Cass?'

'Mmm-hmm?' She turned.

Will considered her for a long moment before he said, 'Diana has been chasing a part in one of my films for months now. I've never dated her.'

See, now, she didn't actually need to know that. 'If you say so. It's nothing to do with me. I've already said that.'

'Well, now you know.'

She'd turned away again when he added, 'And Cass?'

'What?' She swung round and frowned at him.

'Don't even *think* about cooking in my kitchen. We'll order pizza. Less chance of a fire that way…' He smiled a small smile at her.

Cassidy found herself smiling back. 'Cute. Go back to work, Ryan.'

The third time she made it all the way into the next room, then, 'Cass?'

Shaking her head and rolling her eyes, she spun on her heel and set her hands on the doorframe to lean back into the room. *'What?'*

The smile grew, his eyes sparkling. 'Nothing.'

Cassidy gaped at him, quirked her brows, and then ruined the effect by laughing. She continued laughing all the way into the kitchen, feeling irrationally light-hearted—until it hit her why she felt that way. Cold water was running over the back of her hand when she realised she was staring into nothing as it sank in. Then tears threatened. Spending time with Will was like riding a rollercoaster.

A part of her really wanted to knock him on his ear, the way he did her. And at some point during the afternoon she'd got sucked in to the possibility of being transformed into the kind of woman she wanted to be. The kind of woman a man like Will Ryan could look at and want for more than a fling. A woman he wouldn't want to leave behind. Regardless of her errant tongue, her chaotic life, her lack of cooking skills and her body issues…

Was one night of trying that woman on for size so much to ask for?

The next thing she knew she was back in the doorway, her hands pushed deep into the pockets of her sweat pants as she waited for him to notice she was there. 'About Friday night…'

Will lifted his brows, 'Yes?'

'I'll go, so long as it's understood it's not a date.'

'It's just a night at the movies in fancy clothes…'

Cassidy smiled somewhat half-heartedly. 'Like you said.'

'Exactly like I said…'

He wasn't going to make it easy for her, was he? As much as she wanted her one night, Cassidy didn't think she could bring herself to beg, so she shrugged as if it didn't matter to her one way or the other. 'Well, I have a dress now. So if—'

'I'll meet you in the bar at the Beverly Wilshire at seven.' He looked at her with his unreadable expression back in place. 'For our not-a-date-but-a-movie night.'

'Okay.' She smiled a more genuine smile.

Then he ruined the moment for her, by turning away and

adding, 'It'll be nice for you to get a glimpse of the glamorous side of Hollywood before you go home.'

He'd said it with a complete lack of emotion—confirming what she'd already known. An affair was all he was interested in. She didn't know that man—didn't want to either. The Will Ryan she'd loved would never have asked that of her.

Lifting her chin, she turned away from the door, determination straightening her spine. Come hell or high water she was going to knock him on his ear on Friday night. It would serve him right. Would show him what he was missing.

And then this time *she* would be the one to walk away.

How did Hollywood's elite ever get anything done when it took a full day to get ready for one night on the town?

That was the main question Cassidy had after almost eight hours of preparation. She'd been waxed, moisturised, filed, painted, plucked, tinted, washed, trimmed, highlighted, styled, blowdried, artfully curled, and polished to within an inch of her life. She had been scrutinised by enough critical eyes to make her feel abnormal, and had make-up applied with brushes so soft they'd almost lulled her to sleep. Then she'd had a lesson on how to walk—a skill she'd been fairly certain she'd mastered a few decades earlier—all while being steered away from anything resembling a mirror.

She really didn't think she had the patience for beauty if it took so much work.

By the time she was zipped into the beautiful emerald-green dress that slid against her ultra smooth skin like liquid, she was almost ready for a lie-down. It was only the butterflies in her stomach preceding Angie's big reveal that kept her from throwing in the towel in favour of pyjamas and a large tub of ice cream.

When she came out of the dressing room Angie and her team of stylists smiled at her like proud parents, while Cassidy wiped her palms together and fought the need to fidget. 'Tell me I don't look ridiculous. That's all I ask…'

'Oh, honey—you have no idea how far you are from ridiculous.'

'Closer to the sublime, actually,' the designer of her dress added in his thick Italian accent as he beamed at her.

Except in Cassidy's world the two words had a tendency to go together.

'Can I look now?' she asked, when she couldn't take it any more.

'After the final finishing touch,' Angie said as she stepped forward with a flat velvet case. 'Can't walk the carpet without the bling, darling…'

The 'bling' took her breath away, and her voice was barely above a squeak when the case was opened. 'I can't wear that! What if something happens to it?'

'That's what insurance is for. How do you think they ever sell jewellery this expensive without it regularly being draped on beautiful women?'

Bless her, but… 'Angie, I'm a realist. If you've managed to make me look even one step above pretty I'll love you for the rest of my days…'

'In that case put the jewellery on and prepare to love me into your next life too.'

With shaking fingers Cassidy carefully withdrew each strand of diamonds and placed them on her lobes, feeling the touch of their coolness against her neck as a matching pendant nestled between her breasts and enough money was attached to her wrist to make her feel the weight of every single cent.

'How much is this stuff worth?'

Angie shrugged. 'A little under a million, I believe. It's the teardrop the size of a small fist in your cleavage that's worth the most.'

Cassidy's jaw dropped.

Angie winked. 'Just a shame no one can take advantage of how good it would look on you when you're wearing nothing else…'

Before Cassidy could make a comment on that, her friend stepped back and studied her with a broad smile. 'You ready?'

'No.'

'Close your eyes.'

'You do know you've been watching entirely too many make-over shows…?'

'I never got the attraction of them till now.' She steered her towards a long mirror covered in a white sheet. 'Close your eyes.'

There was the whisper of a sheet the second she did. Then a pause that made her heart thunder loudly in her ears.

'Angie—you're killing me.'

'Open your eyes.'

The woman who walked through the foyer of the Beverly Wilshire was almost unrecognisable in comparison to the one who had passed out on its marble flooring a little less than a month before. Men followed her with their eyes, women looked at her with a mixture of open curiosity and envy—and Cassidy Malone knew they did, because she smiled at every single one of them.

She even laughed at the concierge who had brought her the cold medicine when he did a double-take. Stepping into a fantasy version of herself was an incredible feeling, and one she doubted she would ever forget.

Since she was living a fantasy, it seemed only fair she include her favourite movie in it too. So she headed straight for the tall stools at the bar and made herself comfortable. Then she ordered a martini while she waited for Will, who played his part to perfection by walking in wearing a dark tuxedo that—astonishingly—made him look even more gorgeous than he already did as he turned a slow circle and failed to find her...

With a deep breath, Cassidy turned her stool and waited for their gazes to lock. When they did the expression on his face was one she knew she would never forget as long as she lived. Looking in a mirror was one thing. Being told she was beautiful was another. But it took Will's reaction to make her truly *feel* that way.

With a confident lift of her chin she slid off the stool, walking towards him on heels that made her hips sway with each step so that the material of her floor-length skirt shimmered in the soft lighting.

Will dragged his gaze from hers long enough to sweep down her body and back up again as she approached him and smiled. 'Hi.'

'Hi...'

Cassidy's smile grew. 'Shall we go?'

'Mmm-hmm.' He nodded, but stayed exactly where he was—still staring at her.

'Are you okay?'

'There's a limo at the front door.'

'Okay.' She lifted her carefully shaped brows in amusement and stifled the need to laugh when the move made him frown and wave an arm out to his side in invitation. 'Are you sure you're all right?'

'I'm fine.' But it looked as if he was clenching his jaw as she stepped past him.

It was only when they were in the back of the stretch limousine that he seemed to snap to his senses; his gaze was openly explorative as he studied every soft curl artfully arranged on the crown of her head and brushing against her neck. 'They changed your hair colour.'

'Highlights.'

His gaze dropped to the strand of diamonds hanging from her ear. 'Who gave you the jewellery?'

'It's on loan.' In an uncharacteristic demonstration of self-confidence she turned towards him and lifted her breasts with a small arch of her back. 'The necklace is a doozy. Look.'

The move had the desired effect; his gaze dropped to the deep 'V' at the front of her dress, where the teardrop diamond nestled in the shadow between her breasts. The frown returned, darker than before. Then his gaze shifted sharply upwards.

What felt like his disapproval, combined with her errant tongue and a martini at the bar, brought the words into the open before she could stop them. 'Angie says it's just a shame no one will get to see me wearing it on its own. When I have nothing else on...'

Will sucked in a carefully controlled breath. 'You—

young lady—are playing a very dangerous game with me right now.'

Despite the immediate reaction of her body, Cassidy looked him straight in the eye. 'Am I?'

'Yes. And you know you are.' He leaned in closer and lowered his voice. 'So—unless you're planning on making love in the back of this limo—I suggest you tone it down some.'

Her eyes widened when she realised something. 'You're *angry*.'

'Drop it, Cass.'

'You are, aren't you? Want to tell me *why*?'

'You know me better than that.'

'Not any more I don't.' She studied each of his eyes in turn. 'What have I done?'

'It's not what you've done, Cass.' Will shook his head, looking at her with incredulity. 'It's what Angie let her team do.'

Just like that, the temporary confidence she'd had shattered. Oh, well, it had been nice while it lasted...

Turning her face away, she managed a low, 'I see.'

'Don't do that.' When he tried to reach his long fingers for her chin to turn her face towards him she moved her head back and looked sideways at him, forcing him to swear beneath his breath. 'You don't get it. Whatever paranoid thoughts you're thinking right now, you can forget it.'

The hurt was almost overtaking her. 'Then explain it to me,' she whispered.

Will looked as if the top of his head was ready to explode. Then he leaned forward and hit the intercom button. 'Stop the car.'

'Sir?'

'I said, *stop the car*.'

The second it pulled over to the side he was yanking open the door and practically flinging himself out. Leaving Cassidy with no choice but to scramble, as carefully as she could in her expensive dress, across the soft leather seats until she could swing her legs out and join him—where he was pacing up and down.

He shot her a dark glare as he ran the fingers of one hand through his hair, the jacket of his tuxedo flapping with his movements. 'Get back in the limo. I need a minute.'

'No.' She folded her arms across her breasts, trying to stop herself shaking. 'You're going to talk to me.'

'*No*. I'm going to take a minute, and then we're going to the theatre, or we'll be late.'

'You can go to the theatre if you want. I'm going home.' She lifted her chin another defensive notch as she inadvertently called his house 'home'. 'I'm not going to humiliate myself any further if I'm not dressed appropriately.'

It was a ridiculous claim. Even Cassidy knew that. If Angelique Warden and her team didn't know what they were doing then no one did—and Will knew that too, if his violent expletive was anything to go by.

'It's got nothing to do with how you're dressed!'

'Then what *is it*?' She took a step closer. 'I can't read your mind the way you read mine, Will. I never could. So you'll need to explain this to me.'

'You won't get it. You haven't been here long enough.'

'*Try*!'

Dropping his arms to his sides, he stopped pacing and stood in front of her, studying her for the longest time before he pressed his mouth into a thin line and she got a low, rumbled, 'You look incredibly beautiful, Cass. You know that. And if you didn't you'd sure as hell have known it from the way people were looking at you in the hotel. You're not stupid.'

It was the most back-handed compliment anyone had ever paid her. 'Well, if it's not the way I look, and it's not the way I'm dressed—'

'You didn't *need* highlights in your hair.' He clenched his jaw and continued staring into her eyes. 'Or to be draped in expensive jewels. Don't you *get* that?'

'What?'

Sighing heavily, Will started pacing again, his voice somewhat calmer than before. 'Obviously you don't…but then why would you? There are millions of people in this city who don't.'

After he'd made three more trips past her Cassidy had had enough; unfolding her arms, she reached out a hand to grasp his elbow and stop him in his tracks. When he looked at her she summoned a small smile of encouragement. 'Get *what*? You're not making any sense.'

He shook his head, his voice softer. 'Forget it.'

When he tried to remove her hand, she turned it and tangled her fingers with his, stepping closer. 'No. Talk to me.'

His words were the very last thing she'd expected to hear. 'You're beautiful without any help. You always were.'

'What?'

'Hollywood has no idea of what beauty is. It has nothing to do with highlights and expensive jewels. Those people who helped transform you were trying to put you into a box you'd never fit.' When she tried to free her hand he tightened his fingers around hers. 'You're unique—as individual as that giant walnut of a diamond hanging around your neck—and there was a time you knew that. If you were trying to remember by allowing those people to turn you into something you're not, then you're going about it the wrong way…'

Cassidy took a shaky breath and avoided the intensity of his gaze as she fought to control the emotions welling up inside her. When she'd blinked enough times to clear her vision, swallowed to loosen her vocal cords, and dampened her lips in preparation, she made another attempt at freeing her hand and was amazed when he set it free.

Then she looked at him. 'You're right. Partly. But I didn't let them make me over to fit into a stereotype, Will. I did it for me.' When her lower lip shook she bit down on it and lifted her shoulders towards her ears. 'I needed this. More than I can possibly make you understand. Because somewhere along the way I *did* forget who I am—and the kind of woman I always wanted to be. But when I looked in that mirror less than an hour ago…'

She had to stop and look away when emotion overwhelmed her again.

'Keep going…'

Shooting a brief frown his way, for the impossibly gentle tone of his deep voice, she took another shaky breath. 'I was proud of what I saw, Will. The woman in that mirror looked like she could do anything she wanted to do—be anyone she wanted to be. I know you probably think that's silly—'

'I don't think it's silly. I think it's sad you didn't know that already.' He waited until she looked at him before asking roughly, 'Did I do that to you, Cass?'

'No.' She smiled a wobbly smile as his face blurred behind tears she didn't want to shed. 'I let it happen to me. That's why I'm the only person who can fix it.'

'Did this fix it?'

'A lot of things are fixing it. Writing again—pitching successfully.' She laughed throatily. 'Debating back and forth with you even helped. I started to remember what it felt like to be *me* again. And I haven't felt that way in a very long time. Then today…looking in that mirror showed me another one of a hundred possibilities. It's why when I leave here I'll leave stronger than I was when I arrived. It's partly why I changed my mind about tonight too—about coming with you, I mean. If I can carry this image off on a red carpet, without falling flat on my face and making a fool of myself the way I have so many times before, then—'

Will reclaimed her hand. 'Come on. We're going to be late.'

'For movie night?'

'Best night of the week, sweetheart.'

Smiling, she let him turn her around and lead her back to the limo. 'Will there be popcorn?'

'If there isn't, I'll find you some. I promise.'

Cassidy had honestly never loved him more than she did in that moment. Not only had he talked to her, he'd listened—and he hadn't psychoanalysed her to death or made her feel foolish; he'd understood. And he'd said just enough to let her know he did.

But then she'd always been a sucker for popcorn too—so long as it was… 'Buttered, not—'

'Not salted.' He smiled one of *those* smiles at her as they got to the open door. 'I remember.'

Standing on her tiptoes, Cassidy placed a light kiss on his cleanshaven cheek, 'Thank you.'

Will looked momentarily confused. 'What for?'

'For the popcorn you're going to get me…'

CHAPTER NINE

IT WAS one of the most memorable nights of her life. Not for the famous foot and handprints outside the Chinese Theater. Not because she managed the red carpet without tripping over. Not because there was a group of California Fortune Hunters in the crowd to support Will's new film, who went crazy when he introduced her to them and demanded photographs and autographs that made her feel like one of the movie stars she was sharing the carpet with. And not just because Will found popcorn, handed her a handkerchief when she needed it at the end of the movie, or stayed by her side watching over her, but allowed her enough independence to stand on her own two feet…

It was no one thing on its own. It was everything.

By the time they were halfway home…no, back to *Will's house*, she mentally corrected herself as she slipped off her shoes and held them in one hand…she felt happier than she had in years.

'Tired?'

Turning her head on the buttery upholstery, she smiled at him. 'I was poked and preened for seven hours—so, yes, I'm tired. But it's a *good* kind of tired.'

'Okay.'

'Your movie was amazing, Will. I loved it.'

Leaning his head back, he turned his face towards her. 'Good.'

Impulsively she lightly punched his upper arm. 'For crying out loud, Ryan. Show a little enthusiasm, would you? The audience loved it too. They all laughed at all the right times, sat on the edge of their seats at the right times... Most of the women in the auditorium were handed a handkerchief at the end...'

'Yeah.' He pursed his lips and nodded firmly. 'You can keep that, by the way.'

'I only blew my nose once. And I did it delicately.' She pouted on purpose.

'The people in the row in front and behind us appreciated that, I'm sure. But the once was one time too many. It's all yours now.'

Now, see—*this* was the Will she'd missed the most. The Will whose eyes sparkled in the dim light; the Will with a loose bow tie and the top button of his shirt undone; the Will whose familiar boyish sexiness was lit up, then gone, then lit up, then gone in the headlights of passing cars...

When he reached for a loose curl and wrapped it around his forefinger Cassidy let her guard down for the first time since she'd arrived. 'Just in case I never get a chance to say it again, I'm proud of you, Will. You made it. You did everything we talked about and more...'

His hand stilled. Then, without answering, he turned his hand over and ran the backs of his fingers over the sensitive skin of her neck, watching the movement with one of his unreadable gazes. When he reached the hollow between her neck and shoulderblade he turned his hand again, tracing the very tips of his fingers towards the edge of her dress.

But when he began tracing that edge downwards... 'What are you doing?' It was a moot question, but she asked it anyway, her low voice thickly threaded with physical awareness.

'You know what I'm doing.' Changing direction, he caught the necklace between his thumb and forefinger and followed it down to the heavy pendant in her cleavage.

The touch of his knuckles against the curve of her breast made her squirm on the seat. 'Will—'

'Schools don't go back for another month.'

The rumble of his voice was seduction itself. But she still knew what he was offering her—even if he was trying a different angle. 'No, they don't. But—'

Cupping the diamond for a moment, he lifted his gaze so she could see the dark pools of his eyes. 'Checking your list of excuses?'

'What list?'

'The one you have to tell you why you can't get involved with me again.' Long fingers flexed away from the diamond and purposefully brushed her skin.

Cassidy felt the impact of it clean to the soles of her feet. 'I don't have a list of excuses.'

'Liar.'

'They're not excuses.'

'Liar.' The hint of a smile she saw on his face filtered through into his voice, and then he moved his fingers again. 'I can feel your heart beating...'

The heart that was causing such an ache in her chest again when he told her, 'Do you know how a lie detector works, Cass? I do. I had to research it for a script one time. It measures a person's breathing rate, their pulse, their blood pressure and perspiration levels. Right now I can read three out of four of those with you. So, while your head may be frantically searching that list for your next excuse, your body tells me something different. But then you never could lie to me, could you?'

No, she couldn't. Not that she'd ever been much of a liar to begin with. But he'd always been able to read her. It was why it had taken so much effort to hold stuff back from him since she'd come to California.

'They're not excuses, Will.' And that wasn't a lie, because they weren't. They were valid reasons. But then she couldn't tell him that either. Because by telling him she would be inviting him to ask what they were.

'Then why is your heart beating so fast?'

Cassidy reached up and closed her fingers around his hand on the pendant, tapping into a little of her newfound confidence as she lifted her chin. 'Stop it.'

When Will angled his head, her breath caught. But he didn't lean in to kiss her—instead he studied her face for the longest time, before coming to a realization. 'You're hiding something from me.'

Her soft laughter sounded nervous even to her own ears. 'Don't be ridiculous. Why would I need to hide something from you?'

He'd already got entirely more information from her than she'd ever planned on giving him. She'd talked about her doubts and fears and insecurities—granted, sometimes he'd guessed some of them, and *then* she'd talked about them, but it was still more than she'd planned. Heck, he'd even got details of how ordinary her life was when compared to his. Though, judging by his earlier reaction to her make-over, Hollywood maybe wasn't his idea of utopia…

'There is something, though.' His deep voice sounded almost hypnotic in the intimacy of the dimly lit limousine.

Working on prising his long fingers away from the pendant proved a mistake on her part, when Will simply released it and captured her hand in his, between her breasts. If he really could feel her heartbeat then he would know it was racing…

Her plea was barely above a whisper. 'Don't ruin tonight for me, Will. *Please.*'

While he weighed it up in his mind his face shadowed. The movement of the limo stopped. When Cass looked through the tinted windows she saw they were home.

She frowned. No, not *home*—they were at *Will's house*. She really needed to stop doing that.

Turning her attention back to the intense man beside her she twisted her wrist and tugged sharply. 'Let me go.'

For a moment she thought she heard the word 'no', but then her door opened and their driver stood back to let her out, leaving Will no choice but to set her hand free. Cassidy bolted for the door on her bare feet—only to sigh with frustration when she got there and remembered who had the key.

As the limo pulled away, briefly catching her in its headlights, she saw Will's dark silhouette approaching. He took his own sweet time about it too. When he got to the door, instead of opening it he leaned on the frame, turned the key over in his long fingers and studied her beneath the lamp. Just long enough to make her squirm inwardly and feel the most basic of instincts that left her torn between fight or flight.

'Open the door, Will.'

Closing his fingers tighter around the key, he asked again, 'What are you hiding from me?'

'It's almost midnight. I'm tired. And I'm not hiding anything. Key, please.' She held out her palm and waggled her fingers for the key.

'Not till you tell me what it is.'

The calm tone to his voice did nothing to stop the frustration building inside her as she took a measured step closer to him. 'Do I have to come and get the key?'

'You could *try*.' His voice dropped an octave, sending a sharp spark of awareness through her body.

'Don't. Make. Me.'

Folding his arms across his chest, he angled his head a minute amount. 'Yeah. That's an empty threat, isn't it? All talk no action. That's your biggest problem, isn't it? You're afraid to step up to the plate.'

'What?'

'You heard me.' He rocked forward and dropped his chin, fighting hard to keep the smile off his face. 'You talk the talk, Malone. Always did. But the truth is you're a Tootsie Pop.'

Her eyes widened. '*Excuse me*?'

Will nodded. 'Yup. So I'll open the door when you tell me what you're hiding.'

Cassidy laughed, but it had an edge to it that weakened the tone she'd been aiming for. 'You—'

'I'm the most annoying man on the planet, you hate me—yada, yada. Yeah, you've said—several times…' His mouth curled into an almost cruel smile. 'What happened to all that talk back there about being the confident woman you always wanted to be? I happen to know a little about confident women, Cass…'

'Yeah, I'll just bet you do.' When he pretended to search the air above her head for an answer she scowled at him.

'Confident women have the guts to reach out for the things they want. They take chances. They lay it on the line. You used to be that woman, Cass…'

Cassidy's scowl became a frown when he looked at her again. 'Hadn't you heard? I'm now a *Tootsie Pop*.' Whatever a Tootsie Pop is…

'Yes. You are. But not a good one. You have to work too hard at it. You see, a Tootsie Pop is a lollipop that's hard on the outside and soft on the inside—'

'Oh, I get the analogy.' Her gaze lowered, looked pointedly from one of his hands to the other as if she was trying to remember which one he had the key in. 'What I don't get is when you decided bullying me again was the best way to get me to open up. Give me the key, Will.'

He waited for her gaze to rise, controlling his smile before he calmly challenged her. 'Come and get it.'

Her jaw dropped and a strangled squeak of outrage sounded low in her throat.

Will pushed away from the doorframe and took a step forward, his voice lowering. 'Or tell me what it is you're hiding from me.'

She worried her lower lip as she avoided his gaze, taking a deep breath as she aimed for a version of the truth that might get her out of trouble. 'I *am* attracted to you, Will.'

'But?'

'That was a confession, in case you missed it. Score one to you.'

'No, I got it. I'm just wondering what it's leading up to. Because there's more, isn't there?'

She scowled at him again. 'Do you *have* to do that?'

'Do what?'

'Play the *I can read you like a book* card?' She lifted a hand and tucked a curl behind her ear. 'It's incredibly ir-ritating. And you don't know me anywhere near as well as you like to think you do. Not any more.'

'You might be surprised.'

'I don't *want* to be surprised. I *want* to be not standing outside your house.'

Unfolding his arms, he lifted his hand to tuck a matching curl behind her other ear. Her soft intake of breath made his fingers still for a second before he dropped his hand back to his side. 'Whatever it is you're hiding, it's getting in the way.'

Somewhere in the red haze clouding her vision Cassidy had a moment of clarity. 'You're *trying* to pick a fight with me.'

'Am I?'

A second clue slipped into her mind. 'Because every-thing else has failed.'

'Everything else?'

'This is what you do, isn't it? You deflect.'

Will clenched his teeth, and she could almost see the anger expand inside his chest. His tone was deathly calm. 'Like you are now?'

How could she have been so blind? Cassidy laughed at her own stupidity. 'You've made this all about *me*, haven't you? What is this? Your way of proving you can have me any time you want?'

'You're walking a very thin line now, Cass.'

'Am I?'

To her astonishment he slid the key into the lock, swung the door open and stepped inside. Walking away from her. *Again*. Well, not this time.

Slamming the door behind her, she raised her voice. 'Giving up so easy, Will?'

'Leave it be, Malone. I mean it.'

But she couldn't. She followed him down the hall, continuing to push. It was his own fault, she told herself. He'd pushed and prodded and tried every trick in his seduction handbook to get to her since she'd arrived. He couldn't even be content with the fact she still wanted him—oh, no, he had to push some more. While offering her some quick affair. To do what? Get it out of their systems?

Didn't he know it would cheapen everything they'd had before?

'But then walking away is what you do best, isn't it?'

'If I were you I'd quit now.' The deathly calm tone of his voice told her just how angry he was. And when Will was really angry, he placed it behind an impenetrable wall.

So Cassidy did what she'd always done. She pushed. 'Or what? You'll leave? A tad unlikely, seeing this is your house.'

He turned on his heel so fast she didn't have time to react. The next thing she knew he was striding back towards her, his eyes glinting dangerously as he finally lost control. 'You sent me away!'

'You didn't look back!'

There was sudden silence, both of them breathing hard, the combination of anger and pain palpable in the air between them. Then their mouths were fused together, lips slamming back against their teeth, forcing them to open up and tangle in a battle to take the upper hand. Cassidy didn't know who kissed who first, and she was still so angry she could see red behind her eyelids, but it didn't stop her from throwing her arms around his neck at the same time as he hauled her into his arms and crushed her to him. It wasn't soft or gentle or cautious or exploratory, because passion didn't know any of those things. All it knew was blinding need and desperate wanting and hungry desire and—

With a high-pitched moan of frustration she dragged her mouth from his and shifted her arms to push her palms against his wide chest. He let go. She stepped back. And slapped him.

She'd never slapped anyone before. As he flinched, and her palm stung, her eyes widened with the horror of it. She was opening her mouth to apologise profusely when Will's expression darkened, his mouth twisting wryly.

'*Finally*. Now we're actually getting somewhere.'

Cassidy cocked her head. '*Oh?* Getting me to slap you was part of your great plan too, was it?'

'I didn't *have* a plan! But if slapping me is what it takes for you to let out whatever it is you've been holding back, then *bring it on!*'

Everything in her rebelled against the idea of slapping him again; it had never been an option for her. Instead she grabbed two fistfuls of his tuxedo lapels and hauled him back again, picking up where they'd left off—only this time with duelling tongues. Will turned them, pushed her against the wall. She let go of his tuxedo and started undoing the buttons of his white shirt, reaching for heated skin.

'Slow down…' The words were muffled against her

mouth, and then he groaned and tried again, using his hands to set her back a little. 'Cass. *Wait.*'

Frowning in frustration as he lifted his head, she dropped her chin to focus on freeing the buttons faster while she demanded, '*Why?* This is what you wanted, isn't it?'

'*No.*' Frustration equal to her own sounded in the rumble of his rough voice as one hand landed on hers to still them. 'Not like this.'

'But this is what we do best.' She raised her chin and sought out his mouth again.

He ducked out of the way. 'What is *that* supposed to mean?'

'You said it. It's the one area we never had any problems.' She tugged on her hands in an attempt to free them, while pushing closer into his chest. 'I agree. You win. Congratulations.'

Will looked so stunned it was almost funny. Then he shook his head and his frown returned, impossibly darker than before. 'I *win*?'

'You wanted an affair. We'll have an affair.' She sought his mouth again.

He took a step back and placed her at arm's length; literally. 'I wanted *what*?'

'An affair! That's what all this is about, isn't it?' She frowned back up at him. 'Call it whatever you want to call it. It's purely physical. Nothing more. And, yes—I do remember what we were like together—so, yes—I do know how good it will be. We're both adults, right? And pretty soon I'll be gone again. So—hey—why not take advantage of it while I'm here?'

'You think that's what this is about?' Shaking his head, he

stared at her with a look of incredulity. 'At what point did you *ever* hear me suggest we had some kind of affair? It's *purely physical*? Are you even *listening* to what you're saying?'

When he let go of her and took a step back Cassidy frowned all the harder; the beginning of a major headache was forming at her temples. 'You know I have to go home—what else can it be?'

'I just asked you to stay in the limo—or did you miss that part?'

'You didn't ask me, Will.' She racked her brain to remember it clearly—just in case she'd misinterpreted it. But she hadn't. 'You don't ask. *You tell.*'

'We're having this whole argument because of semantics?'

Cassidy was rapidly losing the plot with him. Her voice was threaded with what almost sounded like hysteria. 'You've done nothing but bully me since I got here! At what point has *any* of this ever been my decision? A contract I signed almost a decade ago brought me here. A script we had to produce has kept me here. Not once—*not once* during the whole time, Will—have I been allowed to so much as choose what time I want to eat! Today was the first time I did something on my own—and look how well *that* went down with you.'

During her tirade she'd looked anywhere but directly at his face, swinging her arms at random points in the air while she fought the need to cry again as she let it all out. When her words were met with silence, she finally looked at him. What she saw stunned her. He looked as if she'd just completely knocked the wind out of him.

Even his voice was flatter than it had ever been before. 'Well. There it is. That'll be what you were hiding from me.'

No. It wasn't what she was hiding from him, darn it! How could he be so incredibly dense?

Taking a short breath, he nodded. 'You should have said something. I could have bought you out of the contract and then you would never have had to go through all that torture, would you?'

Oh, come *on*! What did she have to say to make him understand? It wasn't that it had been torture—well, not all of it. There had been times, yes, but it was the constant battle of trying to resist falling for him again that had been the real problem. Especially when he'd been so very hard to resist! And in actuality it had been a moot point, because—

Wait a minute. *He could have what?*

Pushing his hands into the pockets of his dress trousers, Will looked her in the eyes and told her, 'You're not a prisoner here, Cass. If you didn't want to make the trip you'd only to say so. One line in an e-mail would have done it, and you would never have had to see me again. If you don't want to see the script through to the end then fine; any minor rewrites from here on in shouldn't be that big a deal.'

He'd shut himself off again. The realisation made her throat close over. She didn't want them to end like this. She hadn't wanted them to end the way they had last time either.

'*Will*—' She stepped towards him.

But he stepped out of her reach, the small increase in distance as agonising to her as it had been to watch him walk away from her before. 'You can leave whenever you want. You always could.'

When he walked towards the door Cassidy followed him. 'Where are you going?'

'Out.'

'It's after midnight.'

'New York isn't the only city that never sleeps.' He yanked the door open, then stopped and looked over his shoulder. 'Let me know your flight times and I'll make sure you get to the airport.'

'Don't do this. Not again.'

The low plea was enough to get him to turn round, one hand holding onto the door as he looked her straight in the eye and told her, 'That's just it, Cass. I didn't do it last time either. You've made more choices along the way than you give yourself credit for.'

CHAPTER TEN

WILL had never considered himself a complicated man. He knew what he wanted and how to get it. He had worked long and hard to get where he was, and he had the life he'd always dreamed of—more or less. But then he'd never viewed Hollywood with the same rose-tinted glasses Cass had. She'd been the first person in his life outside of a movie screen to make him believe in magic.

When he'd first met her he'd found it amusing, her Tinkerbell-like enthusiasm for all things cinematic. But over time she'd smoothed off his rough edges and made him believe in things he never would have without her. He'd needed her more than she'd probably ever realised. Having her push him away had been the hardest thing he'd ever had to deal with. So what had possessed him to think it would be okay this time…?

Thing was, she'd only had to be back in his life for a matter of days and he'd known. He'd known he *still* needed her.

Taking a deep breath, he glanced upwards at the cloudless sky. What was he doing? He'd spent the night on an uncomfortable sofa in his office when he had a perfectly good bed at home. *Home.* When was the last time he'd thought of somewhere that way? It was the answer to that question that had brought him looking for her.

But when he found her bags packed in her room he felt his anger rising. *Not this time*. She thought he'd never looked back? Well, she was wrong about that. And he wasn't spending the *next* eight years of his life looking back. This time they were getting it out in the open—whether she liked it or not.

The fact he couldn't find her anywhere in the house or see her on the beach turned his determination to panic. Then he thought of the night before and searched his jacket pocket for his cellphone,

'Angie? Will. Is Cass with you?'

'No. I had my PA pick up the dress and jewellery. Is something wrong?'

Will turned a circle in the living room and tried to think of where she might have gone. 'So you didn't speak to her?'

'No.' There was a brief pause, then, 'You had a fight, didn't you? I swear, Will, if you break that girl's heart—'

What was it with the universe suddenly deciding he was the bad guy? It made Will sigh heavily. 'How long have you known me now, Angie?'

'Five years. Why?'

'I'm the guy you're constantly accusing of never getting involved—remember?'

Another spell of silence, then Angie said, 'Never got over her, did you?'

'Let me know if she calls you.'

With her promise made, he considered going back upstairs to search her bags for her passport. But he wasn't going to go through her things. She wouldn't have flown home without them. So she had to be somewhere. He searched for a note—which was dumb. Because after their angry words why in hell would she leave him a note? It would be nice to think she would have if she'd got on a plane. But hadn't he said to let him know? He was pretty sure he had…

For a man who made his living from words, he apparently had a very poor grasp of them in real life. *Just physical*! Where had she got *that* from? He was going to ask her that. He was going to ask her a lot of things.

After pacing up and down for ten minutes he decided to try the beach again, tossing his jacket over the back of one of the sofas and rolling up the sleeves of the only shirt he'd had as a spare in his office as he slid the glass doors shut behind him and jogged down the wooden stairs onto the sand. Which way? If he was Cass, would he have gone left or right?

He shook his head—yeah, it had always been so easy to get inside that head of hers. If it wasn't for the fact she couldn't lie he would have spent half his life asking dumb questions like *What are you thinking?* But then he'd never had to do that back in the day, because she'd always been so open—something completely alien and fascinating to him at the same time. Discovering she'd got so guarded over the years had been quite a shock to his system.

Looking skywards again, he vowed if he had to fly halfway across the planet to talk to her then so be it. And then he lowered his chin and forgot to breathe. It couldn't be. For a split second he thought he was imagining what he was seeing. He told himself he wanted her to be there so badly that his heart must have somehow convinced his brain to tell his eyes she was there. But would his imagination have conjured up an image of her looking so sad? It never had before. Would he have seen her slumped shoulders or the slight hint of red to her nose that suggested she'd been in the sun for too long? Any time he'd ever pictured her it had been smiling and laughing, the way she had that day on the O'Connell Street Bridge in Dublin, when he'd *had* to kiss her. Not just needed to or wanted to but *had to*.

'*Cass…*' He said her name at the same time as she lifted her chin and saw him. If he'd conjured up the image of her then he didn't care; his feet were already carrying him to her, his voice as calm as he could manage to keep it. 'You're still here.'

Oh, yeah—that's great, Ryan. Let the woman think you want her to go.

He tried again. 'I saw your bags.'

She couldn't look him in the eye. Her shoulders lifted in a brief shrug as she took a shaky breath. 'I don't even know your address to call a cab. How pathetic is that?'

It wasn't pathetic. It was another example of what an inconsiderate oaf he was. Because she was right. He had been pretty controlling of their environment of late. He just hadn't realised it. 'Twenty-one-eighteen Shoreview.'

When she looked sideways at him he frowned. He was still giving her the impression he wanted her to leave, wasn't he?

'I said to call me and I'd make sure you got to the airport.' *Still* giving her the impression he wanted her to leave. He was a genius. He could do better than this. 'Do you want to go home?'

There. That was better. Now he was letting her make her own decision. Then he rethought that, and added a shrug. 'You could stay…'

'It's tempting.' She smiled out at the ocean. 'I've been out here walking for the last hour. It's beautiful. I can understand why you live here.'

Will glanced over at the house that had felt more like a home in the last month than it ever had before, then took a step closer to her and pushed his hands into his pockets so they wouldn't be tempted to reach for her. 'I knew the first time I saw it that it was somewhere you would love. You always had a thing for the sea…'

Long lashes flickered as her gaze travelled up to meet his, silent questions written across the chestnut depths of her eyes. She had amazing eyes: fathomless, soulful, bright with intelligence. They were especially amazing when she was laughing, or trying to hold laughter back. Will remembered how amazing they had looked the first time she'd told him she loved him.

Then she dropped her chin and hid her eyes from him. 'I've been thinking about some of the things you said last night.'

'Yeah. I've been doing some thinking too.' When her lashes lifted he tried a small smile on for size. 'We said a lot.'

She nodded. 'We did.'

'I never meant to make you feel trapped here. I genuinely did think it would make it easier to work on the script. And as for the food thing—you never eat when you're working; it was always me who had to remind you to take a break and eat something. I guess I fell back into old habits.'

Her finely arched brows rose. 'I never thought of it that way. You're right. That *is* the way we used to be when we were working. I still have erratic mealtimes, and I eat way too much junk. I've probably eaten healthier here than I have in years.'

Okay. This was good. So he took another step forward—then faltered when she frowned a little and looked away. Too much?

When she sighed he tried not to look down at the rise and fall of her breasts. He'd never been able to look at her without wanting her. How hadn't she *known* how beautiful she was? He would never understand that. Any more than he would forgive Angie for changing the hair he'd always loved so much. It had been bad enough seeing so much of it cut off since the last time he saw her. When he'd known her before it had been halfway down her back, and sometimes when she was lying on top of him they would kiss surrounded by a cocoon of flower-scented hair. Will wondered how long highlights lasted. Not that there was anything wrong with them *per se*, it was just that he preferred her hair the rich auburn of before. Then he thought about how she might take it if he told her how to have her hair… Okay…might not help him stay out of trouble.

'I guess the fact I'm still here shows how much braver you are than me…'

What? He frowned at her profile. What did *that* mean?

Before he could ask she elaborated. 'I always wondered how you did it. Walked away like that without looking back. I tried to do it this morning, but even if I had known the address to call for a cab I don't know that I could have. Not without clearing the air first.'

It was a 'give with one hand, take away with the other' situation. On the one hand she'd just told him she hadn't been able to leave without seeing him—which made his heart swell in his chest. But on the other she'd basically told him she still blamed him for their break-up, because *he* left. He was pretty sure that was what she meant—in a roundabout way, with a backhanded compliment about him being brave.

Will had something to say about that. 'I don't know what you remember about that day. But if you look back maybe you'll think about everything that went before it. No matter what I tried, you kept pushing me away. You—'

'I know. You're right. I *did* send you away.'

He wasn't expecting that one. It brought him forward another step. A step immediately counteracted by Cass, when she stiffened, turned, and waited for him to accept the silent invitation to walk and talk. So he did.

Waves fizzed against the hot sand, dragging back out to sea to be replaced by the next as Cass pushed her hands into the pockets of her light trousers and watched her bare feet as they walked side by side.

'I always knew one day I would have to take on the care of my parents. That's what happens when people wait till later in life to have a child. And my dad was never the same after Mum died. I just never knew that he would end up sick at the very time we had big decisions to make about *our* lives…'

Will walked silently at her side and let her talk it through. The fact they had time to do it was enough for him. She was still there. That was what mattered most.

Cass took a deep breath and lifted her gaze from her feet to stare down the endless beach. 'We shared the dream of coming out here and being a success. We came at it from different angles, but we knew that. I guess the movie knocked some of the wind out of my sails, but not you. You wouldn't give up. Braver than me.' She smiled briefly at him. 'Like I said.'

'We were supposed to do all this together.'

'I know.' The smile wavered and he saw her look skywards. 'I guess a part of me always took some small comfort from the fact one of us made it. I'm proud of you.'

She had no idea what it meant to hear her say she was proud of him. He wouldn't have cared had it been anyone else. From Cass it meant everything. She was the proud parent, the teacher who'd made a difference, the foster parents who'd got it right with him in his last home, and the first woman who had ever made him feel love all wrapped into one when she said those four simple words. With those words the last remnants of the boy who had never thought he would amount to anything had been laid to rest.

Will swallowed hard and battled with the need to hold her. He had to. But he couldn't. Not yet.

'In the end I had to choose between two people I loved.' She took a shaky breath, 'I knew you would make it without me, Will. I think a part of me always knew that. My dad needed me.'

'*I* needed you.' He'd always thought she'd understood that.

The next shaky breath she took caught on a sob. 'When I sent you away that last time I never thought you would go. I didn't want you to. But I couldn't make that decision for you either. It wouldn't have been fair.'

Just like always, her hurt became *his* hurt, making him frown hard at her profile as a lone tear streaked down her cheek and she rubbed it away. 'You made the decision for me. I would never have left if you hadn't.'

She smiled sadly. 'Maybe I knew that. Everything was

so mixed up. It hurt so badly—every time I look back on that time all I can see is hurt. Maybe it was easier to hate you for leaving than it was to face up to my part in it. I just…I never thought…'

When she stopped, placed her hands on her hips and dropped her head back to take several ragged breaths, Will took his hands out of his pockets in preparation.

'See.' It was half-sob, half self-recriminating laughter. 'This is exactly why I've avoided talking about this for so long. It *still* hurts.'

Will could barely breathe. His chest was too tight. He even had to clear his throat before he could speak. 'What was it you never thought, Cass?'

Sniffing, then swiping at her cheeks, she finally looked him in the eye. And smiled a smile that broke him in two. 'I never thought you would do it. And I've spent all morning trying to figure out if in some twisted way it was a test that I set up for you to fail. But I don't think it was. At least I hope it wasn't. I just never—even when I was sending you away and the words were coming out of my stupid mouth—I never for one second thought you wouldn't so much as look back. Or come back. I don't know what it was I expected you to do. All I know is I waited. I waited for a very long time. Maybe a part of me never stopped waiting. Then, when the e-mail came…'

Tears were streaming down her face as she got to the end and she let them flow, not trying to wipe them away or hide them. Will knew a babbling Cass was a nervous Cass—it was one of the quirks he'd always found the most endearing. But she wasn't babbling this time. She was clear and lucid between catches of breath and the odd break of her voice. So it wasn't babbling. It was her finally telling the secret she'd been hiding from him. All of them.

'I was so very in love with you. I don't even think I knew how much. Not until you were gone. Then it was too late.' She lifted her shoulders again, her voice smaller than before. 'Because you never looked back.'

Will tried to form a coherent sentence in his head before speaking. There was less chance of messing it up that way. He opened his mouth…

'No.' She held up a hand in front of her body. 'Don't say anything. That's not why I'm telling you all this. I'm telling you because we never had closure last time. And I can't do that to either one of us again.'

When he stayed silent she smiled in appreciation and nodded her head, wiping her cheeks dry before dropping her arm to her side and looking back out to sea again. 'I can't stay here and have an affair with you, Will. What we had before means too much to me to taint it with something less. So everything I said and did last night with regard to the whole physical thing— If you could try and forget about it, that would be great.'

'Can I speak now?'

Her gaze shifted to tangle with his, the first hint of amusement sparkling in her expressive eyes. 'You're asking for permission?'

Will pointed out the obvious. 'The "don't say anything" instruction you gave me might have something to do with that. So is it my turn to speak now?'

'Is there going to be sympathy in there anywhere. Because I'm not sure I could take it.'

It was her ability to exasperate, fascinate, amuse and

completely distract him from rational thought in equal measures that had first attracted Will to Cass, so he fell back into habits of old as his way of dealing with it. Reaching for her shoulder, he turned her round to face him, ignoring the fact the sea was washing over his shoes.

'Shut up, Cass. And listen. It's my turn.' When she cocked a brow at him he smiled at her. 'I tried being polite about it, but you took too long giving me permission to speak. All you did was remind me why I never ask for it…'

When he was sure he had her undivided attention, he let go of her shoulders and pushed his hands back into his pockets, frowning a little when her gaze dropped to watch the movement and she looked as if she might be figuring out why he did it.

'This whole I never looked back thing? It's rubbish.'

It brought her gaze back up to find his at speed. 'What?'

'You heard me. I've never stopped looking back. If you hadn't sent me away the way you did I would never have left. Or at the very least I'd have gone ahead of you and waited. All you had to do was say the word. I'd spent my whole life being sent away by people. You knew that. You were the very last person I expected to do it to me—technically I maybe should have been able to deal with it better after so much practice…'

The look on her face floored him.

'But, no, I didn't deal with it better. I don't think I've ever dealt with it.' He lifted his brows in question. 'Do you want to hazard a guess why that might have been?'

Her lower lip trembled. 'Because you loved me the way I loved you.'

Will nodded, his voice soft. 'Because I loved you more than I'd ever loved anyone. I didn't even know what love was until you.'

When more tears slipped free, his hands immediately came out of his pockets to frame her face and brush them away with his thumbs. 'Don't do that. I hate it when you do that. I loved you, Cass—I did. So you tell me how I could feel that much and never look back. No one could. There were dozens of times I tore it apart in my head to see what I could have done differently, but the simple fact was it was already done.'

'I know,' she sobbed.

Stepping in closer, he lowered his head at the same time as he used his thumbs to lift her chin. Then, when he was looking deep into her eyes, he took a deep breath. 'I knew when I sent you that first e-mail there was a chance we'd end up here again.'

'I felt the same way when I opened it.' She smiled tremulously.

'We're different people.'

'We are.'

'But we're the same too—if that makes sense…'

Cass nodded. 'It does.'

'It was when you hid under the pillow,' he told her.

It took a minute. Confusion clouded the bright light in her beautiful eyes until she got it. 'When I had the cold and you wouldn't go away?'

'Yes.' His thumbs brushed across her cheeks as he smiled. 'That's when I knew I was in trouble again.'

'It was?'

'Mmm-hmm. Then I tried every trick in the book to get

you to stop trying to hide from me. Have I ever mentioned you can be really hard work?'

She laughed, and the sound was musical and lighter than before. 'It's okay. I'm well aware of that fact, thank you.'

There was more to say, but it was no good. He had to kiss her. Using his thumbs, he tilted her head back a little more while he closed the last inch between their bodies. Then he searched her eyes, hesitating for a brief moment until she silently willed him not to stop. When he lowered his head she met him halfway. Her felt her hands gripping handfuls of his loose shirt at either side of his waist as his lips moved over hers. There was no doubt about it. This part was right. No arguing with chemistry.

Threading the fingers of one hand into her glorious windswept hair, he moved his other hand from her face, traced down her throat, over her shoulder, and then down her back so he could wrap an arm around her waist to draw her closer. Cassidy moved her hands and wrapped her arms around him to bring him closer still. And even the fact that the curves of her body seemed to fit perfectly into the dips and plains of his had always felt right to Will. Another sign that she was made to be there…

He lifted his head enough to mumble, 'Are you going to slap me again?'

She pulled back a little more and grimaced. 'I'm so sorry I did that.'

'And I shouldn't have lost my temper.'

It made her smile. 'Forget about it. I lose mine every…what?'

Will lifted a brow, his mouth twitching. 'Actually, you've improved with age. It used to be every three, four minutes…'

'Funny guy.'

He wasn't kidding. Chemistry like theirs combined with artistic temperaments and stubborn streaks? Oh, there had been fireworks, all right. But whoever it was who said not to play with fire had sure as hell never had as much fun with it as Will had.

'Now. About this supposed affair I suggested.' It took considerable effort not to chuckle when she grimaced again. 'Are we chalking that one down to the problem you have with over-thinking and letting it drop?'

Cass nodded enthusiastically. 'Please, yes.'

'Good—because that's not what I've been aiming for at all.' He flexed his fingers in her hair, cradling the back of her head and watching the reaction in her eyes. 'I was determined to take it slow with you this time—but to hell with it. I want you to stay. You had me with the pillow, Cass, but you knocked me on my ear last night with that dress. Do you have any idea how many guys were on my hit list before we even left the Beverly Wilshire last night? I'd have taken them on—you know that about me.'

In a heartbeat the Cass he'd fallen in love with a decade before was back, her smile lighting her up from inside. Right there, under unforgiving California sunshine, with her wind-blown hair and barely any make-up, and a slight sunburn on her nose and her lips swollen from his kisses, she had never, *ever* looked more beautiful to him. There wasn't a woman on the planet who was a patch on her, as far as he was concerned.

She lightly smacked his back. 'Now you know how it felt to find you with your complimentary female in the dried goods section of the supermarket.'

'You *were* jealous.' He grinned like a fool. 'I hoped you were.'

'No dastardly plans, huh?'

'Nope. I just want you to stay. I love you, Cass. I loved you before and I love you again. Maybe I never stopped.'

Sliding one arm free, she almost tentatively touched the very tips of her fingers to his cheek. He felt the slight tremor of her touch. The uncertainty was so at odds with the confident woman he knew she had in her that it felt as if she'd wrapped those same fingers around his heart and held it in the palm of her hand.

For most of his life he'd felt as if there was something missing in his life—he'd struggled and fought to find it, piece by tiny piece, each part of the puzzle hard-won but never quite enough to fill the void. For a long time he'd feared he was destined to live his life alone. But, despite how far he'd come and how much he'd learned along the way, he realised there and then that he'd never once felt whole the way he did when he held Cass in his arms.

Her eyes warmed to a darker shade of chestnut, and her voice was sure and even. 'I love you too. I never stopped. So, yes, I want to stay. I'm still here, aren't I?'

Will kissed her fiercely, with all the emotion he'd been holding so carefully in check, and then he held her tight and took a shuddering breath.

'You scared me last night.' He exhaled the rough words into her hair, and felt his heart kick against his ribs when she made a sound that was half-laughter, half-sob against his neck. 'I thought we'd got it wrong again.'

'Me too.'

He kept hold of her and closed his eyes as relief

washed over him. 'We'll get it right this time, Cass. I promise.'

The husky words brought her out of hiding, her head lifting so that when he looked at her he could see deep into her eyes. 'We'll get it right because we'll talk like we're talking now. We don't have to try and hide anything from each other any more. And this is worth fighting for—right?'

'Now who's the bossy one?'

'Right?'

'*Right.*' Will took a step back in water that was up to his ankles, setting her back a little before bending over and scooping her up off the ground. 'Now, we have eight years of making up to do.'

'*In one weekend?*'

'I was thinking more in terms of the rest of our lives…'

THE WIFE HE'S BEEN
WAITING FOR

BY
DIANNE DRAKE

Now that her children have left home, **Dianne Drake** is finally finding the time to do some of the things she adores—gardening, cooking, reading, shopping for antiques. Her absolute passion in life, however, is adopting abandoned and abused animals. Right now Dianne and her husband Joel have a little menagerie of three dogs and two cats, but that's always subject to change. A former symphony orchestra member, Dianne now attends the symphony as a spectator several times a month and, when time permits, takes in an occasional football, basketball or hockey game.

With all my heart I dedicate this book to Jason, and all
the brave ones in the battlefield, wherever it may be.

CHAPTER ONE

THE sound of laughter wafted though the walls of Sarah's cabin. People in the hallways were anxious to get underway, were planning the holiday of their lives, with expectations of fun and adventure on this cruise. Not only expectations, but so many dreams were invested in a few simple days. They would eat all the marvelous foods fixed by the gourmet chefs on board. See new sights they'd only seen in picture books. Make new friends. Visit the various ports and come away with gifts and mementoes of the wonderful time they'd had on this cruise—things they wouldn't think of buying back home—like hideously large straw hats and brightly colored plastic gecko lizards. Memories to last a lifetime.

But for Dr Sarah Collins, none of that was going to happen. Staring out the porthole, she sighed the same sad sigh she'd been sighing for months now. It never changed, no matter where she went or what she did. It simply never changed.

Continuing with the task of tucking her clothes into the closet and tiny bureau, she wondered about taking part in some of the shipboard activities, then immediately wiped that out of her mind. Sure, it was a holiday, just like the last one had been and the one before that. Thanks to a conservative lifestyle while she had been a practicing doctor, and a lucrative sale of her part of the medical practice after she'd decided not to practice medicine any longer, her life had been a succession of holidays this past year, skipping, without thought or too much planning, from one to another, like she hadn't a care in the world.

Quite the contrary was true, though. That's all she had— cares, memories, sadness. Which was why her life had turned into a series of events requiring no commitment. What better way to avoid reality than by going on holiday? Over and over again.

This was her first cruise, though, and she wasn't sure why she'd chosen it. It was so…populated. Hundreds and hundreds of people. Planned activities. Normally, she stuck to herself. A self-guided foot tour of Paris was perfect as no one paid any attention to a single woman passing her days wandering the streets, tourist sights, museums, and her nights tucked into a cabaret corner, spending all evening nursing one or two glasses of wine, listening to the cabaret singer spill out her own version of the blues. In those moments she felt a connection to the singer, understanding how life had a way of slapping you down the way the singer was depicting in her words. But all too soon the night and the music would end and Sarah was on to the next day, next destination. A rental car to see the castles of Scotland, where no one took a second look at a solitary tourist passing though. A hike through the Canadian Rockies and bicycling up the coast of Nova Scotia. Both very nice, and quite solitary.

Then this. To be honest, she couldn't explain what had gotten into her, booking a cruise. Two weeks long at that. Maybe it was the boredom factor finally creeping in, or her lack of companionship these last months. Normally she was a very social person, loved being around other people. Maybe that's what was getting to her—the isolation. Or maybe she'd just run out of ideas and this had seemed easy.

Whatever the case, she was here, in a tiny little cabin with sparse amenities, not sure about her decision. For her to find all the amenities a cruise offered, she'd have to leave her cabin and mingle with the other passengers, and while that did seem appealing, it was also more frightening than anything she'd taken on in the past year.

Just thinking about what she was about to embark on caused Sarah's hands to shake, made her break out in a cold sweat.

Damn, it was happening again.

The walls were closing in on her. The ceiling inching down. Room spinning.

Deep breath, Sarah. You know what it is.

Gripping the edge of the bureau, she hung on praying for the feeling to pass. This had been a stupid, crazy idea! Even entertaining the notion that she could endure two weeks on a ship was totally insane. Yet here she was, getting ready to set sail, and having another panic attack over it.

Breathe, Sarah. One more deep breath and you'll be fine.

Two weeks of this, either cooped up and alone or mixing with so many people that even the thought of it nauseated her.

Another breath. You can do this.

It hit her all of a sudden. Once they set sail she couldn't get off. Bad thought. Wrong thought. Her pulse was racing now, her breaths so shallow her lips were tingling.

"Got to get off." The urge to run was hitting her so hard and violently it nearly choked the breath out of her. She had to get off. Now! Couldn't wait. Forget the clothes, they were only clothes. They could be replaced.

Sarah bolted for the door, fumbled the latch with shaking hands, then finally threw it open, looked first to the left, then to the right to get her bearings. Elevator…to the right, she thought. She had to get there. There was still time. Had to be enough time. She hadn't heard the all-ashore warning, had she?

Running hard, zigging and zagging in and out of the other passengers on their way to locate cabins, she did make it to the elevator and managed to squeeze in just as the doors were about to shut. "Excuse me," she gasped, wedging her way between a buxom older lady smelling of gardenias and wearing a large purple hat that took up enough space for two people and a hard body in a white uniform she didn't care to investigate. "Could I just have a little more room?"

Too many people crammed in, too many different cloying perfumes, too many voices… "More room, please," she begged again, just as the elevator started to spin. Not literally. She knew that. It was her head spinning. Damn, she'd meant to eat something this morning…last night.

Stupid! She was a doctor. She knew better. But she recognized a good case of low blood sugar when she felt it, and she felt it. *As soon as I get off the ship*, she promised herself. She'd go and find the closest little café to the dock and have herself a decent meal. Except the claustrophobia left over from her panic attack combined with the wooziness of her hypoglycemia were conspiring to bring her to her knees. As the elevator dinged its way from deck to deck, without anyone getting off, she was glad for the crowded conditions now as there was no way she could make it to her knees.

But her body was trying to make her collapse. Voices getting louder…smells stronger…ringing in her ears. Head spinning…no place to fall except into the immense bosom of the purple hat lady or into the hard body behind her.

In the end, the decision wasn't Sarah's to make. As the elevator jolted to a stop on yet another deck, her head took its last spin and she sank directly into the arms of the hard body, who had the good sense to hold her up until everybody was off the elevator. Then he scooped her up into his arms and carried her out.

She was vaguely aware of him, vaguely aware that she was babbling something incoherent. She knew that she wanted to get off the ship and go someplace where she could be alone again. But all the vagueness lasted mere seconds, then nothing. Sarah had passed out in the arms of a stranger.

"Everybody, out at the next stop," Dr Michael Sloan ordered, as the dark-haired woman slumped against his chest. She wasn't unconscious yet, but he'd bet his medical license that would be the next thing to happen.

He'd noticed her when she'd got on. Pale, nervous. Panicked look on her face. Or maybe frightened. Whichever it was, she'd squeezed in and the instant the doors had shut he'd noticed her breathing. Shallow, rapid. All indicators of someone who didn't want to be there. Panic attack, maybe. Or someone in some kind of real physical distress. Then she'd gone and slumped into him, right into his arms, like she'd had it planned, and now the only thing he could do was hold onto her until they could get off. Then he'd take a look, see what the problem was.

As the doors parted, the dozen or so people crammed into the elevator started to file out while he kept a tight hold on his new patient. He'd never before had one drop into his arms the way this one had. In fact, he couldn't recall that he'd ever had any woman swoon like this, whether or not she had been sick. Too bad this one was sick, because he liked the way she smelled. Fresh, something fruity, he thought as the last three people left, leaving him enough room to lead her through the doors.

Yes, he definitely liked her scent. It wasn't the heavy, sickly sweet scent of expensive perfume he smelled so often on the ship. Turning in the direction of the doors, he prepared to exit. "Now, somebody, please hold the door open for me."

The woman with the monster purple hat wedged her ample body in the door opening to prevent it from closing as Michael started to assist his patient through the elevator doors, but after two steps her full weight sagged against him and he had no other recourse but to pick her up and carry her out.

"Get off," she mumbled at him. "Want off…now. Have to…off…"

"We are. Right now," he replied. "We're getting off right now."

"Got to go… Can't stay…"

"That's right. We're going to my office," he replied, as she tucked her head against his chest. "I'm the ship's doctor and I think I need to have a little look at you to see what's going on."

"Want to go…please, let me…"

"Don't worry. I'll get you back to your cabin once I've given you an exam," he said, already deciding she might be in the throes of hypoglycemia. That happened a lot. People got excited about the cruise, then forgot to eat. The next thing that happened was their blood sugar whacking out. It wasn't uncommon and usually very easy to fix. "When was the last time you ate something? Do you remember?" She looked particularly frail, he thought, and a good several pounds under her ideal weight. Pretty, though. Add another ten pounds and she'd be voluptuous. For a moment he envisioned her looking vibrant—her face with some color in it to better contrast with the raven black of her hair, her dark brown eyes filled with something other than anguish. The more he studied her, the more he was taken by her beauty.

Then she shifted in his arms, laid her hand on his chest and for an instant he felt a tingle, which immediately snapped his attention back to his professional assessment of her. Without a test, hypoglycemia was still his first call. That's what he had to keep his mind on, that he was carrying a patient to his office, not a beautiful woman to his bed.

Although it had been a long time since he'd had a woman there, no matter how she got there—walking on her own, carried in his arms, or somersaulting.

"Too loud. So many people…" she mumbled, snapping him back once again. "Don't want to—"

"Can you tell me if you have low blood sugar?" he interrupted, his voice rather stiff and husky. "Have you ever been diagnosed with a condition called hypoglycemia?"

Instead of answering, she merely sighed, then snuggled in a little more. And snaked her arm up around his neck, causing another tingle to skitter off the tips of her fingers and run down the full length of his back.

Michael cleared his throat heavily, like that would clear away the tingle. "Have you been diagnosed with…" He tried again, but her other arm went up, and now what should have been a simple hold on a patient looked more like a lover's embrace. But only for a moment, then both her arms went limp and her hold on him vanished.

His patient had fainted again.

Sarah finally opened her eyes, squinting into the overhead exam light, before she twisted her head to the side and opened them fully. Where was she? Why was she here? "What's that?" she asked, spotting the IV stand with its bag hanging next to the bed, not yet realizing that it was anchored into her arm.

"Sugar water," came a voice from the other side of a blue-and-green-striped curtain. "Your blood sugar was low so we're giving you something to bring it back up to normal."

Curtain, hard bed… She glanced around as the surroundings started making sense to her. Medical equipment. Now it was all coming back. Panic attack, hypoglycemic episode. She'd gotten into the elevator. It had been crowded…she did remember that much. The perfume, the large woman with the purple hat. Then she'd keeled over, hadn't she?

An involuntary moan slipped through Sarah's lips as her recall returned in full and she remembered collapsing straight into the hard body's arms. Now here she was in the ship's hospital. As a patient, though. Not as a doctor.

"We did a little test," he continued.

Well, of course he would, she thought, not too surprised by his verdict. This was the hospital and he was a medic of some sort. "How low was it? My blood sugar?"

"Forty-two when I brought you in. Normal values start at eighty, and run all the way up to one-twenty. But you were well under the norm, which was why you passed out."

She knew all that. Her days as a practicing physician might be over, but her medical knowledge was certainly as good as ever. It had been only a little over a year since she'd quit medicine altogether, and yet she still read the journals to keep up, even though she had no intention of returning to practice again. But old habits died hard, and her love of medicine hadn't diminished one bit.

Naturally, she wasn't going to explain all that to the medic. No need to. As far as he was concerned, she was merely another tourist on holiday who'd gone and done something stupid, like forgetting to eat. And, actually, that's what she was, wasn't it? The perpetual tourist? "I don't suppose I've eaten anything for a while," she admitted, almost too embarrassed to say so since she did know better.

"How long ago?" he asked.

He had a nice voice. Soothing. Deep. The kind of voice a patient would trust. "Two or three meals, I think," she stated, although she was pretty sure she'd skipped maybe one more than that. "I was…uh…excited about the cruise. All the arrangements, last-minute details." Such a lie. Over this past year she'd neglected to eat as many meals as she'd eaten. Truth was, she had no appetite. She would eat occasionally, but only enough to sustain her, to keep her blood-sugar levels intact. Except this time she hadn't even done that much, and she was mildly embarrassed for messing up that way. "As soon as the dextro…um, the sugar water is in, can I get off the ship?"

"I'm afraid you were still pretty groggy when the ship set sail half an hour ago. Which means you're on a cruise now."

Michael stepped out from behind the curtain, stopping at the foot of the bed. "And from the looks of things, you could probably use the rest."

Handsome man, she thought. Strikingly so. Tall, a little over six feet, broad shoulders, athletic build. Dark brown hair, with eyes to match. Nice smile. But his eyes were…well, she couldn't tell. They weren't unfriendly, but they didn't sparkle. "Believe me, I've had plenty of rest." That was an understatement. She'd had nothing but rest since she'd quit her medical practice.

"You were trying to get off the ship, weren't you? That's why you were so frantic in the elevator. You weren't going to stay and take the cruise."

"I changed my mind. Decided I didn't want to…" That sounded like a silly explanation, didn't it? She'd spent thousands of dollars to book a two-week cruise, then changed her mind minutes before setting sail. It sounded silly enough that he probably thought her addle-brained.

"It could have been the hypoglycemia talking. The lower your blood sugar gets, the more that can alter your thinking. Once you've rested up, got a good meal in you, and your blood sugar is staying normal and not fluctuating, you'll change your mind and start enjoying all the things we have to offer here."

"Not necessary. I'll be fine, um… I didn't catch your name."

"Sloan," he said. "Michael Sloan." He walked around the bed, extending a hand to her. "In case you're wondering, I'm the one you collapsed onto in the elevator."

She'd already guessed as much. Somehow she had recognized the hard body, even though this was the first time she'd seen his face. An amazing face. "I'm Sarah Collins," she said, taking his hand. Nice, soft. Good touch for a doctor…for anybody. "Like I was saying, it's not necessary for me to stay here and take up your time or your hospital space. I'm fine now. Ready to have the IV out so I can go back to my cabin, since it seems I'm taking a cruise. Or, at least, the first leg of it."

"Well, my hospital space is your hospital space. You're my first patient of the cruise and I think I'd like to hang onto you a little while longer just to show the ship's captain that I'm earning my keep." He chuckled. "And by the time we've reached the first port you might decide that taking a cruise isn't such a bad idea.'

It wasn't such a good idea either. "Well, you weren't the one who started your cruise with such a bang the way I did, were you?" she said, her voice sagging into disappointment. It really didn't make any difference where she was—on a cruise in the Caribbean, on a camel somewhere in Egypt, in a cyclo in Cambodia. It had all been the same lately. One place after another, and she'd hardly noticed any of it. "But thank you for doing the gallant thing and bringing me to the hospital. I suppose if I had to collapse into somebody's arms, it was a good thing I chose a doctor's."

"It was either me or the lady in the purple hat."

He smiled at her and his eyes flickered into a genuinely little sparkle. Not much, but it was there. Nice eyes, she thought. Nice sparkle, too, although very short-lived. Come and gone in an instant. "So what's your best guess on how long I'll be here?" she asked.

"I want to do another blood test in about ten minutes, then we'll see."

"Have you done a blood test since the initial one?" she asked, trying not to sound so clinical. What concerned her was that a reading of forty-two wasn't too far from critical or even near-death in some cases. She recalled a patient at her clinic not all that long ago who'd gone into cardiac arrest at a blood sugar of thirty-five, and couldn't be revived. Just another reason to quit medicine, she rationalized. Things that should be easily reversed weren't always what they seemed. One small speck of melanoma should have been easy to remove, easy to treat. A little case of being overtired should have been cured by a couple days of rest.

But what should have been didn't always happen. Or, in her case, didn't ever happen.

"Your blood sugar's seventy now. Good, but not good enough to be up and wandering around yet."

"Then how about I go back to my cabin right now, go to bed and order something sweet from room service?" That was the easy way to do it, then she didn't have to be bothered by anyone, including the doctor.

"How about you stay right where you are for another ten minutes, then we'll decide what you'll get to do after that?"

That worked too, she supposed. It wasn't like she had someplace else to go, or anything else to do. And she really did want to prove that old saying wrong, that doctors made the worst patients. It wasn't her aim to be a bad patient. Dr Sloan was only doing his job and she didn't want to give him any grief over it. In other words, she wanted to be the kind of patient she used to like treating, so she'd stay there and take his advice. "Ten minutes," she agreed, then shut her eyes, not so much to sleep as to simply block him out. This past year she'd stayed away from a lot of things—life, commitments, friends—and the one thing she'd assiduously avoided at all costs had been anything medical. Dr Michael Sloan, handsome as he was, standing there with his stethoscope around his neck and a chart in his hand, was definitely medical. And definitely someone to avoid.

Too bad. Something else on her list of things to avoid was becoming involved in another relationship. Two so far, and all she'd done had been to prove what a miserable failure she was. She'd had two wonderful men in her life and the best she'd done in both relationships had been to fail them. Miserably.

So what was the point of even looking, when that's as far

as she'd let it go? Honestly, buying one of those brightly colored plastic gecko lizards the tourists all seemed so thrilled over didn't seem like such a bad idea for a relationship. At least she wouldn't let a chunk of red, yellow and green plastic down.

Or kill it.

Well, she wasn't sleeping. Trying hard to pretend she was, perhaps, but he knew better. In spite of her attempt to even out her breathing, her eyelids were fluttering—a dead give-away that she was awake and faking sleep.

Michael chuckled as he returned to his office. Something big was bothering her, but he wasn't going to guess what it was. Wasn't even going to pry. He was a doctor whose commitment to his patients was only as long as this two-week cruise. He took care of their physical woes while they were on the ship, then said goodbye to them as he welcomed aboard a new bunch. That's all he was here for—to treat them and leave them—which suited him just fine. So if there was something about Sarah Collins that needed figuring out other than a case of hypo-glycemia, he'd leave that puzzle to someone else. Lord knew, he was the last one to figure out anybody...espe-cially himself.

"Repeat a finger-stick in about five minutes," he instructed Ina Edwards, one of the ship's nurses. "And let me know what it is."

"You OK, Mike?" she asked him. "Your leg? Can I get you something?"

Old enough to be his mother, Ina doted on him. And while she meant well, and he appreciated the concern, it annoyed him. He was fine. Perfect. Just dandy. Except people didn't want to believe that. One war injury and a couple of years later so many pieces of his broken world still weren't back in place. But he didn't take it out on those who cared about him. He merely smiled his way through it. People cared. They wanted to show compassion he didn't deserve, though, considering what he'd done.

Sighing, Michael faked a smile at Ina. "I'm fine, thanks. Just not prepared to start duty so early into the cruise. Normally they don't start coming in until after the first round of bon-voyage parties. Hangovers and all that."

"Well, I can go fix you a cup of tea," she offered, not to be put off. "I brought my own special blend on board again. The one you like."

It was bitter. Harsh in his belly. He hated it, and usually poured it out when she wasn't looking, but Ina was hard to refuse. Sometimes he wondered if she was in cahoots with the other women in his family who wanted to over-mother him. "I'd love a cup," he lied.

"Cream?"

Cream did it no earthly good, and it was a waste of good cream. "I'd love cream," he said, still forcing a polite smile.

That was all Ina needed to be pleased, as she rushed away to brew up her hideous potion, leaving Michael to take Sarah Collins's blood test. Well, that didn't matter, did it? It was a simple finger stick. Took ten seconds. But there was something about her…something that bothered him. Maybe it was the way she'd clung to him when in the elevator, or the little tingle he'd felt when they'd touched.

Or maybe it was the haunted look in her eyes. He knew that haunted look on a deeply personal level. Saw it in his own mirror sometimes.

Yes, that had to be it. Someone afraid. Someone numbed. He didn't often think about the battlefield these days, or all the wounded men he'd treated during those months on active duty. Grueling hours, hideous wounds. Another life altogether that he didn't allow to spill over into this one. What was done was done, and he wasn't going back. Now he worked on a cruise ship, drank insufferably bad tea with an overly protective surrogate mother and spent his off-duty hours in the lounge on the Lido deck, listening to bad karaoke and drinking diet cola.

"This won't hurt," he said to Sarah, as he pressed the barrel of the lancet device to the index finger on her left hand, then pushed the button to let the lancet prick her.

She flinched involuntarily, turning away her head when he squeezed a drop of blood from her finger and smeared it on the test strip. Probably squeamish, he decided. "Are you on this cruise with someone else?" he asked, as he counted down the seconds for the results to register. "Friend, family member, group tour?" *Spouse?*

"Alone," she said. "It's the best way to travel. You get to go where you want, do what you want. No compromises, no one impinging on your time."

Spoken like a true cynic, he thought. Or somebody badly burned by life. "One hundred and one," he pronounced. "I think you're good to go, so long as you don't overdo it."

Sitting up, then swinging her legs over the side of the bed, she said, "Believe me, I never overdo it."

"If anything, I suppose you could say that you underdo it. Which is why I'd like to have you check in here three times a day so I can do readings. For a couple of days anyway. And since there's always food available, I'd like to see you eating five or six times a day."

She laughed over that. "What you'd like to see and what I'm able to do are two entirely different things, Doctor. I'll take better care of myself until I get off the ship. That's a promise since I don't want to bother you again. But I'm afraid that doctor's orders are falling on deaf ears otherwise. I can't eat that many times a day."

"Small meals," he said. "Constant fuel for your body, so your blood sugar doesn't fluctuate so much." Was that a small spark of defiance flickering in her eyes now? Did the lady have a little challenge in her? "Unless you like being a patient in here. Because if you don't take better care of yourself, we're bound to meet under these very same circumstances again." Not that it would be a bad thing, the part where they met again, anyway. But he surely didn't want it to be under these circumstances. And now that he knew Sarah Collins was here, on the ship, all alone…

No! He didn't do that. Hadn't even been tempted before. He knew others of the crew indulged in little shipboard flings, but he didn't. Even though the emotional scars had long since healed from his last try at something more enduring than a casual fling, he didn't indulge at all now, and he was surprised that Sarah had brought out that little beast in him, especially with the resolution he'd made. Well, time to put the beast away. Michael Sloan was off the market, didn't look, didn't touch. Didn't anything! Not until he knew what came next for him.

"OK, so maybe you're right. But I don't like your prescription, Doctor, so here's my compromise. I'll eat my three meals a day, maybe have a small bedtime snack, but that's still up in the air, depending on how I feel at bedtime. And I'll stop in here once a day to have my gluco…blood-sugar level checked. Not the three times you wanted." She smiled sweetly at him. "That's my final offer."

"Most people don't defy doctor's orders." He liked it that she did.

"And most people don't go on a cruise to avoid social interaction, which is why I'm here, Doctor. To avoid social interactions, or even professional ones such as yourself. Once I get myself accustomed to the ship and its schedule, I'll be fine. I'm sure you'll be very busy tending patients who really want your attention once this cruise gets well underway, so there's no need to bother about me. I know how to take care of myself."

"No, you don't, or you wouldn't be lying here in my bed right now, arguing about it." He charted her latest blood-sugar result then set the clipboard on the stand next to the bed.

"I can't force treatment on you, and I'm not even going to argue with you about it. You know what I want, and it's up to you to decide how you want to take care of yourself. You can do it the right way, or…do whatever you want to do." With that, he spun around and walked away. No use arguing with her. She was already dead set on what she intended to do and, as pretty as she was, that didn't always translate into smart. Which seemed to be the case with Miss Sarah Collins.

Or maybe not. He couldn't tell. She'd be back, though. One way or another—following doctors orders, or going against them—she'd be back. He was counting on it.

Sarah returned to her cabin under the escort of a nurse named Ina. She was a nice sort, had even fixed her a decent cup of tea, which had hit the spot. Ina probably would have stayed to tuck her into bed, but Sarah opted for a shower in preparation for going for a late-night meal. OK, so she was going to be good and eat the way she was supposed to. Either that or have herself another time of it in the hospital, and while she certainly had nothing against the hospital—it looked to be magnificently equipped—she had a thing against medicine in general. Loved it, hated it, wanted it, wanted to avoid it.

Mixed feelings all the way around, and the best way to avoid that was to avoid the issue causing the problem. Which was why she'd eat, which was why she'd consent to one, *maybe* two blood tests a day. Her mother used to say something about an ounce of prevention being worth a pound of cure, and since with her condition a pound of cure came in the form of a hospital and a good-looking doctor, she would opt for the ounce of prevention. For a few days. Then she'd get off the ship and see what else she could find for herself. Maybe Japan. Or, better yet, Hong Kong. Nobody there would force food and blood tests on her.

After a quick shower, Sarah finally gave in and went off

in search of a light meal. Off the beaten path…not in any of the main dining rooms, or at the continual buffet of lobster and fruit and so many other delicacies it nearly caused her to go queasy thinking about all the choices. No, she stayed away from all the main sources and instead opted for a dark, cozy little lounge on the Lido deck where one of the passengers, who was a little too inebriated to show good sense, was attempting a tune on the karaoke, and doing a miserable job of it. He was singing about an anguished phantom and sounding more like a walrus with bellyache. Which suited Sarah's purposes as the lounge was practically empty.

She ordered a small salad and a cup of seafood chowder, and settled into one of the back booths to wait, trying hard not to listen to the off key warblings that were getting more off-key by the moment. Shutting her eyes, she leaned her head against the back of the booth, fighting away the image of the good doctor, which had been lingering there a while longer than was comfortable.

Bad impression, she decided. That's why she kept thinking about him. He'd made a bad impression on her. But the images there were anything but bad, which was why she decided to force her concentration on the second verse going on at the front of the lounge. More off key than the first. And much louder.

At the point where it became nearly unbearable Sarah decided not to wait around for her food. She wasn't hungry, and she could eat in the morning. So she opened her eyes, started to scoot out of the booth, only to be stopped at the edge of the seat by a large form she recognized from the sheer size of him, since in her little corner of the lounge it was too dark to see much of anything. "Spying on me?" she snapped.

He placed a cup of chowder down in front of her, along with her salad, then wedged himself into the seat right next to her, pushing her back from the edge. "Apparently, I am," he said, handing her a soup spoon.

CHAPTER TWO

"So, WHAT do you want, Doctor? What do you *really* want?" She was a little flattered by his attention, actually. It had been a long year avoiding everybody with whom she'd come into contact, and there were so many nights when she would have enjoyed a dinner companion, a male companion especially. No strings attached, separate checks, light conversation, going their separate ways at the end of the meal, of course. Someone to share a little space with her at the same table, someone staving off the appearance that she was so pathetically alone.

She wasn't antisocial, even though it appeared she was. Just cautious these days, as getting involved came easily to her. Easily, but with such a high price…costly mistakes she was bound to make again if the occasion arose. And she simply didn't trust herself to do otherwise, which was why she kept to herself now. "Did you follow me here, or do you moonlight as a waiter when you're off duty in the hospital? Are you serving up syringes of penicillin by day and dry martinis with a lemon twist by night?"

He laughed, raising his hand to signal the waitress. When he caught her attention, she gave him a familiar nod, then scurried off to the bar. "Some might think that's the same thing, one cure being as good as another. When you're on holiday, a ship has amazing opportunities, with so many things to do. But when you're on a ship for your employment as well as your living space, those opportunities are pretty limited and the space gets rather small, the longer you're confined to it. I don't fraternize with the guests in the planned social activities, don't date them, don't play shuffleboard with them, don't serve them drinks either. Most of the time I try to keep to places where there aren't so many people hanging around. Keep the separation between crew and guests intact. And right now this seems the place to do it."

"Sounds…dull. So many things to do, and here you are with me, probably the one and only avowed antisocial passenger on board. Not very interesting at all, Doctor. Not for a man who could have other choices, if he so wishes." She glanced at the waitress who was giving him an admiring appraisal, then at a table with three well liquored-up women, all of whom had that same look for him. It seemed the good doctor did have his opportunities if he cared to take them. "A number of other choices," she said.

"If you *want* those choices."

"And you don't?" She arched a curious eyebrow. "That surprises me."

"It surprises me too, sometimes. But it avoids a lot of complications in the long run and who needs complications when you can have all this?" He pointed to the karaoke singer standing under the dim blue light on the postage-stamp-sized stage, singing his off-key heart out.

"Sounds like a been there, done that to me. Once burned, twice shy, or something like that."

"It's that obvious?" He said that with a smile, but that wasn't at all the impression she was getting from him. There was something deep, something disturbing in his voice. Some sadness, maybe? Or wistfulness? It was a hauntingly familiar tone, and one she recognized from her own voice when she wasn't trying so hard to mask it with something lighter, something less truthful, the way Michael was trying to do.

Something compelled her to hear his voice again, to elicit that emotion from him once more, but as she opened her mouth to speak, the karaoke singer hit a particularly loud, startlingly sour note that caused even him to sputter, then giggle an apology into the microphone—but not quit singing.

Michael cringed visibly, and this time the smile that spread to his face was genuine. "You can see why there aren't so many people around here."

The moment was gone. It was too late to try and discover something she had no right to discover. "Well, I think earplugs are a good remedy," she said lightly, shaking off the building intensity and finally relaxing into the moment between them a little more. His motives seemed innocent enough, and she did understand how this was a good place to come if you were seeking solitude on a crowded ship—nice, dim room, secluded entryway making it easy to overlook, perfect low-key ambiance, comfortable booths arranged intimately so they gave the seeming appearance of aloneness. This one in particular, tucked in behind a column, was especially private, which was why she'd chosen it. For a moment it crossed her mind that this might be Dr Sloan's regular booth for all the same reasons she had taken to it. "Or maybe he could do with an adenoidectomy." Meaning the removal of the little piece of tissue located where the throat connected with the nasal passage. Often adenoids were the cause of nasal congestion, thick breathing or, in some cases, a nasal-sounding voice.

Michael shot her a curious look. "You know what an adenoidectomy is? I wouldn't think that's too common a term."

Her comment had been too medical, especially when she was trying to hide from everything that connected her to medicine in any way. But sometimes it just slipped out. Natural instincts coming back to haunt her. Well, that was a mistake she wouldn't repeat. "I don't suppose it is common but a friend of mine had it done," she lied. It had been a patient of hers, so in the longest stretch of the word maybe that hadn't been a lie after all. "Opened up her nasal passages quite nicely, helped her stop talking through her nose, breathing easier…." Too medical again. "You know. Whatever goes along with that kind of surgery." Sarah watched, out of the corner of her eye, to see if he believed her, which apparently he did because he turned his attention to the waitress who was on her way over to the table with a soda and a sandwich. She placed them on the table in front of him, bending much too close for anything other than what she had in mind, which had nothing to do with serving him food, practically slathering him with a come-hither smile. Of which he took no notice.

Most men, having it flaunted in their faces that way, would at least look, but Michael Sloan did not, which made Sarah wonder all the more about him.

Michael and the waitress chatted for a another moment about someone who worked in the business office—she still showing the same interest in him while he showed none in her—then when the waitress had decided that she was wasting her time she scampered away to wait on a another customer. That's when Michael returned his attention to Sarah. "It's like a little city here. Everybody knows everybody else's business."

Like the waitress who knew what Michael wanted even though he didn't have to order it? Briefly, Sarah wondered how much business the waitress and Michael knew about each other, and if his lack of a show of interest in her had been for appearances only. She was young, blonde, built the way every good plastic surgeon wanted his surgical enhancements to turn out. Of course, he'd already denied involvements or, as he called them, complications. Still, a man like Michael…good-looking, smart… She wondered. "The same way it is in a hospital," she said, trying to sound noncommittal.

"Do you work in a hospital?"

Damn. She'd slipped again, when she'd promised herself she'd be more careful. Twice inside two minutes. Something about him eased the tension right out of her, made her feel almost normal again, and she was going to have to be very careful around him. "No, but I like to watch those hospital shows on television. They're very…realistic. Make you feel like you're really there." Ah, the lie of it all, but the look of mild amusement on his face told her he'd bought her rather impaired explanation.

He chuckled. "Real life wrapped up in an hour, minus time out for commercials, once a week. Everybody gets cured or killed at the end, don't they? Or falls in love and lives happily ever after. Well, you are right about one thing. Gossip prevails in the hospital, too. Sometimes it can get so bad it's like it takes on an existence of its own."

"Which you can't live without?" she asked.

"That might be putting it too strongly. Personally, I can live without it quite nicely, like I can live without a good cup of strong, black coffee if one's not available to me. But for some people a little good gossip can start the day off with a bang, the way a good cup of coffee can."

"If you indulge," she said. Somehow, she didn't see him as the type.

"Which I don't. In the gossip, anyway. Can't say that I'd turn down a good cup of coffee, though."

She was glad he'd redeemed himself with that one because she didn't want to picture Michael Sloan as petty in any way, and gossip could be so petty. Being the brunt of it herself over her break-up with Cameron Enderlein, she knew. "So why did you choose a cruise ship?" she asked, knowing she probably shouldn't get that involved. But it seemed right to her. The mood between them was pleasant enough, his company nice. And she desperately missed companionship, not only in a personal way but in a medical one. It had been such a long time since she'd talked medicine with anybody, and while this wasn't going to go into any medical depth, it seemed harmless enough on a superficial level. An encounter with someone from her own profession was stimulating. Then, after tonight, she'd get lost in the ship's crowd, and he'd get busy in the ship's hospital, and that would be that. So it didn't matter. "Rather than a hospital or a clinic somewhere, why here?"

"It's a good job," he said, this time his voice the guarded one she'd already heard bits of before. "The facilities are excellent, patients are usually pretty nice, and I like the tropical islands. Oh, and the food is great." He picked up his sandwich and took a bite of something that looked to be a huge Cubano—pork, vegetables, and a whole lot of other ingredients that added up to one large meal between two pieces of bread.

And one large avoidance, too, she thought as she picked at her salad, finally spearing a grape tomato. But what was it to her? If he didn't want to tell her, she didn't care. They weren't friends, after all. They were barely acquaintances.

"So what kind of job do you do?" he asked, after he'd swallowed and taken a drink of his diet cola. "Wait…let me guess." He leaned back in his seat, folded his arms across his chest and studied her for a moment.

Studied her so hard she blushed under his scrutiny. Good thing the lights in here were dim and he couldn't see her reaction.

"I don't take you to be a lady of leisure," he said. "You've too much purpose in your eyes."

If only he knew how wrong he was. She'd been nothing but a lady of leisure for the past year, and there was absolutely no purpose in her eyes. Maybe once, but not any more.

"Am I right?" he asked, when she didn't respond to his first guess.

Rather than answering, she played his game and busied herself with her soup. If he could indulge himself in a little avoidance, so could she.

"So the lady isn't going to answer. Which means I'll have to take a wild guess. You're too short to be a fashion model, you don't eat with enough passion to be a chef, this is October, which is the middle of the school year so you're not a schoolteacher, and you're too pale to be a professional golfer."

"A golfer?" She laughed over that one. "Where did you come up with that?"

"I'm a doctor. I saw your muscles when I examined you. Very nice, but not overly developed. I can picture you swinging a golf club."

"I'll just bet you can," she said. "Sorry to disappoint you but I don't have a golf swing and I don't play golf. Never have."

"Well, that narrows the field down, doesn't it?"

"That ends the field, Doctor," she said, scooting toward the other side of the booth. This was entirely too enjoyable, and it would have been easy to spend another hour or two here, chatting about nothing and enjoying everything about it. Which was why she had to leave.

"Call me Michael, please," he said, not trying to stop her from leaving.

That surprised her a little. She'd expected a small protest from him, or maybe even an offer to walk her back to her cabin, which she might have taken him up on. But as she climbed out of her seat, he stood and offered a polite hand to her, then turned and signaled the waitress back over to refill his glass—both with the same insouciant effort. All casual, all impersonal, as was his goodnight to her.

"I want to see you in the morning for a finger stick," he said. "I'll be on duty at eight."

She nodded, offered him a half-smile, and scooted out of the lounge to a popular song being mutilated by a short, round, bald-headed Elvis impersonator who sounded like he needed an adenoidectomy, too.

* * *

She slept in, avoiding the morning finger stick, and when, at nearly ten, she heard a knock on the cabin door, she assumed it was Michael, coming to do her blood work. But she was wrong. It was one of the ship's medical technicians. Cheery smile, bright face, she was more than happy to poke Sarah's finger. "It's a little low," Paulina Simpson said, showing the monitor to Sarah, who read the blood-sugar result at sixty-five. "You need to eat something," Paulina continued, fishing some sort of breakfast bar out of her pocket. "Doctor Sloan told me to bring this along, that you'd probably need it."

"Dr Sloan thinks of everything, doesn't he?" Sarah said amiably.

"He's a good doctor. Most of the docs come and go, work a few weeks here and there, but the cruise line likes Dr Sloan because he keeps coming back. He's reliable. The patients trust him and he does an outstanding job."

A bit of a crush from the med tech, too? Sarah wondered.

"And he's received commendations from the cruise line," the girl went on.

Well, so much praise on Michael's account was all well and good, but that still didn't put Sarah in the mood to deal with him. For what it was worth, she felt a little slighted, being passed off to a tech when she'd expected the doctor to come calling on her. "Well, tell Dr Sloan thank you for the breakfast bar, but that I'm doing fine on my own and I no longer require medical attention."

Paulina arched a puzzled eyebrow, then nodded. "He said you'd say that, so he gave me this." She handed over a slip of paper.

Sarah took a look at it, then handed it back. "Tell Dr Sloan I don't need a diet guide, that I'm quite capable of eating what I need, when I need it. But I appreciate his concern."

"He said you'd say that, too. So…" she pulled a small glucose monitor from her other pocket and handed it to Sarah "…he told me to give you this, so you can check yourself at any time. Although he would like to take a daily reading of his own, just to see how you're doing."

Apparently, there was no getting away from Dr Michael Sloan, even when he wasn't present. If he went to all this fuss over a simple little case of hypoglycemia, she could only image how he'd react to a serious illness. Good doctor, she decided, adding her own silent praise to Paulina's as she remembered the days when she'd been at least that persistent with her own patients. "Tell Dr Sloan thank you for the glucometer, and that I'll use it. And that if he insists, I'll allow him to do an occasional test, too." She didn't really need it, but who was she to interfere with a doctor doing his duty?

Too bad he was hiding away on a ship, she thought as she unwrapped the breakfast bar. The world needed good doctors like Michael. Of course, she was hiding away on a ship too, wasn't she? And by most accounts she'd been a pretty good doctor herself.

It was turning into a long day, and the hospital was getting busy. Predictable conditions, the lot of them. Upset stomachs, seasickness, diabetic upheavals from people going wild over so much food available to them. People underestimated their stamina on a ship and he got to patch up the results. It was very different from general surgery, and sometimes he did long for the days when he'd spent his life in the operating theater.

But now… "Take two of these pills this afternoon, and two more before you go to bed. If you're still nauseated in the morning, come back and see me and we'll try something different." He handed the bottle to the fifty-something woman, and watched her leave the examining room, her face a little less green than it had been when she'd come in. "And no seafood for a couple of days," he called after her, remembering that this particular incident of gastric upset had come after a rather large consumption of lobster for lunch.

He couldn't blame her, really. Cruises were all about over-indulgence. Of course, there was Sarah, who wouldn't indulge at all. He was willing to bet she hadn't eaten a thing since her breakfast bar. She was a hard one to figure out. Last night, in the lounge, after she'd relaxed a little, she'd seemed like she had been enjoying his company. He'd certainly enjoyed hers. But just when things had finally slipped into a nice, casual mood, she'd upped and left him there. It wasn't his place to ask her questions, but he was curious. He saw all kinds of people on the ship. Lonely widows and widowers, people getting over the break-up of a relationship, people pressed with tough life decisions running away for a while to think. And people who were simply on holiday. As for Sarah, well, he wasn't sure where she fit in. Normally he was pretty good at telling, but he couldn't get a reading on her. Other than the fact that he liked her, and something about her drew him in, he simply didn't know.

One thing was certain, though. She didn't want a personal relationship in her life as much as he didn't want one in his. That alone made a shipboard friendship seem appealing. "Hello," he said to his next patient, as he stepped into the examining room to have a look at a casualty of a volleyball game—a soft-looking fortyish man who didn't exercise at home but who took the opportunity to start once he'd hit the high seas. "I understand you hurt your back? Maybe twisted an ankle, too?"

The man, who was sitting on the edge of the exam table with his bare, skinny legs sticking out from under the sheet draped over his lap, nodded, looking up from his bent-over position. "Guess I'm a little out of shape." he admitted. "Haven't played in a while."

Michael wasn't going to ask how long that translated into. Instead, he took a look, diagnosed a few strained and sprained muscles and sent the man off to the spa to spend the afternoon in a whirlpool. It wasn't a precise medical therapy exactly, but why not give the man what he'd come for? Something he didn't have in his real life.

So, after what seemed like an interminably long day of routine aches and pains, Michael signed the next watch over to the following doctor on duty, a competent general practitioner named Reese Allen, and headed for his quarters. His leg ached a little more than usual, although it shouldn't, and it was time to get off it for a while. But as he walked down the corridor to his cabin, which was adjacent to the hospital, he changed his mind and caught the elevator up to the sundeck. He didn't actually get outside much on these cruises, and right now he felt the urge for a little sun on his face. And he knew the perfect place. It was amidships, in a little tuck-away behind one of the bars that didn't usually go into use until dark. There were a few deck chairs there, maybe three or four, and no one ever lounged there because there was no real view, unless you enjoyed looking at the back bar or the bottom side of the little rise holding the deck chairs with a perfect view of the pool. Good spot, he thought, heading off in that direction. Very good spot. He'd spend an hour, maybe two, go to the lounge and have Hector fix him a Cubano for supper, then…well, nothing came after that. He didn't make plans, although the thought of a little time spent with Sarah Collins suddenly popped into his mind.

It was a wish that came true almost immediately as he rounded the corner to his little tuck-away and found her in one of the deck chairs. Just her. Nobody else was around. She was there, stretched out almost elegantly in the chair, wearing a simple, one-piece black swimsuit that exposed beautiful long legs, even though they were pale. The black of the swimsuit complemented her black hair and the milky color of her skin was a startling, sexy contrast. Sarah had on black sunglasses, through which she was reading…he couldn't tell what, for sure. It looked like a copy of the *New England Journal of Medicine*, but she snapped it shut and tucked it into her big straw bag the instant she saw him. It was probably a fashion magazine, he decided as he headed toward her. Or another of the women's specialty magazines available from the ship's store.

She tilted her head down and gave him a long, cool glance up and over the top of her dark glasses before she finally spoke. "So, you *are* spying on me."

"I admitted it once, and I'm sticking to it."

"Have you come to do a blood test? You're so dedicated that you'll chase your patients down no matter where they're hiding?"

"I'd like to say yes but, unfortunately, I don't have my medical equipment with me. I'm afraid I'm off duty right now, too."

"Somehow, I doubt that you're ever *really* off duty," she said, that cool stare of hers continuing. It was cool, but not unfriendly. More like wary. "You strike me as one of those doctors who lives and breathes his work. Dedicated beyond reason. Otherwise why would you become a ship's doctor? I don't imagine you can ever really get away from it here, can you?"

"Actually, I have this little hiding place where I go so I *can* get away. No one knows about it, no one goes there, except…"

"Me?" she ventured. "Just like I know about your booth in the karaoke lounge?"

"It is funny, isn't it, how we keep bumping into each other in all the places no one else wants to go? You know, the secluded places."

"I'm antisocial," she reminded him with a hint of a smile tweaking her lips. "What's your excuse, other than you're spying on me?"

His leg was starting to ache even more now, that dull throb he despised that had never completely gone away, and he really needed to sit down. He hated it when this happened.

The reminder, the memories…of so many things he wanted to forget. *Damn, he hated it!* "My excuse is that I've been coming here for the better part of a year now."

She arched her eyebrows…beautifully sculpted eyebrows. Everything about Sarah Collins was beautifully sculpted, in fact. "Well, then, by all means, you should sit down."

"And interrupt you?"

"You're assuming that you being here would interrupt me."

"Would it?" he asked, summoning every bit of determination he had to fight off the inevitable limp that came when he was tired…fight it off long enough to take the last ten steps toward the deck chair next to her. Gritting his teeth, he took one step, then another. Sure, it was a vanity thing, being self-conscious like he was. There was no disgrace in his disability. But, damn, he had the right to hold onto a little vanity, didn't he? His limp caused questions, which required explanations. And the whole sordid story, once he'd explained it, brought pity, which he didn't want. Especially not from someone like Sarah Collins. So he took another few steps toward her, until he finally reached the chair. Then he sat, letting out an involuntary sigh of relief. Two hours off his feet, and he'd be fine. But one thing was sure—those two hours were going to be spent right here. He didn't have it in him to get up again. So if Sarah stayed, he'd spend them with her, and if she didn't stay…

"There's nothing to interrupt," she said. "I was doing exactly what you intend to do, enjoying a little sun well away from the crowds. Having someone else doing the same alongside me wouldn't be an interruption."

"But an intrusion, perhaps?" he asked, shifting to find a comfortable position.

"I don't think you're an intrusion. But if that becomes the case, I'll let you know." With that, she pushed her sunglasses up again, making her intention not to converse quite clear.

Then, out of the blue, "You don't snore, do you?" she asked. "Because if you do, that's an intrusion."

He chuckled. What was it about her that he liked so much? She put up walls, and she wasn't engagingly friendly either. Polite when interaction was forced on her but remaining at a distance. And so damned intriguing that he didn't even care if they spent the next two hours lounging next to each other without speaking a word.

The truth was, he liked Sarah Collins.

While she hadn't been looking for him, not consciously, on some unexplainable level she wasn't displeased that he'd found her. On a limited basis, Michael Sloan was rather pleasant company. Sarah found herself wishing, just a little, that she could talk in-depth about medicine with him, though. She'd just read a brilliant article in the *New England Journal* on advances in medication used to treat hypertension, and she would have loved some lively discussion on that with a colleague. But she had to remind herself almost daily that she'd left medicine behind her, then content herself with the void in her life that that decision had caused.

Unfortunately, the passion hadn't left her, which was why she wasn't engaging him this very moment. She stayed away from medicine because she could so easily be drawn back.

Although, as a doctor, she had noticed his limp. She hadn't stared, of course, especially with the way he had been trying so hard not to limp. Male ego, probably. In her experience as a doctor, the one thing she'd learned well was that men preferred to grit their teeth and bear it rather than admitting a weakness. Actually, that's what had almost killed Cameron. He'd been tired, he'd been losing weight. He'd blamed it on working too much, even though she'd asked him to have himself checked out. *And he a doctor!* Well, the dreadful truth had turned out to be leukemia. The other dreadful truth was that she should have insisted on him getting checked, then kept on insisting when he'd refused. Even tied him up and dragged him to a clinic, if she'd had to. But she hadn't. Probably because avoidance and denial had been easier.

Luckily for Cameron, his ending turned out to be a happy one in so many ways. He'd beaten his cancer, found a perfect wife and now they had a family.

It seemed, though, that the good doctor lying next to her right now was much the same as Cameron. Too stubborn, or too large an ego…she didn't know which. But it was on the tip of her tongue to say something to him. To ask him what was wrong, and if he'd sought medical attention. Which was none of her business. Still, he'd shown a sufficient amount of pain to someone with a trained eye, and whether or not she was calling herself a doctor these days, she was concerned. "Do you ever get time off?" she asked, not sure how to broach the subject without seeming too medical about it.

"Between cruises. A few days here and there."

"Nothing sustained, though? Maybe a few weeks where you can go and treat yourself to some real rest? On one of these tropical islands where we're going to stop on the cruise, perhaps?"

"Social worker," he said.

"What?"

"Last night, I was trying to figure out what you do. My guess right now is social worker. You show just the right amount of concern for other people's concerns, which would make you a very good social worker."

"Well, I'll take that as a compliment because I admire anyone who has the dedication to be a social worker but, no, that's not what I do. And I'm not a librarian either, if that was going to be your next guess."

"I might have. I've always thought librarians have a smoldering, secret sensuality about them, which fits you."

Sarah laughed. "Nothing smoldering in me."

"But there is, Sarah. It's there, and you do a nice job of hiding it, which is why you'd make a good librarian. They have that reserved exterior, but on the inside—"

"Let me guess," she interrupted. "When you were young you had a secret crush on a librarian."

"Not so secret. Her name was Mrs Rowe, and the way she pinned up her red hair, and those tight tweed skirts she wore…" Michael faked a big shiver. "I used to check out books every day. Big books, adult books that I thought made me look intelligent and old. As many as I could get in my canvas bag, like I thought she believed I was taking them home and reading them every night. I was eight, by the way."

"So what brought an end to the love affair?"

"After a couple of weeks, Mrs Rowe asked me if I wouldn't rather have books from the children's section, then she handed me one about a precocious monkey and told me I'd do better with that than the one on quantum physics I was attempting to check out."

"She was probably right, unless you were a child genius."

"Not even close."

"Then I'd say Mrs Rowe had good insight."

"And a good figure, too," he commented under his breath.

Sarah laughed. "Not to be missed, even by a boy of eight." Which further proved her theory about men. They were not all alike, as some people said, but they were certainly similar in some ways. Even now, as he shifted in his deck chair, she saw a little grimace of pain on his face, yet, come hell or high water, he wasn't about to admit it.

Well, back to the original premise and she was sticking to it. It was none of her business.

She was still concerned, though.

CHAPTER THREE

SARAH hadn't planned on going ashore, yet when the passengers started to leave the boat to spend a few hours browsing the shops, seeing the sights and eating the food in Nassau, on New Providence island in the Bahamas, she'd changed her mind and followed along after them. Her cabin was small and she wasn't enjoying her private time there as much as she'd thought she would. While it wasn't her intention to join in with any of the activities on board ship, she wasn't exactly avoiding some minor mingling…walking about, nodding a pleasant hello here and there, making idle chat where it was necessary.

Something about the sea air had caused this change in her, she supposed as she took one last look in the mirror before she dashed out the door, amazed that in only two days she'd taken on a little color. She'd probably gained a pound or two, too, since eating seemed to be the number-one cruise pastime for just about everybody, and the good doctor did keep watch over her to make sure she did her fair share. Michael deserved his due credit, though. Her blood sugar had been perfect three checks in a row now, and she was actually feeling better—not so tired all the time. His vigilance reminded her to take care of herself. That was the reason she was going off the ship this afternoon. For the first time since she couldn't remember when she actually wanted to take a walk, soak up some of the local culture. Her past holidays had been lackluster affairs overall, where she'd showed mild interest at best and, more commonly, no enthusiasm whatsoever, and while she wouldn't go so far as to admit to any enthusiasm over this little outing, she wasn't dreading it as much as she could have.

Too bad Michael wouldn't be coming along. At least, she didn't think he would be. What he'd told her at the start of the cruise, that he didn't usually fraternize with the guests, was holding true. She'd seen him only in passing since they'd spent a couple of quiet hours together in the deck chairs, and even her blood tests were done by somebody else and reported to Michael who, in turn, relayed messages back to her through somebody else.

Well, it didn't matter, really. She would have enjoyed spending more time with him, catching the edge of a medical conversation where she could, but it didn't seem that it was meant to be. Admitting she was disappointed was an exaggeration, but in all honesty she wouldn't have objected to bumping into him on the docks. As it turned out, however, a casual enquiry of the medical technician who'd last tested her blood revealed what Sarah wanted to know—the medical crew probably wasn't leaving ship at this port of call.

Oh, well…

Once Sarah was off the ship, she had several choices. She could see the area by taxi, take a walking tour, hire a horse-drawn carriage, or the one that appealed to her the most—take a jitney, a small bus overcrowded with locals. It made frequent stops, went to the areas the tourists avoided, and she was in the mood for that. She didn't want to shop, didn't want to see the museums or the city's renowned colonial architecture. She didn't even want to go have a dolphin encounter—swimming or snorkeling with trained dolphins—which was a very popular attraction. Instead, she wanted to ride, and watch. Meaning, be alone again. But that was fine. It was a beautiful day, the air was warm, and this sure beat staying in her cabin, reading another medical journal.

So Sarah caught the jitney, and was rather amazed by it. Bright green, small, and chugging along loudly and smokily, like it was about to roll over and die at the side of the road, it wasn't comfortable transportation, but the thirty or so people squeezed into a space that should have accommodated twenty or so didn't mind the inconvenience. In fact, they all got rather chummy as the bus bumped its way through town, stopping at various street corners, letting people out, then letting other people back on.

From her rear seat which she shared with a plump woman named Mimmie and her chubby son who answered to the name Delroy, Sarah stared through the bus window at tourists scurrying into the various shops, some on the tourist map, some not. They were lining up at the doors of all the recommended cafés, happy to queue simply to have a taste of the local food, and flock into the Straw Market for the best of the best souvenirs. After fifteen minutes of being pinched against the side of the jitney, though, with Delroy smearing his sticky red lollipop up and down her arm, Sarah decided it was time to get off and find something better to do. Maybe take a walk through the botanical gardens.

So, at the next stop, she managed to squeeze her way past Mimmie and force herself through the standing passengers until she was down the aisle and out the door. Mimmie followed right behind her, though, with Delroy, who made sure his lollipop came into contact with the back of Sarah's white shorts at least five times. But once they were on the sidewalk, and Sarah was sure Delroy's candy was not attached to her shorts, she started to head down a side street, paying more attention to a street map than she was to her surroundings. Behind her, when she heard the sound of the jitney rev its clanking engine, she assumed it to be off on its route, but all of a sudden the sound of a horn, followed by screams of hysterical men and women, split the air.

Her maps slipped from her fingers and slid to the ground as Sarah spun around.

What was going on? It was hard to tell from where she was, but multitudes of people were running to surround the jitney, and those on the bus were scurrying to get off. And Mimmie…Sarah caught a glimpse of the woman trying to shove her way through the crowd, screaming at them, crying, pounding people aside with her fists.

Warning hairs on the back of Sarah's neck prickled and she immediately broke into a run, pushing herself past even more people crowding in to see whatever was happening. When she reached the jitney, she was still at the rear of the congested knot, but even from there she heard someone shouting about the little boy. Then a blood-curdling scream pierced the noise of the crowd. "Delroy!"

"Let me through!" Sarah cried. "I'm a doctor."

Some people moved for her, others didn't. "Let me through," she cried again. "I have to get through. I'm a doctor!"

All of a sudden, the crowd stepped aside for her, almost creating a corridor that led her straight to the front of the bus where Delroy laid sprawled, unconscious, most of the way under the bus, with only his toes sticking out. His mother was on her knees at his side, wailing, pulling on him, trying to get him free.

"Don't," Sarah warned her. But Mimmie was so frightened she was comprehending nothing but her son's dire injury. "Don't move him," Sarah said anyway. Once she'd dropped to her knees she immediately checked Delroy for a pulse. A quick press to the femoral artery in his groin, which was the only pulse point she could reach without actually crawling under the bus, did reveal a pulse, but not a good one. It was thready, cutting in and out like his heart was deciding whether it wanted to keep beating or quit. "He's alive," she told Mimmie, who was still tugging on Delroy's arm.

She had to get the woman to stop. "Somebody, please, don't let his mother move him," she called to the crowd. "I need help here. I need someone to hold his mother back." With that, two women jumped forward and wrapped arms around Mimmie, forcibly pulling her away from her son. She struggled for a moment then, with big tears rolling down her cheeks, looked pleadingly at Sarah. "Please, *please*, help him!"

"He's alive," she told the woman. "But he can't be moved."

"He must come out from under the bus."

"No, he has to stay where he is." There was no time to explain, no time to waste trying to calm a tortured mother when the pulse she was feeling under her fingertips was fluttering even more tentatively now. "I need an ambulance," she cried to the crowd, not sure what the procedure was in Nassau. Then she bent down, pressed her cheek to the black pavement to see what she could of the little boy.

Nothing was trapped under the bus tire. That was good. But he was pressed very close to it, just inches away, with his shirt actually caught under the tire, and nothing about him was moving. That was bad. Head injury, perhaps? At the very least, internal damage. And here she was without a medical kit. This was the first time she'd regretted that since she'd left her practice. Funny thing was, it was still intact, still packed with all the necessities, sitting just inside her apartment ready to go, like it had always known she'd back for it someday.

Today was that day! And now she had to get closer, had to have a look before anybody touched the child or moved him. So, without another thought, Sarah got down on her belly and inched her way slowly along the pavement under the bus, trying all the while to forget that she'd been claustrophobic lately. Her hands were shaking, her head going light...all the classic signs of a panic attack coming on. Except she couldn't do that. Had to get control. Had to save a life.

Breathe, Sarah.

She inched even farther in, stopping every second or two, taking a look at what she could see from her angle, feeling for a pulse point, running her fingers lightly over the boy's body for an assessment.

You're the doctor. This child needs you. She couldn't let him down. Wouldn't.

As she moved her way alongside his limp body, she saw that Delroy still clutched the red lollipop in his hand, and that caused a hard lump to form in her throat. "We're going to get you out of here, Delroy," she said to the boy, even though he wasn't conscious. "Then take you to a hospital, where they'll give you a brand-new lollipop. Is red your favorite color? I like green." She felt stickiness over his abdomen, and was sure it wasn't from his lollipop. Hopefully, it was only blood from a cut, and nothing significant.

His breathing was shallow and rapid, and her own breaths were fighting against her, trying to go shallow and rapid, too. *Don't quit now, Sarah. You can do this.* "When my mother used to buy a bag of lollipops, my sister and I always fought over who got the red ones, even though I really wanted the green ones. But because Annie wanted the red, so did I. Do you have any brothers or sisters, Delroy?"

She was nearly at his shoulder now, sickened by the twist of his right arm. It was a bad break, easy to diagnose even from her awkward position. Not a compound fracture, though, thank God. No broken skin, no bone sticking out. But it would require surgery. She couldn't even imagine how many bones had been crushed in his little arm, and there was no way to tell. "Looks like you're going to have to use your left hand for your lollipops for a while," she said, doing a second check of his arm just to make sure she hadn't missed an area where the bone might have been protruding. Under here, in the dark, it was hard to tell, but her second check confirmed her first impression.

Pulling herself a little closer to Delroy, Sarah reached across his body, trying as best as she could to make an assessment of other injuries, but it was difficult, given that she was so far away and still in such an awkward position. She decided that once she reached his head she'd try to get over to the other side to do the same exam as she'd done on the right side.

"Pupils?" someone called from behind her. Somewhere not under the bus.

"Haven't assessed them yet. Don't have a light." The voice was familiar, but it was hard to tell through the noise of the crowd.

"It's on its way," the man shouted. At that moment a small flashlight was thrust, with some force, under the bus, and she grabbed it, grateful that a medic had finally arrived on the scene. Now, if only she had enough room to push herself up to her knees for this. But she didn't. This was an exam she had to do either on her belly or her side.

"Are you medical?" he yelled. "Do you need help under there?"

Was it Michael? It sounded like him, and she prayed that it was. She needed someone she trusted, needed someone who was calm to help her get through this. "Michael Sloan?" she called. "It's Sarah. Sarah Collins, from the ship." Gently pushing back one of Delroy's eyelids, she flashed the light in his eye to see pupillary reaction. She studied it for a moment, then did the same for his other eye. Not responsive to light. A very bad sign. "I think we have a head injury here. His pupils aren't equal and reactive to light. He also has a broken arm, not a compound fracture, though. At least, that's the best I can tell. And that's all I can see so far. Oh, and there's not enough room for two of us."

"Sarah," he called, crouching at the edge of the bus.

She glanced at him for a moment, glad to see his face, even though it was streaked with worry. "I don't suppose I mentioned that I'm a doctor, did I?" she asked, knowing full well she hadn't. These days, if it didn't come up in conversation, she didn't bring it up. Even in the company of another doctor. *Especially* in the company of another doctor. That made avoidance all the more easy.

"Do you need a cervical collar?" he called back, rather than responding to her confession.

"To get him out, yes. And a backboard." She did a quick check of Delroy's pulse. Weaker. In her gut she knew he had internal injuries, too, some kind of bleeding somewhere, but she couldn't get a good feel of his belly to check for rigidity. "And I think he's bleeding inside, so I'll need an IV set-up ready to go once he's out of here."

"But he's breathing?"

"Shallow, rapid. Do you have a blood-pressure cuff?" she called, on the off chance that Delroy's other arm wasn't broken and she could take a blood-pressure reading.

Within seconds, a blood-pressure cuff and stethoscope were tossed under to her. But she was on the wrong side to use them, so she scooted all the way around the boy's head and over to the left of his body, praying that his injuries there weren't so extensive. A quick check of his arm revealed it she was safe to use the cuff, so she fastened it on, pumped it up then took a reading. "Damn,' she muttered, not hearing a thing. She tried it again. "Eighty over forty," she finally called. Deathly low. She desperately needed to get an IV into Delroy, to give him fluid volume to offset the internal bleed she guessed was causing his blood pressure to bottom out. "What are my chances for an IV right now, before we move him?"

"None," Michael called. "We've got assistance en route, but it's going to take a while."

"MAST?" Even as she asked, she knew that anti-shock trousers would not be available. Once they went onto the patient and were inflated, they tamped off the internal bleed and kept the blood pressure a little more stable.

"No."

"Other options?"

"Is he ready to move?"

"Not until he's stabilized. So far I've got a head injury, a critical break to his right arm and I have a feeling it might be compartmentalized." Bleeding inside the bone. "And I'm thinking there could be internal damage. And I haven't checked all of him." The boy's last minutes were ticking away, she feared. Moving him would almost surely kill him if she didn't get him stabilized, yet there was no way to stabilize him under the bus. "Look, Delroy," she said, wiggling herself close to his ear. "What I need for you to do is fight this. Really fight it. It's going to take us a while to move you, but we're going to get you to the hospital as soon as we can. So don't give up. You fight this, and I promise I won't leave you."

"We need to get him out from under there and have him ready for when the medics arrive," Michael called.

"Can we get the driver to move the bus?" Delroy's best chance was to be completely away from the bus so when ambulance arrived they could get right to the emergency care, but she wasn't willing to risk his life by pulling him out. As fragile as his pulse was now, and as shallow as his breathing had become, that would mean sure death. She didn't know that for sure, of course, but that was her gut feeling and for now she was going to go with her gut feeling.

"It's too dangerous. One wrong turn…. Are you're sure there's no room for me under there?" Michael called back. "Maybe with two of us bracing him…"

"No room." She wished there was room, but that simply wasn't the case. She trusted Michael out there, though. Even though he seemed so far away, she trusted his presence, trusted his judgement, trusted his opinions. He made her feel…safe, like everything was going to be fine. When that feeling finally took hold, all the panic inside her that had been bubbling up to the surface getting ready to explode simply vanished. She needed that. Needed it desperately. "Look, Michael, I know you said it's too dangerous, but you've got to find someone to drive the bus off us."

"No way in hell," he called. "That's crazy!"

"We'll be fine." Funny how she sounded like the calm one now. "There's enough clearance room." Barely, but it could work.

"The driver's sitting on the sidewalk, sobbing. He can't drive. I *don't want* him to drive."

"Then find somebody else who can. We can't bring Delroy out in his condition, but we need better access to him. So find somebody to get the bus off us."

"Sarah, no! That could get both of you killed if something goes wrong."

"What kind of doctor were you before you were on the ship?" Honestly, she didn't know, and it was an odd time to ask, but she had a hunch about him.

"Surgeon," he yelled back.

Just as she'd thought. Nerves of steel. He was the one to do it. "You do it, Michael. *You* get the bus off of us. Because if you don't…well, you know the consequences." She waited for him to refuse, but there was no response for a minute. So she worked her way down the left side of Delroy's body, finding what she thought was a broken femur. It just kept getting worse and worse for the poor child. "Well?" she finally called out to him.

"Look, Sarah, I don't want to do this. But I've got to trust that you know what you're doing."

Like she trusted that he knew what he was doing.

"I was getting the keys. So now tell me what you see on the bus. Your proximity to the wheel. Clearance above you."

Sarah gingerly rolled over on her back and looked up at the undercarriage. She wasn't a mechanic, didn't know what was what, but she was a good judge of distance, and this distance was much less than she'd guessed. "Eighteen inches clearance in most places. And as we lie here, the child has about twelve inches to his left, which would be the driver's side. He's not touching the tire, but it's close, and I can't get him lined up and any further away from it. Also the tires are turned to the left and the one on the driver's side tire is sitting in bit of a pothole, so before you move you'll have to straighten the tires or you'll run over his leg. And his leg is already fractured, I just discovered." Sarah drew in a steadying breath, counting, more now than ever, on Michael's calm composure to get her through this. "There's more clearance on the right side. You'll be fine there." But it was so close on the left, she wondered if an inexperienced jitney driver could do it.

"And where will you be during this?"

"I'll get back in line with his head." That was the best place, as coming back alongside of him would only increase the risk of her getting run over. "Have you ever driven a bus, Michael?"

"No."

"A car?"

"Yes?"

"A big car?"

"Does a big truck count?"

Sarah scooted on her left side, making her way back up along Delroy's body, aiming for a position where they would be head to head. As she scraped her way along the rough pavement, it was only then that she realized if Michael turned even a fraction of an inch in the wrong direction, he could run over them both and there would be no one to stop him. By the time she could yell directions to someone on the outside who would yell directions to him, it could be too late. But there wasn't another choice. Right at this moment she had to trust Michael like she'd never trusted another person in her life. And after so long of not trusting anything or anyone, it felt good. Surprisingly good.

"Look, Sarah, why don't you come out from under there and let me see what I can do. Maybe someone else out here can drive the damned bus…"

"I promised Delroy I wouldn't leave him, and I'm not going to?" This point was not negotiable. Amazingly, Michael didn't argue about it, like she'd expected he might. She liked it that he listened to reason. In her estimation that made him a much better doctor than she already knew him to be because he knew the value of giving support to your patient no matter what the situation.

Now all she needed was for him to be a good driver, too.

Suddenly a flashlight scanned the area from behind her. She couldn't turn to look at it even though she desperately wanted to see his face again. But she couldn't get herself into that position while he assessed his so-called surgical field before he performed this most critical operation. "So, what's your assessment, Dr Sloan?" she asked, trying to sound light about it. "Minor surgery required? Or major surgery?" After this was over, she'd need a *real* holiday.

"Major surgery, I'm afraid. Your *bit* of a pothole is a little larger than I thought, and it's going to be a problem."

"Meaning?"

"Meaning I've got to gun the engine to bump out of it. The driver's called his company to send a qualified driver out to do this, so maybe we should wait."

"But how long will it take for him to get here? I don't think we have time to wait." She listened for a moment and heard the far-off wail of a siren. The ambulance? She desperately hoped so.

"A few minutes," he said. "Look, Sarah, this is too dangerous…"

"I know the risks, Michael. We're running out of time, though, and I trust you to do this." She placed her fingers to the pulse in Delroy's neck. "So please trust me when I tell you that we have to get this done now. We're losing ground under here."

Michael didn't respond for a second, but finally he exhaled in an audible sigh. "Then I guess we don't have a choice, do we?" he said, snapping off his flashlight.

"No, we don't." Steadying herself for what was to come, Sarah put a reassuring hand on Delroy. "It's almost over," she said to the boy. "Just another minute, and they'll have this bus off us then we'll get you to the hospital." She said a silent prayer that it would be soon because as she laid her hands on Delroy's head, her fingers went to the pulse in his neck yet again. It was even weaker. Irregular now. In another few minutes there would be no pulse.

"Brace yourself," Michael called. "I'm not familiar with the gears, so this could be a little rough. But you'll be fine."

She raised her head just enough to see his feet as he walked away. *Well, Sarah, for someone who said she'd never work again as a doctor, you've sure jumped back into it in a big way.*

Shutting her eyes, she laid her face to the pavement and stretched both her arms ahead of her to make contact with Delroy as the bus's gears engaged. Then she drew in a deep breath and held it.

"Damn," Michael muttered, climbing into the jitney driver's seat. Of all the people in the world, it had to be Sarah under there! And why the hell hadn't she bothered telling him she was a doctor before now?

It was odd, but he didn't have time to think about any of it because there was a critically injured kid down there. And Sarah. And here he was at the wheel of a vehicle he'd never been inside before, let alone driven, scared to death, and ready to drive it anyway, no thanks to the real driver, who was still incoherent, getting more and more hysterical by the minute. Naturally, no one in the crowd had admitted to knowing how to drive one of these things either, of all the rotten luck. So there he was. In the hot seat, quite literally.

Damn! All he'd wanted to do was come ashore for a conch fritter from Clarice's Café and do a quick check of her daughter's leg.

Those things didn't take nerves of steel. This did, and as he studied the gears, trying to figure which did what, he forced himself not to think about the fact Sarah was a doctor who, for some strange reason, hadn't disclosed that fact to him. *Gears. Concentrate on the damned gears!*

That's exactly what Michael did for the thirty seconds before he jumped off the bus and dropped to his knees to tell Sarah what he'd decided. "I'm going to move the bus forward, rather than going backwards—it'll give me better momentum to pop the wheels out of the pothole. I just wanted you to know that the entire jitney's going to roll over you so you'll be prepared. Oh, and after it does, I'll expect an explanation."

"An explanation?"

"Of why you didn't tell me you are a doctor."

Michael didn't wait for her response to that. Instead, he climbed back into the jitney, sucked in a deep breath, turned the steering-wheel until the tires were straight, then depressed the clutch slowly, giving the engine enough gas to rock it, but not enough to get the tire out of the rut. He was too cautious. He knew that. But he lived cautiously these days. Still, he had to try it again, skip the caution and get it right. Sucking in yet another deep breath, Michael gave it another go, punching the gas pedal much harder this time. The bus rocked forward even harder, but still not enough. Damn it, it wasn't going to work! To get up the momentum he needed, he'd have to practically floor the gas pedal, and in doing so, the tire would pop out. But in that moment the bus would also be totally out of his control. And Sarah… He forced that thought from his mind, replacing it with another.

"I need help," he shouted, jumping from the jitney. "I need people to push this bus forward. Enough people to get behind and push it when I hit the gas pedal." This would work. He knew it! "Push it just enough so that we can get the front tire out of the hole."

Immediately, the majority of the hundred or so people who'd gathered there to watch ran to the back of the bus. Too many, of course, but he'd get a good line of men from the group, and that would do nicely. With the sound of the siren getting closer, he guessed they'd just about make it by the time the medics arrived.

"Damn," he muttered, steeling himself for what he had to do. Battlefield surgery had been easy compared to this.

The first time the jitney engine revved, Sarah held her breath, but nothing happened. The second time, she actually looked up, saw the bus try to move forward, then sit itself back down in the hole. Delroy was struggling for breath now, and it occurred to her that if he quit breathing altogether, she was in no position to attempt any sort of resuscitation. She'd have to pull him out from under the jitney, risking injuries that might kill him to perform CPR. "Just another minute," she said to the boy. "In fact, maybe we should count it off together."

She glanced out to the feet of the crowd. They were running away now. She couldn't imagine why. Clearing a way for the ambulance? It still didn't sound so close, but she hoped the people out there were making way for it. "One. Two. Three." She counted long, drawn-out seconds, thinking about Michael in between the protracted count, conjuring up his image, trying to find his sense of calmness. She didn't want to get to sixty and depended on Michael's distraction to keep her away from it because she feared that at sixty Delroy would give up for good.

Back in the driver's seat, Michael depressed the gas pedal and the crowd at the rear started to push. It took only a second for the wheel to come out of the hole, then he inched the bus forward, deathly afraid that he lacked the proper sensitivity in his right foot to do this. Actually, his right prosthetic foot. He could drive just fine, but the reflexes governing the movement in a prosthetic leg certainly weren't like those of a real leg, and he'd had more than his fair share of speeding tickets where he'd depressed the gas pedal too hard, trying to figure out the delicate adjustments to life without a limb. So, as sweat beaded across his forehead, he drove, hoping he was better than he gave himself credit for.

The jitney moved forward slowly and, thank God, went as straight as an arrow. At least his steering wasn't impaired, he thought as he looked into the rear-view mirror to see if he'd cleared Sarah and Delroy yet. He'd instructed the crowd not to converge on them, and so far everybody was hanging back. But he didn't see them yet, even though it seemed like he'd driven miles.

His hands ached from the way he gripped the steering-wheel—white knuckles all the way. And the sweat dripping down his face stung his eyes. If muscles could scream, the ones knotting in his shoulders and neck would do that as he forced the bus forward, willing himself to concentrate on the driving and not on Delroy. Not on Sarah.

"Eyes forward," he warned himself, even though he wanted to look in the rear-view mirror again, wanted to finally see them lying on the ground, safe and secure. "Eyes forward. Keep it steady." Just another few feet. That's all it was. All it could be. Just another few feet…another few inches.

Michael drove until he heard cheers coming from the crowd, yet even then he didn't look in the mirror until he'd driven well past the place where Sarah and Delroy were stretched out. When he finally came to a stop and applied the brakes, he slumped over the steering-wheel for a few moments, willing himself to breathe normally again, willing

his heart to settle back down. Then and only then did he
gamble a look at the two forms lying on the ground. And
when he'd finally convinced himself that he hadn't run over
them, it took him another few seconds to force himself out
of the driver's seat.

Once he was out the jitney door, Michael was greeted by
the cheers of the crowd...*they were actually cheering him.*
But he ignored them in his haste to make his way back to
Sarah. When he reached her, he dropped to his knees and
began an immediate assessment of Delroy.

A glance out of the corner of his eye caused him to turn his
head to Sarah. "You OK?" he asked, trying to sound unaffected by the whole event, even though the sight of her there
on the ground affected him in ways he hadn't expected. She'd
been so...vulnerable. And so trusting. Her mistake. People
shouldn't trust him. He'd proved that a long time ago and so
far nothing in his life had changed. He wasn't worthy of being
trusted. Just ask the loved ones of the two men who'd trusted
him to save their lives, and he hadn't. Those were families who
knew just how far that trust went, where he was concerned.

"I'm fine," she said, pushing herself to her knees. "But I
was wondering, were you following me again? Or do we just
have this uncanny ability that makes us turn up at the same
place at the same time?"

Uncanny, maybe. Something he was going to have to
avoid in the future, definitely.

"Is the hospital good?" Sarah wrung her hands, watching the
ambulance pull away with the patient she'd held onto for the
past thirty minutes...thirty minutes that had seemed like a
lifetime.

"Actually, yes. Prince Hospital has about four hundred
beds, I think. It's the public hospital here, and they have just
about every service you can imagine—general practice,
surgery, obstetrical, emergency, intensive care. Delroy will

be in good hands there, and if they feel they don't have all the support he needs, they'll transfer him to one of the hospitals in the States."

"If he lives," she said despondently.

"He'll live." Michael brushed away a dead twig that had tangled in her hair. "So, why didn't you tell me you were a doctor? Here I was, explaining hypoglycemia and all its complications to you, and you're a… What kind of medicine do you practice?"

"I don't practice medicine now, but when I did I specialized in internal medicine and family practice as a partner in an immediate care clinic."

"But you quit?"

He seemed to want an explanation, but she didn't talk about it. Not to anyone. "Burned out," she said. It was a simple explanation and people accepted that much better than they would the real reason. "Probably wasn't meant to be a doctor in the first place so I got out of it."

"Well, you sure could have fooled me, because the doctor under the bus seemed like someone who *should* be a doctor. Someone who cared enough to risk her life."

"Well, we all have our opinions, don't we?" That seemed a little snappish maybe, but she didn't want to talk about it. Not with Michael, not with anyone else. Right now she just wanted to go back to the ship, clean herself up, grab something to eat, and spend the rest of the day in her cabin. "Look, I'm sorry. I don't mean to be rude, but after what just happened…"

"I totally understand about the way you feel. Not about why you left medicine. But if you don't want to tell me, I won't ask. OK?" He frowned. "Are you aware that you're in need of some medical attention? I mean, a doctor would be, but as you're not a doctor now…"

"Really subtle, Michael. But I'm still not going to talk about it." She glanced down to the cuts and scrapes all over her legs and arms. "And I'm fine. When I get back I'll stop by the ship's hospital for some antibiotic ointment and bandages."

"Well, as you're not a doctor and I am, I'd like to get all the dirt washed off those cuts before that," he said, pointing to the hose-drawn carriage making its way down the opposite side of the street. "The streets aren't very clean here, in case you didn't notice."

He was attempting to humor her, to lighten her mood. Trying hard. Charming. Close to being irresistible. But she had to resist. That's what she did now…resisted. "I don't see any kind of facility nearby, so I'll be fine until I get back."

"Right there," he said, pointing to a picturesque little café not three doors away. "I was on my way to make a house call there anyway, so if you don't mind going with me…"

She glanced at the horse clip-clopping its way by her, then at the scrapes on her knees. She really didn't want to go, but there was no telling what was already festering in her wounds. And, yes, that was the doctor in her prevailing on her common sense. Wasn't it amazing, though, how Dr Michael Sloan always seemed to be on the spot when she needed him? Funny, how that worked out.

Funny, but nice. "OK, I'll go with you. But no doctor questions."

Taking her arm, he pulled her through the crowd of people that was finally beginning to disperse. Admittedly, she liked the feel of clinging to him. He was sturdy, and she hadn't had that in a very long time. It felt good.

"Are you being mysterious or stubborn?" he asked, as they approached the cottage door.

"I said no questions."

"You said no *doctor* questions. That wasn't a doctor question."

She glanced up at the smile spreading across his face. Yes, this felt good. Maybe too good.

CHAPTER FOUR

"You're the one who rescued Mimmie's boy, aren't you?" Clarice Rolle's high-pitched voice drifted over the noisy crowd while she ushered Sarah and Michael through the tiny café at the front of the wood-frame building. It was filled to capacity with people staring at Sarah, many of them patting her on the back and smiling as the three of them made their way down a hall and through a door into Clarice's living quarters in the rear. It was all very cozy—the café, the flat. Tidy, and immaculately clean, it was a nice, friendly place that Sarah immediately liked, both parts to it done up in different shades of blue—the café in an array of bright blues and the flat in more subdued shades.

"I was under the bus with him," Sarah admitted to Clarice, wishing she wasn't the center of attention now. Although an admission wasn't necessary with the way she looked. She was a mess, head to toe, covered in a mixture of dirt and blood and whatever else had come off the street, all of it ground into her tattered clothes, into her hair, her skin.

"Well, it was a brave thing going to help him like you did, when you could have been hurt yourself," Clarice said, giving Michael a frown and a shooing gesture that told him he clearly was not wanted or welcomed in the bedroom into which Clarice was leading Sarah. Once she'd shut the door, practically in his face, she said, "Now, you go clean yourself up in the bathroom, take care of those cuts and scrapes all over you, and I'll go and find you some fresh clothes to put on."

"That's not necessary," Sarah said, for the first time noticing that the leg of her shorts was split right up the middle, almost to her hip line. It was, quite literally, hanging in shreds, revealing much more of her leg than she cared to reveal. "I can just wash off."

"With your clothes hanging on you the way they are, showing off more than they cover now, I don't think you'll want to walk through the streets that way. Men being what they are, and this is such a crowded town with all the ships docking here…" She gave her head a wary shake and pointed to Sarah's knit shirt, which was torn halfway down from her neckline. "But don't you worry. We're about the same size, so I've got something you can put on." Clarice said, "and it wouldn't be polite of me not to take care of you after what you did for Mimmie's boy."

Sarah studied Clarice for a moment. It was optimistic, thinking they were about the same size. Clarice had a perfect figure, and she was diminutive, the way Sarah had always wanted to be. Sarah, in comparison was…larger. Taller, bigger bones, bigger everything. But Clarice was right about the way she looked. Her clothes were so close to being indecent, with so many rips, and covered by so much blood. "Thank you," she finally said. "I'd appreciate it. And I'll be glad to pay you—"

"That's not the way we do things here," Caprice interrupted. "We take good care of our friends, and you're a friend now."

"A friend," Sarah murmured, shutting the bathroom door. It had been a while since she'd considered anybody a friend, or even been anybody's friend. Cameron had been the last, and look what she'd done to him. Even thinking about that ugly period in her life caused her hands to shake as she turned

on the water in the sink, then splashed some of it in her face.
She couldn't think of it…wouldn't think.

Focus, Sarah.

The room was getting smaller, starting to spin.

Just breathe.

She gripped the edges of the washbasin to steady herself.

One breath at a time.

The wobbling was starting in her knees.

You can stop this.

She knew she could. It was only a panic attack. Mind over
matter. She was in control. In control… Sarah held her breath
for a moment, then let it out and turned to focus to the face
in the mirror, and to the small abrasion on her left cheek. It
was red, but not bleeding. Nothing too deep, nothing that
mattered. Neither was the tiny cut along her right jaw.
Insignificant again. Especially when she thought about
Delroy, and all his injuries.

Besides the major ones, he'd been a mass of cuts and
scrapes, some that would, no doubt, leave scars. And then
there were the emotional scars. He had so much trauma to
overcome, so much recovery ahead of him. Perhaps she would
try and get his address so she could check in on him from time
to time, just to see how he was doing. Not as a doctor, but
as…as someone who'd shared an experience with him.

Cleaning herself up to where she was presentable took
Sarah nearly ten minutes, dabbing gingerly at all the spots
that were now becoming sore. But after they were clean, and
after she'd made the assessment that everything was superficial, she took one final look in the mirror, hoping she could
hold everything together until she was back in her cabin.
These panic attacks…she hated them. They made her look
weak, feel weak. Feel out of control. And for someone who'd
owned an immediate care center, which had depended on her
always being in control not just for herself but for everyone
working for her, she absolutely despised what she'd become.

That face in the mirror…she hardly even recognized it any more. Didn't want to recognize it.

Disgusted with herself on many levels, Sarah put on the clothes Clarice had left on a chair outside the bathroom. Admittedly, now that she was clean again, she did feel a little better. But the clothes Clarice had chosen for her…hot pink *short* shorts, with much less fabric in them than anything she'd ever worn in public, with the exception of a swimsuit. And the top…pink and blue floral, bright colors, in a stretchy knit fabric—much less fabric than the shorts—that left nothing to the imagination about her breasts, now that her torn bra was in the trash can. Clarice's idea of a shirt pulled tight across Sarah, showing off the precise outlines of her nipples, and it didn't come within a good hand's width of covering her belly button, it was so short.

"Well," she said, assessing herself in the mirror, not sure she wanted to walk back through town to the ship dressed *this* way. But what other choice did she have, other than her own clothes, which were filthy, and in shreds? Probably discarded already, as Clarice had carried them off the second Sarah had handed them out the door in exchange for what she had on now. Which turned out to be the case she found out once she'd stepped out of the bathroom. Her old clothes, bra included, were already in the incinerator.

"You look beautiful," Clarice said, smiling her approval at the way Sarah wore the outfit.

"It's a little…small, don't you think?" She tried tugging down on the shirt but all that did was reveal more breast.

"But you can wear small. Better than me. I've lost so much weight these past months, worrying about Lachelle the way I've been doing, that my clothes practically hang on me."

Well, nothing about this outfit was hanging on her. Sarah took another look down at herself, and decided to make the best of it. "You have a daughter?" she asked.

"She's out with Dr Mike right now. He's supposed to be

examining her, but they play more than anything else, when he comes to look at her leg."

"He makes houses call?" That seemed odd.

"Every time the ship docks here. He keeps an eye on Lachelle's progress, especially now, with her growing so much. She's wearing a new one and he wants to make sure it fits her properly."

Sarah didn't follow that. "A new what?"

Clarice looked surprised by the question." A new leg," she said, like Sarah should have known. "My Lachelle has to have a new leg made for her when she has a growth spurt, then Dr Mike comes to check, to make sure the fit is good and that Lachelle is working with it properly. I trust him more than I do the public clinic here."

So, the child had a prosthetic leg. And Michael had been on his way to visit her, which was why he'd carried his medical bag with him. She'd wondered why he'd happened to have it but that explained a lot. He was making a house call of sorts, and lucky for her he was. Lucky for Delroy, too. "How old is Lachelle?" Sarah asked, on her way to the bedroom door.

"Ten. Eleven in two months. Big girl for her age. Looks more like fourteen, she's been developing so fast."

Such a rough age, growing up. Almost into adolescence, all those hormonal changes going on. And a prosthesis to contend with. Her heart went out to the child. "But she gets along well with it…with her new leg?" She asked that, rather than asking if Lachelle had other disabilities.

"She gets along beautifully. Better than I would if I'd had the accident and ended up the way she did. She's good in school, she plays with her friends, rides a bicycle. Dr Mike introduced us to a very good man who specializes in prosthetics for children, and that has been a blessing for us because he knows just what Lachelle needs."

Once Sarah had stepped out into the hall, she immediately heard the giggling of a young girl. And deeper, more resonant laughing she took to be Michael's. It was interesting that the ship's doctor had one special patient here in Nassau, but as it was really none of her business, she wouldn't ask how that came to be. Even though she wanted to.

"Delroy went straight to surgery," Michael reported, once Sarah stepped into the living room. "No word yet on how he's doing other than he's still holding on well. Not conscious, but they said that his vital signs were much improved."

"He's my friend," Lachelle piped up. "We go to school together, and play together."

"Do you like him better than me?" Michael asked, the corners of his mouth turning down to feign hurt.

Lachelle giggled. "He's here all the time. You're not. So I have to like him better when he's here. But I like you better now, and every time you come to visit me because you bring me candy."

"So now I understand," Michael said. "You're fickle. Do you know what that means?"

Lachelle looked puzzled for a moment, then her face brightened. "It means I can like Delroy better when he's here, and I can like you better when you're here."

"But what if we're both here together?" Michael asked. "Then what would you do?"

"I'd like whoever's closest to me the best," Lachelle said, with perfect ten-year-old logic. "Especially if he has candy."

Michael was seated on a wooden chair and Lachelle was standing across the room from him, smiling for all she was worth. She was a beautiful child. Smooth black skin. Black hair, dark brown eyes and a smile that could have melted even the coldest heart. It gave Sarah a little tug, thinking about how she'd wanted children, first when she'd been married to Kerry, then again when she'd been engaged to Cameron. She was almost thirty-five now, and while the longing hadn't gone away, the expectation had. "And what if I'm the one who's closest to you?" she asked Lachelle.

"I might like you best, but I don't even know you." She looked Sarah over, head to toe. "But you *are* wearing my mama's clothes, so I suppose I *could* like you, too."

"Well, I'm Sarah," Sarah said.

"And you're a doctor, like Dr Mike," Lachelle said, quite matter-of-factly. "I'm going to be a doctor, too. An orthopedic surgeon. Dr Mike says that when the time comes, he'll help me find the best medical school."

It crossed Sarah's mind that Michael and Clarice might be involved, as there was no sign of a permanent man in this house. Not here in this room, not in the bedroom either. Michael certainly did seem like he had an important place in this family, though, especially with the way Lachelle seemed to adore him. "Well, I'm sure he'll have some very good suggestions."

"And I'll work with children like me, who have had amputations. And like Dr Mike."

That's right. Michael was a surgeon. She'd forgotten all about that. "I think you'll make a fine surgeon," Sarah said, as she watched Lachelle walk cross the room. She was in shorts, not at all self-conscious about showing off her prosthetic leg. It came over the knee and stopped at mid-thigh. Not the old, clunky kind that imitated the real thing, but a lightweight metal variety that showed it for what it was…an artificial limb. A functional part of the body meant to work, not look like it was real. The newer ones were easier, had more precision to them. While she wasn't an expert in the field, she'd done enough reading to know that technology had come a long way these past few years and the science involved in making a leg or an arm was as close to being exact as you could get. Anyone wearing one could expect high function, and high function seemed to be the case with Lachelle, because her limp was barely noticeable as she moved with all the agility of any ten-year-old. She seemed quite athletic, in fact.

"Fritters, Dr Mike?" Clarice called from the hallway. "Or a salad this time?"

"Why do you even bother to ask?" he asked, standing up.

"And what will you have?" Clarice asked Sarah.

"Excuse me?"

"Conch fritter? Conch salad? Conch chowder? We have conch just about any way it can be eaten, and if you know of a better way than I have to fix it, tell me and I'll fix that."

"Conch?' Sarah whispered to Michael. "What's conch?"

"Shellfish. You know, the big shell you can hold up to your ear and hear the ocean in it? That's a conch shell."

"Cannot," Lachelle said.

"Can too," Michael argued.

"Cannot," Lachelle said again.

"You go bring me a conch shell and I'll show you how you can hear the ocean in it." It was an old myth, but a fun one.

With that, Lachelle took him up on the challenge and went running out of the room. Sarah watched, amazed by her speed down the hall. With a pair of long pants on, no one would even know she'd had an amputation.

"So, what kind of conch do you want?" Michael prompted, taking Sarah by the arm and leading her down the hall that went into the back door of the little café.

Once inside, she did have to admit that it smelled wonderful. And she was actually hungry. Crawling under that jitney had worked up quite an appetite in her. "What are my choices again?"

In the end, she settled on the fritters—little pieces of conch dipped into batter and fried, then served with a spicy sauce. Good choice, she discovered after the first bite. "It's amazing," she said, sitting across from Michael at a little table in the kitchen, one used by the cooks and servers when they wanted to take a break. The dining area was full, and a line of people waiting to get in spread all the way down the sidewalk. That's what made this private little dining nook work out perfectly for them. "I had no idea there was such a thing as conch."

"It's one of my favorite parts of the cruise, even though it's not served on the ship."

"That, and sitting alone in a karaoke bar," she commented, as a drop of the dipping sauce dribbled down her fingers and she unconsciously licked it off. "Funny, how we keep turning up in the same places, isn't it?"

"Maybe I *am* following you," he teased. "Maybe it's not a coincidence after all."

"If you are, you must be disappointed with what you're seeing, because I'm not at all an interesting person. I keep to myself and don't get involved in much of anything. I don't sing karaoke in the lounge, don't mingle with the people on the ship, don't get wrapped up in the group tours off the ship. Meaning I'd think you could find someone better to follow than me."

"Actually, I think you're interesting. The fact that you're a doctor has caught my interest, anyway. And keeping that little bit of information from me when I was treating you is even more interesting. Of course, I can't ask you about that, can I?" He arched a playful eyebrow.

That was a definite hint, but she wasn't going for it. She liked Michael well enough, even felt oddly attracted to him—likely because they shared the same profession—but that didn't call for some kind of revelation, where she laid out the details of her husband's death and her fiancé's cancer, then explained that she'd quit medicine because as a doctor she'd realized how very little she could do, even when it had been for someone she'd loved at the time they'd most needed her. That she was a failure in the things that mattered,. No, that was none of Michael's business, so she avoided the conversation altogether. "I collected stamps when I was a little girl, but I didn't tell you about that either," she said. "People are entitled to their privacy, Michael, and your knowing that I was a junior philatelist is private."

"Is that why you didn't ask about Lachelle? You're respecting her privacy?"

"If I ask questions, then I have to answer questions. And I don't want to answer questions, so I don't ask."

"Well, it keeps things simple that way, doesn't it?"

Rather than nodding, she stuck another piece of conch in her mouth and chewed.

"Car accident. Her father was driving, and they were hit by someone driving a truck. Her father was killed immediately, and Lachelle was thrown clear, but her leg couldn't be saved. They tried for months. She had several surgeries, but the infection got the better of her. She was brave about it, though. Very pragmatic for someone so young, but you've seen how she is...brighter than most children her age. And very well adjusted."

Better adjusted than most adults, too, Sarah thought. "So, you and Clarice..." she started to ask, but stopped. She didn't ask, she didn't answer. Although she was interested in the relationship.

"We're not involved romantically, if that's what you were going to ask. Not Clarice and me. Not me and anybody. And in the spirit of being mysterious or stubborn, let's just say that I don't do it, I don't talk about it and I don't answer questions about it either." He paused for a moment, then frowned. "Where have I heard that before?"

"OK, I get it. And just so you'll know, I wasn't curious about your relationships," she lied. In truth, she was, but they'd established their lines now. No crossing over them. "I was just curious how you two met, and how you came to be a consultant for her daughter. Since you're on the ship, it seems it might have been difficult for you to find the time."

"In case you hadn't noticed, that's a doctor question. But you're the one who won't answer doctor questions, aren't you, so that makes me the one who does."

His teasing was downright sexy. This was a man who had the power to distract her in ways she probably didn't even know about. "You don't have to answer anything. In fact, we can have a mutual understanding that we discuss weather and the ship's shuffleboard game, and nothing else."

"Except I like to answer doctor questions."

"Unlike me," she said. Michael wasn't subtle in the least, and he didn't even try hiding the fact. But she was curious about what he *was* hiding. Unfortunately, she couldn't ask.

"You said it. I didn't. And just for the record, Lachelle and I met in a clinic in the States. One for amputees."

That made sense. He the doctor, she the patient. Sarah was glad for the girl because Michael seemed to be a compassionate man. "I'm glad it was you there with me today," she said. "Even when I was practicing medicine, that kind of rescue wasn't at all like anything I'd ever done, so when I found out that the person helping me was you...you don't know how happy I was to have you there. I was scared to death, and there's nothing mysterious or stubborn about that."

"Well, to be honest, I'd much rather be treating a good case of heartburn than driving a bus with two people underneath. But if me being there made you feel better, I'm glad I was."

"You did a good job, Michael. I think that if you ever decide to give up medicine you might find another career in driving a jitney," she teased, even though her hands were shaking again as she thought about what had happened. This was pleasant though, eating informally here in the kitchen with someone she really did find herself liking more and more all the time.

"So, what career do you find yourself in now that you've given up medicine? And for the record, that's not a doctor question. It's more about lifestyle, and you didn't put that on the taboo list."

"Maybe it's not specifically a doctor question, but it's getting awfully close to the edge."

"Close, but not over."

She stared at him for a moment, the expression on her face giving away nothing. "I'll concede you the point. Just this once."

"Just this once?"

He cocked a playful eyebrow. And infuriatingly, playful eyebrow. The gesture was pure sex, filled with all the innuendoes something so simple could be, and it was all she could do to drag out the answer. "I, um…I have no career at the moment. I'm just…I'm just living life as it comes." He knew exactly what he was doing to her, taking pleasure in it, damn him. "Going on holiday, seeing the sights." To avoid the spell he seemed to be putting over her, she stared intently into the dipping sauce. "No real plans yet, which is fine because living day to day is all the challenge I want. I have the money, and the time, so why not?" She instantly regretted giving him so much insight into her life, but Michael was so easy to talk that her talk turned into babbling.

"I'm a little surprised by that. You don't seem like the kind woman who'd want to be idle for very long."

She dragged another conch fritter through the dipping sauce, then debated whether or not she could eat another bite. Rather than deciding, she simply held onto it for a minute. "I'm not idle so much as I'm doing all the things people promise themselves they'll do once they retire and never get around to doing for whatever reason. I just decided to take an early retirement and start on my list now, rather than later." Not a good explanation, but it would do. And true to her fashion, it skirted the truth.

To keep from answering another of his questions, she popped the conch into her mouth, instantly regretting it as she was so full already. But she forced herself to chew, then swallow. Then she stood. "Look, I think I'm going to head back to the ship now. I know we've got another three hours in port, but I'm not really in the mood to be a tourist any more today."

"I'll go with you," he offered, dropping his napkin to the table and standing up, too.

"You don't have to. I'm sure Lachelle would love to spend

more time with you. And maybe you see other patients here…"

"Lachelle is out playing with her friends, and I have no more patients."

She wanted to ask if he and Clarice might like some time alone, in spite of his denials of a romantic relationship with her, or anybody else, but out of respect for his personal boundaries she didn't. "You don't have to babysit me. I'll be fine. No more crawling under jitneys unless absolutely necessary."

"I have duty in an hour," he said, heading over to where Clarice was giving instructions to one of the cooks. "So we may as well walk back together. And with the way that outfit looks on you, you probably need a male escort to protect you."

He eyed her up and down, not in the clinical way a doctor would but in the way a very appreciative, very hungry man might. Like the man he would protect her from on the street. None of that was lost on her, and she did have the decency to blush. But Michael didn't see that as he was busy giving Clarice a very circumspect kiss on the cheek. Definitely not the kiss of a lover.

For some strange reason Sarah felt better about that. But it did make her wonder, because a man like Michael shouldn't have sworn off that kind of relationship the way he'd claimed he had.

Sarah said her farewells to Clarice, then to Lachelle, who was in the yard when she and Michael stepped outside. "You coming back with Dr Mike next time?" the girl asked, as she hugged Michael around the waist and pretended she wasn't going to let him go.

"I wish I could, but I've got someplace else to go after this cruise." She wasn't sure where. The truth was, she hadn't made any plans. Not in a very long time. Something would come to her, however. It always did. "But the next time I'm in Nassau, I'll be sure to come see you." She had no plans to return to Nassau, but she could. Living the way she did, there was nothing to stop her.

After walking a few blocks, dodging the blatant comments from strangers about the way she looked—mighty hot mama, they were calling her—and shrinking from the blazing stares, Sarah and Michael finally retreated to the relative privacy of a cab for the rest of their journey back to the ship. But in the cab, an old rattletrap of a car that smelled of human bodies and tobacco and had badly ripped seats, she and Michael barely spoke, which was odd as the condition of the seat practically forced her into his lap, they had to sit so close to each other. Good thing she'd had a quick bath, she thought as her shoulder wedged into his arm.

"So, have you ever been to the Bahamas before?" he finally asked, as it became apparent they were stuck in a traffic jam, going nowhere any time soon.

"No. Never been on a cruise, never been to the Bahamas." Stiff conversation. *Very stiff.*

Another minute passed before he spoke again. "If you don't consider it private, could I ask where you're from?"

"Chicago, born and raised." She might have asked him the same, but at that moment the cab lurched forward several car lengths, then stopped again. "Do I make you nervous?" she asked impulsively.

He bent to her ear. "You don't but your clothes do."

She glanced down, shocked by what she saw. Her short shorts had crept up as far as they could go. Likewise her shirt. In attempting to get settled in the back of the cab, apparently her clothing had…shifted. Indecently so. "You're a doctor," she whispered back, trying to force her clothes back into the right position as the cab driver glanced in his rear-view mirror to see what all the whispering was about. "This shouldn't disturb you."

"I'm not on duty. I'm allowed to be disturbed."

That was kind of cute, actually. And she was flattered. Not

so much that she'd ever wear these clothes again, though. Or anything like them. But after being so long without a man, it was nice knowing that she still did have the power to attract one. Too bad she didn't want one. But one year married to one man, then a year and a half engaged to another…the third time wasn't going to be the charm. She simply wouldn't let that happen.

"I thought I might find you here," Michael said, sliding into the seat next to her. The same dark corner of the same karaoke lounge. Tonight the singer wasn't so loud or off key. And a few more people had found this hidden little gem, so they didn't have most of the place to themselves like before. But Sarah'd been there an hour, in her regular out-of-the-way booth, sipping ginger ale and wondering if he might meander in.

"It's as good a place as any to spend time," she said, watching the waitress take note of Michael. She literally perked up, primped her hair a little, tugged the neckline of her black blouse a little lower and undid an extra button. It was clear that Michael could have his pick of them if he wanted. For a moment she almost regretted the boundaries she'd established, because she sure wanted to ask him why he didn't want his pick. Especially with a waitress who was doing everything she could, except make an announcement over the karaoke machine, to attract Michael's attention.

"Not really," he said, as he gestured her over to the table. "But it's a habit that won't get you into trouble."

Oh, I see trouble, Sarah thought as the waitress slithered her way up to the table.

"The usual, Doctor?" Heidi asked. She was almost breathless, and it wasn't from over-exertion.

"I'm not in the mood for a Cubano tonight. Just bring me a diet soda and a basket of pretzels." Heidi looked almost crestfallen as she scampered away, like she took Michael's change in order personally.

"That's not a proper meal," Sarah said, trying to sound light about it. "After all the lectures you've given me on the subject of proper dietary habits…"

"Do you always listen to what the doctor says?" he asked, relaxing into the booth. "Because you don't seem like the type."

"Depends on the doctor. I've known a few whose word I'd take as gospel, and a few I wouldn't trust as far as I could throw them."

"So, when the pretzels arrive, if I were to tell you that they are a perfectly balanced meal, lots of vitamins, good nutrition, would you take my word for it?"

Sarah didn't even hesitate. "I'd take your word, Michael. I may not practice as a doctor any longer, but I'm still a pretty good judge of one." The next thing out of her mouth would have been something about why such a good doctor was limiting himself to a ship's practice, but Heidi plunked down the basket of pretzels at that moment and Sarah shoved one in her mouth before she asked a question that would, on some level, involve her with Michael in something more than a casual chat in a dark little karaoke lounge.

"Delroy's in Intensive Care," he said, picking up a pretzel, studying it for a moment then dropping it back into the basket with a weary sigh. "They removed his spleen, surgically repaired his arm, splinted his broken leg, stitched up numerous cuts. He has a concussion, but he's beginning to stir so they don't anticipate permanent brain damage. Oh, and they discovered four broken ribs. His surgeon told me that one was so badly separated that if Delroy had been dragged out from under the bus, the rib would have gone right though his lung, and he'd probably have died on the spot, owing to all the other injuries and blood loss. You had a good instinct with that one, Sarah. You saved the boy's life."

"That's good."

Michael didn't answer for a minute, and when he finally

did, he seemed almost angry. "Did you hear what I said? I just told you that you saved the boy's life, yet you seemed…unaffected. I don't understand that. I'm emotionally drained, and I wasn't under that bus. You were, and you're so…"

"Uninvolved," she said, trying to sound detached and dispassionate when, in fact, she was so elated that Delroy would recover that what she really wanted to do was grab Michael, hug him, kiss him. But what she was putting on for him now was part of the facade, and she was good at it. Well practiced. "I did what anybody would have done, but that doesn't give me any kind of a bond to the boy. I'm glad he's going to be fine, and that's all there is to it." Except the part of her that wanted to get up on the table and dance. That's the way she used to be, though. Good news for the patient became her own good news. Bad news, and she suffered right along with them.

But not any more. Sarah Collins, retired doctor, forced herself to stay uninvolved.

"I don't believe that," he said. "I was there this afternoon. Remember? I saw you under the bus, saw the way you held onto that child and protected him. Saw the way you wouldn't leave him even when your own life might have been in danger. So you can tell me you're uninvolved all you want, but those are words, Sarah, that I wouldn't trust as far as I could throw them."

"Why does it matter to you?" she snapped, as she started to scoot around to the other side of the booth. It was time to leave. Time to retire to her cabin and figure out what she was going to do. Stay, or leave the ship? Michael was becoming too personal, and if she wasn't careful, she'd get personal right back at him. She was seriously considering it. He was more tempting than anything in a long, long time and that's what scared her, because part of her really wanted to give in to the temptation. A big part of her did, anyway. "Why do you even care what I do, or how I feel? If I say that I'm not involved with Delroy, who are you to question me…no, accuse me of lying about it?"

Michael grabbed her by the arm before she could scoot to the other side of the circular booth. "I'm not sure who I am, Sarah. Not sure why I care. But I do."

She wrenched free. "Well, don't. People who care for me end up…" She didn't finish her sentence. Instead, she got up and walked away. Just like she always did now.

CHAPTER FIVE

SARAH stared up at the row of coconut palms on the hill above the fruit plantation. She was totally isolated from the other cruise passengers who'd come ashore here in Jamaica. That was by design, of course. While people were running off to go rafting and bird watching, she'd decided to wander off on her own and stay away from the main flurry. Theirs wasn't the only ship in dock at the moment, and there were tourists everywhere, but she never considered herself a true tourist, so traveling along the dusty roads by taxi to destinations no one else cared to see suited her just fine.

The ship would be there for twelve hours to give its passengers an opportunity to experience Montego Bay both during the day and at night, when it came alive in ways only Jamaica could come alive. But by the time evening rolled around she intended to be back on ship and, truth be told, the only reason she'd come ashore had been that twelve hours in dock seemed like such a long time. She wanted to avoid Michael, and that would be hard to do on a practically empty ship, as they kept bumping into each other on a full ship.

The ride was jarring as there were giant potholes in the road, but Sarah barely noticed as her attention wasn't on where she was going. The taxi driver, a friendly man named Frank, was trying frantically to engage her in some way, talking incessantly about the countryside as they bumped their way from place to place, and she responded politely in the places that called for a response, although she just wasn't in the mood. So after two long hours of a tour she wasn't interested in, she asked Frank to drive her back to the ship, where she paid him a generous tip and went back to her cabin.

What was the nature of her latest discontent? The list was getting longer, she feared, and Michael had taken his place on it. Maybe at the top of it.

Two hours after her return to the ship, two hours of fretting and pacing the confined space of her cabin, always on the verge of a panic attack, Sarah decided to go out in search of a bite to eat. Something, anything, to get her out of that cramped space. Her first thought was the karaoke bar. Michael would be on duty so she wouldn't bump into him there, and at this late hour of the afternoon no one would be singing. So it would be a perfect place to be alone. Yes, perfect, she thought as she hurried down the corridor to the elevator.

After she punched the button, she stared at the floor, folded her arms across her chest and waited several seconds, until the doors parted. When she looked up, Michael standing in the center of the elevator, grinning at her. "Margueritaville," he said. One simple word and nothing else.

"Isn't Margaritaville a song?"

"It is, but I said Mar-*guer*-itaville, not Mar-*gar*-itaville." He gestured her into the elevator, but she stepped backwards as the doors started to close. Undaunted, he punched the "open" button, then wedged himself against the right door so it wouldn't close again. "I heard you'd come back early."

"I saw everything I wanted to see," she said. Everything she could see, with her thoughts so scattered. She was restless, and the reason was standing directly in front of her, looking so handsome she wanted to melt into his arms like she had that first day, only this time doing it on purpose. "One place is pretty much like another, and I did exactly what I wanted to do."

"Well, you ought to take a look at your face because, judging from the expression there, you haven't done anything you wanted to do in a long time."

"Why me, Michael? Why do you keep coming after me?"

As the elevator alarm started to sound, he stepped off. "I'm not coming after you, Sarah. But it's a pity that you isolate yourself so much you can't accept a simple gesture of friendship when it's offered."

"Is that what this is? A simple gesture of friendship? Because you've got hundreds of other people on the cruise who are probably clamoring to be your friend, and I'm the one who's not. Yet here you are, forcing something on me that I simply don't want."

Rather than being put off by that, as she'd expected he would be, he stepped even closer to her. So close she could smell the slight muskiness of his aftershave. "Your shell isn't as hard as you think it is, Sarah. I'm a student of human nature, and as you're saying one thing, your eyes are saying something entirely different."

She snapped her head up, glaring at him. "So, what is it you want from me, Michael? Sex? Is that what this is about? I'm the lady you've chosen to fulfill your needs on this particular cruise? Or maybe I'm the challenge you've picked to conquer? Are you taking bets on the outcome? Because if that's the case, how about we go back to my cabin, then you can strip me, throw me down on the bed and do whatever you want to satisfy that urge, or win that bet, and we can move on from there? You can go find your next conquest and I can do what I came on this cruise to do."

Anger sparked in Michael's dark eyes, but just for a second before his usual genial expression returned. "Apparently, I have a higher opinion of you than you have of yourself. Which is a pity, Sarah, because it's got to be miserable living the way you do, always pushing people away. Especially since that's going against your true nature."

She straightened her shoulders, still trying to hang onto her defiance, even though it was beginning to slip away. "You don't know a thing about my true nature."

"I know you've called to check on Delroy several times. That tells me something about you."

"You don't think I have the right to be concerned?" she snapped.

"The Sarah you're trying to be wouldn't be concerned. The Sarah I think you are would be. So you tell me, am I close to your true nature?"

This was crazy! She didn't have to argue with him. Didn't even have to speak to him, yet here she was, standing in a deserted corridor, pulse rate rising, breath coming shorter and shorter, nipples probably hardening, all because Michael made her respond in ways she'd thought dead a long time ago. She hadn't been with a man since Cameron, hadn't dated, hadn't kissed, hadn't even been alone with a man, and she did recognize her starving biological urges. Especially in her crazy responses to Michael. But that's all they were. Urges. She could control them.

She hoped.

"My true nature, Michael, is what I want it to be. It's whatever suits me at the moment."

A wicked little grin played across his face, on his lips, in his eyes. "So when you invited me to your cabin to let me throw you down on the bed and strip you naked, was that your true nature? At least, true for that moment?"

"You'd be disappointed in my true nature," she said flatly, trying to avoid the way he was baiting her now. It wasn't a sexual thing, but he was trying to goad her into something, and she didn't want to be goaded.

"I hardly think so, Sarah. But that's not why I came looking for you."

So this really wasn't an accidental encounter. Her heart did skip a beat knowing that, which was why she had to fight even harder now to keep herself under control. "Whatever it is, you shouldn't have," she said stiffly. "And just so you'll know, I don't date, don't get involved with men—"

"You think that's *not* obvious?" He chuckled. "You wear it like a banner. It's on your face, in the way you hold your body, the way you pull back even from people passing by you who are paying no attention to you whatsoever. Look, Sarah, I can respect the distance you want. I don't know what caused it and I'm not going to ask because I do believe that people have the right to be the way they want to be."

"And in your opinion, I'm being miserable. Is that it?" she snapped.

"Are you?" Before she could respond to that, he thrust out his hand to stop her. "No, don't answer that. It's none of my business."

She studied him for a moment, not sure what to make of this little quibble between them. It wasn't so much that they were arguing as establishing their ground rules. But for what? And for some reason, she didn't believe the boundaries being imposed were all about her. Michael kept his distance, too. His boundaries were as obvious to her as hers were to him. Which made this safe. So, maybe that was good. She liked him, and at another time in her life would probably have gotten involved with him.

For now, though, two people with strong boundaries worked. It broke up the monotony in her life, gave her that medical connection she still hungered for, and there was the added bonus of his company. She enjoyed it. Sexual attraction had definitely been in short supply in her life lately, and she did recognize it for what it was.

In other words, this alliance was safe, and safety was all she really wanted. "Tell me again why you came looking for me?"

"Margueritaville," he stated, like he had the first time. "I thought you might like to go there with me."

"Aren't you working?"

"I'm off duty for the next eight hours, and there's this nice cantina I try to get to here whenever I have the time. Good food, great music. And just so you won't consider this a date, I'll be going there even if you don't." A wide grin spread across his face. "And we'll take separate taxis, if that appeases your need to keep this casual."

How could any one man be so infuriating in one breath and so absolutely irresistible in the next? Even though she'd never heard of the place, all she wanted to do now was go to Margueritaville with Michael. In fact, she wanted it so badly it was like this was the only thing she'd ever wanted to do. "How about we take one taxi, and split the fare?"

"If you pay the taxi driver's tip," he said, still grinning, but more with his eyes now. Which caused goose-bumps to go wild up and down her arms.

"Both ways?" she asked, trying to keep a straight face, because his smile bought out a smile in her. "Because that doesn't seem fair to me."

"Sounds like we've got something to argue about in the taxi, doesn't it?" he said, then spun around and punched the elevator button. "I'll meet you on the dock in fifteen minutes." There were no gallantries after that. Michael merely stepped into the elevator and engaged himself in chat with a young couple who were clinging to each other so tightly it made Sarah think they might be honeymooners. He didn't look at her as the doors started to close, didn't acknowledge her in any way. Professional demeanor, she thought as she stood there, watching him, even doing some bold-faced admiring that he could see if he looked at her. Then, in the very last instant before the doors came together. Did he actually wink at her?

Margueritaville turned out to be a pleasant town sitting

right on the coastline. It was nearly dark when they arrived, but lights twinkled from every window along the street they traveled, giving the place a nice, welcoming feeling. It was congested, though, with tourists making their way down the coast to see the little town with the name that so closely resembled the popular song. "So which came first," she asked Michael, "the town, or the song?"

"The town, by a long stretch, and they're enjoying the popularity of their name now."

"How did you find it? By the name, like everybody else does?"

Michael leaned forward on the seat and gave the taxi driver instructions to turn at the next corner. They did, straight into a dark little alley. "Marguerite is my mother's name. I saw it on the map first time I came down here, and when I had the chance, I came here to have a look."

Halfway down the alley, Michael tapped the driver on the shoulder, and the cab came to a stop under a single light jutting out from the wooden building. True to their agreement, he paid his half of the fare, then jumped out of the cab, leaving Sarah to pay her half, as well as the driver's tip. Although, in his defense, he did go around and open the taxi door for her. But rather than offering her a hand as she climbed out, he stood back. More distance, she thought, and she wondered if that was on account of her wish to keep up the boundaries or his.

"Why are we going in the back way?" she asked, following him to the door.

"Less crowded."

"Like your booth in the karaoke bar?"

"You mean the booth you choose for yourself when you can beat me to it?"

He held the door open for her as she passed by him. Once inside, she ran straight into the wall, it was so dark in the corridor. "Don't they use lights in here?" she asked, backing away from the wall and thrusting out her hand to locate where she was and which way to go. But what she encountered, rather than another wall or obstacle, was Michael's chest. Strong, muscular, her palm flat on his chest, she drew in a ragged breath, but didn't remove her hand. Instead, she kept it there as his chest rose and fell with a breath. Then another breath. Then another.

Finally, she pulled back, but before she could pull back from him more than an inch or two he took hold of her wrist, and she was overcome with a rush of sexual twinges like she'd never felt in her life. Not with anybody.

All from an innocent touch in the dark!

Yet she made no move to pull away from him. Instead, she fought to keep her breathing steady as he pressed his way past her in the tight little hallway, pushing her back against the wall for that instant as their bodies met. And in that moment crazy, aroused thoughts ran through her mind… She wanted to, right there, like she'd never wanted to with any man in her life. Wanted to even more when she felt his hand skim up over her ribs and slide its way under the knit top she was wearing—the one Clarice had given her that she'd vowed never to wear again.

Sarah bit her lip to keep from sucking in a sharp, loud breath because she feared the least little sound would break this spell, and she didn't want it broken. Barriers were down, and she didn't know for how long. And while they were down she wanted everything from Michael that she could have.

Tilting her head to the side, she felt the nuzzle of his lips just at that tender spot where her neck and shoulder connected, and the liquid heat from something so simple melted down through to her very core, arousing her to the point that she pressed her hips against his, and felt his erection hard against her. She gasped, in spite of her resolve to be quiet, and that only intensified the pressure on her as he ground into her even harder.

Sarah was ready for him, in this dark little nook, even as her eyes were adjusting and she could see the outline of his body so close to her, pushing harder in such intimate ways. The feel of his fingers pushing away her bra to find her nipple, the feel of his lips on her jaw...

Somewhere in the distance the sound of shattering glass broke the mood, and Michael backed away from Sarah as quickly as Sarah adjusted her disheveled clothing. "Sounds like a tray of bar glasses," Michael said roughly, then cleared his throat. "Bet somebody's going to pay for that."

The liquid heat still flowing everywhere—through her breasts, between her legs, Sarah was able to answer only with a nod and something that amounted to a squeak. This was...incredible. Incredible and stupid! She was about to do, well...anything, everything, with Michael in the back hallway to a bar. That wasn't like her. She'd never been wild like that. Never been driven to the point of such extreme desire that it would compel her to do such an impulsive, crazy thing. Worst of all, the heat wasn't going away fast enough. She still wanted Michael. "Do they have tables here?" she asked, finally finding her voice. "Because I need a margarita in a big way. Two of them!"

Michael chuckled. "Can you imagine what would have happened if we didn't have boundaries?"

"I understand hormones and lust," she said stiffly.

"If that's what you want to call it." He took hold of her hand once more, but this time pulled her along the corridor until they entered the kitchen, where he greeted the cook, a man named Emilio, an assistant cook called Juan, and a large woman—not large in weight so much as stature—all decked out in multicolored scarves and large, jingling gold hoop earrings and bracelets. The woman had dark, smooth skin and bright eyes.

"I wondered when you'd be getting 'round to see me, man," she said to Michael. "I knew da boat was in, but I've been waiting all day to see the doc, and I was gettin' disappointed he wasn't comin'."

Michael dropped Sarah's hand and rushed over to give Evangeline, the proprietor of Evangeline's, a big hug. "Do you think I'd miss the chance for some of your jerk chicken?"

"You crave Evangeline's jerk chicken the way you should be craving a woman," Evangeline said, her jolly chuckle rolling out over the entire kitchen. Jerk chicken was a typically spicy Jamaican recipe, and a favorite of the locals as well as tourists. "The way you should be cravin' that one," she said, pointing to Sarah.

Sarah blushed, wondering if Evangeline had witnessed what had almost gone on in her back hall.

"You know you and your jerk chicken are the only things I've been craving tonight," Michael said, casting a sideways glance at Sarah. "And some good reggae music."

"You get the chicken and you get the good music, but you know you don't get Evangeline. I like my men…older. With lots of money. You're good-lookin', Doc, but I've got other needs you can't take care of." She cast a sly wink at Sarah. "But I'm guessin' what her needs are tonight, and it's not chicken and reggae."

Evangeline sauntered away, still laughing, while Sarah was coming to the decision to catch a cab and return to the ship. But Michael didn't give her an opportunity to slip back out the way they'd come in. As if he'd guessed what she might be planning, he grabbed her by the hand and pulled her the rest of the way through the kitchen into a dim room full of people, all sitting at tables or at the bar on the other side of the room—a bar backlit in blue. The place was packed, there was barely room to squeeze through as a saxophone wailed something so rhythmic on stage that most of the people in the club were clapping and stomping along to the music.

"How are we going to find a place to sit?" she shouted over

the music. Deep down, she really hoped they wouldn't find a seat so they could leave. Or they'd find only one seat, for Michael, so she could leave by herself. As it turned out, Michael had a cozy little booth reserved for him, back in a secluded corner, of course. They'd no sooner squeezed into it when Evangeline appeared at the table with two tall glasses—one with a fruit juice concoction she placed in front of Michael and one with something yellow for her.

Evangeline gave her a toothy grin as she passed the glass over. "From what I saw of you in the kitchen, I think you'll be needing this. It's Evangeline's specialty." She actually tweaked Sarah's cheek before she walked away.

"That means she likes you," Michael said. Or, actually, practically shouted as he was sitting on the other side of the booth. "I remember the first time she tweaked my cheek…" The rest of what he said washed away in the noise and, to be honest, Sarah didn't really care. She was so uncomfortable being there now, after what had almost happened, that she was happy to turn her attention to Evangeline's drink and lose herself in it. What had she been thinking, giving in that way? Never mind that it was in a public place!

Well, it wouldn't happen again. And Michael's suggestions to take two taxis…that's exactly what she intended to do. Take her own taxi back to the ship as soon as she finished Evangeline's rather tasty rum extravaganza.

OK, so he'd screwed up. The moment, and the opportunity, got the best of him, but it wasn't like anything had really happened between them. To look at Sarah, though, someone might have made assumptions about all kinds of things having gone on in Evangeline's back hall. Sarah looked guilty, and she wore that guilt even now, twenty minutes later. But, damn it, it just wasn't that big a deal. They'd flirted a little. Well, maybe flirt wasn't accurate. But they'd stopped. That's all that counted.

Sarah was sitting across the table from him, and she hadn't looked up from her drink for the last ten minutes. Hadn't really drunk any of it either. So what the hell was he supposed to do now? This was supposed to be a nice evening out for her, something to relax her and help take her mind off what always seemed to be bothering her, but it wasn't working.

"Want some chicken?" he asked, shoving the plate across the table to her.

She looked up, giving him a blank stare.

"The chicken. You should try some," he said again, only this time louder, trying to cut through the noise all around them.

Judging from her expression, she still didn't hear him, though. Or didn't want to. Normally the noise level in there was a blessing. He always slipped in the back door like he'd done tonight, come to this booth and eaten his chicken. Alone. There was something to be said for being alone in a crowd. Of course, most of the time Evangeline never let him be entirely alone, even though tonight she was staying away. Deliberately, he guessed. And for some reason, even with Sarah sitting across from him, he'd never felt so alone here as he did right now. "The chicken," he shouted, then finally gave up and scooted around to the other side of the circular booth. Surprisingly, she didn't push herself away from him, but she did cringe when his arm brushed against hers. "Look," he said, bending toward her, yet taking particular caution not to touch her. "I'm sorry about what happened."

It was an opening, and he waited for her to respond, but all she did was give him a stiff nod. Well, so much for trying to approach her. One little lapse in good sense had ruined her evening which, in turn, was ruining his as he'd truly thought she might enjoy this. So maybe they should simply return to the ship and promise to avoid each other for the rest of the cruise. Or perhaps he should send her back in a cab, alone, while he stayed and enjoyed the routine he'd established over the months—jerk chicken, reggae and a pleasant way to relax.

"Do you want to go back to the ship?" he asked. "Since that little faux pas in the hall is bound to ruin at least one of our evenings, maybe you'd be more comfortable having yours ruined somewhere else." OK, so that was harsh but, damn it, he was trying to make up for his mistake and she wasn't giving him an inch. So why keep trying? "How about I just call you a cab, and we'll pretend it never happened?"

"Pretend it never happened?" she sputtered, finally turning sideways to look at him. "How can you pretend something like that never happened?"

The way the dim light overhead caught the glint of her hair, the angry spark of what had to be the most beautiful eyes he'd ever seen… Honestly, he wasn't the least bit sorry about what had almost happened. If the truth be told, he'd been aroused to the point that he'd have probably pushed her into the little broom closet just inside Evangeline's back door and broken a promise he'd made himself nearly two years ago. "You can quit dwelling on it, then enjoy the food and the music, that's how."

"It's that simple for you?"

"Look, Sarah, what happened…happened. Apparently, we've got some pretty good chemistry going between us, and we let it get away from us for a couple of minutes. It happens. We're humans. Hormones flow. I've apologized, and I'll apologize again, but if you want to know my true feelings, I'm not really all that sorry. I enjoyed it and if the situation presented itself again, I'd probably do the same thing." Against his dictates, but not so much against his will. Sarah was the first woman who'd turned his head since his self-imposed ban on women and his whole relationship avoidance, and he didn't really object to his feelings toward her as strenuously as he should. Or wanted to. Probably because she put up enough barriers for both of them that he felt relatively safe with her. If he couldn't resist her, which it seemed he couldn't, at least she'd resist him. "But that's all I can do. Say I'm sorry and give you an option…to stay here with me and enjoy the evening or leave and do whatever you want to do."

He hoped she'd stay, but from the long pause he was pretty sure she wouldn't.

After nearly a minute, Sarah finally spoke. "It wasn't just you," she said so quietly he had to lean in close to hear her. "I was ready to do something I've never done before, in such a public place. And I'm not like that, Michael. But for a minute I forgot who I was and where I was…"

"And that's so bad?" he asked, for his sake as much as hers.

"I'd like to think that I have more control," she admitted.

"Have you ever just let yourself go, Sarah? Been spontaneous about anything?"

"I think the way I live *is* spontaneous," she said defensively. "You know, living for the moment, that kind of thing. That's me! That's all I do, living in the moment, going with the flow."

"Very rigidly," he argued. "You strike me as a woman who'd much rather make plans and live by the rules."

"Rules are made to be broken, and plans are a trap. My only rule is that I'm not allowed to make plans. Why bother? They don't work out. Trust me, I've lived that life before, and been disappointed by it. So why put myself through anything like it again?"

"Maybe you're right. Why put yourself through it?" Broken plans only caused pain, and he'd had his share. Sarah was right. Plans were a trap, which was why he'd avoided making them himself. Once was enough. In life, in love, he didn't make plans any more either. Not even in the short term.

Michael finally broke through the barrier between them, scooting so close to Sarah they were sitting hip to hip. "I've lived that life before, too. Tends to make you a bit cynical, I think."

"Ah, the man who knows."

"What I know is that you can plan your life down to the smallest details, live by that plan and count on it to be your beacon. As long as you're headed toward the light you're doing fine, things are going to work out. Then one little thing happens…" *Like having a leg blown off by a landmine and watching your buddies die beside you while you're helpless to do anything…* "And it all changes. Goes straight to hell. All your plans are gone, everything you've hoped and dreamed for vanished, and you suddenly find yourself in a position you can't even conceive of. Your meticulous life, the one you could picture in a panoramic view, isn't yours any more and you're left wondering what comes next. What the hell are you going to do now." Something he'd been wondering from the day the doctors had released him from rehab and sent him out into the world to face whatever it was he had to face. Eighteen months between the hospital and rehab, living in an altered reality, and he'd been totally unprepared for his new reality. Even after a year of living inside his new reality, he still wasn't prepared for it.

"You speak from experience," she said.

Michael cracked a bitter laugh. "We all have experiences that mold us, whether or not we want them, don't we?" Like a fiancée who had been repulsed by a less than perfect body in the man she'd supposedly to loved, one who hadn't even pretended to be sympathetic or unaffected when she'd seen him without his prosthesis. That had been an experience that truly had molded him, and not in a good way, for future relationships. It was another one of these things that fit into the category of why bother to put himself through it? He'd already seen the results. Didn't need to repeat them.

"Want them or plan for them. You know what they say about the best-laid plans…" She finally picked up a strip of the chicken and took a little nibble, caught off guard by the spicy heat of it. Coughing as she tried to swallow it, Michael shoved his fruit drink over to her, frowning as she took a greedy gulp. Yes, he did know about what happened to the best-laid plans. The problem was, he hadn't planned on Sarah. She was the sexiest woman he'd ever known in his life, and if he wasn't careful, some of his best-laid plans were in serious jeopardy of going astray.

Thinking about his current course as he picked up a strip of jerk chicken, Michael wondered if now wouldn't be a good time to actually form a plan...a plan to *not* get involved. He also wondered if he was drawn to Sarah because he was more like her than he cared to admit. In her, the sadness and isolation was so easy to see, but what he saw in her...was that what other people saw when they looked at him?

Sighing, Michael tossed the chicken strip back onto the plate then leaned back in his seat, still taking care not to accidentally brush Sarah's arm or bump her hip. Distance was best, and he was going to have to be very careful to keep his.

"I'm sorry I overreacted a while ago," she said, just when he was about to give in to the melancholy crashing down on them. "You're right. It's chemistry, and I shouldn't be such a prude about it, because under normal circumstances it's a good thing for most people. A wonderful thing. But in my life those kinds of things never happen."

"Because you don't allow them?" The way he didn't allow them any more?

"Honestly, yes. Keeping focused always seems to work best for me. There's no need for me to be any other way because what I am, what I do, suits me."

No, it didn't, and he could see that very plainly. Even now, as she toyed with another piece of chicken, licking a little of the spicy-hot marinade off it first, then licking her lips and letting her tongue wander across her bottom lip, he was as aroused as he'd been in the hallway. More so, because he could see her now, see all the sexy insinuations of her movements…insinuations she didn't even know she was making. Right at that very moment he wished he had some of her focus, because if he wasn't careful he'd find himself in the same position he'd been in earlier in the dark hall, and even he had only so much restraint he could call on to save himself. The best-laid plans were about to fail him.

But deep down didn't he want to fail in this one? Of course he did! He was a man, after all. And she was…well, everything he'd ever dreamed of in a woman. And, damn it, human nature did prevail, his disability and his checkered past notwithstanding. "I know you've got your resolve, but are you ever tempted, Sarah?" he asked, his voice much lower, much more seductive than he'd intended it to be. "Maybe you don't ever give in, but are you tempted to? I mean, like right now. After what happened in the hallway…"

She glanced into his eyes, very seriously. "Yes, I get tempted. You could have had me in the hall, Michael."

Well, that certainly wasn't what he'd expected from her. Wasn't what he'd needed either because in the next instant she was in his arms…whether he pulled her there or she'd gone voluntarily, he didn't know, but the temptation melted away all resolve as his lips crushed hers and he tasted the slight heat of the spice still lingering on her lips. The pull was too great to resist, even though he knew he should pull back and leave well enough alone. But what he knew and what he did were two different things as his tongue forced her lips apart, only to join with a tongue that was as eager as his to probe.

As he caressed her upper lip with his tongue, moving it in slow, delicious circles, she reached up to stroke his hair, running light fingers through it at first. Then as he nipped softly at her lip, she pulled with some vigor until he tilted his head back and away from her, but only enough to allow her to kiss his neck then his jaw. Sweet mercy, he'd never felt anything like it! The way her tongue played gently up his throat, over his jaw… The plan be damned. He'd deal with its demise later.

Once she reached his mouth, she was the one to do the probing this time, to run her tongue over his lips, to delve inside and once she'd found his tongue to suck it with a potent energy like no one had ever done to him before. And if he had been aroused before this, he was now aroused to the point that he was uncomfortable, and had this not been a public place they would have been past the point of no return. But this *was* a public place, a fact that niggled in the back of his mind as he returned a forceful kiss to Sarah, his full, open mouth taking hers in a greed he'd never before known as both her hands snaked around his neck and pulled him tightly to her, as tight as human beings could possibly be without being inside one another.

And as the kiss should have been diminishing, she arched herself back into the booth seat, pulling him along with her, causing him to shift to a position that was nearly on top of her. His arms wrapped around her as she turned sideways into a semi-straddle and her knee came up over his thigh. Because they were in a dark, secluded booth where the only people who could see them were the ones who wanted to, he pulled Sarah up over his lap until she was fully straddling him, looking down, pressing her hands to his cheeks and lowering her mouth over his. Tongues sought tongues again, nipping, probing…harder, faster, the urgency growing until Michael moaned the moan of a man who couldn't take it any more. He was at his limit, and so was Sarah as she pulled away, looked down at him with longing in her eyes like he'd never seen before, then slid off his lap.

Without a word she straightened her clothes, slipped out of the booth and left Evangeline's.

That evening, needless to say, they returned to the ship in separate taxis.

CHAPTER SIX

ONE more day, and they'd docked again. A good many people had gone ashore for various expeditions and shopping, spending their few hours milling about, but Sarah hadn't gotten off ship this time because there hadn't been anything she'd really wanted to do. Neither had Michael. She'd seen him in passing once since two nights ago in Evangeline's. He'd been strolling along the deck, pushing a patient in a wheelchair down to the cabana chairs, and he'd been so caught up in casual chat with the old man he probably hadn't even noticed her. Or hadn't wanted to. Whatever the case, the instant she'd seen him, she'd turned around and hurried off in another direction.

It wasn't like she was embarrassed, though. Because, oddly, she wasn't. What they'd done in the booth at Evangeline's had been the culmination of what they'd started earlier in the hallway, which had been the climax of some pretty pent-up feelings. She understood. And Michael was right about it, too. They did have chemistry going on between them. What was the point of denying it? And if he thought that she couldn't be spontaneous, well…he'd seen her at her spontaneous best that night.

Truly, it did surprise her that she'd acted that way. In the dozens of times she'd replayed that little scenario in her mind since then, she hadn't found an excuse for what she'd done other than she'd simply wanted to. *With Michael*. No one else had ever stirred that little wild streak in her like he had and she'd returned to the ship a very sexually frustrated woman. In her mind she'd had herself naked with him over and over—in her cabin bed, in the shower, the dark hallway at Evangeline's and even in the booth. In some of her fantasies they were even in their private little section on deck, behind the bar. And those kisses weren't bound by what was proper in public either.

Even thinking about that now was dangerous because it put her in a mood to be reckless, and if there was one thing she wasn't, it was reckless. She could be. Maybe she even wanted to be, but recklessness led to other things. A brief, sexually satisfying affair might have been just fine.

But she wasn't wired that way. She knew it. For her, anything less than full commitment with all the trimmings simply didn't work. Although, with her history, full commitment didn't work out so well either.

So, skipping any embarrassment that might have normally occurred at such wanton abandonment of everything she'd worked so slavishly to keep in order, it was best to hold Michael at a distance now. Put what they had into its proper perspective, rationalize it into what it was—a moment of lust—and let it go at that. Oh, and be grateful to know *that* part of her was still alive. She'd figured it was long dead. After Kerry, then Cameron, she'd wanted it to be dead. Willed it away to a dark, dusty corner, never to surface again.

Sarah was happy it had surfaced, however, because this was the first time she'd felt normal in so long. Now that she knew she was relatively fit in those ways, however, it was time to ignore it all again. Time to steady herself with a deep breath, hold her head up high, and get on with her life…whatever that was.

So now not only was she avoiding Michael, she was avoiding all their usual places. There was no point in being around him, even though she wanted to see him. Which was why she couldn't. Or wouldn't. No need to put herself into a situation where she might accidentally bump into him, when it was just as easy to avoid him altogether.

On a ship this large, after all, avoidance was fairly simple. Which was her reason for being there in the first place—to make her life simple by taking a detour around everything that adversely affected her.

So now here she was, all alone on the promenade deck, going for a stroll on a perfectly beautiful evening. Being alone wasn't such a bad thing, really, even though the people around her did make her uneasy, all those couples on romantic interludes, walking hand in hand, stealing the occasional kiss, embracing in hidden alcoves, doing what couples should be doing on a night such as this. The sounds of happiness off in the distance added to the ambiance— lively music filling the empty spaces, laughter bubbling through the air, both coming from the people enjoying themselves at the formal dance being held in the grand ballroom this evening.

She'd received an invitation to attend, with a little note tucked inside telling her that the ship had a limited number of escorts available for those who were alone on the cruise. In her fantasy, the invitation was from Michael, but in reality the stamped scrawl on it was a fuzzy blue duplicate of the captain's signature, probably put there by one of the ship's office staff and never even seen by the captain himself. "For the best," she murmured.

Sarah strolled casually along the railing, looking out into the water at the reflection of the ship's twinkling lights dancing off the gentle waves made by the ship as it glided along its way rather than watching other people doing the things she was, surprisingly, envious about. She should have flown back home. That chance came up earlier today, yet she hadn't even so much as flinched when the announcement had been made. Now she was wondering why she'd stayed here, given her troubling proximity to Michael. Perhaps it was that she had to be somewhere, and on board a cruise ship was as good a place as any.

Or maybe it was because of Michael? Something to do with her growing attraction?

No, that wasn't it. Absolutely, positively, could not be! He was handsome. Had a nice personality. He was an outstanding doctor. *Wonderful, amazing kisser.* But all those things combined weren't enough to sway her over to the side she so arduously resisted—the side where she found herself solidly involved with someone again. Been there, done that, twice now, and she couldn't go back. Sure, she was an emotional wreck over the choice she'd made to stay unattached in every way, because she loved being involved. Loved everything about it. But once with Kerry, then a second time with Cameron…

Sarah truly didn't believe in the third time being the charm, which was why she was a mess now because, deep down, she really did want to give that third time a chance. But being a mess was easier because the only pain was self-inflicted, which was much easier to endure than what she already had.

"Did you know you've become quite famous?" A bright, chirpy voice from behind her interrupted her thought. "People are talking about what a brave thing you did to help that little boy, the way you put your life on the line to save him."

Sarah spun around to face her admirer, not because she wanted any kind of a conversation with the woman but because she wanted to be polite. "I wasn't really brave. I think I just did what anybody would have done under the circumstances." What her natural instincts had led her to do.

"Well, from what I've heard, there weren't a lot of people stepping up to help, Sarah. And you were the one who went under that bus and stayed there when they had to move it off him. I'd say that's risking your life."

The woman looked vaguely familiar, but Sarah couldn't

quite place her. "Do I know you?" she asked. "Have we met before?"

"We haven't been properly introduced, but I suppose you could say we met that day in the elevator, when you nearly fainted in my arms and Dr Sloan caught you. My name is Martha. Martha Grimes."

Now she remembered. The lady with the big, purple hat.

"I heard mention that you were a doctor," Martha continued. "That explains why you did what you did for that child. Even though you're trying to be modest about it, it's in you to be brave like that, to help somebody in distress. I know how it is. My husband was a doctor and he'd have done the very same thing you did."

"A doctor," Sarah murmured, still trying to be polite to Martha yet not really in the mood for conversation.

"A very good doctor. Gone a year now. It was so sudden. He hadn't been sick a day in his life, then all of a sudden…"

Martha's voice was positively sad, and in the light shining down on them from one of the lanterns hung along the walkway Sarah could see the woman's eyes pooling with tears. Her heart went out to Martha because she, too, knew the pain of loss in the same deep, personal way.

"What kind of doctor was he?" Sarah asked gently.

"Obstetrician." Martha's voice was filled with pride as she fought back the sniffles. "I was his office nurse, helped him deliver babies until I started having babies of my own." She swiped at a stray tear trickling down her cheek. "Now here I am, on a cruise my husband and I should have been taking together, only I'm with the Ladies' Purple Hat League. We do gardening in public areas to make things beautiful. Planting purple flowers…" She started getting tearful again, and fumbled through her purse for a tissue. "Purple pansies and petunias our specialty."

"Purple flowers, like your purple hats," Sarah said sympathetically.

Martha laughed. "You can't miss us, can you? We do tend to stick out wherever we go." She was still dabbing at tears, sniffling again and biting her bottom lip to keep from crying harder. "You'll have to forgive me. I'm new at this…at being alone. It's not easy being all by myself after forty years of marriage."

Yes, that was something Sarah understood all too well. Married to Kerry only a little over a year, she'd wept for months after he'd died. She couldn't even imagine what it would be like to lose the person you loved after forty years with him. Poor Martha. Yet she was getting on with her life through her Purple Hat League, which was more than Sarah could say for herself. It was commendable, not that *she'd* ever don a purple hat herself, but she did admire Martha for what she was doing, fighting her way through while her heart was still breaking. "Look, would you care for a ginger ale? I know this nice little lounge…"

Before she could finish, Martha pulled Sarah into her ample bosom and practically squeezed the breath out of her. Ten minutes after that and they were tucked away in Sarah's favorite booth, sipping ginger ale and chatting like old friends. Well, one old friend and one woman who wasn't saying so much. But Sarah didn't have to say much around Martha, and Martha didn't seem to notice. Even so, she truly could have done a lot worse for a companion. Martha Grimes was a pleasant, if not overly talkative woman, and she actually seemed to enjoy the karaoke singer, who was doing a particularly agreeable job.

Twenty minutes of ginger ale, chat and karaoke had passed before Sarah saw Michael approaching her. Maybe it was a good thing she had Martha here with her tonight, because he looked especially attractive in a well-worn, faded pair of blue jeans that hugged him in all the right places and a cream-colored cableknit sweater that accented everything she liked accented in a man. "Michael," she said, giving him a cordial nod, even though her pulse was racing when he stepped up to the table.

"Sarah," he said, just as cordially. He glanced at Martha, turning on a much broader smile for the older woman.

Sarah made the proper introductions, explained that Martha was one of the ladies in purple hats, then let Martha launch into her explanation of why they wore purple hats and what kinds of flower varieties they planted, while Sarah sat back and observed Michael…her observations first coming as a woman but then as a doctor when she noticed that he seemed particularly tired tonight, and that his limp was far more pronounced than before. The doctor in her took over completely as he stood there awkwardly, listening to Martha ramble on and on. It wouldn't be proper to ask him how he was feeling, even though she was tempted, because that could signal involvement and that was the last thing she wanted, especially after what had happened two nights ago. But he was a doctor, too. If he needed help, wouldn't he get it?

Silly question. Doctors were the worst when it came to getting help for themselves. Cameron came to mind in that category. He had been an excellent doctor, her medical partner actually, and someone whose skills and decisions she'd trusted implicitly. Yet when his symptoms had started, he'd written them off as fatigue. Fatigue! Weeks and weeks later, it had been discovered he'd had a well-progressed case of leukemia. That was the one single experience that had taught her how the worst patient of all was a medical doctor. Especially a doctor diagnosing himself the way Cameron had done. So it was only normal that she didn't have much of an expectation of Michael paying attention to what was going on with himself. Yet it wasn't her place to get involved, even if she was bothered by the way he favored his right leg, shifting his weight off it then back onto it, and wincing slightly as he did so.

"Michael, I, um…" she started, but was interrupted by

Martha scooting her way out of the booth. The karaoke machine had just become available and Martha was on her way to have a try at a Beatles classic. As she breezed by Michael, he finally sat down next to Sarah. "She seems nice enough," he said in a lackluster voice, keeping quite a distance from her.

"She's lonely. Widowed only a few months, and she doesn't know what to do with herself. I don't think planting purple flowers is very fulfilling for her."

"It's nice that you've befriended her."

His voice was so stiff it was almost unrecognizable. After convincing herself that what had happened at Evangeline's was nothing to be embarrassed by, was it possible that Michael was embarrassed? "Not befriended so much as I do sympathize with her. My husband died a few years ago, and I know how it feels to be so…alone. Not knowing where you're going or what you're going to do. It's frightening. You spend half your time hoping no one will notice you and half your time praying they will."

Michael looked shocked by Sarah's admission…properly shocked. "I didn't know, Sarah! I'm…I'm sorry."

"I appreciate it. But you couldn't have known because it's nothing I bring up in the course of normal conversation. You know, *Hello, my name is Sarah Collins, and I'm a widow.* It makes people uncomfortable. They don't know what to do or say around you, and they feel embarrassed or awkward because they're unsure about what's proper under the circumstances, so it's best left private, I think." It was something a man who'd had his tongue down her throat should know, however.

"How long were you married, if you don't mind me asking?"

"Just over a year."

He nodded, the way people usually did when they heard the story. However, most of them prodded her for more information about Kerry's death, asked tacky questions, made insensitive comments like *Well, thankfully you'd only been married a year. It would be so much harder on you if you'd been married longer.*

"I know words really are never enough, but I *am* sorry, Sarah," he said again, at the same time Martha hit an operatic note in a range the Beatles had never achieved and people in the lounge spontaneously jumped to their feet, applauding her. "I do have some idea what it's like going through what you did, and I know it's not easy, no matter how long you were married. Losing someone you care about…someone you love—is hard. Cruel. It hurts on so many levels, and I'm sorry you've had to go through that."

"Thank you. It was quite a while ago, but I do know how difficult it is to get over it, which is why I thought Martha needed a friend tonight. She's not doing so well yet, and she shouldn't have to be by herself."

"Your husband. Was he a doctor?"

Sarah shook her head. "An engineer. He built bridges. Had quite a good reputation for it, actually. In fact, I met Kerry on a bridge. I was strolling, totally absorbed by the sights of the river down below, and he was strolling, looking at ways to overhaul the bridge, totally absorbed by the support structures. He literally bumped into me—the movable romantic force meets the immovable scientific one, we always said. I discovered his melanoma…on our honeymoon."

"Was it metastatic?" Cancer that had spread.

She nodded, amazed by how easy this was. What was it about Michael that made this so easy when telling other people had always been so difficult? "Stage four." Meaning severe. "It wasn't diagnosed in time, unfortunately. We did everything possible, he had every treatment. But the different things we tried couldn't keep up with it. In the end, the cancer spread to his bones, then to his lungs within a matter of a few months. Kerry's oncologist thought it had probably been there a while, but by the time I discovered it, it was already too late."

"They do go unnoticed much of the time," Michael said, taking hold of her hand and giving it a squeeze.

"Yes, they do," she said simply. That much was true, but a fiancée should have noticed it some time during their six-month relationship and subsequent two-month engagement. It had been a tiny speck just under his armpit—but she hadn't seen it. New love, with all its excitement and urgency, didn't really have much to do with physical exams, and with so many other wonderful places and sensations to explore, she'd just never looked there. Not until their wedding night, after they'd made love for the first time as husband and wife. Totally satiated, Kerry had lain back on his pillow, his hands cupped behind his head, grinning at her with all the content-ment in the world, and she'd seen it. There were no words to describe what she'd felt at that moment. How could there be words to describe what, as a doctor, the newly wed wife had known she'd found? "Well, it looks like our diva has left the stage," she said, deliberately changing the subject as Martha headed back to the table, taking a bow every few steps of the way as the people in the lounge continued to applauded her.

Michael took that as a hint, and pulled away from Sarah.

"You don't have to go," Sarah said, disappointed that he was. He was easy to talk to. Easier than anyone she'd ever known in her life, and that included the two men she'd loved.

"I'm afraid I do. It's been a long day. Two of my medics are sick and I only stopped here to grab a sandwich to take back to my cabin. I've got to be back on duty in four hours and I need to get some sleep. Any other time…" As he stood, he brushed his thumb over her cheek. "Any other time, Sarah," he said on a wistful sigh, then turned away.

"Can I help you?" she cried out impulsively as the karaoke revved back up with a duo intent on butchering a ballad. "Can I help you in the hospital?" Volunteering for medical duty hadn't been her intention, but she was worried about Michael. He needed more than four hours of sleep, and his limp as he left the table was even more pronounced than his limp toward the table had been a few minutes earlier. "I can do, well, whatever you need me to. Lab work, general checks, anything. I'm not busy, and I could…"

He turned back to face her. "I appreciate that, but we're fine so far. We still have adequate coverage with the staff we have, even if we're putting in longer hours."

"Longer hours, and you're not looking good, Michael." There, she'd said it, even though she hadn't meant to. But it had just popped out. "You look…tired."

He opened his mouth to say something, then changed his mind as Heidi, the waitress, wiggled her way up to him and handed him a white paper bag with his sandwich in it. He thanked her, said goodnight to Martha, who'd climbed back into the booth, then he took a long, hard look at Sarah, but said nothing. All he did was smile, then walk away.

"Nice-looking man," Martha commented. "Downright handsome. You two are friends? Maybe even something more? A shipboard romance, perhaps?"

"We met that day in the elevator, when I collapsed in his arms. That's the extent of our relationship," she lied, even though they'd met in some fashion, personal or impersonal, almost every day since then. Was that enough to call him a friend? Was their volatile chemistry enough to call it something more? The fact that she rarely revealed that she was a widow to anybody, including Martha, and it had been so easy talking about it to Michael probably did make him a friend. She'd admit to that much and draw the line there, because one step over it put her back at Evangeline's, and that was something she really didn't care to explore further.

So, for the duration of the cruise, Michael Sloan was her friend. That was a decision with which she was satisfied.

But what would happen after the cruise?

Would he go off to his world and she back to hers?

Somehow that seemed inevitable, yet Sarah caught herself wondering if it would seem strange to book herself on the next cruise after this one, just to spend a little more time with Michael. "He's a nice man," she agreed on a melancholy note. The starkest truth of her world was that she might yearn, but she would never touch again.

"You two look so good together," Martha said. "The way my Robert and I did when we were younger."

Maybe that was true, but she'd looked good with Kerry, too. People had commented on that, especially on their wedding day. And she'd looked good with Cameron, something that had been said over and over at their engagement party. How did that old saying go? Was it, once bitten, twice shy? Could she change that to twice bitten and third time scared to death?

The truth was, she was attracted to Michael in ways she'd never meant to be attracted again. She would like to look good with him. No, she would *love* to look good with him, a sentiment that was speeding up her pulse rate and turning her respirations rapid and shallow. *That was the problem.* "You know what, Martha? You have a lovely voice. After these two guys get off the karaoke, I'd love to hear you sing again."

He'd worked harder than this, but he couldn't remember a time when he'd worked in a more distracted condition than he was right now. Sarah was on his mind all the time. After going for so long without any emotional involvements, finally convincing himself that he could get along fine without one, here he was, thinking about something that just couldn't happen. Not now. Especially not with someone who'd already known more than her fair share of tragedy. How could it be fair to her, dragging her into his own tragedies?

Knowing that he had to put an end to this kind of wasteful thinking, however, wasn't stopping him from imagining all the things he wouldn't allow himself to have. And as his patient load was growing, and as he wandered from patient to patient, treating all the common shipboard maladies over-taking passengers, he couldn't help but wonder how it might have been to work alongside her. She'd volunteered, after all. So he could have said yes, could have taken her up on her offer then scheduled her to work when he worked, saying, of course, that he was duty bound to keep a close eye on her as she wasn't a regular ship's employee.

Duty bound! Just like he'd been duty bound to seduce her in Evangeline's hallway then, later on in the booth, kiss her like he'd never kissed another woman. After all that, there wasn't an excuse on the face of the earth that he could use to keep Sarah at his side—not one she'd believe, anyway. Especially when the only thing he really wanted to do was finish what they'd started that night. Wanted it so badly he wasn't even sure he could work alongside her and remain un-affected.

Except there was one big thing standing in the way of letting her work with him, as much as he'd wanted to accept her suggestion…one big thing that set him right back into the professional frame of mind. Sarah had never confided her reason for not practicing medicine now, and that was a huge concern. While he couldn't imagine Sarah ever doing anything wrong as a doctor, anything that would have had devastating results or even have gotten her sanctioned in some way, he did have to know about her background and her reason. That was ship's policy, and he had to be careful with the way he proceeded as the responsibility of the ship's hospital was solely his. But more than that, as a responsible physician, it was his own personal policy to know about the people who treated his patients. So, with the remote pos-sibility that she could have had her medical license revoked, which he doubted, he couldn't allow her to work. As much as he would have liked to. *Loved to!*

"We've had thirteen new people come in with generalized aches, low-grade fever, lung congestion in the past three hours," Ina, the nurse in charge, reported to him. "Most of them can stay in their cabins and no one feels all that bad. Oh, and we're having the normal lot of over-eaters, people who are seasick, pulled muscles, that sort of thing. Nothing you wouldn't expect to see."

Michael sighed, looking at the growing stack of patient charts on his desk. That was the part he truly hated—the paperwork. "Well, you can't do much about the people with the flu-like symptoms, but you'd think some of the others would apply common sense with their eating habits, wouldn't you? I mean, the stomach's only got so much elasticity to it, and it gets to a point where it won't stretch any more. And then their food choices…" He faked a shudder. "Like I said, no common sense at all."

"Like you have when you eat those huge, porky, greasy Cubanos every day?"

"And what's your point?" he asked, chuckling.

"Other than the fact that you have horrible dietary habits yourself, and that you're in a rut with what you eat? Probably nothing, unless you want me to say something about the way you've look lately, because that's not too good. Or the way you've been limping, because that's not too good, either. Or the overall rut your whole life is in, which isn't healthy for you, Mike. You're too young to be acting like an old man. Which is what you're doing."

"I already have a mother, Ina," he said, trying to sound good-natured, even though he was a little put off by her observations. He'd have been even more put off if they weren't true. But they were, and he knew it. He was in a rut in so many ways, and it was easy to get lazy like that. Easier than trying to crawl out of that rut. It was all taking its toll on him, too, both physically and emotionally. Especially these past few days.

"And your mother's not here, seeing what I'm seeing. So, until she is…"

He thrust out his hand to stop her. "I'll eat better and sleep better. Is that good enough?"

"I won't tell you how to run your personal life, but at least have someone look at your leg. Because you need that, too."

Touchy subject. He didn't really talk about it unless someone like Ina forced him to. "My leg is fine," he snapped. It did tend to bother him the more tired he was. His emotional turmoil was beginning to drag him down physically. But there was an easy cure for that and maybe he'd take a week off after this cruise was over, just to rest. It was all part of the same restlessness.

"No, it's not, or you wouldn't be so grumpy about it."

"If you weren't such a damned good nurse, I'd fire you," he grumbled.

"If I weren't such a damned good nurse, I wouldn't care what's going on with you. But I am, and I do, and you know I'm right, even if you won't admit it out loud. So, how about a cup of tea?"

Ina's hideous brew from hell. He really should tell her how bad it was, declare it a hazard of some sort, then take her teapot and throw it overboard. But he wouldn't be that unkind to someone who thought she was doing a good thing, even if that good thing turned his stomach. "I'd love a cup of tea," he said, fighting back a cringe.

An hour later, back in his cabin, he rinsed the aftertaste of Ina's tea from his mouth and turned on the shower to let the water warm up. Now that he was off duty again, he had eight blessed hours before he went back on duty, and he intended to spend each and every one of them with his eyes closed. Unless, of course, he got called back, which was a possibility with another of his medical crew taken ill in the past hour.

Pulling off his white uniform shirt, Michael dumped it into the laundry bag and was starting to unzip his pants when a knock on his door stopped him. His first thought was that he was already being called back and he hadn't even been off fifteen minutes yet. "I'm coming," he called, grabbing his shirt out of the laundry bag. He was shrugging it back on as he opened the door, expecting to see Ina standing there with another cup of tea. Instead, he saw Sarah.

"I don't want to bother you," she said, "but I wanted to talk about my offer. I heard someone else on your crew is sick." Her eyes raked over his chest. "And I…um…I wanted to tell you that I'm serious. If you need me to come and work…"

Two of the purple-hat ladies, obviously lost and wandering down a passage where they weren't supposed to be, took a look at Michael in his half-dressed condition, then started to titter. "Come in," he muttered, grabbing Sarah by the hand and pulling her into his cabin, then shutting the door behind him.

"I'd expected something bigger," she said, looking around the room. "Since you practically live here, I thought you'd have larger quarters than the passengers have."

He laughed. "They're large, if you're not claustrophobic and don't have a lot of personal possessions." Which he did, but they were in storage back in Florida. His real life all locked up safely while he lived this life.

"I meant what I said, Michael. I want to help in the hospital. Whatever you need me to do is fine."

Maybe he would take up her offer. With the right permissions, it could work out. Having a little more time with her wasn't a bad incentive either. "Can you give me ten minutes to shower, then we'll discuss it? I'd like to get myself cleaned up before we talk about anything, if you don't mind."

"Should I come back later? Or do you want to meet me somewhere else?"

"No. This if fine. Just make yourself comfortable here. Like I said, ten minutes."

Michael disappeared into the bathroom and Sarah could hear the water running. She sat in the single chair in his cabin, feeling awkward, three steps away from his bed, fighting back the fantasies assailing her. On top of that, the purple-hat ladies outside were probably spreading rumors that turned her fantasies into reality, but the truth was that, she really had come here to offer her services again. *That's all!* While she didn't want to return to work on a regular basis, the urge to get back into it for a little while was taking over, and getting back into it with Michael at her side certainly had more than its fair share of appeal.

But right now, as she waited, she was so close to his bed she could smell the slightly musky scent of his aftershave, probably permeating his sheets. Musky sheets. Then all of a sudden she was picturing his bare chest, and the way his partially zipped white uniform pants had ridden low on his hips, revealing the sexiest patch of dark hair trailing below his belly button.

All of a sudden she felt hot. Jittery. It wasn't a panic attack this time though. Not in the traditional sense, anyway, as the panic she was feeling had much more to do with a dormant libido waking up—waking up, screaming—than it did the walls closing in on her. Which they weren't doing, amazingly enough.

Walk, Sarah. Just walk it off.

But she didn't want to walk out of his cabin as the reason for her being there was, truly, to offer her help. It was genuine. She did want to help.

Shake it off before he comes back. Shake what off? The fact that she could picture herself between the sheets with him? That her cheeks were flushed? Or that her hands were shaking?

Or that she was merely giving in to all the silly romantic

notions of a cruise and this wasn't at all about Michael? That
was probably the one she didn't want to shake off, the only
thing in these past few days that made any sense to her.

Except knowing that and walking straight through his
door, back into the corridor, back to her cabin, were things
that didn't seem to mesh so well because here she was, still
ignoring what was becoming increasingly obvious to
her…almost as obvious as the steam that was seeping into
the room from underneath the bathroom door.

She was getting hotter by the minute. Steam, yearning,
raw emotions, both old and new, it all caused her to jump up
from her chair and start pacing. Back and forth, round and
round. The space was too small to take many steps, but she
walked from one end of his bed to the other, back and forth
to his closet, to the cabin door, forming a precise rhythm to
her steps so she could count off the cadence rather than think
about anything.

This is crazy, Sarah. OK, so a little thinking was sneaking
in.

You're attracted to the man, so why not admit it?
Especially after she'd crawled all over him already. But was
this more than a physical attraction? That notion was slipping
in, which scared her. Admitting to something physical was
one thing, but to something more…

"Too much thinking," she muttered, deciding this wasn't a
good idea. She still wanted to volunteer, but she couldn't stay
in his cabin. The feelings and awareness were squeezing her
out. She'd leave him a note, telling him she'd catch up with him
later.

Good idea. Get out of his cabin before he was out of the
shower because Michael in the shower was too potent an
image for her to deal with.

In a hurry to leave, Sarah searched the nightstand next to
his bed for a piece of paper and a pen, but no luck. The was
nothing on the little table in the corner but a stack of medical

textbooks. So she decided to check his closet, not to go through personal belongings or anything like that, but to see if what she needed was in there.

When she opened the door, her eyes went immediately to the array of white uniforms hanging in a neat row. *He looked so good in his uniform.* Then to the few off-duty clothes he had hanging there. *He looked good in those, too.* She didn't see a pen on the shelf, and when she glanced down she saw shoes, and a…

Dear God! It was a prosthetic leg.

Michael's limp!

How could she not have recognized it?

The way she hadn't noticed Kerry's melanoma or recognized Cameron's leukemia. That's how!

Taking two steps back, she bumped straight into Michael. She turned, stared him straight in the eyes, then drew in a sharp breath. "I changed my mind. I don't want to work for you."

After that, Sarah walked very calmly to Michael's door, turned the handle, then left the cabin. And slumped against the wall outside while her whole body began to tremble.

How could she have ever thought she could be a practicing physician again when she couldn't even see the things she should have, the things that were so close to her?

CHAPTER SEVEN

MICHAEL stared at the cabin door for a moment, then finally
looked into his open closet. What he saw first…his running
prosthesis, one made especially for the hard, pounding run
he liked to have three times a week, four if he could fit it in.
Was that what had caused Sarah's reaction? She'd seen it,
been repulsed, then left?

Surely she'd known about it, hadn't she? He always
limped a little, even on his best days, and Sarah did have a
trained eye, so she must have noticed it. Then again, maybe
she hadn't. And it wasn't like he'd slipped a mention of his
injury into his casual conversations, because he never discussed it with anyone. Not even Ina. But he didn't keep his
amputation a secret either. If someone asked a question it, he
answered. Sarah, though…he'd really thought she would
have known, would have seen it.

Or perhaps, deep down, he'd hoped she wouldn't.

He hadn't been involved with anyone as a casual friend,
or even as a lover, since he'd been jilted after his injury.
Emotionally, he wasn't ready for it yet—a fact of which he
was painfully aware. Something else he was just as painfully
aware of was what he had to do before he could ever hope to
have a semblance of a normal life again. But that had much
more to do with the circumstances surrounding his injury and
not the injury itself. Sometimes, though, it all blurred

together…the loss of his leg, the loss of his dream, the loss of himself all tied up in there somewhere.

Could, or would, he ever let himself fall in love again? Yes, he had thought about what could happen if he ever did, thought about what kind of woman would be attracted to someone like him, to someone disabled the way he was. He tried not to, though, because he wasn't at a place in his life where any of that would fit in.

Of course, he'd be lying to himself if he said it didn't bother him—not the injury itself as much as what might come about as a result of it. That wasn't the reason he'd avoided any number of women who'd made advances these past months since he'd come to work as a ship's doctor. Or the reason he'd avoided even looking at them. Heaven knew, he wasn't a saint when it came to that part of his life. Wasn't even close to it. He'd had relationships, long and short. He'd had his share of casual flings, short and shorter, too. Quite a vigorous, healthy past, all things considered. Yet right now getting involved in *any* manner wasn't right, not when he had so little to offer someone.

So little to offer himself, for that matter.

But Sarah…she was different. Someone who intrigued him. Someone who had captured his interest and held it. Someone so sexy and yet so vulnerable he couldn't even begin to imagine what it would be like to have a woman like that in his life for a little while, maybe even for ever. He hadn't meant to look, hadn't meant to go any further after he had. Just look at him, though, all caught up in thoughts he simply didn't need to be having. Sarah was on his mind in ways he didn't want, and couldn't control, and he was disappointed by her reaction to his prosthetic leg. More than disappointed, he was surprised.

Better to find out now, he supposed, unable to shake off the letdown seeping through him as he sat down on the edge of the bed, getting ready to sleep. What had he expected, though? It wasn't like this was the first time someone was turned off by him. It wouldn't be the last time either.

Sinking back into the pillows, Michael stared up at the ceiling for much longer than he cared to before he finally dozed off. But it was a fitful sleep that overtook him, not at all restful, and when he woke up seven hours later he felt agitated and restless—much worse than he had before he'd gone to sleep. Naturally, the first thing that came to his mind when he opened his eyes was Sarah.

"Damn," he muttered as he crawled out of bed. Here it was, another day, another dozen or so patients to see, and he just didn't have the energy for it. Didn't have the energy for any of it.

And that had nothing to do with the fact that in spite of everything, in spite of not knowing what he wanted to do with his future, he still loved being a doctor. Loved it, lived it, breathed it like it was the very oxygen he needed. No, his lack of energy for it today had nothing to do with the job itself but with all the uncertainties of it he'd yet to face. The time was coming, though. He could feel it in his bones. Or maybe it was the way he couldn't get Sarah off his mind that was causing the change in him. Perhaps seeing how adrift she was in her life made him realize just how adrift he was in his own.

Whatever the case, as he trudged off to work that morning he felt the changes coming.

"Morning, Mike," Ina said brightly as he walked through the hospital entry. She immediately handed him a cup of her special brew, the way she did every morning.

This morning, though, Michael didn't even muster a polite smile when he handed it back to her. "No more tea," he told her, rather gruffly.

"But I thought you liked my tea."

She sounded positively hurt. Hurt, like the way he still felt after Sarah's reaction last night. No reason he should feel that way and he couldn't explain why he did. But rather than think about it, or even deal with Ina and her repulsive tea, he simply took the mug back from her and continued walking on to his little office, where he had himself one good look at the growing stack of paperwork he needed to do and slumped down into his desk chair, really hating this day, even though it had barely begun. "Have Dr Monty see patients for the next hour while I try to get caught up with all this mess," he called out to Ina, who was organizing patient charts in the outer office. "And if he doesn't have anyone come into the clinic first thing this morning, tell him to go ahead and do rounds in the hospital."

"Doctor Monty is sick this morning. Flu symptoms. He called in about fifteen minutes ago and said he won't be back for at least twenty-four hours. Twenty-four, if he's lucky."

Michael let out an exasperated sigh. "Another one?" This was beginning to worry him because it had all the makings of some kind of virus spreading through his crew. And as the crew succumbed so went the passengers. "Dr Griswold? I know he just went off duty, but I need him back on, at least for the next hour."

"You're right. He just went off duty, but he's not feeling too well either, and I have an idea he's already in bed." Ina stepped into Michael's office. "I didn't want to be the bearer of bad news, but we're down by well over half our staff now. You're the only doctor out of four who's not sick, and besides me there are only two other nurses left. And if you want my opinion, I think we could be working up to an outbreak of norovirus." A highly contagious virus resulting in gastrointestinal upset and other associated belly symptoms, that usually lasted between twenty-four and sixty hours. Norovirus was notorious for spreading quickly on cruise ships because everyone lived at relatively close quarters, and while it wasn't an illness with a serious outcome, it was one that turned into a huge inconvenience for the passengers and an even bigger headache for the medical staff.

"Normal symptoms?" he asked. "I'm assuming it's running its normal course."

"Not yet. Most of the complaints so far are achiness, feeling tired, that sort of thing. But you know what happens next!"

He did. Hundreds of sick people, all confined to their cabins, all of them feeling like they were going to die even though they wouldn't, all of them wanting a doctor's attention, even when they didn't really need it. He'd heard about norovirus hitting ships—hitting them hard and knocking down hundreds—but this would be his first time, if norovirus was, indeed, what this was, and he wasn't looking forward to it. It wreaked havoc on a ship's medical facilities, not to mention its medical crew, which was already turning out to be the case, it seemed. "But *you're* feeling OK?" he asked Ina, trying to sound light about it, even though he was getting worried that she could be correct about her diagnosis.

"Maybe that's the question I should be asking you. Are you feeling OK? Because with the way you look this morning, not to mention the fact that you're grumpier than I've ever seen you…"

"I'm fine," he said, his voice completely flat. "Just dandy." Michael took a sip of his tea and maybe it was because he was getting used to it, or maybe she'd varied her usual atrocious recipe, but it didn't taste so bad to him. Was that a symptom of the virus he feared they were being infected with? Perhaps the first thing to go was the sense of taste.

"Well, from what I'm seeing, you're *not* fine, so is that because you don't feel well and you don't want to admit it, or is it personal? Something to do with that lady doctor you've been sniffing around after?"

"I'm not sniffing after the lady doctor," he snapped. "Or anybody else."

"You're not?" She snorted a laugh. "Just listen to you! I've never seen you act this way, Mike, and I've known you since you were a medical student." She'd worked at the hospital where he'd served his residency, and had proved herself the best nurse he'd ever seen. Opinionated, bossy, but the kind of nurse he wanted at his side, which was why he'd hired her out of retirement when he'd taken this job. "If I didn't know better, I'd say…"

He gave her a deep scowl, meaning to stop her. "*Don't* say," he cracked. "Don't say a word. Not *one* word!"

"Grumpy *and* touchy," she persisted anyway. "I think she's really got you bothered, doesn't she?"

"Wouldn't matter if she does. She has a problem with…" He gestured to his right leg.

"You already got naked with her?" Ina asked, sounding almost excited about it. "It's about time you get back into life, act the way a normal man is supposed to."

"No, I didn't get naked with her, not that it's any of your business. But she discovered my running prosthesis in the closet, and that's as far as it went. She took one look and she was out the door."

"And you hadn't told her about your injury? Aren't you the one who tells the children at the amputee clinic to be honest about it?" He volunteered at a clinic in Florida when he had the chance…a few hours here and there. It had become something he looked forward to more than just about anything else in his life.

"Honest, yes. But I've never told them to just blurt it out without provocation. It's not exactly easy to drop the topic of amputation into casual conversation, you know, *Hello, my name is Mike Sloan and I have a right below-the-knee amputation.* Yeah, that's really going to impress someone."

"The *right* someone won't care." Ina shook her head and folded her arms across her chest. "But you're looking for any reason you can find not to get involved, and you sabotage your relationships, Mike. People do care. Old friends, new friends…people who wanted to be there for you after you were injured. You've shot them all down, and even now, if you meet someone and it looks to be a promising situation, you do something to kill it. And don't deny that, because you know you do. It's on purpose, and I'm not only talking about with the ladies. You push everybody away, and if I didn't just love you to pieces in spite of your attitude, you'd have pushed me away a long time ago, too."

Maybe what Ina said was true, all of it, but he wasn't going to admit it. "I don't have time for relationships."

"Because you don't want to make the time. But I've seen the way you look at Sarah, and it's a look I haven't seen in you before. Not back when you were a medical student, not since then either. Honestly, I've wondered if you might be falling in love with her, and now I know."

"Know what?" Michael snapped.

"That you're falling in love." She was so sure of it she almost seemed cocky. "Or you've already fallen in love. Too stubborn to admit it to yourself, though. And now you think you've got a reason to back away from it, just because of the way she reacted when she saw your prosthesis. You're probably glad of the excuse, aren't you? Glad Sarah gave you a reason not to have to come up with something yourself."

"Since when have I given you permission to get involved in my personal life?" he grumbled. "It's none of your damned business, Ina."

Rather than being offended, Ina laughed. "Like I said, now I have my answer. So, what are you going to do about it?"

"What am I going to do about a woman who's repulsed by the fact that I'm missing part of my leg? I think that already answers the question, doesn't it? There's not a damned thing I can, or will, do." The hell of it was, his leg wasn't even the problem.

"Not a damned thing to do except sit around and be

grumpy. Which you're very good at, Mike. And getting better at all the time. I'm betting it's not your amputation that turned her off, though. She probably got a big dose of your attitude."

"I'm not grumpy," he practically yelled.

Ina smiled at him with all the love of a mother, and her voice turned gentle. "Falling in love's not always easy, is it? But if it's meant to be, you'll find a way to work it out. Don't give up on it yet, Mike, and most of all, don't give up on yourself. You're quite a catch if you'll allow it, and if I were twenty-five years younger, I'd be giving that Sarah a run for her money. *A serious run.*"

They weren't docking anywhere today, but her bags were packed and ready to go for tomorrow. Aruba. She'd leave the ship there, spend a little time then fly home and start all over again—the cycle of her life now. For her, the cruise had ended, and so had the delusion that she could go back into medicine. One little incident with the boy under the bus, and she'd fooled herself into believing that something had changed, that all her imperfections had vanished. But, as she'd soon discovered, nothing had changed. Nothing at all. She was still the same Sarah Collins who had a confounding way of not seeing the flagrantly obvious—a horribly danger-ous trait in a doctor.

"You're looking distracted this morning," Martha said. They were having breakfast together at an outside buffet near the pool. It hadn't been Sarah's idea to do it, as she'd have preferred staying cooped up in her cabin all day, having her meals delivered to her there. But Martha had come knocking on her door bright and early, and Sarah simply hadn't had the heart to refuse the woman a few minutes of conversation and companionship over buttered toast, fresh fruit and juice.

"I'm…um…I'm thinking about leaving the ship tomorrow and flying home," Sarah said, almost reluctantly. The truth was, leaving was purely an intellectual decision. It was the only practical thing to do under the circumstances. In her heart she wanted to stay, though. Yet she never let her heart win. Not any more. "It's something I've been thinking about from the start, but now's the time, so I'll be leaving once we arrive in Aruba."

Martha's eyes widened. "You're not having a good time? Or is this about a personal matter?"

A little bit of both. Even though it was something she couldn't put into words. "The cruise is not what I expected. I think maybe I'm more the type who prefers to keep my feet flat on the ground." Along with her heart.

"We're only halfway through. It would be such a shame to give it all up now. But I think it has to be difficult being here alone, the way you are. At least I have my purple-hat group."

Sarah grabbed a piece of ripe pineapple and offered it to Martha, hoping that would distract her from what Sarah believed would be the inevitable offer to join the purple-hat bunch as a way to keep her from being alone. "For some people, being alone is difficult, but I don't mind it so much. It keeps my life simple," she said. "And over the years I've learned that staying simple works best for me. I'm sure it seems dull to some, but I don't mind dull, because there aren't any complications."

"But the complications of friendships, and especially of a serious relationship…that's what turns a dull life into something that sparkles." Martha reached across the table and gave Sarah a friendly pat on the hand. "Sparkling is nice, Sarah, but I don't think you believe you're entitled to sparkle, do you?" Before Sarah could answer, Martha continued, "Look, some of the ladies and I are going to take a photography class they're offering on the ship. You're welcome to join us but, in my opinion, you'd be smarter chasing down that good-looking Dr Sloan. He's much more interesting than a snapshot, and as you're not going to stay with us much longer I think your time would be better spent with him." With those words, a definite sparkle popped into Martha's eyes.

"I don't get involved," Sarah said, without explanation.

"Life isn't much fun without involvements. Planting purple flowers certainly isn't something I've ever aspired to, but if I didn't have my purple flowers, and the other ladies who plant them along with me, I don't know what I'd do. After my husband died I didn't think I ever wanted to be involved with anything, ever again. But just look at me now!" She reached up and cocked her purple hat. "I had to make myself get involved, had to force myself to put this ugly hat on my head and take that first step out my door, and I haven't regretted a minute of it since I did."

"I've been involved," Sarah said, "and it's not all it's cracked up to be. For me, I think the regret would be taking the first step out the door." She shrugged a gloomy feeling washed down over her, and turned her attention to the fresh papaya juice she'd been nursing for the past several minutes. The truth was, being involved was everything. She just didn't have the heart to try it again.

Sarah spent another ten minutes lingering over a breakfast she wasn't in the mood to eat, listening to Martha ramble on and on about all the things she'd done with her purple-hat friends, before she decided to head back to her cabin and…and do what? Spend the day sleeping, or staring at the walls? Those were probably her best options, even though they didn't seem much of a way to spend her last day at seas. The thing was, what came next in her life? She'd leave the ship, spend a few days in Aruba, then what was she going to do after that? Take another trip? Was there really anything left that she truly wanted to see?

The answer to that question was so obvious, she didn't bother mulling it over in her mind. She didn't want to go anywhere, didn't want to see anything, didn't want to do anything. It was all as plain as that. Her life had become stagnant, and she hadn't even realized how much so until that day she'd crawled underneath the bus. Then it was like the floodgates had opened, and for one brief moment, she'd thought she could get back everything she'd always wanted. She wanted to work as a doctor again. Wanted it so badly it was turning into a physical ache. Wanted to diagnose and treat patients, again, wanted to be part of the whole medical community the way she had once been.

But the medical community deserved better than what she could give them, and that was always the bottom line that came back to flog her. She couldn't have what she wanted. Couldn't even come close to it.

When breakfast was over, Martha trotted off to her purple-hat ladies and Sarah headed back to her cabin. On the way she stopped and leaned against the ship's rail, simply to stare out at the ocean. It was one vast surface with so little on the top of it and so much underneath, all of it coming from nowhere, going nowhere. Like her.

"It's amazing, isn't it?" Michael said, stepping up beside her. "The first time I ever saw the ocean I was five years old. I went to the beach with my parents, and I think I spent most of the day trying to see the other side of the world. I knew it had to be out there somewhere, if only I could look a little harder. Once I was sure I spotted the other side of it, then it turned out to be a freighter making its way slowly across what I knew had to be the very edge of the world. I couldn't take my eyes off it, and I ran along the beach as it started to disappear, trying to keep it in my sight. I just knew that if I lost sight of it, it would fall off."

"But it didn't," she said, her voice wistful as she continued her stare, now visualizing a five-year-old spending his day doing the very same thing.

"No, it didn't. But I used up my whole day worrying about the people on that ship, worrying about what was out there at the end of the world. I could have been playing in the water with my brothers or building sandcastles or picking up sea-shells, but instead of doing the things a child should have been doing I found myself a little ridge and just sat there and watched. Wasted a perfectly good day doing nothing, as it turned out."

"Was it really a waste?" she asked.

He chuckled. "Actually, that was the day I announced to my parents that I wanted to be a doctor. Just like my father was, and my grandfather. In my five-year-old mind, I thought I could help all those people who were about to topple off the end of the world. Put bandages on them and make them better after their fall."

The way he made her feel better as she was toppling. "Then I'd say you were a little boy with strong convictions. When I was five I wanted to be a ballerina. When I was six I wanted to be a teacher. Then at seven an archaeologist. It was a pretty long list by the time I got to college, which was when I finally had to give it some serious thought and decide what I really wanted to do. But I'm sorry to say I didn't enter medical school with the conviction of a five-year-old boy who wanted to save a ship's crew from a terrible fate. I simply liked the science involved in medicine. Thought it was amazing. Thought the workings of the human body were the most interesting thing I'd ever encountered in my life." She turned to face him. "Look, Michael, I wasn't running away from your prosthetic leg," she said. "I know it probably looked that way to you, but that wasn't it, and I'm sorry I left you thinking so."

"It wouldn't matter if you were," he said, without a trace of defensiveness in his voice. "People react how they react. I've learned to deal with it."

"Or avoid it?"

"Has anybody ever told you how blunt you are?" he said, a hint of amusement in his voice.

She laughed. "It's been mentioned a time or two." She was dying to ask him about his injury, but so far he didn't seem willing to talk about it, other than in the vaguest sense. He'd said what he'd wanted to say, and that's all there was. "Blunt, stubborn...one of the technicians who worked for us at the clinic called me Dr Ice. She didn't know that I was aware of the nickname, but I wasn't bothered by it. It took me a long time to learn how to appear unaffected and, apparently, I was pretty good at it."

"Nothing about you seems unaffected to me. In fact, if your technician had seen you go under that bus with Delroy, and stay there the way you did, she'd find something else to call you. He's doing better, by the way. Good progress, according to his doctor."

Behind them, the frantic pounding of feet on the deck caught her attention for a moment, as one of the organized exercise groups fast-walked their way around the deck, their heel-toe, heel-toe rhythm almost precise as they passed by where Sarah and Michael were standing. As their footsteps faded she thought about how much she liked being here with Michael this way, and how she didn't want to leave. Which was exactly why she had to. Anything else got her involved, and she was so on the brink of doing just that she felt like the ship that five-year-old Michael Sloan had watched sailing along the edge of the world, ready to fall off. She was attracted to Michael Sloan, and it was about so much more than his ability to fill her medical longings. From that very first moment he'd caught her... No musings. No regrets. She plainly couldn't do this. "Look, Michael, about my offer to help you... I'm leaving tomorrow instead. I've already sent a message to the ship's captain telling him that when I go ashore in Aruba I won't be returning."

"Why?" His voice was stiff. That relaxed feeling between them was gone.

Should she tell him that she had feelings for him in a way

she didn't want to? Or tell him the same thing she told every-body else—that it was time to move on? That was always the easiest excuse. Very impersonal and precise, and no one could argue against it. But with Michael she didn't want to be impersonal and precise. She didn't see any other way, though. "My life is full of reasons, Michael. None of them really make any difference. I just do what I do, and moving on is part of that."

"Avoidance?" he snapped.

"Now aren't you the one who's being blunt?" Sarah smiled sadly, thinking about how true that was. But it was about self-preservation. She understood that better than she understood just about anything else. If you didn't avoid things, you opened yourself up to the possibility of being hurt, and she'd already had too much pain in her life.

He chuckled, but there was a sharp edge to it. "I've been called stubborn a time or two also."

"But never unaffected. The little boy who wanted to save that ship could never be unaffected. Neither could the man he turned into."

"Look, Sarah, if I weren't in trouble, I wouldn't say this, but I am. Most of my medical staff is down sick, and I need you to stay here and help me until the cruise line makes other medical arrangements. I've cleared you working here under emergency provisions through the ship's captain, who cleared it with the cruise line. So, until help arrives I'm authorized to do what I have to do to take care of the passengers and crew and for starters that's putting you to work. But I've got to warn you up front that we're looking at some hard hours ahead. There's a pos-sibility we might have an outbreak of norovirus on our hands."

Sarah certainly knew what that was. Back in Boston, at her immediate care clinic, she'd treated a rash of people with norovirus, all of whom had jumped a quarantined ship that had been docked a few blocks from her office. "I take it you're confining them as they get sick?"

Michael nodded. "Both the passengers *and* my medical crew. If I had my way, I'd confine everybody on board, sick or not, for the next three days and let the whole damned thing run its course. Which they won't let me do. And to be honest, if this thing plays out the way it usually does, nobody's going to be allowed off the ship in Aruba anyway."

"Then I don't have much of a choice, do I?" The truth was, as much as she wanted to avoid practicing medicine, this unexpected opportunity excited her. Norovirus was simple. And she would have a little more time with Michael. That was, perhaps, the real reason she accepted. Around him she didn't feel quite so unaffected. In fact, if she wasn't very careful, he had the power to affect her in ways she'd thought she'd never be affected again. Only if she let that happen, of course. Which she wouldn't. "When do we start?" she asked, the gloomy shroud that had entangled her suddenly blowing out to sea.

CHAPTER EIGHT

"THREE passengers, all with non-specific complaints," Ina announced as Sarah followed Michael through the hospital doors. "Headaches, muscle aches, fever with unknown origin, several of them with some respiratory distress. That kind of thing. I've got them all in exam rooms, having their vitals taken and their medical histories assessed." Her glance darted from Michael to Sarah then back to Michael, and a thin little grin spread over her lips, even though she didn't break her cadence. "We've had calls from two more passengers who will be coming down here shortly, again non-specific complaints."

Sarah frowned. "Noro usually starts with quite a kick rather than non-specific complaints. This seems odd."

"But there are so many variations of it," Michael added. "Currently, there are five *known* specific norovirus groups that are divided into thirty-one smaller groups. The symptoms we usually see at the onset are generally the same, to varying degrees, but who knows? Viruses mutate so quickly these days we could be looking at a variant that hasn't been identified, or just a new version on an old theme."

"Well, identified or not," Ina chimed in, "the captain is on his way down to the hospital to see what we're dealing with. He says he wants a full report."

Michael nodded. It was premature to attach any major significance to this little rush of illnesses, but the captain should be made aware that there was a similarity, just in case it turned out to be something major. In the meantime, there were still the normal ailments to treat, and people were beginning to line up in the Emergency clinic to be seen. "Sarah, could you take over regular duty in emergency? I think that will be pretty much what you did working in an immediate care clinic. I'll back you up if you need it, look in on the patients already staying in the hospital, and I'll also take anyone coming in we think could be in the early stages of whatever this is. And, Ina…" He simply waved her off, as she was already on her way back to her nursing duties and needed no further instruction.

"Do I have a nurse?" Sarah asked.

"We're stretched pretty thin there, too. Besides Ina, we have two other nurses, and I'm going to try and keep them on general duty, triage, that kind of thing, if I can. If you need a nurse to assist you, call Ina and we'll see what we can do." He stepped closer, and took gentle hold of her arm. "You're going to do fine, Sarah," he said, his voice practically a whisper. "I know this isn't what you want to do, but I appreciate you helping me. It's safer having two doctors available." She looked worried, in spite of the fact that she was forcing herself to smile. But there was nothing else he could do at the moment.

Sure, it would have been nice working side by side with her, just to help boost her confidence a little. Or simply to spend a little time with her any way he could get it. That just wasn't going to happen today, though, and he wasn't worried about leaving Sarah on her own. She was a good doctor who, for whatever reason, didn't trust herself. That much was evident. He trusted her, though. And for now, that had to be enough. It would have been nice knowing what had caused the fear and doubt in her, but that was a story for another time. At present there were other priorities, and trusting Sarah was one of them. She was good. He was sure of it—sure enough to put the lives of his patients in her hands.

Her pace was slow at first, he noted. By the time she was ready to start her medical duty, there were half a dozen patients lined up waiting to be seen, and she took her time seeing each one. He really didn't have time to stop and observe, not that he would have, but he did catch occasional glances of Sarah as she performed a routine procedure or simply talked with a patient. What he saw was amazing. She had such grace…something to which the patients were naturally drawn. He could see that in the easy smiles that came over their faces once they were greeted by Sarah—the smiles of a patient who truly trusted the doctor. It was nice, and he would have loved standing back and watching, but Captain Regard was waiting for him now, and it was time to have a frank discussion about what was happening. In the past half-hour another ten patients with the same non-specific complaints had wandered in. And in that same amount of time, Dr Allen, one of the first people to go down with this unknown ailment, had spiked an extreme fever and developed a suspicious heart rhythm—so much so, they'd had to put him on a monitor.

If this was norovirus, it was definitely an unknown strain, as the formerly non-specific complaints were now becoming specific, and they weren't anything like norovirus. That had him concerned.

Captain Thomas Regard was a distinguished man. Tall, with silver-gray hair and piercing blue eyes, he carried the demeanor of ship's captain quite well, except that when Michael set eyes on him, that demeanor was diminished. Captain Regard looked gaunt, tired, and as he approached Michael's desk, he practically fell into the chair opposite it. "Report," he said, his voice weak. "Tell me what's going on here. Why are most of your medical personnel down?"

"Symptoms?" Michael asked in return. "Tell me your symptoms."

Regard shook his head. "It's nothing. I'm due for some holiday time after this cruise, and once I've had a little rest I'll be fine."

"I have twenty people saying the same thing right now, Tom. And you're looking like every one of them"

"Is it norovirus?" the captain asked, his haggard face creasing into a frown. Noro was the scourge of so many cruise ships these days that it was well known to people, like Captain Thomas Regard, who had absolutely no medical knowledge whatsoever, except for Norovirus.

"Initially, that's what I thought. But now, I don't know. I'm inclined to think we've got something else going on…something in its very early stages. And based on what I'm seeing, the symptoms aren't even close to norovirus."

"So tell me what to do, Mike. You're the doctor here, and it's your call. Should we be alarmed?"

"Well, twenty's not an alarming number, if it doesn't go beyond that. But that's twenty people who've all come down with something I haven't been able to identify yet. I've got them confined to quarters but something's telling me that I need to bring them into the hospital to watch them even more closely. Especially if it's not norovirus, which is what I'm inclined to think right now."

Captain Regard nodded, although it was clear by the expression on his face that he didn't have the vaguest idea what Michael was talking about. "So, what about docking and going ashore in Aruba? Should we skip that port?"

"Yes," Michael said, without hesitation. "I don't know if we're dealing with something infectious, and I don't want to risk taking it ashore. So, at least for this port of call, we need to stay on ship."

"You know how that's going to go over, don't you, keeping the whole ship away from the next destination when only a handful of the passengers are sick? People aren't going to be happy." He let out a sigh. "And if I didn't feel like hell right now, I'd probably try and argue you out of this, but I do, so I won't." He started to stand, wobbled, and sank back down into the chair. Michael was immediately at his side, laying a hand on the captain's forehead at first, then taking hold of his wrist to feel his pulse.

"You're burning up with fever. And your heart rate is too fast. How long have you been sick?"

"About a day. But it'll pass," the captain said. "I'm going back to my quarters for a short nap now, and I'll be fine."

"You're off duty, Tom, and I'm admitting you to the hospital," Michael said emphatically, helping the man up from the chair.

"I need to—"

"There's nothing you need to do right now except rest and let me be the doctor." He expected an argument. The man had an exceptionally robust personality, but at this moment he had no fight left in him as he practically slumped against Michael, without uttering another word. Five minutes later, Captain Thomas Regard was the twenty-first patient on the charts for whatever this outbreak was. And there was no denying it. This was definitely an outbreak of some sort. As much as he hated admitting it, Michael was admitting it now.

"Your blood sugar is three times the normal value," Sarah said to the woman on the exam table. Mrs Margesson was the fifth over-indulger she'd seen that morning. Too much good food, too little willpower, and the result for a diabetic could be devastating. "Your blood sugar is registering at three hundred, and you need to be closer to one hundred."

The woman grinned sheepishly. "I ate a few sweets last night and had a pastry or two for breakfast this morning," she admitted. "I didn't think it would hurt me."

Sarah patted her patient's hand. "It's not much fun to

come on a cruise and not be able to eat everything they have available, is it?"

Mrs Margesson shook her head. "The food is so…good."

Wasn't this the same lecture Michael had given her, only in reverse? Eat more, Sarah. Don't let your blood sugar go so low. And hadn't she argued with him? Maybe this was some kind of retribution, being confronted with, well… herself. *Patience, Sarah*, she cautioned herself as she prepared to argue logic with a woman who was clearly more interested in a chocolate-covered éclair than she was a medical lecture.

"It's hard to resist," Gertie Margesson continued.

Sarah smiled, thinking back to the way Michael had handled her little blood-sugar situation. He really was an excellent doctor. She admired that in him. Wanted to emulate it right now. "Here's what I'd like to do, Gertie. First, I want to get your blood sugar back down to a normal level with some insulin. You're not so high that you're in any danger, but I really don't want you getting any higher because you do risk having a stroke in the short term, and I'm sure your own doctor has advised you of all the long-term side effects." Blindness, kidney failure, nerve damage, heart disease, circulatory problems leading to possible amputation…

Amputation! Was Michael a severe diabetic? That certainly was a consideration, and something she needed to watch him for since in the next little while he was going to be working more hours than he normally did. His blood sugar could go out of whack with extreme fatigue. "So, here's what you need to do after we've got your blood-sugar level back in order. I want you to watch your diet more closely, stay away from the sweets on a regular basis, restrict your carbohydrates overall. But just so you won't deprive yourself, I want you to go ahead and have a little indulgence every other day. Keep it moderate, though, and balance it out with a better choice of foods all the way around. In fact, I could have the ship's dietitian sit down and have a chat with you, maybe draw up your own special menu if you'd like. Also, you need to keep a record of your blood sugar. Test yourself three times a day and bring me the results every morning. If you're good, I'll give you the go-ahead for that little treat. If your results aren't so good, we'll hold off until they are. Can you do that?" She looked Mrs Margesson straight in the eye.

"That's asking an awful lot of me," Gertie replied, none too happy with any of this. She wanted more, but she needed less, and Sarah had a hunch that this wouldn't be the woman's last trip to the ship's hospital with a diabetic-related crisis.

"But you'll try," Sarah said.

"I'll try, but don't expect too much. I'm here on a holiday, and that includes my diet, so I'll be good when I get home."

Ah, yes. Put it off until tomorrow. She'd heard that excuse hundreds of times over the years. Deny the obvious now, promise to do better next time, and in the meantime hope the side-effects of what you're doing now don't do you in.

Wasn't that the way she was living, though? Didn't she put everything off until tomorrow, then the tomorrow after that? Didn't she keep promising herself that she'd make a decision about her life? Well, she understood Gertie Margesson's circumstances because, in a way, they were just like hers. Only Gertie did it with food, while she was doing it with avoidance. Yes, that old bugaboo she and Michael had already talked about. "I'm sure you do much better when you're home, Gertie, but if you don't do better here you might not make it home. Diabetes has serious consequences if you don't manage it properly. So, it's your choice. I can't control how you eat. Can't watch every bite you take. All I can do is try and fix you up if you hurt yourself, and hope it's enough."

Gertie looked like she'd been slapped in the face. Maybe it was a harsh pronouncement, but it was a true one. And for someone who had a history of missing the obvious, the way Sarah did, one thing she wasn't missing here was the fact that she had an uncooperative patient who truly believed that her actions today didn't have a significant bearing on her life tomorrow.

If only that were the case. But Sarah knew better, and all she had to do was remind herself of Kerry, and of Cameron.

After Gertie departed, not at all convinced by Sarah's little admonition to do better or else, there was no one left to see, so she wandered off in the direction of the clinic where Michael was working, ready to offer assistance. On her way, she glanced into one of the private patient rooms in time to see the man in the bed go completely rigid, then begin to thrash about so hard the bed rattled.

A seizure?

Sarah was immediately at his bedside, trying to turn him on his side in case he vomited up his stomach contents, but what she saw wasn't a seizure. The man was so cold his body was shaking as hard as a body could shake. And he was literally going stiff.

Rigor? "I need help in here!" she called, as the man frantically grabbed at her hand. His hand was icy. So were his cheeks, she found as she laid her hand on his face. His body was literally in the throes of what happened when someone froze to death, and it was hard to hear his heart beating as she pushed her stethoscope to his chest, he was thrashing and shaking so badly.

She listened for a moment, heard his heart beating rapidly, but not critically so.

"What do you need?" Ina asked, rushing in. She took one look at Captain Regard and ran right back out of the room.

"You're going to be fine," Sarah said, wrapping a blood-pressure cuff around the man's arm. "As soon as I make an assessment, we'll get you warmed right up." But what was making him so cold? That was the question she couldn't answer yet.

"What the hell?" Michael sputtered, running into the

room. "Fifteen minutes ago, when I admitted him, his temperature was spiking to four degrees above normal."

"And now it's dropped," Sarah said, stepping back as Ina shoved her way in to take Captain Regard's temperature. "To the point of rigors. What was your admitting diagnosis?" she whispered, pushing Michael out into the hall.

"Didn't have one. He's like the other twenty-five people we've admitted now, and I'm pretty damned sure it's not norovirus."

"Too bad," Sarah said. "With noro we know what to do." She breathed out an exasperated sigh. "Look, I know you're in charge here, but I think we need to set up an isolation ward until we can figure it out. Keep these people separated from everybody else, get the lab work started, treat the symptoms until we know what we're dealing with."

"His temperature's rising," Ina called out.

"Start an IV, normal saline for now. And get him on oxygen." Michael ran a frustrated hand through his hair. "And do the same for everybody else who's come in with the captain's symptoms."

"He's the captain?" Sarah asked.

Michael nodded. "Between us, I'm worried about how many of the crew are going to come down with this."

"What about medical supplies?"

"We're OK for now. Hope it stays that way until help arrives."

"Which will be when?"

He shrugged. "They're telling me soon, but not saying what that means. I have a suspicion the company is looking at its reputation, and sending in medical reinforcements to a ship with a couple of dozen patients with an undiagnosed illness is just bad publicity. They'll take care of us, but let's just say they'll be careful at first." He squeezed her arm. "I'm sorry I got you into this, Sarah."

"I'm not," she said, as one of the nurses ran by, carrying

an IV set-up. "Look, Michael. Can you spare me for a few minutes? I have an idea."

"Dr Sloan, the patient in number three is spiking a fever," the other nurse called from down the corridor. "And we have an ankle sprain in Emergency."

Before Michael could answer Sarah, she bolted out the door and ran straight to the elevator. Minutes later, she crashed through the doors to the photography class and ran toward the front of the room. Looking out over the group, she saw a sea of purple hats. "Martha," she called out, spotting her friend in the crowd. "I need your help. Now.' Then she turned her attention to the rest of the ladies, who were whispering among themselves, wondering what was going on as the photography instructor assumed an angry frown over the intrusion. As Martha came forward, she whispered, "I don't have time to explain, and I don't want to cause a panic, but we need medical personnel in the hospital. *Now!*"

Martha acknowledged with a quick nod, then followed Sarah to the back of the room and waited until she had left before she looked around to see who in the class also had a medical background. Fifteen minutes later, after she'd discreetly called out four more purple hatters, the little troop of retired nurses marched their way into the ship's hospital, ready for duty.

"We're not going to put you in the ward where we're isolating the ones with the undiagnosed illness," she told Martha, who was wiggling her ample body into a pair of blue surgical scrubs. "We don't know what we're dealing with and I don't want to put any of you at risk, but what I'd like you to do is manage everything else that's coming in, which will allow Michael and me and the nurses already exposed to tend to the others." Which now numbered thirty-two.

"We don't need five nurses in the ER clinic," Martha stated. "So I'm coming with you."

"But we don't know what we're dealing with yet," Sarah argued.

"And if you get yourself too rundown, you won't be in any condition to find out. I know what I'm doing, Sarah. I spent my life working at a doctor's side, being in the thick of it, and that's what I do best."

Sarah gave the woman a big hug. "I think this is called getting involved," she said.

"In more ways than one." Martha chuckled. Backing away from Sarah, she grabbed an IV set-up from Ina, who was on her way into Dr Allen's room, and hurried to get to work.

"Where the hell did all those ladies out there come from?" Michael asked, minutes later, on his way back to the captain's bedside. Tom Regard's fever was on the rise again, and if the pattern repeated, he was about to drop to a nearly life-threatening cold shortly after.

"Purple hats, every last one of them. Desperate times call for desperate measures, and as you already had permission to find qualified help on board, that's exactly what I did."

"Well, I'll be damned," he said, as he swabbed the captain's arm, readying himself to take a blood sample. "We wouldn't happen to have a lab tech in the bunch, would we? Once I get the blood samples, I need someone to run them. My lab tech just checked herself into the hospital."

"Let me go and ask Martha."

Nine hours later, the crisis had not let up, and the slow trickle of patients into the emergency clinic continued. The cruise line was concerned now, and everything they needed was en route. Of course, with nine purple-hat nurses, two purple-hat lab technicians, and a retired purple-hat doctor who'd been called in by Martha and had subsequently taken total charge of all non-essential medical care, the hospital was functioning pretty well.

Captain Regard was doing better, after a simple prescription of acetaminophen, but he wasn't out of the woods. And unfortunately, Dr Allen had taken a critical turn. Michael hadn't left his side for the last hour as the man seemed to be suffering a serious cardiac crisis. Of the sixty-three patients they had in isolation now, seven were considered critical, nine were serious, and Dr Reese Allen, a man much too young and vital to be in his condition, was in a critical condition.

"Mike needs to take a break," Ina confided to Sarah. "He's not helping anybody, wearing himself out the way he is. But he won't listen to me."

"He's dedicated," Sarah said wearily. She'd been off her feet ten minutes, and was allowing herself twenty more, barring an emergency.

"Dedicated to the point of being foolish," Ina snorted. "Loosely translated to mean stubborn as hell."

"You've known him a long time, haven't you?" Sarah asked.

"I was the first face he saw the first time he stepped foot in a hospital. He was…different from the other medical students. They all huddled together, scared, timid, not sure which end of the thermometer to use. But Mike…he stepped right out, distinguished himself." She chuckled. "All full of big plans for his life."

"He was materialistic?"

"Not at all. Mike was about as altruistic as anybody I'd ever met. He always wanted to make a difference. Wanted to do something good with his life. Had so many goals, so many things he wanted to do as a doctor."

And he'd ended up here on a cruise ship? It wasn't a bad thing, and cruise ships did need medical personnel. But she seriously doubted that working on a cruise ship had been one of his goals, so what had happened to change him? His leg?

Sarah wondered about that, and she wanted to ask. She might have, but Ina dashed off in pursuit of an IV refill, leaving Sarah alone for the remainder of her break. At least, she'd thought she was going to be alone, but no sooner had Ina gone than Michael wandered into the doctors' lounge, and dropped his lanky body onto a sofa there, letting out a weary groan as he lifted his legs up over the armrest. "If I weren't so damned tired, I'd complain about how uncomfortable this sofa is," he said, as his eyes shut. "Oh, and *don't* let me sleep. I'm better off sleep-deprived than I am grabbing a quick nap."

"Medical school days," Sarah commented casually, giving him the full scrutiny of her medical expertise, studying him from head to toe while he wasn't looking. Such a handsome man. Better than handsome, actually. He was the kind of man who took away your breath at first glance. Rugged, even a little hard around the edges, he looked like a man who'd seen a lot of living. Of course, that was only conjecture, as she knew practically nothing about him. "Back then I was up for a quick nap anywhere, even standing up, if I had to."

He chuckled, but didn't open his eyes. "I remember once, I was so tired that I literally fell asleep sitting at a patient's bedside. When I woke up, a full hour later, I was still sitting in the chair, but had tilted over, with my head actually on the bed. She said I snored."

"And she didn't wake you up?"

"She felt sorry for me. I think she also figured I'd be a better doctor if I were a little more rested. So she let me sleep there, and even kept other people out so I wouldn't be disturbed."

"I think my worst was the elevator. I got on, leaned back in the corner, and apparently rode up and down for fifteen minutes before somebody was kind enough to lead me off." He looked none the worse for the wear, she thought, still trying to make a casual observation. In fact, for all the hours he'd put in, he looked rather amazing. "Can I get you something, Michael? To eat, or drink?"

"Damn it, Sarah! I can get it myself! What the hell makes you think I need or want you to wait on me? I mean, who the hell do you think you are to me?"

That was a mood swing she hadn't expected out of Michael. His mood changed so drastically, so quickly, it took Sarah a moment to realize that it had actually happened, and when that finally sank in, she was left wondering why. What was so dark in Michael that made him so defensive? "I wasn't suggesting that you *couldn't* help yourself, Michael." She struggled to tamp back her own flare of temper. "But I'm at the end of my break and you're at the beginning of yours, so I thought I'd do the polite thing and—"

"And what?" he snapped again. "Save me steps? *Poor Michael. Look at the way he limps*. Is that it? My leg makes me incapable of taking care of myself? Is that how you see it, because if it is, save the pity, Sarah. I don't need it. Not from anyone, and especially not from you!"

Well, this was certainly a little hotbed of something she'd stumbled into. Problem was, she couldn't hang around and find out what it was about. Duty called and medical emergencies took precedent over bad moods. "Good thing I don't generally give pity," she said, standing up. "And just so you'll know, Michael, I'd have made the same offer even if you didn't limp. Call me crazy that way, but I do like helping people when I can, and whether or not you want to admit it, you looked like…and still do look like…you need some help. But not from me. I'm out of here. Back to work. If you want something, get it yourself!" She headed toward the door but stopped before she got there, then turned back to face him. "You know what, Michael? We all have problems right now, and while yours may legitimately be worse than most of the others, it's not right to take it out on me…or anyone else who's simply trying to be kind. I know you're in charge here, but I'd suggest you get your bad mood under control before you come back to work because none of us needs to deal with that along with everything else going on." Harsh words, but she was glad she'd said them because he needed to hear them. He could bask in his damn bad mood another time, but right now he had more important things to think about.

As Sarah stepped into the passage, Michael let out a frustrated sigh. "Don't go," he managed, pushing himself part way up to look at her.

"Why shouldn't I?" she asked, without turning around. She had so many feelings swirling around….anger, hurt, frustration. *Confusion.* They seemed to do so well together in so many ways, her and Michael, yet there was always an intense wariness between them, one that neither of them had penetrated yet, and she wasn't sure what to do about it. Or if she even wanted to try doing something. He wasn't the only one with problems and complications in his life, and if they hadn't been in such close proximity, she would have left. Right then. Left the ship, no looking back. Well, that wasn't an option, was it? She wasn't going to jump overboard, and the doctor in her compelled her to be here, with Michael, to take care of these people. So that was it—no choices.

"Look, Sarah, I think I owe you an explanation," he continued. "And an apology for being so bad-tempered with you just now."

"No, you don't owe me a thing," she said. Finally, she turned to face him. "Except civility."

"People patronize me. Treat me like I lost my intelligence with my leg."

She wasn't surprised, but that still wasn't a good enough reason for his attitude toward her. *Who the hell do you think you are to me?* She'd thought she was his friend. Maybe a little more. Silly her. "Maybe they do, and I'm sorry for that, but I'm not like that, Michael, and you know it. And I resent being the one you pick on because you're feeling bad."

"Look, could we pretend that I never came into the room and made a total idiot of myself?"

She did want to. But the things he'd said had cut so deeply

she needed time to figure it out. "The deed's done, Michael. But go ahead and pretend anything you want to, if it's easier for you."

Propping his head up on the armrest, Michael studied Sarah from that position for a moment, without making any effort to get up. "You're an odd woman, Sarah Collins."

"In a good or a bad way?"

"I don't think there's anything about you that could be odd in a bad way."

"So I should take that as a compliment, that I'm odd in a good way? A sincere compliment, I hope, seeing that you're trying to redeem yourself from being a total idiot."

"You're straightforward," he said. "More so than anybody else I know, except Ina. Most people won't even mention my disability, yet you seem to have some insight. And some gall to ague with a cripple, which, I might add, most people won't do."

"In other words, you beat them up and they let you?"

"I don't beat them up, as you think. Most of the time I get better results beating myself up."

She wanted to ask. Dear God, she wanted to ask. But there wasn't time. "You said I had insight into your disability? Remember, I had a husband with terminal melanoma, so I suppose that did give me some insight. Oh, and in case I hadn't mentioned it before, after Kerry died I got myself engaged to a man with leukemia. More insight there." Lots of it, for a very long time.

"Did he…?"

"He didn't die, but we didn't make it." She forced a half-smile, then left the room. There would be time for talking later. If Michael wanted to talk. If *she* wanted to talk.

"I'm sorry," he called after her. "Please, Sarah. Forgive me."

She turned back to the room to accept his apology, just in time to see Michael nod off. No snoring, though. The patient whose bed he'd slept on all those years ago must have lied about that. Not that it mattered, because when would she and Michael ever share a bed?

CHAPTER NINE

"You let me sleep for two hours!" Michael said, as Sarah sailed past him to admit the next patient.

The toll had now risen to seventy-six, and even though most of them were a long way from being critical, she was past the point of being tired. Her feet hurt. So did her head, her shoulders, her back. As well as everything else. But she was running on pure adrenalin now, so wired that even if she'd had the chance to sleep, she probably couldn't.

"You needed it, and we were slow. We're keeping those patients with the minor symptoms to confined to their cabins with instructions to check back in with us if their symptoms get worse. And I'm not patronizing you because of your disability. Just giving you my medical opinion." She flashed him a grin. "Which, in this case, was valid. You look better."

"I don't get you, Sarah. You didn't want to practice medicine so you quit it, yet when you're given the opportunity to work again you blossom."

"Sometimes it's not so much about what we want to do as what we have to do." Before he could ask what that meant, she turned down a side corridor leading to the small lab area and disappeared into the cubbyhole where Helen Weinstein, a seventy-something retired lab technician, was busy examining blood samples. "Anything yet?" Sarah asked.

"It's a nice lab, very modern, but limited in its scope. I'm seeing a run of elevated white cells, elevated blood sugars, but nothing really significant other than that. And I don't have the equipment to test for many of the specific conditions I'd like to. But I've got some bacterial cultures incubating and maybe that will tell us more. Unfortunately, they take time."

"Do you think it could be bacterial? All along we've been going on the assumption that it's some kind of virus, but if it's bacterial that would make the way we're treating this entirely different." She did a mental check of all the various symptoms they were seeing, and while there was some commonality, there wasn't enough to be conclusive. But the possibility that this could be bacterial did raise some interesting questions, such as where was the point of origin? In a virus it didn't matter. One person got it, they coughed or sneezed and spread it to another. It was contagious from person to person. Bacteria weren't contagious like that, so if this mystery illness wasn't being transmitted that way…

"What if it's not viral?" she asked Michael a few minutes later as they passed in the hall, practically bumping into each other they were both moving so fast in opposite directions.

"Then we don't have enough broad-spectrum antibiotics to treat everybody who's ill, and we'll have to evacuate them to a hospital. What makes you think it's not a virus?"

"Something Helen Weinstein said."

"Who?"

"The purple-hat lady who's running the lab now. She said she's not seeing much of a commonality in the blood samples. Nothing is really popping out at her and she doesn't have the right equipment to get too specific. But she's growing some cultures, and I think that's certainly something to think about. Food-borne and water-borne bacteria occur all the time."

"In the form of gastric upset normally."

"Except most of our patients have respiratory symptoms to some degree, and practically none of them have gastrointestinal problems. And it's causing system-wide problems…blood in the urine, abnormal blood sugar. I just saw one patient with an elevated blood sugar who swears she's not diabetic, yet her blood sugar is extremely high. So I did an A-one-C—" a test averaging out blood sugar levels "—and she's normal. In fact, she's perfect. But her blood sugar's hovering at three hundred and fifty right now, so something caused it to get that high."

"And you're inclined to believe your patient isn't simply over-indulging, like so many of the others are?"

"I'm inclined to believe her."

"Just like I'm inclined to believe Reese Allen didn't lie on his physical exam to work on the ship when he said he had no history of heart disease, yet he's just a tick shy of a heart attack."

Sarah frowned for a moment, then her frown line changed into a more thoughtful expression. "A couple of years ago Cameron and I had a patient who complained about lingering flu. She said she'd had it for a month and couldn't shake it, and she decided it was time to see a doctor. She didn't have a regular doctor so she called us to schedule herself in, but she missed her appointment, and I got word that she'd been admitted to the hospital in a critical condition. Her symptoms…" Sarah's eyes widened. "They were all over the place, Michael. But we never saw her and, to be honest, I didn't give it a thought as she never requested that either of us take her case while she was hospitalized."

"Well, most of our patients do have flu-like symptoms," he said. "Among other things. Do you think anyone might remember that case you mentioned?"

"My ex-fiancé." It wouldn't be an awkward phone call because there was no animosity between them, but talking to Cameron again would bring back memories of things she'd have rather forgotten. Dark days in her life she wasn't particularly proud of. "I guess it's time to give him a call, isn't it?" she said drearily.

"I can do it, Sarah. I know it's not always easy, facing people from your past. I've got a few of those ghosts myself."

"No, it's not easy facing the people you let down, is it?"

Michael was quiet for a moment, then he forced himself to speak. "You're being too hard on yourself," he said, his voice unusually strained. "I'm sure that whatever happened between the two of you isn't as bad as you think it is."

Spoken like a man who hadn't come to terms with his ghosts. Her heart did go out to him. It was hard, living with something terrible in your past. Not standing by someone she'd loved while he'd been experiencing the worst tragedy he'd ever faced, and needed that support to help get them through, was her ghost. Along with all the emotional distance she'd built. "What happened between the two of us was worse than you could imagine," she said, as she walked away.

It took ten minutes before the call went through to Cameron. He was a small-town doctor now, married to a veterinarian, and from what she'd heard he was thriving in every way possible. Marriage and fatherhood agreed with him, and she heard that the instant his cheery voice burst onto the line with, "Sarah! It's great to hear from you again. How are you doing? I understand you've been on an extended holiday."

"And I understand that you've got quite the life going for yourself," she said, avoiding any talk of herself.

"Everything I've always wanted. Health's good, too. Full remission, and I'm feeling better than I have in years."

She was happy for him. So happy, in fact, that tears began to slide down her cheeks. Cameron had never been bitter, had never held any feelings of anger toward her, and she could hear that in him now. He was such a wonderful man. He deserved a wonderful life. "You deserve all the good things you've gotten," she said, fighting to hold her voice steady as she swiped at the tears with the back of her hand.

From behind her, Michael gave her a tissue.

"Look, I'd love to catch up with everything you're doing, and maybe we can in the future, but I'm in the middle of a medical situation right now, and I need some advice."

"You've gone back into medicine?" Cameron asked. "Sarah, I'm so glad you finally realized that nothing was your fault. Not my illness, not the way I put off treatment, not the way we turned out. I've felt terrible, knowing you'd quit the practice and sold your half of it because of me, but now that you're back...where are you practicing, by the way?"

She closed her eyes, picturing Cameron. Just a shade shorter than Michael, he was muscular but not large, and he had dark brown hair, but not as dark as Michael's, with... Funny, she couldn't remember the color of Cameron's eyes any longer. Michael's were a haunting dark brown, but were Cameron's brown too, or green perhaps? How could something she'd seen so often have simply slipped from her mind? But the more she thought about Cameron now, the more his image blurred until he was indistinguishable from Michael. Then he was Michael, in her mind. "I'm not exactly back in a practice, but I'm helping out in a cruise ship's hospital, and we've got an outbreak of something I thought you might remember from a couple of years ago."

Cameron chuckled. "I always picture you more as staid. You know, someone who wanted an orderly life, personally and professionally. Wouldn't have ever guessed you'd wind up as a ship's doctor, but if that's what you like, I'm happy for you, Sarah. Now, tell me about this outbreak."

Sarah went into details for the next several minutes, telling Cameron everything she knew, which wasn't nearly enough. But when she was finished, she held her breath, hoping he remembered their similar case. "It was odd," he said, "because it didn't come to us in an outbreak, and normally legionnella, or legionnaires' disease, comes in an outbreak where numbers of people are affected. Like what you've got going on there. Without the tests I can't say for sure, but it sure sounds the same to me."

"Oh, my God," she whispered, a new sense of dread coming over her now. Legionnaires' disease could be fatal, yet it was also highly treatable if caught in time. She'd never treated a case herself, but now all the varying symptoms were making sense to her. Incubation period was right, the ship's conditions were certainly favorable to it… "That's not what I wanted to hear."

With those words, Michael stepped up behind her, slipping a steadying arm around her waist as Sarah said thanks and goodbye. After she'd hung up the phone, she stayed in his partial embrace. "Legionnaires' disease, if it's full-blown, and Pontiac fever if it's not." One would require strict medical treatment, and the other would run its course in a matter of a few days. Both were the same illness, but they attacked in differing degrees, hence the different names. The only good news in this whole mess was that legionnaires' was not communicable from person to person.

"So now we X-ray everybody to see who has pneumonia and who doesn't, get the ones who do on antibiotics, keep treating the various other problems people are having, and hope no one else comes down with it."

"And find the source," Sarah said, relieved that the medical mystery was possibly solved but dreading the next phase of what they were going to have to face. Right about now a nice little secluded booth in a dimly lit karaoke bar sounded awfully good, and she wondered if she and Michael would ever meet there again. Probably not, considering the way they'd been last time they'd sat together in a dark booth. "Let me go and see who, among our purple-hat nurses, has experience in taking X-rays."

There came a point when the body just gave out, and Michael had reached that point finally. He hated the fact that he didn't

have all his endurance back yet. He'd spent months in reha-
bilitation, then months after that working alone, retraining
himself in all the strenuous physical activities that had once
come so easily, but now, when it mattered, he wasn't up to
it. He had to take a break. Even after that two-hour nap
sixteen hours ago, he had to take a break. And he was disgusted with himself for that.

OK. So he was weak. He admitted it. The prosthesis had
to come off for a while. No getting around it, unless he
wanted to cause himself even more trouble. But, damn it, why
now? They had just over a hundred patients, the preliminary
diagnosis stage was still in progress, the tests and X-rays
were under way, and he needed to be there to make sure his
hospital ran as efficiently as it could, given the fact that he
was the only staff physician left healthy. But he had to walk
out. Had to turn his hospital over to Sarah and Dr Emma
Needham, one of the purple-hat ladies, and limp away.

*Had to go off and take a nap, just like that day when he'd
done the same thing to his medics and got them killed.*

Even now, thinking about it made his pulse quicken. Made
him break out in a cold sweat. "No distractions," he warned
himself, forcing himself to think about the technicians who
would shortly come aboard to find the source of the bacterium
and establish its nature once and for all. He mentally tracked
the next hours to come. He would take a short nap, then make
a transport manifest for his sickest patients. After that he
would assess those with the milder form of the illness and give
them the option of leaving or staying. Yes, that was the course
of action he'd be taking, and as for the rest of the cruise…
Actually, at this point he didn't give a damn about what
happened. As far as he was concerned, they could turn the ship
around and head back to Florida, to their port of origin, and
end this cruise. Most likely, that would be his recommenda-
tion at a meeting called for the ship's senior personnel in a
couple of hours since, as of yet, they had no idea where the

bacteria were multiplying. It could be anywhere…ventilation shafts, showers, hot tubs. Anywhere with a water source, which meant it was still a danger for all the guests.

Too tired to remove his clothes, or anything else, Michael slumped down into his bed and simply stared up at the ceiling. Sleep wasn't eluding him as much as he was fighting it off. He wanted to feel the ache for a while. It reminded him of all the things that had turned his life over, and he did need to be reminded from time to time. Some of that beating up he did to himself. Brent Mullavey, Greg Warren…his friends. Men he'd counted on. Men who'd counted on him. Their images were always on the edge of his mind, where they needed to be. He should have let go of them months ago. The military doctors who'd taken care of him had told him it was time to do that. But he couldn't…

"Four hours now, and I'm worried," Sarah said, as the ship's maintenance man pulled out his master key and inserted it into the lock on Michael's door. Michael had gone to take a break four hours ago and hadn't come back. To be honest, she'd been so busy she hadn't really noticed how long he'd been was gone until Ina had pointed it out. After that, she'd been in quite a panic, trying to find someone to come open his cabin door.

"He's going to hate this." Ina's voice was more worried than wary as she huddled behind Sarah, gripping her medical bag so tightly her knuckles were turning white. "Mike is a great guy, but he hates intrusion into his personal space. He's private that way. Doesn't want people interfering." Worry changed to panic on Ina's face as the maintenance man fumbled with his keys, trying to get the lock to open. "Can't you hurry?" she snapped.

Sarah's own worry was evident in the way she balled her fist and struck the doorframe each time Bruno, the maintenance man, failed to open the door. Then finally it gave and they were in. Sarah first, followed by Ina, then by Bruno.

"Michael!" Sarah called out in her mad rush across the cabin. Ina ran forward too, but Bruno, who might not have recognized a critically ill patient, did recognize the fact that an unresponsive patient wasn't good.

"Can I go get something for you?" he asked.

Sarah dropped down onto the bed next to Michael and immediately felt for his pulse. Fast, weak. And he was burning up with fever. "Go to the hospital and have someone bring a gurney down here," she said. "Tell them stat. They'll know what that means."

Ina, who was in the process of strapping a blood-pressure cuff to Michael's arm, cast Bruno an impatient glance as he hesitated for a moment to watch what they were doing. "Stat means immediately," she said, her voice razor-sharp.

"Legionnaires'," Sarah said on her way to the bathroom to fetch a basin of cool water. "I need him set up with an IV so we can get an antibiotic into him immediately. Acetaminophen, too, to bring down his fever. Can you go get that? I'd rather get it started here before we move him."

"Blood pressure's low," Ina reported. "But not abnormally. And I'm on my way to get the IV set-up. Does he need oxygen?"

"Probably not," she called from the bathroom. "His breathing seems fine for now. Wouldn't hurt to support him once we get him to the hospital, though." Sarah returned to Michael's bedside, carrying a basin of water after Ina left the cabin, immediately stripped off his shirt and applied a washcloth to his head, then one to his chest. Nice mat of soft, dark hair, she thought as started to removing the rest of his clothing to help him cool off. "Somehow I'd thought that the first time I saw you naked would be something other than this." Unzipping his white uniform pants, she slid them down over his legs. "Actually, that night at Evangeline's, I would have been very happy to see you naked, maybe in the broom closet or even under the table."

She paused for a moment, looking at his prosthesis. It was the first time she'd seen it, and she was amazed by the technology. She'd witnessed the working of a trans-tibial prosthesis on several occasions in her medical practice, but seeing it now on someone she knew, someone she cared about… Blinking hard, Sarah shook all that out of her mind as she removed his shoes, then his prosthetic leg. "I'll bet you're thinking I'm going to remove your underwear," she said, draping a sheet over his body for modesty's sake. "But I won't. At least, not while you're unconscious like this."

Would she have been so bold as to say these things to him if he'd been conscious? Probably not. That wasn't in her nature. Of course, what she'd done with him at Evangeline's wasn't in her nature either. But she'd been thinking these things, and more, for a while, and talking to Michael did make her less nervous as she examined him.

Another check of his pulse revealed nothing different from the first time. It was a little off but not dangerously so. And listening to his chest really didn't reveal any congestion, which was good, even though pneumonia was always a worry where legionella bacteria was concerned. Yet here he was right now, another case of non-specific symptoms, which meant the bacteria could be attacking just about any of his systems in ways she couldn't detect under these circumstances. That scared her, not just for Michael, but for everyone on board. "Look, Michael, I know this probably isn't the best time to iron out our differences but, to be honest, I probably wouldn't even say this if you could hear me. Or maybe you can. Who knows?" She laughed nervously as she sat down on the bed next to him. "But that night at Evangeline's…I'm not usually like that. Normally I'm pretty reserved, but you're so right about the chemistry. It's there. We've got it. To me, though, it goes beyond chemistry, which is why I would have… Well, what I'm trying to say is that, for me, it takes more than chemistry. At least, under normal circumstances. And I'm trying to figure it out…figure out what made me act that way. But I don't want you to think that I'm loose, or anything like that, because I'm not. It's just that I think I might be…" No, she couldn't say the words to him, not even when he was unconscious. Couldn't tell him she might be falling in love. That was too complicated, even for a man in his condition. And especially for herself.

Sarah pushed a stray lock of damp hair from his forehead, dipped the washcloth in the basin of water she'd set at the side of the bed, then reapplied it to his forehead. "Not that anything between us could ever happen," she continued. "But I want you to know that just because I shut people out of my life, it doesn't mean that I'm not normal in those ways. *Because I am.* You proved that." More than she'd thought anybody could.

She laid her fingers to his pulse again, not because there was anything she could do so much as she simply wanted to make contact with him. *Physical* contact to reassure him, on some level, that she was there with him. "You're going to be fine, Michael. I don't know what you went though that got you injured so badly, but I promise that I'll see you though this." She had no other choice. Whether or not she wanted to admit it, she loved him, and if there was one thing she was good at, it was standing by the men she loved. In the physical sense, anyway.

So maybe he had to hear that. Maybe she had to go against everything she'd held back from herself and tell him. Because, God forbid, if he died… No! She wouldn't think like that. Wouldn't make the same terrible mistakes she'd made before either.

Suddenly it was all so clear to her. Mistakes from the past…mistakes she wouldn't repeat. She had to do this because she didn't want the regrets, and in a life filled with them what she felt for Michael wouldn't be turned into another. Bending down to his ear, she whispered, "I do love you, Michael. I don't know what that means yet, but I think I've loved you almost from the moment I collapsed in your arms."

It felt good. Amazingly good. And right. Sitting back, pleased with her decision, she was dipping the washcloth in the basin to sponge off his chest again when Ina ran into the cabin, followed by a brigade of purple-hat volunteers pushing the gurney. Because Michael was a large, robust man, it took every woman in the room to lift him onto the gurney, but once they had, they whisked him away to the hospital, leaving Sarah behind to close up his cabin. As she started to pull the door shut, she took another look at his prosthetic leg. It didn't make him less of a man, didn't make him anything other than who he was. And it didn't matter to her. But she had a disturbing feeling that it mattered to Michael in more ways than she could understand. Maybe more than he could understand, too.

In a life full of ups and downs with her past relationships, she was fully aware of why she held back from getting involved in another one again. But was she looking at the reason Michael held himself back? That might have been part of it, she decided. Somewhere deep down, though, he had other demons. She was sure of it. Someone with her fair share of demons knew the symptoms when she saw them.

"Michael, you're in the hospital."

Of course he was. That's where he worked, and it was time to get up from his nap and get back to it.

"You're going to be just fine. Your temperature's come down now, your vital signs are stable, and there's no sign of any permanent damage."

Damn, he hated taking naps. Normally he felt worse afterwards than he had before. That's why he didn't nap very often, because he always came out of it feeling like hell. Like he did now.

"They found the source of the legionella bacteria. It wasn't on the ship after all. It seems that the hotel where so many of the passengers and crew stayed the night before the cruise launched had the bacteria cultivating in their ventilation system. Everybody who stayed there breathed it in."

He'd stayed there, but apparently he'd escaped the effects. Opening his eyes to Sarah, Michael wondered how she'd gotten into his cabin. "How long did you let me sleep this time?" he muttered, raising his hand to visor his eyes from the bright light overhead and for the first time noticing the IV in his wrist. "What's this?" he sputtered, now trying to sit up.

Sarah laid a gentle hand on his shoulder to keep him down. "Normal saline now, with a piggyback of an antibiotic in another three hours."

It didn't make sense. He'd gone to take a nap. Just a few minutes off his feet then back to work. But he'd heard Sarah's voice waft in and out. He remembered that. Had it been in his dream? And why the IV? "What happened?" he asked, fighting to remember, to clear the fog that had settled over his brain.

"You got sick. The cultures were positive for legionnaires', and you came down with it. You've been sick with low-grade pneumonia these past couple of days, lapsing in and out of consciousness. But the pneumonia's cleared and you're on the mend."

"Am I still on the ship?"

"You're in Miami. You were transported with the other patients. Everything's under control now."

Under control. He was lying flat on his back in a hospital again after he'd vowed that no matter what happened to him he'd never go back to another hospital as a patient. "When can I leave?" he asked, turning slightly sideways to take in his surroundings. It was a private room, not a critical-care unit. That was good.

"If you keep responding to treatment, maybe in a week or so."

"You've stayed here with me the whole time?"

"I promised I would."

He vaguely remembered that promise. Or he thought he did. "And everybody's fine? All the people who contracted…" Glancing up at her face, he knew the answer she was fighting desperately to hide. "How many?" he choked.

"We can talk about that later."

"No. We can talk about it now. How many people did we lose?"

Drawing in a long, ragged breath, Sarah took hold of Michael's hand. "Just one. I'm sorry, Michael, but it was…"

"Reese Allen. The bacteria lodged in his heart, didn't it?"

She nodded. "The medical examiner said that he did have a weak heart and that was the easiest thing for the bacteria to attack. He also said he didn't believe Dr Allen was aware of his heart defect."

"And I came close to dying?"

Sarah nodded again. "Because you've had so many surgeries in the recent past. They weakened your system and the legionella bacteria love to attack a weakened system."

He didn't know what to say, and even if he had, he didn't have the energy. So he shut his eyes and drifted back to sleep, but not before something flashed through his mind. *I've loved you almost from the moment I collapsed in your arms.* Had he dreamt that? Dreamt that in Sarah's voice? "Go away," he murmured as he drifted off. "Go away, Sarah."

He was sick, grumpy, probably frustrated by the inconvenience of being confined to bed, which was why she wasn't taking his mood personally. In her experience she'd dealt with much worse. So taking a break was good, and in a while, after she returned to Michael's room, maybe he'd feel better. Maybe he'd be in a better mood, too.

Both Ina and Martha had been at her side almost constantly these past days. They'd become friends she'd never expected to find in a life she'd never expected to find. Bright spots in so much uncertainty.

"I think he's waking up again," the nurse on duty said three hours later as she poked her head into the doctors' lounge, where Sarah had practically taken up residence this past week.

"Thank you." It was tough, not knowing whether she should go back to him now or leave him alone for a while longer. The last couple of times he'd woken up he'd just told her to go away. Nothing else. And, frankly, that's what she expected this time. Ina said it was because he wasn't ready to face the truth. But was it the truth he feared? Or did he fear her? Did he really love her, the way he'd said he did every time he'd woken up these past few days. He'd told her, he'd told Ina and Martha, he'd told any number of nurses... But that had been delirium, and, as much as she wanted to believe it was something else, she wasn't going to allow herself to believe it. He was a very sick man. That's all it was.

But it had been nice to hear, nevertheless. Now she wondered if he remembered some of the things he'd babbled, and that scared him if they were true. Or made him feel guilty if they were not.

Why were the deepest personal feelings, like loving someone, the hardest to admit to? Why were they the ones that scared you the most? Rather than making life better, they became a complication, which didn't seem right. Vulnerability, she decided. The hardest thing to do was to make yourself vulnerable to someone else. But it was also the nicest, because that's where the true bond started—a bond she'd thought about over these days sitting at Michael's bedside. A bond she truly wanted with him. But now she was scared, too. Which took her right back to her original question. *Why were the deepest personal feelings, like loving someone, the hardest to admit to?*

"You should go to him," Martha prompted. "He needs you now more than ever."

"And be kicked out again."

"It's not personal, sweetie. You know that."

Sarah signed wearily. "But what it if is? I think he either remembers some of the things he said…"

"Or he's afraid of some of the things *you* said. Is that what's bothering you? That you opened yourself up to him so much? Made yourself vulnerable?"

"You heard?" How could that be? Yes, she'd told him she loved him, told him that several times. But she'd been alone. So how could Martha have known?"

Martha chuckled. "No, I didn't eavesdrop on your conversations with him. But it's in your face, Sarah, in the way you look at him, the way you respond to him, the way you touch him when you're taking care of him. So, tell me, how could you *not* sit at the bedside of the man you love without telling him that you love him?"

Martha was right about that. She couldn't. "Do you think he heard me, and he doesn't want to deal with me now?"

"I think he doesn't know *how* to deal with you, sweetie. He's a lot like you, the way he tries to keep to himself and push everybody away. If you want my opinion, though, I think you pierced his armor and he doesn't know what to do about it. The way he pierced yours. Only he changed the rules by getting sick. He needed you and you were forced to give in to your feelings for him in order to help him." She smiled. "Which gives you an advantage he hasn't had. It's amazing, isn't it, how sometimes the worst situations bring out the best truths?"

Truths she didn't know what to do with. Sarah took two steps toward the door, then turned back to Martha. "Falling in love shouldn't be so hard. I thought if I ever did it again it would be…I don't know. Maybe without problems? You know, something simple."

"If it's without problems, or simple, then it's not true love. And what you feel for Michael is true love, isn't it?"

"True love. That can't work itself out." She shook her head. "It's so complicated, Martha. I don't handle true love as well as it should be handled. I let people down, do the wrong things for what I believe are the right reasons, and end up just making a mess of it. I'm not sure I've got it in me to do it again."

"Which is why you keep to yourself. Not trying is easier than taking a plunge into the great unknown. Well, I don't know what happened with your late husband, sweetie, or that other gentleman you told me about, but from what I've observed with the way you've been with Doctor Sloan, I'd say you've done everything perfectly and the greatest unknown should be how you'll survive without him *and not* how you'll let him into your life. I think you're the hardest critic of yourself, even though you've got no call to be that way now. Yet words aren't going to make you believe that, Sarah. It's going to take time, and patience, and the love of a good man that lets your heart truly trust again…and that includes trusting yourself. So you'd better go to him while he's awake and tell him you're not going anywhere."

Sound advice, except running away would have been the easiest thing to do. Leave, and never come back. Her heart was fully committed, though. And she was so tired of running. So very tired…

"Michael," she said quietly as she slipped into his room and took her regular seat by the side of his bed.

His eyes fluttered open to her. "Have I told you that I love you, Sarah? Have I told you yet?"

"Yes," she said, realizing he was on his way down again. "And I love you, too." Her love wasn't the blear that comes from a spiking fever either.

"Good," he murmured, as he slipped away. "I'm glad you do."

* * *

"He's gone?" Sarah stared at the empty bed, still not believing what she was seeing. "Michael's gone?" He wasn't ready. Wasn't well enough yet.

"Checked himself out an hour ago," the nurse said. "AMA." Against medical advice. "We tried to convince him to stay, but he refused, and there was nothing we could do to stop him. Dr Sloan called a private hire to take him, then left."

She couldn't believe it! "Do you know where he went?"

The nurse shook her head. "All he said was that he'd consult a doctor when he arrived at his destination. No word where that destination is, though."

She'd been gone four hours. *That's all.* Four lousy hours because she'd needed to take a walk, get some fresh air. So she'd gone back to the hotel in which she hadn't slept, taken a shower, then had a stroll on the beach. Four hours, and he'd taken full advantage of the time! "How was he, physically?"

"Weak, but coherent."

He'd been coherent for the past day and a half. Coherent and totally unresponsive to her. Every time she'd gone to his room he'd spent his time staring out the window or faking sleep. She'd known he was improving, and she'd hoped that his attitude would improve too, but apparently that had been nothing more than wishful thinking on her part. Obviously, he'd planned on leaving, on walking away from her the first chance he got.

"He did leave you this note." The nurse handed Sarah a sealed envelope, but Sarah didn't want to open it there because she knew what was inside would make her go to pieces. She wanted to be alone for that. Alone, the way she should have stayed all along.

Sitting on a bench in the lush tropical garden outside the hotel, with the scent of gardenias and salt water in the air, Sarah stared at the ocean just across the way for nearly twenty minutes before she finally tucked her little finger under the envelope's flap and ripped it open. Inside she saw the white sheet of paper, and it took her another ten minutes to pull it out and open it up.

Dear Sarah, it started.

She drew in a deep breath, bracing herself for the pain that was inevitable.

Sometimes, these past few days, I've heard myself telling you, telling everyone else that I love you, and I do. I want you to know that it wasn't crazy talk from a man who was out of his head. You said you loved me almost from the moment you collapsed in my arms and I've held onto that through my delirium. And, yes, it's true what they say about how some people, when they're unconscious, can hear what's going on around them, because I did hear you. Everything you said to me. And here's the funny thing. I fell in love with you almost at the same time you did, when you collapsed in my arms. You looked up at me with so much trust, and you were so beautiful, how could I not?

You had such a wall around you, though, which kept you safe. But it kept me safe, too, from the very same things you didn't want in your life. Except we had that chemistry, didn't we? Nothing to deny there. Which made it so tough for me, because I can't have a relationship with you...and it has nothing to do with you.

You have such a good, kind heart, Sarah. There's so much to give deep inside you, and I would love, with all my heart, to be the one to take what you want to give, but I can't. My life isn't worked out, and I can't drag you into it.

You need to live your life for yourself now, Sarah. I don't think you've done much of that because you are such a dutiful, faithful woman. But to the wrong man this time. Please know that I won't stop loving you

even though, with a small piece of my heart, I do hope
that you can find it in yourself to stop loving me.
      Let your heart tell you what to do. Listen, Sarah. It
won't let you down.

Too numb to cry, too numb to even breathe, Sarah stared
at the ocean for another hour, clutching Michael's letter to
her chest, before she finally got up and returned to her hotel
room. Then she packed, and finally went home to Boston.
Home, for the first time in a year.

CHAPTER TEN

IT WAS a nice cabin, and she'd been sitting in her parked rental car, down the road from it and out of view, for the past hour, trying to gather up the courage to do this. It had been a month now, and she had to. He'd had his space, she'd had hers, and with every breath she'd drawn during those long, empty days she'd come to realize just how much she wanted him in her space. That's all there was, and if Michael was worth loving the way she did, he was worth fighting for. This time it was different, though. Her future wasn't slipping down a drain the way it had while Kerry had been dying, or while her relationship with Cameron had been ending. With Michael she had no future unless she went after it. And she wanted to go after it. Give herself that chance to fight for it and, if nothing else this time, walk away knowing she'd done everything she could.

But that scared her, because she didn't count on him having a change of heart. And this would be the very last time. If he succeeded in pushing her away this time, he'd never let her get near him again. She was sure of it.

He loved her, though. She knew that more than she knew just about anything else. Michael Sloan did love her. Which was what made this the most important thing she'd ever done in her life. So now it was time to prepare herself for all the things that had to be said, and do whatever it would take to fight for *them*. For Michael and herself as a couple.

Gritting her teeth with the resolve she'd been working on this past month, Sarah turned the key in the ignition and headed down the road after what she wanted.

"I like it here," she said, stepping up to the porch rail where he was perched, looking out over the lake. He looked good. Rested. Healthy again. "It's peaceful."

"It's not mine," he said flatly. "I don't need a home, with the way I live. Borrowing one is just fine. Better than owning, as you don't have any permanent ties."

She chuckled on the outside even though she winced internally. He was so hard now. Pulled so far into his emotional scars she wasn't sure she knew how to break through. "You sound like me. No need for permanent roots. Just go wherever the urge takes you." Except her urge took her only one place now. No matter how this turned out, her days of wandering were over.

He didn't respond to that. Neither did he make a move toward her. Didn't even look at her, but, then, she didn't expect him to. Although she'd really hoped for something else…open arms, maybe? It would have been a nice start, she thought on a sad note. "How are you, Michael?" she finally asked, breaking the icy silence between them. "I've been worried." He hadn't returned her phone calls, but she'd never quit calling so he'd had to expect this…expect that at some point she'd come here. She'd half expected to find that he'd moved on without leaving a forwarding address. So maybe his still being here was a good sign. She desperately hoped so.

"Why the hell can't people just leave me alone? Did it ever occur to you that I'm out here at this lake, all alone, cut off from society, because I want to be?"

"Actually, yes. It did. When Ina told me where you were, she also mentioned that you didn't want to be bothered. Which is why I came."

"To bother me?"

"Yes, to bother you. Because I know some of your isolation has to do with me, and I don't want it to. So I had to come find you, to tell you…"

"What?" he snapped, finally turning to face her. "That you love me? Because I already know that. So what can you tell me that I *don't* already know?"

The pain was so stark in his eyes it shocked her, and broke her heart. But this time she couldn't quit, couldn't back away like she had before. Couldn't let him bully her into backing away. "I know what it's like to live with a different image of yourself, to have something you counted on taken away."

"My leg?" He barked a bitter laugh. "You don't know anything, Sarah. Not a damned thing!" Spinning away, he walked through the French windows back into the lodge, and was halfway up the stairs by the time she'd caught up with him.

"I do know, Michael. I know what it's like to watch the man you love lose his body image by bits and pieces. To go from a large, athletic man who competed in marathons to one who weighed barely a hundred pounds, who'd lost all his hair, whose skin just hung on his bones. I lived with that, and loved a man who was going through it. So don't tell me that I don't know, because I do."

"It's not about my leg," he insisted, but this time his voice wasn't so sharp. Turning to face Sarah, he stared down at her but didn't attempt to come back down the stairs. "And sometimes it gets to the point where body image just doesn't matter any more."

"It never does, Michael. More than once, when he didn't know that I could see him, I saw Kerry stand at the mirror and look at himself. And cry. The tears weren't for the cancer, but for the losses he could see in that damned mirror. Inside he was still the same man, but on the outside he was ravaged by an illness he couldn't control, and the visual reminder was as much a part of what he was dealing with as was his cancer.

Maybe even more, since it was a constant harbinger even on the days when he wasn't feeling so bad.

"And I wasn't there for him, Michael. Oh, in the physical sense I never left his side. But there's something more…the things that needed saying. Things he needed to say that I *couldn't* hear. Things I wanted to say that I was afraid to. Which is why I'm here. There are things I need to say now, things you need to hear, and I won't do to you what I did to Kerry." She fought back a strangled sob, angry that she was reduced to tears. She didn't want to be because it made her vulnerable, and for Michael's sake she couldn't be vulnerable in this. He needed her strength…her complete strength. A strength that had faltered for Kerry, and even for Cameron.

Bracing herself, she fought off the tears stinging her eyes, threatening to spill. She wouldn't cry, wouldn't give way to her emotions. *Not this time*. "So you can run away, Michael, but I'll just follow you."

"I'm sorry," he said, his voice barely above a whisper. "I don't want to hurt you, Sarah. I never wanted to do that. But you don't understand. I just…just can't do this."

"Then make me understand. You owe me that much, Michael. If you love me, like you said you do, then you owe it to me to make me understand."

"Maybe I do."

The resignation in his voice was thick, but not as thick as the lines creased into his face now. Michael looked like he'd aged ten years in the past few minutes and she couldn't help but think that her coming here had caused that.

"But even if I do make you understand, I still can't make it right for us, Sarah. What's broken is inside me, and it can't be fixed. I've tried, but nothing changes. And words are only words. They don't make the deeds go away."

She swallowed hard, still looking up the stairs at him. "After Kerry died, when I was engaged to Cameron, he put me off. I knew something was wrong with him…as his fiancée, as a doctor, I could see it. It showed in every way I looked at him, but yet when I mentioned it to him, asked him if he was feeling well, asked him if he'd had a physical check-up lately, he put me off, the way you're trying to do now, Michael. And I let him because, for me, it was like Kerry all over again, and I didn't want to go through that. With Kerry, when our time together was coming to an end he desperately wanted to say so many things to me, to make sure that I would be taken care of. That was important to him and I know it was his biggest worry, yet I would never let him talk about it because I was so adamant about avoiding the obvious, *that my husband was dying*. I lived in the delusion that if I didn't talk about it, that would somehow change things. Like you're doing, I think. So in the end, when Kerry and I most needed to talk, to say everything we'd thought we would have a lifetime to say, I couldn't do it. I wasted so much time, Michael. Time I'll never get back. Things I'll never get to say to the man I loved so dearly. Things I'll never get to hear him say to me. Then Cameron…I knew he wasn't well, but I didn't push it, even though he was in denial. For me, it was safer. And, trust me, I know denial. But when I should have been talking to him…" She paused, blinking back the inevitable tears.

"It was a doomed relationship before that, and one that was just hanging on by a fraying thread when his diagnosis of leukemia was finally made. So there I was, engaged to marry a man I knew I'd never walk down the aisle with and trying hard to be the support he needed in a difficult time for him. Avoidance is such a hurtful, terrible thing to do to yourself, or to someone you care about. We became so…estranged, because there were so many things that needed saying. Honest feelings I just couldn't face up to, and Cameron needed that honesty from me, especially when he was so sick, but I was holding back again.

"It was bad for both of us. Yet I couldn't leave him, even though I was on the verge of it when his leukemia hit, and I truly believe that the strains we were putting our relationship through at the time made his condition worse. Or, at least, caused him undue stress he didn't deserve, and which he didn't need, going into chemotherapy. But I stood by, and it was horrible for both of us because I think we both knew that we would have already ended the relationship if not for his illness.

"But the thing was, Cameron never knew about Kerry. Cameron was my rebound love after Kerry died and all Cameron ever knew was that I'd been married before. I never told him more than that and he never asked. Then one day, when Cameron was having a particularly bad bout from his chemo, I told him about an herbal tea that had always settled Kerry's stomach when he had been going through the same thing. It just slipped out. I hadn't meant it to, but there it was."

"And that's when you ended your relationship to Cameron?" he asked.

She shook her head. "That's when he ended his relationship with me. He said I should have told him, and he was right. And I let him down, Michael, just like I did Kerry. I avoided too much, and Cameron sent me away at a time he needed someone to be with him. I could have stayed as a friend, but we were past that point."

"Twice, Sarah… I don't know what to say."

"There's nothing to say. Life doesn't come with guarantees, does it? I was angry and bitter both times, but mostly hurt. It was easier to run away than face up to so many bad decisions. So I ran."

"But both of them made their choices too, Sarah. I don't want to speak ill of your husband, but it was his choice to *let* you avoid the things you didn't want to face. He could have insisted on having those talks you never had, to say those things that never got said. But I have an idea that his choice was to protect you from them because you were so afraid of them, the way it was Cameron's choice to ignore his symptoms even when you were telling him to get help."

"But if I'd been stronger... I wasn't strong enough to help them through the way they needed to be helped. *And that's the point.* My inadequacies are the reason I quit medicine. I was there for them, but not enough, and not in the right way. Which is the same thing as failing them."

"It's not about your strength, Sarah. You are strong. I've seen that. What you've gone through, twice, are the kinds of things no one is ever prepared to deal with, and sometimes it's just a matter of getting through the best way you can. You can't keep condemning yourself for that."

"But it wasn't supposed to be about me. Not with Kerry, not with Cameron. Cameron said that if he'd known what I'd gone through with Kerry he'd have let me go long before he did. I think he knew that the friction we already had between us worsened his condition. I tried, Michael, but it wasn't right between us. But I didn't want him to..."

"To die alone?" he asked, his voice tender. "The way you didn't want me to die alone?"

Finally, the tears broke, and she took an angry swipe at them. "People were hateful after Cameron broke it off. They accused me of terrible things, even though Cameron defended me and told everyone that he was the one to leave me. But no one believed that. They simply assumed that I couldn't take it. Or didn't want to." She ducked her head as Michael walked down the stairs then straight over to her and pulled her into his arms. "Which is why I came here today. I have a terrible history of not saying the right things, or not saying anything at all, and I can't do that again, Michael. Not with you."

"And this time you didn't run, even though that's what I've been trying to force, telling you to leave me alone."

She nodded, as the tears streaking down her face blotted against his sweater. "I let down the people I love. I don't mean to, but that's how it works out. How can I be a good doctor when I can't even do what I need to do for the people I love? Twice, Michael. I've failed twice. I missed the obvious, let myself be talked out of something I knew, couldn't bring myself to say or hear the right words... Those are all horrible traits in a doctor. When I took my oath I vowed to do my best, and that includes seeing everything, insisting when the patient is protesting, saying what needs to be said and, most of all, listening. Without the ability to do those, I can't be a doctor."

"So why are you here now, Sarah?"

"Because I couldn't fail you, Michael. I fell in love with you and I had to tell you. I know you heard me say it when you were sick, but I wanted you to hear it when you were well. I thought that maybe, if you loved me like you said you did, hearing it from me again would help you get through whatever it is you're going through. Maybe it would give you something to hold onto. As simple as that. I used to go around thinking there was always enough time, but there's not. And I don't want to make any mistakes with you. Not like I've done with everybody else. So, I do love you, and that's why I'm here." She felt his body go rigid against hers. "I know you have feelings for me, but if the reason you've been resisting me is because of your leg..."

He pulled away from her, but not to retreat up the stairs, like she feared that he might. Instead, he marched to the other side of the room, to the liquor cabinet, where he pulled out a bottle of something she thought to be Scotch.

"I don't know if we can work it out between us," she continued, as he poured a shot in a small glass, then drank it straight down. "But at least I've come here to try. It wasn't easy, Michael. I'd promised myself I'd never get involved again, because that only led to being let down, or to a broken heart. But I'm not one of those people who denies her feelings. I didn't want to fall in love with anybody, but I did fall in love with you. That's why this is so hard for me, because I know how much you didn't want to fall in love with me. But I think you did, Michael. I *know* you did."

He turned around to face her. "I'm glad you've been able to work through your problems, Sarah. I'm sure that in time you'll return to medicine, find yourself a man who deserves you, settle down and have yourself a nice life. But not with me." He started to pour himself another drink, which was uncharacteristic of him. It was an obvious sign she couldn't miss, and he wasn't going to put her off the way Cameron had. She was heart and soul in love with the man who'd given her back the life she'd always loved, and now it was her turn to find a way to give him back his life. But if his disability wasn't the cause of this, what was?

"I've never asked because I figured that if you wanted me to know, you'd tell me. But how did you lose your leg, Michael? What happened?"

"I told you it's not connected to my leg!" he snapped.

"And if you've convinced yourself of that, you're lying to yourself because even if your leg isn't the whole cause of what you're suffering, it plays a part."

"Oh, that's right. This is where you get to be insistent with me, the way you couldn't be with Cameron. Except with me it isn't going to work." He stared at his second drink for a moment before he drank it down. "So you can go now, Sarah."

"Was it something stupid you did to yourself? Motorcycle accident? Some other kind of sport-related injury?" She hated this, but she wasn't ready to give up on Michael yet, not when he was so close to giving up on himself. "Car wreck? Cancer? Diabetic complication?"

"Go away," he snapped, brushing his hand through his hair.

"I read about a climber who got his arm caught by a rock and had to do a self-amputation. Were you a climber? Maybe it was severe frostbite? Tell me, Michael. Tell me what happened."

"It's nobody's business what happened." He picked up the Scotch bottle for a third go at it, studied the bottle with pure revulsion on his face, then hurled the mostly full bottle at the wall. It crashed with a vengeance, sending glass shards everywhere while the butterscotch-colored alcohol ran down the wood panels. "Just go away Sarah," he said, this time the anger all drained from his voice. "There's nothing here for you."

"An industrial accident?" she asked. "Something alcohol-related? Some kind of infection? A compound fracture that wouldn't heal?"

He sucked in a deep, rapid breath and forced it out just as quickly. "A landmine. I stepped on a damned landmine and it exploded. So are you happy now that you know? Happy enough to get the hell away from me?"

Dear God, she hadn't even been close. "You were in the military?" That surprised her, yet in a way it didn't, as exact as he was about his actions, about the way he practiced his medicine. He did have that military precision about him, didn't he?

"That's right. I was military. It was all I ever wanted—to be a doctor in a military hospital like my father had been. From battlefield surgeon to cruise-ship doctor all because I…" He broke off, shook his head and headed for the stairs again, but on the way Sarah caught him by the arm, and wouldn't let go.

"Tell me the rest of it, Michael."

"What makes you think there's more to tell? I got sloppy. Walked somewhere I shouldn't have." With his hand, he made a sweeping gesture toward his leg. "And this is what I got for it. Are you satisfied now?" He shook her off, but she grabbed hold of his arm again, this time fighting to hang on.

"I know what Kerry saw when he looked in the mirror,

Michael. I know what broke his heart. But what do you see when *you* look in the mirror? What breaks your heart?"

"What breaks my heart is a self-centered, selfish bastard who couldn't be bothered to stand by his men. That's what I see." He spun away from her and marched up the stairs, but by the time he was at the top, she was right behind him.

"You forced me to take a good, hard look at myself, Michael. That's how I'm able to come to you now. In the note you left me, when you said that I needed to live my life for myself, that meant something to me because I really haven't ever done that. At least, not much in the past years. When I thought about it, I realized what that life was. My medical practice. *And you*. That's the life I want to live for myself."

"Well, good for you, Sarah. Except you can only have half of that."

"But I don't want half of it."

"Then call me selfish for cheating you out of everything you want, because that's what I am. Selfish. This is all about me, not you."

"You're not selfish, Michael. I've seen that. You care so deeply for people."

"Yeah, like I cared so much that I sent my two medics out while I stayed back and took a nap. Sent them out to die while I went to bed, and it got them killed."

"I don't believe that!" she sputtered.

"Believe what? That I could put myself first? That's what I did. We were all tired. All equally tired, but somebody had to go, and it was my decision to make. So I sent two people out who were as tired as I was and they went the wrong damn way. Traveled into an area that hadn't been cleared and got themselves killed doing it. And the hell of it was, it was a non-essential trip. People had to be transported from a first-aid station to the hospital, but they weren't critical. We could have waited. But I issued the order, and even though my men asked to hold back for an hour or two so they could rest, I made them go anyway."

"But you couldn't have known... I mean, you can't predict the outcome in a war zone."

"Maybe you can't, but you up the odds of making it a bad one when you send war-weary troops out into the middle of it."

"So, how did you...?" She pointed to his right leg. "How did that happen?"

"After I heard the explosion, I ran that half mile to get to them...don't even remember it." He paused, shut his eyes, then drew in a ragged breath. "Rather than sticking to the road, which I knew had been de-mined, I veered off to get there faster, and stepped on a landmine. I don't remember anything after that for about a week. And they gave me a damned medal for doing nothing."

No more words. Michael marched into the bedroom and slammed the door shut behind him, leaving Sarah standing alone on the stairs. She didn't know what to say, didn't know what to do. Turning around, she started back down the stairs, but had taken only a few steps when Michael's words came back to her. *Let your heart tell you what to do. Listen, Sarah. It won't let you down.*

She prayed that would be the case as she climbed those stairs again, then pushed open Michael's bedroom door. "I could say something trite like accidents happen, or there was no way you could have known what would happen, but I won't because your pain goes too deep for that. But what I will say, Michael, is that what happened to you changed you to the very core. I'm not sure you were ever as bad as you think. We all change, get touched by the world in ways we didn't know we could. Maybe you were selfish, staying behind to take a nap. I don't think you ever could be selfish, but I wasn't there so I really can't say. Or maybe it's more a case of you being too hard on yourself. Whichever it is, the Michael Sloan I know right now isn't the one who existed back then, and the one I know now isn't selfish. He's a caring, generous man who loves medicine, and has the pure heart of the five-year-old who wanted to save those people on the freighter. What counts…*the only thing that counts*…is that you make your life matter for something good."

He laughed bitterly. "I'm damaged goods," he said.

"So am I, but you've made me realize that damage can be repaired, or at the very least turned into something better. I know the guilt you're feeling over losing your men…your friends. God knows, I have had my share of loss. But as doctors we know better than most that there are some things we just can't control. That includes death. Even though I know I let Kerry down, I don't think he ever thought I did. Cameron, too. And your men…if they knew you the way I've come to, I don't believe they would have thought you were letting them down."

"But it doesn't matter what they thought, does it? I did let them down. However you look at it, I did."

"That's how *you* look at it, Michael. But what I see is a very brave man who would have given his own life to save them." She walked slowly to the large picture window where he was standing. His back was turned to her as she slipped her arms around his waist and laid her head against him. "We're our own harshest judges, aren't we? You blaming yourself, me blaming myself."

"Sometimes we have to be."

"But there's a time to let go. There's got to be because I always wanted to love again, in spite of not believing I really could. You know, that little speck of hope hiding deep down inside. Then I met you, Michael, and the little speck grew, which really scared me because it's so much easier to live within the restrictions we set for ourselves than step outside them. But everything about you made me want to step outside them. The heart has such an amazing capacity for expanding and changing, doesn't it?"

"Maybe it does," he whispered, "but that's not going to change things between us."

She hadn't expected this to be easy, but she wasn't giving up. "No, it's not. I love you, and I know you love me."

"Look, Sarah, regardless of how I might feel about you, I didn't want to meet you. Not yet."

His voice was softening, taking on the gentle qualities she expected from Michael yet still fighting them. But she wasn't going to approach him again. This time he would have to come to her. "And I didn't want to meet you. Maybe not ever. But there's one unavoidable thing we have to face here. *We met, Michael.* And we found each other over and over on that big cruise ship, even when we weren't trying to."

"At the wrong time."

"Or the right time...the time we most needed to meet. And be together."

"But I can't." He finally turned to face her.

"Why not?"

"I was engaged once, and..."

"And she walked out on you after your injury?" It had been a wild guess, but the answer was in his eyes. "Do you really think I'm that shallow?"

"Not shallow. Duty-bound, maybe. But not shallow."

"Believe me, that night in Evangeline's had nothing to do with being duty-bound. And I'd do it again, in a heartbeat." She drew in a steadying breath, still in for the fight. "That's not me, Michael. You know that's not me."

"Maybe I do, but the life I'd planned for myself is gone and there's nothing left in its place. That's where I am, Sarah. In a place where there's nothing. I want to be a doctor. That's never changed, even though I'll never be a military surgeon again. But I don't know how I'm going to work it out, and I don't know where. Until I do, I can't bring someone else into that uncertainty. Can't bring you. You deserve better."

"Even if that someone else wants to be there with you? Because I do, Michael. I don't know where my life is going either, but wherever it goes, the only thing I know for certain is that I want you to be there, in it. I don't even care about the rest of the details. What I want is you, any way I can have you."

"You *are* stubborn. Of course, I knew that the first time I set eyes on you…the way you defied doctor's orders about your hypoglycemia."

"Not so much defied them as adjusted them to suit my needs." She smiled. "The way I'm trying to adjust *you* to suit my needs."

"How can we do this, Sarah?"

"Together. That's the first step, and maybe the only one we should take right now. I think we're good for that much, Michael. One step at a time, one day at a time."

"I do love you, you know. Every time I've said it, I meant it."

"I know," she whispered, on the verge of tears again. She desperately wanted to run into his arms, but she wouldn't. She'd made every move toward him she knew how to make, bared her soul, allowed Michael into places in herself no man had ever touched, but now it was time for him to want her. She'd taken that first step toward him and now it was his turn to take that same step toward her, so she stood her ground, even though it was very difficult. "And I love you, too."

They stared at each other for a moment, with all the longing of two broken hearts in their gazes. Yet Michael didn't go to her, and she wondered if he would. She still did believe she'd let Kerry down when he'd needed her the most, the way she'd also let Cameron down. Both in different ways, yet both with so much pain. Now she was beginning to wonder if Michael thought that she would let him down, too.

Nothing intentional, nothing planned, but an accumulation of all her inadequacies.

Maybe it was time to go. Maybe the character flaw that Michael had convinced her wasn't a flaw really was after all. And he saw that. "I, um…" she began, then stopped. This time she'd said everything. There was nothing remaining and she had no regrets as she'd told him everything in her heart. Drained her soul dry. After that, there was nothing left to do but to go, and leave Michael to figure it out on his own.

She didn't want to leave him because she feared he would be glad she'd taken the easiest way out. Yet she couldn't stay. Not any longer. So, without another word, she turned and walked through the bedroom door, then down the stairs, each and every one of her footsteps leaden. Halfway to the front door she heard the faint click of the bedroom door upstairs, and a large knot caught in her throat. He'd shut her out, and she'd never get back in. Ten more steps and she'd be out of his life for ever.

She'd only taken five of those ten, however, when he called to her. "Sarah, don't go!"

She held her breath, without turning to face him.

"I don't have any answers," he said. "I know you've never let down the people you think you have…"

"And you didn't let down your men."

"But it's going to take more than words to convince either of us, isn't it? Knowing it on the surface and feeling it in the heart are entirely different."

"Survivor's guilt," she said. "Both of us. It happens. The one who doesn't die experiences guilt over it as part of the way they deal with it. I don't know how to get through it, Michael."

"Together," he whispered. "We have to get through it together."

"Together."

"I don't know how it's going to work out, Sarah. The only

thing I do know for certain is that I want you there with me when it does. More than that, I want to be there with you. Can you accept all the other uncertainties that go with it?"

She nodded. She couldn't speak now as tears flooded down her cheeks. But she heard him walk down the stairs and cross over the wooden floor, and by the time he reached her and pulled her into his arms, she was certain of *only* one thing among the many things she still wasn't sure of. She loved Michael Sloan. Nothing else mattered.

Third time *was* the charm. This was where she was meant to be.

"I love you," he whispered. His entire body relaxed as he held her.

So did hers as she clung to him for dear life, happy and contented. Finally, after so long, Sarah had found her life again, and it was with Michael. Only Michael… "I love you, too."

"You should look at this," Sarah said, tossing the medical journal across the bed to Michael. Things were getting better. They moved forward in small steps each day, always together. She still carried her guilt, so did Michael, and with each other's help they were coming to understand the nature of their guilt and help each other through it. It was amazing how much lighter the load was when it was carried by two. In the rough moments they worked through it together. In the good moments it was perfect.

Being married to Michael was everything she'd ever hoped for. And more.

"You read enough medical journals for the two of us," he grumbled, pulling the sheet up over his head. He'd been off duty for the grand total of an hour and he wasn't anywhere near ready to wake up. Especially since he'd had more than his fair share of cruise overeaters come into the hospital the night before—overeaters like Mrs Grimaldi, who'd made a

light snack of a pound of shrimp, a lobster, and half a chocolate cake. "But you're going to tell me about it anyway, aren't
you?" he groaned.

"It's about a little clinic in a country near Thailand.
They're doing remarkable things for victims of landmines
and other similar traumas."

That caught his attention, and he finally turned over.
"So…"

"So, they're expanding. Opening an amputee clinic specifically for children. Predicting great things, according to the
article you don't want to read."

He reached over, trying to grab it away from Sarah, but she
held it out of his reach and waved it at him just to taunt him.
"If you want it, you're going to have to pay for it," she teased.

"And what kind of payment would the lady like in
exchange for a used journal?"

"I think you know what I want," she purred, dropping the
magazine on the floor next to the bed. She slid down her
pillow just enough so that when Michael came sailing over
her to grab the journal, she was able to do a little grabbing
of her own. "There's really nothing else to read," she whispered in his ear, as she turned ever so slightly on her side and
raised her leg over his hip. "And since I don't have to be on
duty for another two hours, I thought…"

He was instantly aroused. She could see it, the way she
could see the eagerness in his eyes right now that was there
for something other than her. Smiling, she slid on top of him
just a bit more. "I do have something to tell you," she said as
he let the journal fall back to the floor.

"Right now, I'd rather you *show* me…" Before he'd
finished the sentence, Sarah pushed him all the way over on
his back, then straddled him. In a flash, he reached up under
the T-shirt she always wore to bed, one of his, to find her
breasts. "Just like that," he growled, as she wiggled out of the
shirt. "That's exactly what I want you to show me."

"I have something even better," she said, leaning over him until her breasts were in his face. He had only started to nibble when she pulled back and thrust a piece of paper at him she'd grabbed off the bedside table.

"It had better be sexy," he warned, giving her an exaggerated scowl.

"Well, not so much sexy as satisfying, I think."

That piqued his curiosity enough that he grabbed the paper. The instant he laid eyes on it, she sucked in a sharp breath and held it.

The words on the paper were brief, and after less than half a minute he turned to look at her. "I…I don't know what to say."

"Yes, for starters. It's everything we want, Michael. Everything we've talked about these past couple of months."

"They want us to run the children's amputee clinic?"

She nodded. "After I saw the posting this morning I e-mailed them, just to enquire about the position, nothing else. While you were still on duty. They e-mailed back within an hour, wanting more details about us, then made the offer a little while after I told them who we are. They said they checked our credentials, thanks to the marvels of modern technology, and if we'd like a job with little pay, long hours, lots of hard work, and more satisfaction than we could imagine…"

"And how long were you going to keep this from me?"

She smiled. "Just long enough to write this…" She handed him another piece of paper from the bedside stand. This one was handwritten, from herself to Michael. It was a letter of resignation from her position as ship's doctor, giving him two weeks' notice. The reason stated was that she was going to work with her husband in a little clinic near Thailand. "I think Martha will probably come along as my nurse, if I ask her," she said. "And I'd suggest you ask Ina along as *your* nurse, if you know what's good for you."

A sexy grin slid to his lips. "You really think you know me so well that you can anticipate my decision, don't you?" Both letters in his hand fluttered to the floor as he rolled over to face her. "Don't you?"

Laughing, Sarah snaked her hand around Michael's neck. "I do. And just to prove it, I'm making another decision right now that you're going to love."

"Anything you want to tell me about?"

She pulled his face toward hers. "I'd rather show you."

MILLS & BOON®

Want to get more from Mills & Boon?

Here's what's available to you if you join the
exclusive **Mills & Boon eBook Club** today:

✦ *Convenience – choose your books each month*
✦ *Exclusive – receive your books a month before
  anywhere else*
✦ *Flexibility – change your subscription at any time*
✦ *Variety – gain access to eBook-only series*
✦ *Value – subscriptions from just £1.99 a month*

So visit **www.millsandboon.co.uk/esubs** today
to be a part of this exclusive eBook Club!

0914_ST_1

MILLS & BOON®

The Little Shop of Hopes & Dreams

* cover in development

Much loved author Fiona Harper brings you the story of Nicole, a born organiser and true romantic, whose life is spent making the dream proposals of others come true. All is well until she is enlisted to plan the proposal of gorgeous photographer Alex Black—the same Alex Black with whom Nicole shared a New Year's kiss that she is unable to forget…

Get your copy today at
www.millsandboon.co.uk/dreams

MILLS & BOON®

Why shop at millsandboon.co.uk?

Each year, thousands of romance readers find their perfect read at millsandboon.co.uk. That's because we're passionate about bringing you the very best romantic fiction. Here are some of the advantages of shopping at www.millsandboon.co.uk:

* **Get new books first**—you'll be able to buy your favourite books one month before they hit the shops

* **Get exclusive discounts**—you'll also be able to buy our specially created monthly collections, with up to 50% off the RRP

* **Find your favourite authors**—latest news, interviews and new releases for all your favourite authors and series on our website, plus ideas for what to try next

* **Join in**—once you've bought your favourite books, don't forget to register with us to rate, review and join in the discussions

Visit **www.millsandboon.co.uk**
for all this and more today!